DUEL OF FIRE

STEEL AND FIRE 🔥 BOOK 1

BUNKER SERIES

Wake Me After the Apocalypse

Meet Me at World's End

Follow Me to Armageddon

THE SEABOUND CHRONICLES

Seabound

Seaswept

Seafled

Burnt Sea: A Seabound Prequel

DUEL OF FIRE

STEEL AND FIRE 🔥 BOOK 1

JORDAN RIVET

Contact the author at Jordan@jordanrivet.com

Cover art by Deranged Doctor Design

Editing suggestions provided by Red Adept Editing

Audiobook narrated by Caitlin Kelly

Map by Jordan Rivet

Duel of Fire, Steel and Fire Book 1/ Jordan Rivet – First Edition: April 2016

Hardcover Edition: June 2021

ISBN: 978-1-0879-6463-8

❀ Created with Vellum

For Sarah, Brooke, and Rachel.
Thank you for your game-changing advice.

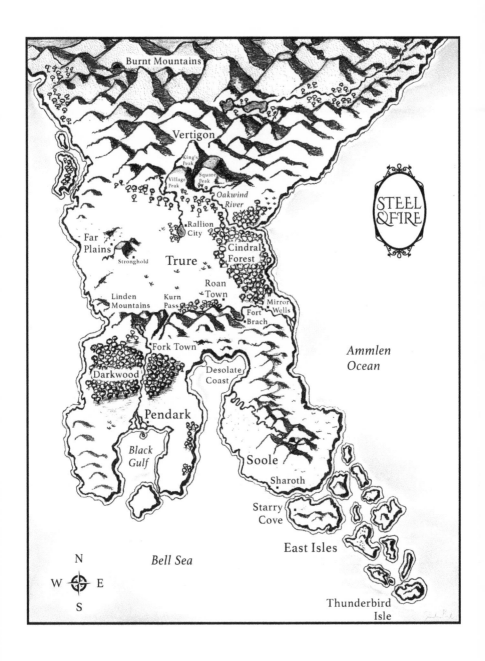

THE REQUEST

DARA struck the practice dummy with a precise lunge. The wooden figure shuddered under her blade. She recovered to a guarded stance. Breathe, retreat, advance, lunge. She stabbed the dummy three times in rapid succession. Arm. Head. Heart.

Her breathing steady, she recovered and checked her form. She couldn't afford any wasted movements. The Vertigon Cup was only two months away, and she had to be perfect.

Breathe, retreat, advance, lunge. Again.

"Practice as you compete." Her coach's words replayed in her head as the air hummed with the quick slice of her blade. "If you want to be the best, you train each time like you are fighting for the Cup. This is no practice duel, no just-for-fun game. Fun is for children. You are an athlete."

Dara hit the dummy again, the blunt point of her sword adding check marks to the battered surface. She wanted to be the best. She had trained for years, sweating through intense workout sessions, fighting opponent after opponent in an effort to show her worth as a duelist. She would not ease up in the final stretch.

Sweat dripped through Dara's hair as she completed her forms. She did a hundred perfect lunges every day before her coach arrived. If they weren't perfect, she started over. After the hundredth one, her arms and back felt limber, though there was a bit of tightness in her left calf. She set her blade on the stone floor and worked at the muscle. It was always cold in the dueling school, even in midsummer, and she hadn't warmed up enough today. She usually ran across the bridges on her way to practice, but today rain fell thick on the mountain, making the boards slippery. She couldn't afford an injury this close to the biggest tournament of the season.

Dara didn't just want to win the Vertigon Cup. She was going pro. She had finished her basic education and graduated to the elite adult division six months ago. Her parents had grudgingly given her permission to continue training in the afternoons as long as she worked in their shop in the mornings. She'd have to start earning her keep full-time soon unless she could pull off a big victory. The prize money was part of it, but if she won the Cup, she could sign with a patron to support her training.

But Dara's coach was late today. He usually came in while she was doing her lunges. Dara put her blade and mask beside her trunk in the corner and sat on the wide brown rug to stretch while she waited.

Rain drummed on the rooftop, and echoes played around the hall. The training space was cavernous, with a wide stone floor and competition strips painted across its length. Ash spread out from the big stone fireplace in the corner, scattered by the wind whipping down the chimney. It was past midday, but the fires blazed in the blustery weather.

Tall windows revealed a slice of the opposite peak. The king's castle stood like a crown on the mountaintop. The rain fuzzed the details except for the piercing lights in the topmost towers.

Dara had the school to herself for now, but soon the other duelists would arrive for their group training sessions and fill the hall with the clash of steel and the shouts of competition. She loved the metallic din, the way it spurred her to perform better in every practice, every tournament. Professional dueling was an obsession—both for Dara and for the kingdom of Vertigon. Swords hadn't been used in war in a hundred years. In fact, there hadn't *been* a war in a hundred years. But the sport had exploded in popularity during the time of peace. Every competition sold out, and prosperous craftsmen and nobles paid dearly to support the best athletes. Top duelists drew more attention on the streets than King Sevren himself, and they lived like royalty by the time they retired their blades.

Only a handful of women in the city ever landed patrons, though—and Dara would be one of them.

She was more than ready, but there was still no sign of her coach. Berg Doban trained some of the best duelists in Vertigon in his school on Square Peak. Dara had been working with him for years, and he was almost never late.

The tall wooden doors banged open, and the other students began to arrive for the group drills. Dara's friends Kelad and Oatin were among the first to stride in, laughing and shoving each other and shaking the rain out of their hair. They were both solid athletes. Kel had a patron already, and Oat was expected to make a top-four finish in the men's division at this year's Cup. But Dara worked harder than both of them.

"Where's Doban?" Kel said, coming over to the stretching rug after chucking his gear in the general direction of his trunk.

"No idea."

"You're usually slicing him ragged by now," Oat said.

"I thought I'd be late today." Dara switched her long legs around and reached for her toes. A strand of golden hair fell into her eyes. "I couldn't run with the rain like this."

3

"Don't know why you bother anyway," Kel said. "Running is for horseboys and valley scum."

"If you ran more, you wouldn't have dropped those last two hits to Rawl in the Square Tourney," Dara said. "You have to build your endurance."

"Don't remind me." Kel flopped onto the rug and stretched a leg across his body, rotating his hips until his spine cracked. Kel was wiry and short for a swordsman, but he made up for it with his fine-tuned precision. He could hit a flea with a running lunge on barely a glance. Plus the crowds loved him, which was almost as important in this game. "I lost a gold Firestick to Yuri because of those points."

"You've got to quit betting on yourself," Oat said. "It messes with your head." He stood above them, working his long arms in a slow circle. Oat was one of the tallest men on the mountain. Looking up from the floor all Dara could see was the black stubble on his chin and his windmilling limbs. He dropped into a long lunge and grinned at her.

"Better than betting on you, Oat," Kel said. "You didn't even duel in the last tournament because of your precious ankle." Kel sat up and stretched his legs out in front of him.

"Don't remind me." Oat grimaced. Being tall gave him a great reach, but he was forever falling victim to twists and sprains. It was probably the only reason he didn't have a patron already.

"You'll get them in the Cup," Dara said.

"Thanks, Dar, but we all know you're going to be the star of the Cup," Oat said. "Coach barely remembers I'm competing when you're on the strip."

"Wish he'd remember when we have drills scheduled. He should have been here half an hour ago."

"Maybe he's—"

The door crashed open. Coach Berg Doban strode in, water dripping from his cloak. All the athletes stopped and stared, their stretches forgotten. Berg strode into the center of the dueling hall and hurled his bag of practice blades across the room. It slid to a stop at the foot of a training dummy.

"Idiot!" he roared. Then he stalked over to his trunk and kicked it open. He reached in to grab his padded coaching sleeve, but he had flung the lid up with such force that it immediately slammed back down on his hand. Berg let out a string of curses and lifted the lid again more carefully.

"Sounds like someone woke up on the wrong side of the bridge today," Kel whispered. "I don't envy you one bit, Dara."

He and Oat went over to their own trunks and quietly began pulling on their gear. The other athletes became very interested in lacing up their boots and adjusting the bends of their blades as Berg grumbled at his coaching equipment. Dara retrieved her blade, glove, and mask and approached him.

"Umm, Coach?"

He whirled around, another curse on his lips, but held it back when he saw that it was Dara. "You are ready?" he said instead. "We drill now."

Dara gulped and darted to the drilling strip marked out in paint along one side of the dueling floor. Berg stalked after her, pulling on the thick coaching sleeve and muttering under his breath.

Berg was a big, square man with big, square shoulders. He didn't look like a typical swordsman. The pros tended to be long and lean, like Dara and Oat, but a few compensated for their shorter reach with other assets. In Berg's case it was his knock-down-walls strength, still visible in his thick shoulders even though he'd grown a bit paunchy around the middle in his coaching years. Berg still had a temper like a cur-dragon in mating season. He was originally from a distant part of the Lands Below, but the dark look that lit his eyes as he crossed the dueling floor had become legendary since his arrival in Vertigon decades ago.

They began their usual drill sequence. Berg didn't need to call out commands, only occasionally correcting Dara's stance as she moved through the basic forms. Advance. Parry. Thrust. He was a demanding teacher. He knew how fierce the competition was this year and how much Dara wanted that Cup victory. But today instead of his usual criticism he praised every move she made.

"Yes, Dara, that is how it's done," he growled as she touched each key point on his coaching sleeve: hand, arm, shoulder, chest. "Yes, you stay focused. That is it. You do not give your opponent time to think in case you miss your target. No guarantees in a duel. You always go for the second and third and fourth shot even if you think you have number one. Yes! That is the way!"

Berg's praise made Dara more nervous than being corrected. Her performance today wasn't much better than their last drill session, when he'd shouted at her for ten minutes for dropping her guard before the arm shot. She tried to focus on keeping her movements efficient, but she missed a handful of hits, the rounded tip of her blade glancing off the padded sleeve. And still Berg praised her.

"Yes. Is okay. You get most, and you try harder each time. Good!"

The dull thud of her hits and the tap of boots on the stone floor filled the hall. The other students must have sensed Berg's mood, because they kept their noise to a minimum. Finally, after what Dara thought was a perfectly ordinary series of compound attacks, Berg removed his mask and wiped the sweat from his forehead with his heavy glove.

"This is it, Dara. You are a serious athlete. You know the way." Despite his words, Berg grimaced, his face reddening. "That young fool is too arrogant. He should be like you." He clenched the strap of his mask in his fist and shook it. "I am wasting my time. He does not see it."

Dara stepped out of the way as Berg hurled the mask to the floor. It bounced away from him and rolled between two young duelists practicing parries. They edged over to a strip closer to the wall.

"Um, who's arrogant, Coach?" Dara asked.

"If he could see you train," Berg ranted. "Or duel! He does not know how much danger he would be in from a swordswoman like you. Too foolish . . ." Berg lowered his eyebrows and studied Dara.

She shifted under his gaze, her sturdy training boots squeaking on the floor. Berg worked with a few pupils privately in the grand homes of the nobility on the lower slopes of King's Peak. Sword masters were in high demand—if your pockets were deep enough. Berg didn't usually talk about his private students, though, and Dara and the others figured training nobles was just a vanity project. Most of the young lords wouldn't stand a chance in a real tourney. Berg continued to stare at Dara without really seeing her.

"Should I join the others, Coach?" she asked.

He started. "No, not yet. Dara, you must help me. I cannot abide this young fool anymore. You will come with me next time. Show him what it is like to duel a real athlete."

"Coach, I've got to stick to my training schedule. Can you take someone who isn't entered in the Cup? I'm sure half of them would be able to beat this fellow." She gestured to the other students working through their usual drills. She was a pro, or at least on the verge of becoming one. She didn't have time to teach lessons to some spoiled noble.

"No, he is very good. This is the problem. He is too confident because he is good, but he does not respect the danger. He must learn."

"What danger?" Dara asked. "The worst that could happen is he gets bruised up in some parlor match in Lower King's. That'll teach him." The mountain was safe, peaceful. No one had fought with true sharpened swords since the reign of the First Good King.

"No, there is true danger for this young fool," Berg said. He looked around at the two dozen students. Kel and Oat were nearest to them. They kept slowing their footwork to glance over. Kel's curiosity burned like a Fire Lantern through the wire mesh of his mask. Oat tapped him on the head with his blade to draw his attention back to the drill.

Berg drew Dara away from them toward the corner where the gear trunks lined two walls.

"You must not speak of what I will say. Do you understand?"

"Yes, Coach."

"The student is Prince Sivarrion."

Dara blinked. "You want me to duel the prince?"

"He does not respect the blade. If a swordsman ever tries to attack him, he will believe he can win. He will try to fight. But he must learn to fear. He will never be the Fourth King if he falls to his own pride."

"But people don't get assassinated in Vertigon, Coach. It's not like the Lands Below here. And if he's already good—"

"You see, this is his problem. He believes he is too good. And the mountain has more dangers than you know." Berg took Dara's blade from her. It was quality steel, flexible, with a rounded tip. During a match, the tip would be rubbed with charcoal to mark the hits on her opponent's jacket. Berg rubbed a hand across the battered guard, the metal cup that protected the duelist's hand. It was a plain design, lacking any ornate etchings or inlays. "Tell me why we fight to ten, Dara."

"That's just the rule for tourneys," Dara said. "Makes an interesting bout for the spectators that won't end too quickly."

"It is more than that," Berg said. "Tell me the target area for a duel."

"Anywhere that can bleed scores a point, even the hand." Hand touches were Kel's specialty. The dominant hand was always the closest target on your opponent. Dara could do them too, but she was better at dependable shots to the shoulder after clearing her opponent's blade with a clean parry. Her style was all about careful precision.

"Yes, of course. Anywhere that can bleed. Prince Sivarrion believes he can win with a single fatal hit if ever he is attacked. He must see that ten hits to the hand, the arm, the toe, will bleed enough to put him in grave danger. And he must see that the fatal shot is not as easy as he thinks against a superior opponent."

"But I'm sure you've taught him all this," Dara said. "Why do you need me?"

"He does not listen," Berg said. "He thinks he listens. But he does not *understand*. I am not so fast as I once was. You are the one to show him."

Dara didn't want a distraction this close to the Cup, and she already struggled to get enough time for practice when her parents needed her in their shop. It worried her that this prince was frustrating enough to send Berg into a rage. But she couldn't refuse her coach. He had trained her for years, and she hated letting him down. Reluctantly, she agreed.

"Okay, Coach. I'll duel him. But would it be okay if I have an extra private lesson in exchange for missing practice?"

"This will be a good lesson for you too, young Dara," Berg said. "It will be worth one practice. Meet me by Fell Bridge at dawn in two days."

LANTERN MAKER'S DAUGHTER

D ARA woke late the next morning, her muscles stiff.
Waves of sound and heat were already issuing from her
father's workshop. Their dwelling was a terraced house built in
the mouth of a cave, with a tunnel leading back toward the
workshop deep in the mountainside. Dara's room was in the
upper part of the house, jutting above the slope of Village Peak.
She had a single window looking out at Square Peak, where
Berg's dueling school was located. When the weather was clear,
she could just see King's Peak, the third and tallest peak of
Vertigon Mountain, off to her left.

Dara rolled out of bed and stretched on the thick woven rug
covering her floor. She twisted her golden hair into a loose
braid over her shoulder while she rotated her ankles, still
thinking through her final bout with Kel last night. She had a
new bruise at the base of her thumb from one of his expert
hand touches. She may have figured out a tell that would help
her counter that particular attack next time. She grinned. He
was going to be mad if she found a way to beat his most famous
move.

She pressed her foot against the stone wall at the back of

the room to stretch out her calf. It was warm this close to the workshop. She laid her hands flat against the stone, feeling the heat and vibrations coming from deep within the mountain. Her father must have been working for hours already. The early morning was when he could focus best, and he needed a lot of focus to practice his art. It would be too dangerous otherwise.

Dara's father, Rafe Ruminor, was a highly respected Fireworker. The mountain was an important source of Fire magic, one of the only known sources in the world. The Fire ran through the roots of the three peaks like blood through veins. Few were born with the ability to wield the molten energy. The Fireworkers of Vertigon used the Fire to craft valuable objects of beauty and power with their bare hands: sticks of metal that could set any substance alight at a touch, heat stones able to clear a path through the depths of a snowstorm, and some of the most glorious forged weapons known to mankind. The potential of such an industry had made it worth building a city atop the sheer cliffs of Vertigon Mountain.

Rafe's specialty was conjured lanterns that would hold their light and warmth indefinitely. His designs were more intricate and beautiful than those of any other Fireworker in the city, and people traveled all the way from the Lands Below for his custom models. Dara's mother, Lima, organized the sale and export of Rafe's Fire Lanterns and also handled the operations of the Fireworkers' Guild. The family business was the most successful Fireworking shop in Vertigon.

There was only one problem: the ability to work the Fire was innate. You either had it or you didn't—and Dara didn't. The Spark typically manifested in children between the ages of five and eight. Dara had waited in vain for her own Spark to appear, but her fingers remained cold and her senses numb.

Dara dressed quickly and thundered down the narrow wooden staircase to the kitchen. It had a wide window and a good view of King's Peak with its multitude of bridges connecting to the other two peaks. The sun was already up, casting sharp shadows over the terraces. Dara hadn't realized how late it was. No wonder she felt as if she could eat enough for three people.

Her mother was waiting for her at their large stone dining table.

"Where were you last night?" she said as Dara dropped into a chair and reached for a bowl of porridge. As usual, Dara didn't look at the chair beside hers, which had been empty for over a decade.

"I went for a run after practice," Dara said. "The rain finally let up."

Lima pursed her lips. "Your father has been up for hours already." She was an imposing woman, with a wide frame and silver-streaked hair tied into a tight bun. She didn't approve of dueling. She wanted Dara to spend her time organizing ledgers at a desk and making connections with important clients. But endless meetings and paperwork were poor substitutes for the magic of the Fire.

"You were supposed to get up early to help with the summer orders," she said.

"Oh, I forgot all about that. I'm sorry."

"Dara, when we said you could train after your education—"

"I know. I'll get it all done before I leave."

Dara was supposed to help her mother in the mornings and train in the afternoons, but she found it harder to jump out of bed for paperwork than for a good run across the bridges. She couldn't conjure up any enthusiasm for the business side of Fireworking.

Dara's disappointment when she found out she couldn't work the Fire had been shattering. And it had come close on the heels of her older sister's death. Dara resisted the urge to glance at the empty chair. Renna had been born with the Spark and had already begun training in the art of Fireworking. The Ruminors would have had a Fireworker in the next generation if she hadn't died. When they realized Dara couldn't Work, Renna was already gone and it was too late for them to have another child.

Dara's mother had been more upset that she couldn't train in the family art than Dara herself. At least her father tried to hide it. When Dara was nine, long past the age when Workers typically felt their first link to the Fire, he had suggested that she take up dueling. She had loved it from the moment she first drove the tip of a blade into a target and felt the force of the hit vibrating up her arm.

Rafe had intended swordplay to be a diversion, a consolation until she was old enough to help her mother with the business, but it soon became Dara's one and only passion. She threw herself into training, thriving on the fact that the harder she worked, the better she became. It had nothing to do with some inborn Spark beyond her control. As she got older, her disappointment over not being able to Work the Fire had faded.

"You may need to skip some of your afternoon practices for the next few weeks," her mother said. "The work is piling up."

"Can you hire someone else to help you?" Dara asked.

Lima's pursed lips thinned to a blade-sharp line. "With the current restrictions on the Fire your father can't increase his production enough to support another employee," she said. "His access shrinks every year."

Heavy footfalls sounded outside the kitchen door, and Dara's father emerged from the tunnel at the back of the house. As always, he smelled of fire and metal.

"Hello, dear ones!" Rafe Ruminor filled every room he entered. He was tall and lean, with a strong jaw and golden hair like Dara's. Lima rose, standing almost as tall as her husband,

and kissed his cheek. They were a formidable pair, and it was easy to see why they commanded such respect on the mountain.

"You're up late, my young spark," Rafe said, dropping a heavy hand on Dara's shoulder.

"I ran after training last night," Dara said.

"One day you're going to get injured, and you'll wish you'd spent more time on something besides those swords," Lima said.

"But the Cup is in two months."

"Now, now. There will be time to win plenty of tourneys," Rafe said. He sighed expansively. "Perhaps it is for the best. There may be no business in the future if the Warden continues to parse out the Fire to those who are not worthy of it."

"It can't be that bad," Dara mumbled. "They're just making Firesticks and Everlights."

"Watch your mouth, Dara," her mother said. "You have no respect for your father's Art."

"Of course I do. It's just that—"

"He has toiled his whole life to perfect his creations," Lima continued, warming up to the familiar lecture. "He deserves better than to have his access to the Fire diluted so hacks can sell cheap tricks. If Warden Lorrid would stop granting Fire shares to every new upstart that thinks he can Wield, we wouldn't have this issue."

Dara sighed at the old-fashioned term: *Wield*. Long ago, the Firewielders were the most powerful force on the mountain. They had warred over access to the Fire of Vertigon, drenching the mountain in smoke and blood. But now the power was Worked, not Wielded.

The First Good King, Sovar Amintelle, had been a Firewielder. When he prevailed over the others he designed a system to control the flow of Fire through the veins of the mountain and keep the surviving Wielders in check. His son lacked the ability to Wield, so he assigned a Warden to ensure that no Firewielder could become too powerful and disrupt the peace established by the First Good King.

Now, the Fire was strictly regulated, used almost exclusively for the production of useful objects. It flowed from the Well beneath the Fire Warden's greathouse and through the roots of the mountain. Each Fireworker's shop received a controlled amount of Fire, just enough to create their masterworks. The Workers were also forbidden from creating Fire-infused weapons for anyone but the king, his guards, and the army. This ensured that the famed Peace of Vertigon endured. But the more powerful Fireworkers didn't like the constraints, however necessary.

"Never fear, my dear," Rafe said, washing his hands in the stone basin beneath the window. He looked out at King's Peak across the Gorge. "Perhaps the winds are turning. I may yet be able to protect the noble Art."

Lima squeezed her husband's shoulder and began ladling portions of spiced mountain goat porridge into his bowl. Dara ate hers mechanically. Lima may be formidable, but she was an indifferent cook at best.

As her mother talked about the lantern orders that would need to be completed and delivered before winter, Dara thought about her strategy for her royal duel the following morning. It was always useful to practice against someone besides the regulars at the school. She didn't have high hopes for the dueling abilities of the heir-prince, though.

"What do you know about Prince Sivarrion?" she asked when there was a lull in her parents' conversation.

"Worthless," Rafe said immediately. "His father's sway over the mountain is increasingly ceremonial."

Dara blinked. "Ceremonial?"

"The Fire Warden is the true power here. Sivarrion is at

least smart enough to know that. He entertains himself and lets Zage Lorrid do as he will."

Dara had heard her parents' complaints about the Fire Warden, Zage Lorrid, a thousand times. The king was another story, though.

"Isn't King Sevren well liked?" Dara asked.

"Of course. He's a nice man," Rafe said. "A weak man, but nice. He has to rein Zage in before he allows our best asset to disintegrate into nothingness."

Dara poked at the bits of goat floating in her porridge, avoiding the sight of the empty chair. She knew all too well why her parents hated the Fire Warden. Most of their dislike was personal after what had happened to Renna a decade ago, but they had professional differences with Zage as well. According to her father he was determined to spread the mountain Fire so thin as to be nearly useless. The king purportedly approved of this policy, but she had never thought of his power as ceremonial only.

"Why are you asking about the prince?" Lima asked, her sharp eyes on her daughter. "You've never mooned over his *dashing good looks*, unlike most of the girls in the Village."

"Oh, I heard he likes to duel, that's all."

"He's a lout," Lima said. "*I* hear he spends most of his time drinking in the parlors in Lower King's. He's bound to enjoy other frivolous activities too."

Dueling isn't frivolous. Dara curled her fingers around her wooden spoon as though it were the pommel of her sword. Her mother's disdain for her sport got worse every day. She suspected her parents would object to her going up to the castle the following morning. If she could get away, that is.

"Well," Rafe said, "I suspect the prince will need to watch his back, if Lorrid continues along his current path. Perhaps he should learn to defend himself."

"You think the Fire Warden would do something to him?"

Dara asked. She looked up in time to see her parents exchanging glances.

"We already know what the Fire Warden is capable of," Lima said bitterly. She looked over at the empty chair then, and Dara couldn't help following her gaze. Renna's chair. Her mother kept the wood polished and dust free after all this time.

"Never you mind, my young spark," Rafe said, resting his hand on his wife's arm and leaning toward Dara. "You ought to be more concerned about what the Fire Warden is doing to the family business if you're to run it one day."

"You gave me until the Cup to prove I can make it in the duels," Dara said.

"Just keep your eyes open," Rafe said. "And be wary of taking too much of an interest in the royal family."

Dara finished her meal in silence. Her parents had their own quarrel with the Fire Warden, but could he actually be plotting something against the king's family? Or Prince Sivarrion in particular?

In any case, Dara was quite certain her mother would consider her upcoming duel a waste of time. So how was she going to get out of work tomorrow?

Her mother snapped her fingers sharply. "Did you hear me, Dara?"

"What?"

Lima stood and stacked their emptied bowls. "I said since you're getting such a late start this morning I need you to stay home this afternoon and help me with the ledgers."

"But—"

"No arguments. You have a duty to your family. Meet me in the shop after you wash up."

Dara gritted her teeth and helped clean the bowls while her father returned to his workshop. She wouldn't be able to try out that new idea on Kel at practice after all. She'd have to work extra quickly today if she had any chance of getting away tomorrow morning.

~

After finishing up the dishes, Dara joined her mother in the lantern shop, located next to the kitchen on the ground floor of their dwelling. It was an elegant room, with hardwood floors polished to a shine and discreetly placed mirrors on the walls. Ruminor Lanterns hung from intricately carved arches around the open space. There were only eight pieces on display, which served as samples of Rafe's work. Most clients purchased custom lanterns rather than buying from the showroom. As far as Dara was concerned, the shop didn't really need to stay open all the time. But her mother didn't see it that way.

On one side of the room was a large hardwood desk, where Lima sat with ledgers and drawings spread before her. Lima herself couldn't Work the Fire, like Dara, but she had a knack for drawing. She would sketch the designs based on their customers' requests, and Rafe would bring them to life.

"I need you to double-check all of these orders for me," Lima said, pushing a stack of papers toward her daughter. "We can't have a mix-up like last year when the Morrven and Samanar orders got switched. We almost lost two of our best customers over that."

"I'll be careful," Dara said. She pulled up a chair and sat beside her mother, preparing for a long morning bent over the papers. Her wooden seat was hard and unforgiving, and her body felt crunched and useless as she set to the tedious task of crosschecking the orders. At least the shop was well lit with the steady burn of the Fire Lanterns.

It was midsummer, one of their busiest times as they prepared new lanterns for the winter season. Rafe needed time to complete the work and then deliver the lanterns throughout

Vertigon and the Lands Below. Their customers always wanted the newest and most-fashionable lantern designs despite how long they lasted. But as Rafe was the only one in their family who could Work the Fire, the business couldn't grow much bigger.

If only Renna hadn't—Dara stopped herself from completing the thought. Her parents' grief over her sister's death had only been amplified when they discovered Dara's lack of Spark. She had spent so much of her life trying to make up for something beyond her control, but she was close to breaking free on her own merits. She had to move forward, even if her parents couldn't.

The shop door opened, and a stocky man entered wearing a coat embroidered with ornate threads of Firegold. He swept off his matching hat and bowed.

"Afternoon, Lima."

"Corren. You're early."

"I never keep Rafe waiting. This is my new assistant, Farr."

He waved his hat at the taller, younger man who accompanied him. He had muddy-brown hair and long, bony arms. Dara was reminded forcibly of the scraggly trees that grew on the tougher slopes of the mountain.

"A pleasure." Lima rose and swept forward to offer her hand. The two men took it in turn, and Dara noticed that Farr had burn marks on his fingers. "Rafe didn't mention the purpose of your visit."

"Guild business," Corren said, shrugging his broad shoulders. Corren was a prominent Fireworker, like Dara's father. He specialized in spinning fine threads of Firegold to adorn shoes and other leather and fabric goods. He wasn't a direct competitor, and he had been helping Dara's parents with the Fire Guild for years.

"Anything I should know about?" Lima asked.

"A couple of the Smiths had their supply cut off again

yesterday. We need to talk about how to respond. I don't want to interrupt your work, though. I'm sure he'll fill you in."

"It's all right," Lima said. "Rafe is in the workshop. Dara, would you walk these gentlemen down there? Come right back."

"Yes, ma'am." Dara leapt up, eager to escape her desk. She worked her wrists to loosen the tension in her pen hand.

"You're getting tall, Dara," Corren said as they walked through the back of the shop and down the long corridor that went from wood to stone as they descended into the mountain. "How's the dueling?"

"Not bad. I've got the Eventide tourney coming up in a few weeks, but I'm mostly getting ready for the Vertigon Cup."

"I remember when you first picked up a sword. It was almost as long as you." Corren chuckled. "And now you're all grown up. Any marriage prospects on the horizon?"

"I'm too busy for that at the moment with training and helping out with the business," Dara said.

"Ah yes. The business," Corren said. "You'll make someone a good match, Dara." He gave Farr the assistant a significant look. "I can find my way from here. Farr, give me a few minutes in private with Rafe before I introduce you. You can chat with Dara here." Corren grinned widely and nudged her arm. They had reached the end of the stone tunnel, where half a dozen steps led to the door of her father's workshop.

Dara kept a polite smile plastered on her face as Corren disappeared into the workshop, a wave of heat spilling out into the tunnel. This wasn't the first time he'd brought one of his many assistants to meet her. Corren had long been vocal about his desire to more closely align his business with the Ruminors'. Once he had even suggested that if Dara couldn't Work the Fire herself maybe she could produce a Firesparked baby or two. Her parents had laughed, but they hadn't dissuaded Corren from bringing around his most eligible assistants.

"So," Farr said after a minute, shifting his feet on the smooth stone of the passageway. He opened and closed his bony hands, knuckles cracking. Dara sighed. The last apprentice had been much more charismatic.

"You're a Firegold spinner?" she prompted.

"Trying to be," Farr said.

"Right."

He looked at her mutely, a hulking shape in the corridor. There wasn't quite enough space for her to slip past him and return to her mother. She wondered how long Corren had meant by "give me a few minutes." He probably expected they'd need at least five to agree to marry and make Firesparked babies.

Despite her desire to poke Farr in the toe with a sword so he'd move out of her way, she couldn't offend Corren.

"Any idea what they're talking about in there?" she asked politely.

"Master Corren is going to ask Master Ruminor if I can learn some latticework from him," Farr said, his words coming out in a rush. "I keep breaking the threads, and he wants me to try out something heavier."

"Hmm." Dara doubted her father would agree to that. Like Dara, he hated anything that broke his focus. And he hadn't taken an apprentice since Renna died. He would much rather keep the business in the family.

"So . . . you don't Work the Fire?" Farr asked.

"I'm sure Corren mentioned that," Dara said. Corren had undoubtedly filled Farr in on exactly how valuable the Ruminor name would be to an up-and-coming Fireworker. Even though she was over her disappointment at not having the Spark, she didn't like being reminded of it every time she turned around. "I help my mother with the orders, and the rest of the time I duel."

"Really? I've never been to a dueling show before," Farr said.

"Competition."

"Huh?"

"You mean dueling competition. It's not a show."

"Right. Sorry."

Farr went back to shuffling his feet and cracking his knuckles. Dara held back another sigh. This fellow wasn't promising. She wondered if he liked paperwork. Maybe Lima should be the one taking on a part-time apprentice.

Actually, that wasn't such a bad idea.

Dara looked up at Farr as he took a deep breath and blurted out: "I think you're pretty!"

"Uh, thank you," Dara said. "I need to talk to my mother about something. Will you excuse me?" She didn't wait for an answer as she squeezed past him in the tunnel.

"Will I see you at the next Guild meeting?" Farr sounded a little panicked, and words tumbled out of him again. "The discussions have been quite interesting lately. Lots of developments that could alter the future of our business."

"I'm sure it's fascinating," Dara said. "I don't go to the meetings unless I have to. Good luck with the spinning." Dara started up the corridor then took pity on the poor assistant. She turned around. "Look, Corren can be a bit forceful, but you don't have to try to woo me."

There was enough light to reveal the blush in Farr's cheeks.

"Sorry I messed up. He said I should . . . Never mind. I do think you're pretty, though."

"Thank you. Look, if you're really interested in the Fire Guild, I could ask my mother to talk to you about it. She's been keeping the Guild minutes for a decade."

"I'd like that," Farr said.

"Great." Dara grinned. "In fact, I'll see if she's free tomorrow morning."

"That's really nice of you," Farr said, grinning back. He had a nice, unassuming smile, and it softened his bony features. "I hope I'll see you again."

Dara jogged back up the tunnel to the shop. She should be able to get away for her duel with the prince if her mother was occupied with Farr. For her part, she was tired of suitors and guilds and paperwork. She was tired of trying to replace her sister when she didn't have the same ability. She had to find some way to ensure that she wouldn't be totally dependent on the Fireworking business for the rest of her life. She needed a patron—and a replacement of her own—soon. In the meantime, her mother and Farr would get along grandly. And she had a royal duel to win.

THE PRINCE

D ARA leapt out of bed before the sun rose on the day she had arranged to meet Berg. She had almost been too excited to sleep last night. The familiar buzz she got whenever a competition approached hummed through her stomach as she peered out her window. Mist hung thick over the slopes of the mountain. A few lights burned over on Square Peak, but the castle at the top of King's Peak was still dark.

A low rumble came from deep within the cave as Dara dressed in her usual practice gear of soft gray trousers, training boots, and a darker gray blouse. The cut was more masculine than her mother liked her to wear outside of the dueling hall, but it moved easily and hid the sweat. Dara twisted back her long golden hair and put on a deep-blue cloak. It was too hot for the cloak inside, but the farther she got from her father's workshop, the more she would need it. It may be summer, but it was always cold on the mountain.

Dara slung her gear bag over her shoulder, slipped out of the house, and hurried down the stairs from their porch. Only the howl of the wind and the thud of her boots disrupted the silence. A dozen of her father's lanterns lit the boardwalk, which soon met a winding pathway leading down through the Village and all the way to Fell Bridge. The darker it was, the brighter the Fire Lanterns glowed. The city was often shrouded in mist, and they needed the lanterns during the daytime as much as the night.

Vertigon was built on a grand mountain topped by three steep peaks: King's Peak, Square Peak, and Village Peak. Dara's family lived on Village Peak. It was divided from King's Peak by a gorge lined with orchard terraces. The tallest buildings in the Village were just level with the base of the castle on top of King's Peak. Square Peak was the shortest and widest of the three, located across a much deeper gorge called the Fissure. All three peaks were connected by dozens of bridges spanning the Fissure and Orchard Gorge. Wooden staircases and stone steps cut into the slopes connected the homes and shops built around the three peaks.

The narrow canyon leading out of the Fissure was the only true access to the city high up the mountain. The precipitous cliffs surrounding the rest of the peaks made the city remarkably easy to defend. It had been no simple task for the Founders to build their mountaintop citadel, but once it was established no one was foolish enough to attack it. They had to import any supplies and food not found on the mountain, but the Lands Below were desperate for its primary export—the Fireworks—and they were willing to pay handsomely for the magical objects.

The Village stirred fitfully at this early hour. The *clop-clop* of mountain goats and the rustle of pigeon hatcheries arose as Dara descended from the rocky heights where the Ruminor dwelling was located. A few miners crossed her path on their way to work, and sleepy bridge guards headed the other way, home to their beds in the humble wood and stone houses scattered up and down the slopes of Village Peak. The smell of roasting pigeon, berry pies, and fresh-baked bread drifted from the market, located a bit lower on the slope between the entrances to Fell Bridge and Furlingbird Bridge. Smoke wafted out of the Fireshops, which dotted the Village like glowing coals.

Dara waited for Berg by the bridge, jumping up and down to warm her muscles. Fell was the widest of the bridges across Orchard Gorge connecting the Village to King's Peak. Berg would have to cross from Square Peak first. He lived near his school, which, like many of the dueling schools, had been built on Square because it had more level space than the other two peaks. It was also home to the king's army and a motley patchwork of orchards, cave dwellings, and breeding farms for goats and mountain ponies.

Dara was nervous about her sparring match with the prince. She had never met Sivarrion Amintelle. When she had seen him standing with his two younger sisters, Selivia and Soraline, beside their father, King Sevren, at official festivals, he usually looked bored. She hadn't even known he could duel. She remembered what her mother had said about his reputation for drinking in the parlors in Lower King's, worrying this excursion would end up being a waste of time.

Sivarrion's father, King Sevren, was the Third Good King. His family had presided uncontested over the mountain for a hundred years. The Lands Below had seen succession battles, rebellions, and civil wars in that time, but Vertigon had remained stable in the hands of the Amintelle family. As the oldest child and only son, Prince Sivarrion would have a smooth transition when he succeeded his father one day. It was unlikely to happen for many years, though. King Sevren was fifty years old, and by all accounts he was as hale and hearty as ever.

Dara worked her ankles in slow circles and scanned the narrow road through the Village eagerly. She was more than ready to see what this prince could do.

Berg finally approached through the mist, wrapped in a cloak made from the long black fur of a mountain bear. He grunted a greeting and started across the bridge.

"Good morning, Coach!" Dara said. "What's the prince's style like? Can you give me any—?"

"We talk later," Berg grumbled. "Is too early."

"But I want to know if—"

"Later." Berg pulled his cloak closer around his body.

Dara fell silent. As their boots pounded on the wooden slats of Fell Bridge, she wanted to ask more details about the upcoming bout. She had never gone into a tournament on such short notice before. She couldn't help but think of it as a competition. Berg had taught her well.

Dara doubted Prince Sivarrion would ever engage in a real duel with sharpened blades. Berg was likely getting paranoid as he aged. But she was curious to see if the prince was really as good as Berg said. She studied all the best duelists in the city, and she found it hard to believe he could be *that* talented. The pros trained five or six days a week and went to tournaments on most Turndays at the end of the week. There was no way the heir-prince of Vertigon had that much time on his hands.

The castle loomed above them on the crown of King's Peak. At the top, three towers mirroring the three peaks of the mountain rose behind a high wall. The wall didn't seem necessary given the castle's position, but the effect was impressive. Built from the same dark stone as the mountain, the castle looked as if it were growing out of the rock. The walls had been Fireformed, one of the last great Works using the full power of the Well to mold the stone. Works on that scale were impossible unless the Fire was diverted from every shop in the peaks through a single wielder. It had been decades since such a Work had been performed.

Beneath the castle, the district known as Lower King's Peak covered the slopes with elegant greathouses where the city's noble families and wealthiest residents lived. As Dara and Berg crossed Orchard Gorge and drew nearer to the foot of the peak, tall marble buildings obscured their view of the castle. At the end of the bridge, they descended a few stone steps and nodded at the guard, a sleepy-looking man wearing a thick cloak. The bridge guards were mostly there to make sure no one fell off while drunkenly walking the rails. They didn't need to defend the residents of the peaks. The steep slopes of the mountain did that well enough.

Dara and her coach crossed the broad expanse of Thunderbird Square by the bridge and climbed the quiet streets of Lower King's. At this hour most of the buildings were dark, but at one corner, light and slurred voices spilled out of a greathouse parlor. A young man stumbled out of the door with his arm around a buxom woman. He laughed and shouted back at someone inside the house. The woman glanced at Dara's gear bag and trousers, giggling into the mug in her hand. Dara hoisted her bag farther up on her shoulder and tugged her cloak close. She had never been to a parlor to participate in the revels. She was old enough now at eighteen, but she had seen Kel and Oat try to bout with hangovers, and that had been warning enough. Everything she did was geared toward staying in prime shape for her competitions.

"Keep up," Berg grumbled. He was nearly to a staircase at the end of a steep, winding pathway.

"Sorry." Dara jogged after him, leaving the warm lights of the parlor behind.

"You must make me proud today," Berg said.

"I'll do my best."

"He is fast. Remember this."

"Yes, Coach."

"He has good reach. And don't let the fact that he is a prince intimidate you. If you get a chance to whip him, you take it."

"Yes, Coach." Despite herself, Dara had begun to feel

nervous. She wasn't sure how a simple Fireworker's daughter was expected to act around the heir-prince of the mountain. Fireworkers were important figures in Vertigon, but they were not members of the royal court like the favored landowners. Even so, Dara was determined to win. She couldn't let some noble defeat her, no matter how high up he was. Not if she wanted to call herself a real duelist.

The castle entrance was over a hundred steps above the next highest building, making it an easily defensible position. Dara and Berg ascended the final stairway and arrived at the wide stone slab in front of the castle gates. Dara slung her gear bag to the ground for a moment and rolled her shoulders to work out the kinks. She'd better not get injured today or Berg would really owe her. Nothing was worth messing with her chances to win the Cup, not even a dueling prince.

Berg rapped on a small sally port beside the main gates. A guard wearing the Amintelle sigil on his chest opened the door and let them in immediately. Beyond the walls, the ground sloped upward across an uneven courtyard, all rock until it reached the base of the three-towered castle. A delicate vein of Fire-infused metal ran along the lower wall. In the half-light of the dawn, the castle appeared to be floating on the vein. The castle door was a solid piece of steel wrought with designs every bit as intricate as the ones Dara's father used on his lanterns. Dara caught a glimpse of a crowned figure etched atop a fiery mountain as the doors swung open to admit them.

The entrance hall was tall and bare, with Fire Lanterns hanging from the walls. A handful of servants darted around on soft-slippered feet, polishing the floors and opening the shutters on the high, narrow windows to let in the morning sunlight. They barely glanced at Berg, despite his imposing presence. The guard nodded at them and returned to his post, closing the doors behind him. Berg led the way deeper into the castle.

Across the entrance hall and halfway down a narrower corridor, Berg stopped at an oak door with an ornate iron handle. He looked down at Dara and said, "Give him hell."

"Yes, Coach."

Then he opened the door, and they walked into the most beautiful room Dara had ever seen.

It was a perfectly formed dueling hall. Four windows facing southward allowed the morning light to cut evenly across the dueling strip. The floor was stone with the ideal level of polish, neither too slippery nor rough enough to wear down good dueling boots. A padded stretching rug was positioned beside an elegant wardrobe, with a partially open door revealing a jumble of jackets, gloves, and masks. Two chairs and a stone washbasin sat beside the wardrobe. At the far end of the room stood a row of practice dummies in different positions. Dara couldn't count the number of times she had cursed her own practice dummy as she tried to reposition its heavy wooden arm for a new drill. In this room she could move rapidly down the line and start over again.

The ceilings were high, and a balcony jutted out above the stretching rug directly across from the windows. Dara guessed there were seats up there. Spectators would have a perfect view of the action on the strip.

A rack on the wall by the door displayed one of the most impressive weapon collections Dara had ever seen. There was a sword from each of the major smiths, evidenced by the unique designs of their guards. There were different hilts and pommel types and even two experimental light broadswords. The dueling officials had discussed adding broadswords to select tourneys, but the move hadn't been as popular as hoped. The traditional dueling rapier reigned supreme.

On a separate rack were three blades that looked different from the rest. Dara knew instantly that they were Fire Blades. Contrary to popular belief, true Fire-infused blades didn't glow, but she could tell these ones still had Fire cores. A Fire core could make a blade faster and its tip more accurate, but use of a Fire Blade was strictly forbidden in competitions. And unlike the dueling weapons on the other rack, these blades were sharpened and deadly. Dara had an almost overwhelming urge to pick one up, to feel the bend of the steel and the heft of it in her hand.

"The young fool cannot be on time," Berg grumbled. He had settled into a chair near the wardrobe and stretched his legs out in front of him.

A door beside the stone washbasin flew open.

"Which young fool?" said a jovial voice. The prince had arrived.

He was taller than Dara had expected, nearly as tall as Oatin, and he was built like a swordsman, lean and strong. With his dark hair and high cheekbones, he was handsome, but there were bags under his eyes, his cheeks were unshaven, and his shirt was only halfway tucked into his trousers.

"Prince Sivarrion." Berg stood, but he didn't bow or give any sign that he was worried the prince had heard himself being called a young fool. "I brought a new sparring partner."

"Was that today? I don't know, Doban. I had a rough night. Not much time for sleep." The prince rubbed his eyes and grinned at Berg. He still hadn't looked at Dara.

"You cannot reschedule an attack," Berg said, a vein pulsing in his thick neck. "I am trying to teach you. Why you are wasting my time?"

"Calm down, man. I can still duel." The prince stretched his long arms above his head. "Where is this guy anyway?"

Berg nodded toward Dara stiffly, looking as if he wanted to slap the prince.

"My student, Dara," he said. "You will duel today."

Dara stepped forward, away from the weapon rack in the corner. She inclined her head but followed Berg's lead and did not bow. The prince looked her up and down, eyebrows raised. Finally he laughed.

"Okay, Doban, you made your point. Don't get too cocky or you'll only be fit to fight women. Lesson learned. I think I'll head to bed now. Truth is I haven't slept, and I've got the makings of a powerful hangover."

He turned to go, but Berg flung up a hand. "Stop. The lesson has not yet begun. You will duel now."

The prince sighed. "Do we have to? I'm sure she's great, but—"

"Yeah, Coach," Dara said, not caring that she was interrupting the future ruler of Vertigon. She didn't have to stand for this. "I have better things to do. Why don't you let me get back to training?"

"You will duel," Berg said.

"But—"

"Is training for both of you."

"Fine," the prince said, sighing heavily. "A bout to ten, then?" He went over to the expansive wardrobe and haphazardly pulled out some dueling gear and dumped it on the floor.

Dara dropped her bag and cloak where she stood and began lifting her knees to her chest to loosen her muscles. She was still warm from the walk up the mountainside. Next she shuffled her feet rapidly, her usual pre-match ritual. The prince glanced over at her and shook his head. He sat down and slowly laced up a fine pair of leather dueling boots. When he finished he walked over to Dara's corner to retrieve a blade from the weapon rack. She was twisting her arms in wide circles to warm up her shoulders.

"You ready yet?" he said, pulling out a blade at random and returning to the wardrobe to shrug on a padded dueling jacket. "Let's get this over with."

"In a minute," Dara said. If he didn't want to warm up, that was his problem. She would not risk injury on account of this amateur.

The prince trudged to the dueling strip, blade slung over his shoulder and mask perched sideways on top of his head, and sat cross-legged on the start line. Dara did her final warm-up sequence, squatting in a low guard stance and then leaping up as high as she could. When she caught the prince rolling his eyes, she did five extra jumps. Finally she pulled on her own glove and jacket, buttoning the collar snugly beneath her chin, and rubbed fresh charcoal on the tip of her blade.

"Okay," she said, facing her opponent on the dueling strip.

"So good of you to join me," the prince said dryly. He stood, pulled his mask down, and adopted a relaxed stance with his blade pointed down.

"To ten," Berg said, walking to the judge's circle beside the strip. "But if I say more, you do more."

"Yes, Coach," Dara said. She assumed her guard stance: mask on, right foot forward, left pointed toward the tall windows, knees slightly bent, blade at a perfect angle so the round guard protected her hand. The prince grinned, his sword arm still relaxed in a lazy stance.

"Ready?" Berg raised both hands, palms facing forward. "Duel!"

Dara executed a perfect advance lunge, her hit landing squarely on Prince Siv's chest. He hadn't even bothered to lift his blade.

"One," Berg said.

"Oh, did you say start?" Siv said. "Right, then."

Dara scowled. He had better try. She would never waste an opponent's time like this.

"Ready. Duel."

This time when Dara advanced, Siv skipped back a few paces. She timed his steps, watching for the rhythm that too many duelists adopted out of habit or laziness. Again, she lunged. This time Siv raised his blade to counter her, but not fast enough. Her hit landed on his arm.

"Two!"

"Okay, okay," Siv said. "No big deal."

"Duel!"

Siv countered Dara's third hit, but his parry was sloppy, and the riposte went wide. Dara landed another clean shot to the prince's torso.

"Go easy, will you?" Siv said. "I might throw up last night's libations." He resumed his stance with the same languid air, but this time he kept his guard up. At the call, he leapt forward and drove a quick thrust straight into Dara's chest. He had a fast arm at least. She parried, but too late, and the blade hit the wooden chest plate beneath her jacket with a dull thunk.

"Nice of you to provide a larger target area," he said.

Dara's jaw tensed. She had heard *that* joke more times than she cared to remember.

"Siv, one; Dara, three. Ready? Duel!"

Siv leapt forward again, but Dara countered him, and they exchanged several parries before retreating a step each. Dara bounced lightly, judging the distance better now that she knew the prince's reach. He went in for another attack, and she countered with a quick shot to the wrist. Siv swore.

"Four, one," Berg said. "Wake up, Prince. You are embarrassing me now."

Siv stopped to rub new charcoal on the tip of his blade. Dara could tell he was flustered. She had seen the same look on the faces of dozens of opponents when they stopped to regroup. He hadn't expected to have to work for this. He resumed his stance.

"Duel!"

Dara and Siv picked up the pace, advancing and retreating across the full length of the strip. Dara tried for a toe hit, but she misjudged Siv's speed, and he countered with a shot to the head. Her mask rang with the impact. She got him back next time with a sharp flick to the wrist that had him shaking out his hand and muttering curses under his breath.

They dueled back and forth, trading blows and occasionally landing simultaneous hits, which earned them a point each. Dara began to sweat, more from concentration than exertion. Prince Siv was proving to be a decent swordsman now that he was taking the bout seriously. But she would not let him beat her.

Soon, the score was nine to six, with Dara still in the lead.

"Ready? Duel!"

Dara advanced, dancing in and out of Siv's range, trying to provoke a response. He didn't rise to the challenge, keeping distance with her but not responding when she got too close. She dropped her guard a bit, inviting him to move. They danced like that, neither one attacking as the seconds passed.

"Do something, students!" Berg growled. "You are not—"

Siv lunged. His hands were lightning fast, and he caught Dara on the forearm as she moved her guard. The blow stung, and she knew it would add to her current collection of bruises.

"Hit! Seven, nine."

"I'm coming back," Siv said. "Look out, girl. You can't catch me sleeping forever."

Dara didn't answer. She never responded to taunts on the strip. Some duelists made a game of it as a way to improve their popularity. The crowds loved a bit of banter. But they loved a winner more.

"Duel!"

Siv advanced, but Dara was ready for him. She caught his blade on hers and thrust it toward him with a strong parry. He seemed about to pull back but suddenly changed tactics and lunged again. At the last second, Dara swept his blade out of the way and launched herself forward. Her hit landed on Siv's shoulder, and she stumbled against him.

"That's the bout!" Berg said. "Dara is the winner."

Siv put both hands on Dara's shoulders to steady her. "No need to throw yourself at me."

Dara regained her balance, face red, and retreated to the start line. The prince swept his mask off and executed a perfect salute, but his jaw was clenched, and he didn't meet Dara's eyes.

Suddenly, a burst of applause came from the spectators' balcony above the dueling hall.

"Bravo!"

"Yes, well done. Siv never loses."

"It's about time!"

Two pale faces peeked over the stone edge of the balcony. Two young women had crept onto it during the duel, and now they were looking down at Dara with huge smiles.

"That was great!" one of them squealed.

"When did you scamps get here?" Siv shouted up at the pair, wiping the sweat from his forehead.

"We've been here since you started losing. Oh, wait. You were losing the whole time! To a girl!" The girls dissolved into a fit of giggles, disappearing from view.

"Get down here, will you?" Siv called. He grinned at Dara. "My sisters. They'll never let me live this down. Good bout, eh?"

"Uhh . . ."

"You don't have to be polite. I got my ass handed to me."

"I am telling you this will happen if you are ever attacked," Berg said. "You will underestimate your opponent, or you will be sloppy."

"I know. I know," Siv said lightly. "Let's just hope they catch me on a morning when I haven't been out all night."

Dara frowned. She was pretty sure she could beat Prince Siv on a good day too, even if he *was* quite fast. He wouldn't laugh it off so easily then.

Berg seemed about to argue, but the door beneath the

balcony opened and the two princesses emerged, still grinning madly.

"This is Sora and Selivia," the prince said. "You know my coach, Berg Doban, and his student . . . uh, what was your name again?"

"Dara Ruminor," she said, voice tight.

"Ruminor? Really? Are you related to the Lantern Maker?" asked the older of the two girls, Princess Soraline. She was a head shorter than Dara and a bit plump. She had sharp eyes and the same high cheekbones and dark hair as her brother. If Dara remembered correctly, she would be about seventeen years old now.

"I'm his daughter," Dara said reluctantly.

"Oooh, Ruminor Lanterns are the best! I have two in my chambers," said the other girl. Selivia was already almost as tall as Soraline, though she was four years younger. She had light streaks in her dark hair that looked suspiciously like she'd bleached it herself with a cheap Fire potion.

"Isn't Lantern Maker Ruminor the one the Fire Warden is always complaining about?" Sora said.

"I'm sorry?" Dara said.

"He was saying that your father wants to loosen the restrictions on the Fire so the Workers can have greater freedom to practice their craft," Sora said. "Warden Lorrid thinks he's trying to gain more power because—"

"Honestly, Sora, no one wants to talk about politics," Selivia interrupted. "What's it like to be a female swordsman? Does it hurt when you get hit? Do you always beat the men? Where did you learn to duel like that?"

"Coach Berg taught me everything I know," Dara said. Berg and Sivarrion had gone over to the washbasin. Berg was lecturing the young prince while he dunked his head into the water repeatedly. Princess Selivia still waited expectantly. "Uh, I love the sport," Dara said. "That's all there is to it, really. I'm trying to get good enough to sign with a patron so I can duel all the time."

"Are you learning Fireworking too?" Princess Soraline asked.

"No, that's my family's business, but I don't have the Spark." Dara fought to keep the bitterness from her voice. She was supposed to be past that.

"I wish *I* could learn Fireworking." Selivia sighed, twirling her fingers in her poorly dyed hair. "It's so beautiful to watch them direct the flows."

"It's very dangerous, Princess," Dara said. "Unless you have the Spark the Fire can really hurt you." She tried not to think of Renna. Sometimes it could hurt you even if you *did* have the Spark. "But yes, it's pretty to watch."

"Oh, you can call me Selivia," the girl said, "especially if you're going to be coming here to train. I like to watch Siv bout sometimes."

"I don't think I'll be coming back," Dara said. "Today was a favor to Berg. I have my own training routine."

"Hold on," the prince said, returning from the washbasin. Water dripped from his dark hair and ran through the coal marks from Dara's hits on his chest. "You have to come for a rematch! In fact, Berg and I were talking, and he thinks you should come a few times a week."

"What?" Dara shot a glare at Berg. "I'm sorry, Prince Sivarrion, but I need to maintain my training regimen. I have a big competition coming up, and—"

"I swear I'll be a better match than I was today. You're better than my other dueling partners have been lately."

"Prince Sivarrion—"

"Siv."

"Fine. Siv. I really can't afford to take the extra time out. I usually help my mother with the lantern business in the mornings, and my training—"

"Young Dara," Berg interrupted. "This can be good practice. And our prince needs this for his safety. I will give you joint lessons, no charge to you."

Dara hesitated. Her parents paid her coaching fees for now, but maybe she could put off working full-time in the lantern shop a bit longer if she got some free lessons.

"I'm tired of dueling hobbyists," Siv said. "I want to fight the pros."

"I'll consider it," Dara said. She didn't particularly like Siv, and he would never understand how important her training was. She couldn't afford to mess around with a training partner who wasn't as focused as she was. But the prospect of free lessons was tempting.

"You come three mornings a week," Berg said, as if it had already been decided.

"I work for my mother in the mornings," Dara said.

"She'll make an exception for me," Siv said. He dumped the rest of his gear on the floor in front of the wardrobe and headed for the door beneath the balcony. "I insist you return. Now I'm going to pass out. I could sleep like a velgon bear right about now."

Dara bit back her response. He insisted, did he? They'd see about that. Dara would *consider* it, and no more.

"Please come back!" Selivia said, grabbing Dara's hand as the princesses walked with Dara and Berg to the other door. "You're more fun to watch than Siv's last dueling partner. He was soooo slow."

"And I'd love to hear more about the lantern business," Sora said. She smiled kindly, her plump cheeks rosy.

"Maybe," Dara said. "It was nice to meet you anyway."

With a final wave, the princesses turned to walk deeper into the palace together. Dara was surprised at how casually they treated her. Fireworkers were not nobles in Vertigon, despite the influence they wielded. She wondered if her status as Rafe

Ruminor's daughter put her above the average craftsman's or if the princesses treated everyone alike.

Berg and Dara headed back toward the entryway. The castle was busier than it had been early in the morning, with noblemen and ladies in Firegold-embroidered dresses processing through the halls with their attendants. They didn't even glance at Dara and Berg in their practical, somber clothing.

"You see the prince is not serious," Berg said as they left the castle and made their way down to the outer wall. "You must do this, Dara."

"Coach, my mother needs me in the shop. I can't get away three mornings a week."

"You will try," Berg said. He stopped and placed his big, square hands on her shoulders. He looked her in the eyes, a deep frown cutting into his forehead. "Is for the sake of the kingdom, not just for your training."

"I'll see what I can do." Dara didn't understand why this was so important to Berg. The prince might scoff at the nobles who treated dueling as a hobby, but he himself would never compete in a tournament, much less a real fight. No matter what dangers Berg thought were lurking, she suspected the prince would be fine.

But if Berg was serious about the free lessons, maybe she could extend her training hours even if it took her longer to find a sponsor. If her coaching wasn't costing her parents gold, they might ease up on her a bit about working in the shop. It might be worth spending a little extra time with this insufferable prince for that.

KING SEVREN

SIV flung himself face-first onto his bed. He hadn't realized he was that out of shape. Losing to a girl. Damn. He buried his face in the cushions. He should take off his dueling boots and sweaty shirt, but he wanted to rest for a minute. Or an hour. Or all afternoon.

He'd just drifted to sleep when there was a knock at the door.

"Go away!"

"Sir? It's Pool."

"Go away, Pool," Siv mumbled into his cushions. His body-guard knocked harder.

"Your father, His Majesty the King, has requested your presence as he takes his noon refreshment."

"I know who my father is," Siv grumbled, but he pulled himself up and ran a hand over his scruffy beard. No time to shave. He reached for a dry shirt.

"Sir? I must insist that you accompany me to attend His Majesty."

"Hold your hell irons, Pool. I'm coming." Siv lurched to the door and pulled it open. Pool was about to knock again, but he drew back his hand and stepped aside as Siv exited his chambers. Pool was a dour man, just past forty, with a sweep of gray beside each temple. He had been Siv's bodyguard since he was a little boy, and he had protected him from fun far more often than from danger.

Siv and Pool headed up the wide corridor leading to the castle's main stairwell. His father's chambers were at the top of the central tower. Siv wished he had palanquin bearers to carry him up there. His legs were sore, and his head felt as if he'd accidently left it inside a kettledrum during a thunderstorm. That last goblet of wine was definitely a mistake last night. He shouldn't let Bolden talk him into such things. No one ever needed their last goblet of wine.

Siv climbed the winding staircase slowly. Slices of daylight cut through the windows, which were just wide enough for light and Firearrows. He hadn't been up to dine with his father in more than a week. His mother was visiting her relations down in Trure again, and the king must be lonely.

Siv would much rather be in bed. He'd sleep like a cullmoran as soon as he had half a chance. That girl had given him a run for his firestones—and he didn't like it. Sure, Sel and Sora could laugh about it, but it stung. Stung like a Pendarkan zurwasp.

He was still grumbling to himself when he arrived outside his father's antechamber. The two aged Castle Guards stepped aside after a cursory glance and a nod at Pool, who had followed him up the stairs.

"Get some rest, Pool," Siv said. "You had a long night too."

"Thank you, sir." Pool gave a crisp salute. "I shall return before your afternoon excursion."

Siv shrugged, tempted to cancel his afternoon excursion. What was he supposed to be doing again? Tea with some noble family or other, probably. To be fair, he should have dismissed Pool *before* he had to climb all the way up the stairs, but then

Pool really shouldn't have let him have that last goblet of wine. His head gave an answering throb. *Firelord take you, Bolden.*

Siv's father hadn't arrived, but his serving man was busy setting up the meal in the antechamber. Siv could eat a cur-dragon right about now, but all he saw was a simple stew and a plate of orchard fruits. His father was trying to watch his midsection. Siv sighed, grabbed a plum from the platter, and flung himself onto one of the low couches. If he could get away, he'd head down to the kitchens for a goat pie later. The cooks never said no if he smiled wide enough.

When the king entered, Siv was nearly asleep, his half-eaten plum in danger of dropping out of his hand and rolling across the wide Firegold rug. King Sevren wore chamber slippers and carried a stack of papers, which he dumped onto the couch beside Siv. His thick gray hair stood up in all directions, the surest sign that the queen had been away for too long. His eyeglasses hung slightly askew.

"Sivarrion, have some fruit," the king said, reaching out to help himself.

"Already did," Siv said. "I'm beat. What's this about?"

"Have you tried the West Gorge blue plums? They're excellent this year."

"Yeah. Delicious." Siv popped the rest of his plum into his mouth and sucked on the pit.

"Do you know which orchard was the first to produce blue plums?" King Sevren asked.

"West Gorge?" Siv said around the pit.

"Wrong! Second Slope. It was during the reign of my grandfather."

"Fascinating."

"And do you know why it's important to know this?"

"Parlor quiz?"

"The Ferrington family, which owns Second Slope, also controls one of our primary export hubs." The king continued to bustle around his table, but Siv knew where this was going. He was in for a lecture all right. The first clue should have been that his sisters hadn't been invited to lunch. "The Ferringtons could cut access to the entire citadel if they were so inclined. Or if they felt offended because people"—here the king tipped his eyeglass toward his son—"don't have a proper appreciation for the work they've done to cultivate the blue plums."

"I'm glad you appreciate them, then. Can I go now?"

"Son." The king's tone barely changed, but Siv sat back in his chair. No point pushing it. "Warden Lorrid informed me that you skipped the second half of your lesson yesterday. You told him I asked to see you."

"Uh . . ."

"Now, I know I didn't ask to see you, because I was enjoying a meal with the blue plum family at their orchard estate." The king held up one of the luminous fruits. How was he able to sound so pleasant and still make Siv feel as if he was in trouble? The man was skilled, no doubt about it. "I would have been happy for you to join me," the king continued, "except that I know your relationship with the Fireworkers is even more important. That's why you were supposed to be with the Warden."

"Sorry, sir," Siv said.

The king took a seat beside his son on the cushions, a plate piled high with orchard fruits perched on his lap. "You've avoided too many of your lessons, Sivarrion. This has been going on for some time."

"Zage drones on and on about the history of Pendark. I read Merlin Mavril's account last year, and he makes it a lot more interesting than Zage."

"Zage understands the nuances of how Pendark relates to Vertigon—and how they make use of our Fire exports. Mavril is propaganda written for an adoring Pendarkan audience. Zage himself spent time in Pendark during his youth studying with the Watermight practitioners. You must listen to him."

"I'll work on it." Siv started to stand, but his father stopped him with a word.

"Sivarrion."

Siv sighed. "I know. Responsibility. Duty to the kingdom. Studies. I understand it's important, but I have plenty of time."

"You may think you do, but you need more experience, son. I want you to take a larger role in governance."

"The kingdom is doing fine without me," Siv said. "I know what I have to do eventually. Rule. Reproduce. Be wise and good and responsible. But it'll be years yet before it matters." The last thing he wanted to do was spend even more time studying matters of state. He read a lot. That should be enough for the next few years.

"Becoming wise takes longer than you think," the king said. He popped a small plum into his mouth.

"Sure it does." Siv reached for an apple from his father's plate. "But I've got the perfect model. I'll just become you when I'm old."

The king raised an eyebrow. "Flattery won't get you out of every scenario, you know." His face softened. "You'll find your own way, son. Every ruler does. I don't rule like my father, and you won't rule like yours."

Siv didn't think it would be bad at all to rule like his father. Sevren led Vertigon with an easy hand. He relied on people who were good at their jobs, like Zage the Fire Warden, Pavorran the General, and his buddy Bandobar, the Captain of the Castle Guard. It was all about delegating tasks. There should be plenty of time left for dueling practice and sleeping in.

"So what was more important than both blue plums and Fireworkers?" the king asked.

Siv knew there was no point in lying now that he'd been caught. "I was playing cards with Bolden Rollendar."

"Ah. Another important family. You must be wary of your friendship with him. The Rollendar family doesn't always have the interests of the city at heart."

"I know. Better to keep him close, don't you think?" There was a chance Siv could still spin this his way.

"Perhaps." The king frowned. "But be wary. And don't skip lessons. You know how Zage gets when he's offended." The king and the Fire Warden had worked together since before Siv could walk. He was pretty sure his father would always take Zage's side if the Fire Warden said he wasn't studying hard enough.

"It won't happen again," Siv said.

"Excellent." The king folded his arms. "And another thing: you still smell of liquor. That and sweat."

Siv rolled his eyes. "Now you sound like Mother. It's all part of the game. You don't want me to stop drinking, do you?"

"Goodness, no. But you must be careful of leaving yourself vulnerable. A king can't be seen to be out of control at any time."

"I'm not out of control," Siv said. "In fact, I've already had a healthy training session this morning." He glanced at his father. "And I'm not a king."

"The people's memory of you will remain."

"You'll be king for another thirty years." Siv knew he'd have to be responsible one day. And he would be. He loved Vertigon, the heady mountain slopes, the crisp lines of the bridges, the mist and magic of it. He'd take care of it. Eventually.

The king shook his head. "You know the saying: the people of Vertigon have memories as long as the mountain is tall. They can't see you as an irresponsible young man."

"I *am* a young man," Siv said. He stood, planning to pace around the room, until his head gave a warning throb. He settled for leaning against the table. "I'll have plenty of time to meet with plum farmers and Fireworkers. I want to enjoy my youth while I have it."

"You have duties, Siv."

"As you and the tutors remind me every day . . ."

The king sighed and adjusted his eyeglasses. "Perhaps you should pay a visit to your mother's people in Trure. Your grandfather will put you to rights. It may be time for you to begin seeking a wife there as well. Certainly settled me down."

"I've barely turned twenty," Siv said. "That's years away yet. More importantly, I don't think I should take a Truren wife when the time comes. It worked out well enough for you, but I'm sure our people would prefer a Vertigonian lady for their next queen. It'd be a chance to make extra special friends with a powerful noble family too."

The king raised an eyebrow. "You've thought it through."

"Believe it or not," Siv said, leaning conspiratorially toward his father. "I keep my wits about me when drinking with Bolden. I might have met a promising candidate or two in his company."

"I'm listening."

"Don't want to show all my cards just yet." Siv took a plum from the table and tossed into the air. "But I have an alliance in mind that could pan out." He caught the plum with a grin. "Trust me."

"I want to trust you, son, but in the meantime I need to see you taking some responsibility." The king stood and put a weighty hand on his son's shoulder. He always made Siv feel safe, firmly planted in the soil of the mountain. Siv really did want to please him. Eventually.

"I'll work on it."

"Good. Now, that goat stew is getting cold. Have a bowl."

PRACTICE

W HEN Dara stopped by the Ruminor dwelling after leaving the castle, her mother had still been deep in conversation with Farr, Master Corren's apprentice. They were chatting away about Firesmiths and access restrictions, so Dara avoided any questions about where she had been. She managed to get out of the house again with plenty of time left to meet up with Kel and Oat for a bite to eat before practice.

She found her friends in Stone Market near Furlingbird Bridge, which connected Village and Square Peaks. They were easy to spot in the bustling market because Oat—who was already exceptionally tall—had climbed onto a barrel outside a tavern. He waved his long arms over his head to get Dara's attention.

She pushed her way through the crowd, enjoying the enticing smell of soldarberry pies and fresh-baked bread. A handful of vendors hawked their wares from baskets strapped to their backs, but most had set up permanent stalls along the two levels of the market.

Stone Market was built across two terraces near the bridge entrance, with steps connecting them on either end. A rocky outcropping separated the two levels, and since it was summer people were perched on the stones, enjoying their lunches in the rare sunshine. The steps were extra crowded today. Dara clambered across the rocks to get to the upper level, where Kel and Oat waited.

"It's about time!" Kel said. "The salt cakes are going to run out."

"Sorry," Dara said. "I had to take care of something at home."

"You're always taking care of things."

"My parents need me."

"We need you," Kel said. "I don't have any coins. Can you spot me lunch?"

Dara dug into her pocket with a sigh. "You'd better pay me back," she said. "You're the one with the patron."

"I know, but Lord Bolden does love to gamble," Kel said. "I've got to keep up with him."

"I'm sure that's why," Dara said. "You'd never, ever go out to the parlors, otherwise."

"Indeed," Kel said sagely. "I'd be a regular workhorse if it weren't for my liege."

Oat hopped off the barrel beside them. "Where are we eating?"

"Tollia's?" Dara said.

"Better not," Kel said. "One of the serving women is a dueling fan. Last time I was there I couldn't finish my goat pie with her lurking around and staring at me."

"Sounds like she's a Kelad Korran fan, not an actual dueling fan," Dara said. Kel had a rather mysterious effect on spectators —female ones in particular—but Dara had spent a bit too much time sweating it out with him in the dueling school to see the appeal. He had a wiry strength, but he was also a full head shorter than her.

"That's my favorite kind of fan," Kel said, "just not when I'm trying to eat in peace."

"Rordin's, then?" Oat suggested.

"Rordin's it is."

They made their way through the crowds toward the little pie stall at the far end of the market. The shops displayed fresh-cooked foods, garments, imported wares from the Lands Below, and Fireworks of all kinds. The more established Workers kept their own shops, like the Ruminors, so most of the Fireworks on display in the market stalls were the cheaper kind: Everlights, slim Firesticks for warming hands and beverages, simple Firebulbs, Heatstones, and even small Fireblossoms, which exploded into beautiful, ephemeral flowers to decorate special occasions. There were also metalworks in a hundred varieties. These had been forged using the Fire, like most dueling rapiers, but they didn't continue to burn once completed unless they were Fire-infused.

Dara slowed when they passed Morn Brothers Dueling Supply Shop three quarters of the way down the market. A new line of dueling gloves was on display in the window, each intricately embroidered with a different design. The windows were bedecked in the colors of Bilzar Ten, an accomplished duelist sponsored by the Morn brothers. A painting of Bilzar hung on the wall inside the shop, clad head to toe in his sponsor's gear.

Oat stopped beside her. "I need to get myself some fans," he said. "And one of those equipment deals. Bilzar gets all his gear for free."

"They probably don't make jackets long enough for those gangly arms of yours," Kel said.

Oat sighed, shoulders slumping. "I know. But custom gear is expensive."

"You have fans," Dara said. "What about those three brothers who always wait for you after tourneys?"

"That's true," Oat said, brightening a bit. "They think I'm the greatest thing since spiced salt cakes."

"Speaking of which," Kel said. "Can we move along here? Rordin's cakes go fast."

They purchased goat pies and salt cakes and found a free spot on the rocks to eat. A few people recognized them from competitions, but they were nowhere near as well known as some of the older duelists in the city. Bilzar Ten was just one of the athletes who had managed to parlay their fame into lucrative sponsorship deals with local businesses and noblemen. Kel's patron, Lord Bolden Rollendar, was the son of one of the more powerful nobles in Vertigon. These arrangements were many times more valuable than the prize purses at any given competition. They were essential if you didn't want to work another job in addition to training. Dara had her eye on one patron in particular who signed a female duelist every season.

"What were you and Berg whispering about the other day, Dara?" Kel asked as he licked pie juice off his fingers. "He was looking mighty grim."

"Berg is always serious," Dara said.

"Yeah, but he's been acting suspicious lately too. Haven't you noticed?"

"Suspicious how?" Oat asked.

"I've seen him around on King's," Kel said. "Last time, he pretended he didn't see me and snuck away down an alley by the Fire Guild."

"I'm sure it's nothing," Dara said. Berg had asked her not to mention her duel with the prince. But he *had* left her before she crossed the bridge after the duel that morning. What other business did he have on King's Peak?

"Maybe he's thinking about setting up a King's Peak branch of his school," Oat said.

"Or maybe," Kel said, "he's spying on one of the schools that's already there. I wouldn't mind finding out which moves

Rawl has been working on. I'll probably have to face him at the Eventide Open."

"Doesn't your friend Yuri train with Rawl?"

"Yeah, but he's no snitch," Kel said. "Even when he's drunk. I've already tried to pump him for information."

"So what could Berg be up to, then?" Oat asked.

Dara kept her attention on her salt cake and didn't answer. She had a feeling she was in the best position out of the three of them to find out. She wondered if Berg's strange behavior was connected to his sudden desire to take the prince's training to the next level. She couldn't help feeling curious about what her coach might be up to. She knew very little of what his life was like outside of the dueling school. He had lived on the mountain for longer than she could remember, but he *was* from the Lands Below. It was strange that he should be so worried about the future ruler of Vertigon. Perhaps she should give training with the heir-prince another try after all.

"All I know is Berg will make us do extra squat lunges if we don't head over soon," Kel said, stuffing the last of his cake into his mouth and standing. "Let's get moving." He glanced across the market nervously, and Dara spotted an eager maiden shoving through the crowd toward them. Her feet slipped on the stones, but that didn't slow her down.

"Isn't that Tollia's serv—?"

"No idea. Race you to the bridge." Kel took off before Dara could finish the question, demonstrating his impressive agility as he leapt down the rocky outcropping. Oat offered Dara a hand and pulled her to her feet. They set off after Kel as the blushing serving maid scrambled across the laps of five picnicking bridgeworkers to reach them. By the time Dara and Oat made it to Furlingbird Bridge, Kel was halfway across the Fissure.

A few days later, Dara arrived at the castle to find Prince Siv stretched out on the rug in his dueling hall.

"The swordswoman has returned!" The prince looked more rested than the last time she'd seen him. His brown eyes were a little brighter, and he no longer had bags under them, though he still hadn't bothered to shave. He bent the corner of a page in his book and tossed it aside.

Dara set her gear bag beside the weapon rack, staying near the door.

"Where's Coach Berg?" she asked.

"He's got a cold. He sent a courier this morning. You changed your mind, eh?"

"A few sessions can't hurt," Dara said. She shifted her feet, feeling awkward without Berg there. He was the whole reason she had decided to come back here. The room seemed bigger and grander with only her and the prince inside. She looked up at the balcony, but it was empty too.

"My sisters are out with the cur-dragons this morning," Siv said. "They'll be sorry they missed you. Selivia's your biggest fan."

"Oh. I guess we should start, then. What's your warm-up routine?"

"You're looking at it," Siv said. He reached for his toes half-heartedly.

"It's better to jog or something first. Your muscles are probably still cold."

"If you insist."

Siv hauled himself to his feet and started jogging in a wide circle around the dueling hall. After a moment's hesitation, Dara joined him. He was just another training partner, she told herself. It was just like running with Kel and Oat. She tried to forget the fact that they were in the royal castle.

After a few minutes Siv turned around so that he was jogging backward. He seemed to know the shape of the hall well, because he turned the corners without looking behind him, still studying Dara.

"Sel's been asking around about your stats," he said. "Sounds like you're already an accomplished duelist. Berg could have warned me."

"Wouldn't that defeat the purpose of the lesson?"

"He didn't even mention that you won the Square Tourney last season. Won it outright."

"This is the season that matters," Dara said.

"I guess. I usually only follow the male duelists, though. I'd never heard of you."

"Charming."

"That's me!" Siv turned around again to face forward while they jogged. "So what do you do when you're not dueling?"

"I help my parents with their business."

Dara had slipped out after her father went to the workshop that morning. Her mother had a meeting at the Fire Guild, so she would never know that Dara wasn't in the lantern show-room for the whole morning. She'd need to come up with a better excuse if she was going to keep doing these morning training sessions with the prince. *If.*

"I meant for fun," Siv said.

"Dueling is fun."

"Well, yeah, but you take it super seriously. It's just a sport."

"Maybe to you. Okay, shall we stretch and start some drills?" Dara returned to her corner and began her warm-up routine. Siv kept looking over at her. He seemed to find her amusing somehow. She avoided his gaze as she completed her usual set of exercises. She couldn't let him disrupt her focus.

They met in the middle of the hall to begin the drills. Berg had taught Siv the same form sequences he used with Dara and the others. They took turns going through the movements. Siv was more alert than he had been last time, but he tended to get lazy and drop his guard between the forms. Dara found herself getting frustrated. Maybe this wasn't such a good idea. She could only work with the prince if it meant training every bit as hard as she normally did. And now her coach wasn't even here.

"Shall we bout?" she said finally.

"Easy there. Let's have a water break first."

"I can't stay for long. And aren't you supposed to be ready at any moment? What if you're attacked?"

Siv tucked his mask under his arm. "Do you honestly think that will happen? In Vertigon?"

"I . . ."

"Look, I appreciate what Berg's trying to do, but if I'm going to be assassinated, it will probably be a poisoned goblet or something. I just like to duel."

"You never know," Dara said, remembering what her father had said about the Fire Warden's growing sway over the kingdom. "You should really be ready for anything. There could be dangers you don't know about."

"Sure, sure. Dangers abound," Siv said. He poured water into a goblet from a silver pitcher by the washbasin. "What about you? You're training again this afternoon. Can't you have an easier morning session?"

"I have the Eventide Open in just over two weeks," Dara said. Siv hadn't offered her any water, but she didn't think she should help herself. This was the palace, after all. She'd have to bring her own water skin next time. If there was a next time. "Eventide is one of the last competitions before the Vertigon Cup. I need a strong finish so the patrons will pay attention to me at the Cup."

"Oh right, you need a patron. What's the big deal with them anyway? They just choose the best duelists?" Siv picked a blade from the weapon rack and began rubbing a brick of charcoal on the tip.

"Generally, yes," Dara said. "They also pay attention to who's most popular with the crowds. They want to know who will draw high ticket sales, both for standard tourneys and for exhibition matches."

"So they like big personalities. Tough luck for you, then." Siv grinned and headed for the dueling strip.

"They like winners," Dara said. "All the posturing is a waste of time. I'm going to be the best, and they won't be able to turn me down."

"Sounds like it's about more than winning," Siv said. "You've got to play the game."

"You don't know anything about it," Dara said.

"Hey, think about my father. He's a likable man, and it helps him keep the peace."

"Vertigon would be peaceful no matter who the ruler is," Dara said.

"Not true at all. We Amintelles rule with an easy hand. Squeeze people too tight, and they want to squeeze back. My father knows what he's doing." Despite his casual air, pride and affection crept into Siv's voice when he mentioned his father.

"The duels are different," Dara said. "You don't need to be that likable if you're good enough."

"Let's see how good you are, then," Siv said. "I'm feeling like a human being today. Ten firestones say I can beat you by three points."

"I don't have ten firestones."

"It's an expression. Sheesh, no wonder the fans love you. Duel!"

Dara and Siv dueled. They didn't keep score out loud, but Dara kept a running tally in her head. She suspected Siv was doing the same. She had to work hard to keep the points even. Siv had been right: he was better than he had demonstrated last time. He used his relaxed air as a weapon, which made him a frustrating opponent. Nearly every time Dara thought he had lost focus, he answered her attacks with lightning-fast ripostes and counterattacks.

She always liked facing opponents with different styles. She had trained against the same sparring partners at Berg's school every day for years. Siv used some of Berg's signature moves, but he also threw in unique attacks that Dara hadn't seen in competition before. This would be good practice for her upcoming tournament. There were a few strong women in her division—and more would travel from the Lands Below for the Cup. She had to be versatile. She had to show the patrons she deserved a sponsorship more than the others.

After they had each landed fifty hits, Dara stopped keeping score. She focused on the rhythm of Siv's steps and the angles of her blade. The only sounds were the tap of their boots and the thud of their hits. Sweat seeped through both of their thick jackets. Dara threw everything she had at the prince—and he answered. They fought back and forth across the hall, and Dara lost herself in the thrust and pulse of the duel.

Finally, Siv raised a hand. "Enough, enough! You're in better shape than me." He pulled off his mask and flopped down onto the floor.

Dara hesitated for a second then sat cross-legged across from the prince. Her weapon arm shook a bit, and sweat dripped down her forehead.

"That was a good bout," she said. "You're better than you look."

"Damn right." Siv grinned, running a hand through his dark hair. "So, are you coming back?"

Dara rubbed the surface of her guard. The morning sun was strong now, slanting through the windows of the prince's gorgeous dueling hall. It *had* been a good bout. If she gave her mother a few extra hours of work in the afternoon and stayed later at the dueling school, she could probably get away with training here a few mornings a week. She could tell her mother that Berg had switched her lesson schedule around.

"Only if you give me a bout like that every time."

"Deal." Siv stretched out a gloved hand, and Dara shook it, meeting his eyes for a moment and then looking away.

A bell chimed. It was almost high noon. Dara had lost track of time. She packed up her gear quickly.

"I have to get over to the school on Square," she said.

"Can't believe you're planning to train more," Siv said. He still sat on the dueling floor, breathing hard.

"I have to be ready."

"Well, I'm going to sleep the afternoon away."

Dara remembered what her mother had said about the prince being a lout. But he had worked hard during the duel. Siv's instincts were good, and he had fast reflexes. He could be a good training partner. And she was curious about whether there was any merit to Berg's suspicions. At the very least, she could practice with him until the Eventide Open.

Siv lay on his back and pulled his knees up toward his chest one at a time to stretch, groaning as he stretched out his muscles.

"Maybe you should do more exercise before our next bout," Dara said, "so you can keep up with me."

Siv glanced up from the floor, one foot high in the air. "Maybe you shouldn't tell the prince of your citadel what to do. Especially when it involves exercise."

Dara's cheeks warmed. "I'm sorry, Your Highness. I didn't mean—"

"I'm kidding." Siv chuckled. "Relax. You look like a red-handed cullmoran."

Dara bowed stiffly and reached for her gear bag, biting back the urge to respond.

"Prince."

"Until next time, swordswoman."

She slung her bag over her shoulder and left the dueling hall. A guard patrolled the hallway outside the door, but otherwise the palace was quiet. She headed down the corridor, its straight lines like a giant's dueling strip. It was longer even than Berg's school and flatter than most of the spaces on the mountain outside of Square Peak.

Dara glanced back at the guard, but he was staring at the opposite wall as if it might come to life. She picked up her pace, jogging down the cavernous corridor. There was so much space! She ran faster. It was exhilarating, better than running the bridges because she didn't have to worry about rotting boards and foot traffic. A few servants glanced at her as she passed, but they didn't stop her. The weariness in her legs didn't slow her as she embraced the feeling of running down the long, flat space. Despite herself, she grinned. She could get used to this.

Then she rounded a corner and bumped straight into Zage Lorrid.

Dara recoiled, and her gear bag slipped off her shoulder. The blades inside rattled, the sound echoing around the castle entrance hall.

"I'm sorry, sir!" she gasped. "I didn't see you."

Fire Warden Lorrid was a slight man who seemed to disappear into the shadows in the entryway. He wore a black cloak with a silver clasp shaped like a leaf. He pulled the cloak close around him, studying Dara.

"And what is the daughter of Rafe Ruminor doing in the royal castle, may I ask?"

Dara started. She had only seen the Fire Warden from a distance. His name had been a curse in their house since Renna died, but she was surprised he knew who she was.

"I was dueling with Siv—with the prince. I train with his coach." Dara wished she could disappear too. What had she been thinking, running down the palace corridors?

The Fire Warden frowned, his egg-white forehead creasing. "Is that so? Interesting. I wouldn't expect Rafe Ruminor to want his daughter keeping company with the Amintelles."

"Sir?"

The Fire Warden twisted his fingers in his black cloak, suddenly seeming to loom like a great black dragon. Dara resisted the urge to take a step back. She was surprised the Warden had the nerve to speak of any daughter of Rafe Ruminor after what he had let happen to Renna. Her sister's face rose before Dara for an instant, wide and strong like their mother's. Dara pictured the molten Fire sliding over Renna's fingers like oil as she learned to bend it to her will. Dara had watched her early lessons, sitting on a stone table in the workshop, her legs swinging, as Renna practiced the Work. But she hadn't been there the day it had happened.

"Tell me, Miss Ruminor, do you also Work the Fires?" Zage whispered. "Or perhaps you carry a Fire Blade to your duels."

"No, sir," Dara said. "I'm not a Fireworker. I train with steel."

"Hmmm." The sound was drawn out, as if Zage were humming. "See that it stays that way."

"Yes, sir. I really should be going."

Zage waved a hand. He had a large silver ring set with glittering obsidian on his middle finger. "Be careful what you bring to the castle, Miss Ruminor. Farewell."

Dara fled. She didn't stop running until she reached the bottom of the staircase leading away from the castle. She told herself it was just because she was late, but she couldn't get away fast enough. She shivered, grateful for the sunshine warming the mountainside when she reached Lower King's.

She had spoken to Zage Lorrid. The man who controlled the system regulating the flow of Fire through the mountain. The man who had *lost* control of the system that fateful day ten years ago, allowing the power to surge through every channel in the mountain and burst from every access point like a hundred geysers. Most of the Workers had been able to handle the surge, but not Renna. She was just an apprentice. A child. She had still been learning to control the Fire, managing the careful balance between drawing it into her veins and manipulating it outside her body. Workers spent years achieving that balance before they could create anything meaningful out of the Fire. Renna had been too young, and the surge had been too much.

And Zage Lorrid had been responsible. The king had pardoned him for the Surge, calling it an accident, but that wasn't enough for Dara's parents. They had warned against restraining the Fire. They knew that holding back the power was too dangerous. The Surge proved their fears were well founded, but their daughter had been the one to pay the cost. Thanks to Zage.

Dara looked back at the castle standing proud on the mountaintop. Zage had maintained his position after all these years. Whatever relationship he had with the king, he hadn't been punished. Somehow his power had only grown. What if he wanted more now? Berg was worried about a danger to the king's family. What if that danger came from the man the king had pardoned years ago, keeping him in his employ like a viper in a cave?

Now that Dara had seen him in person, seen his glittering eyes and felt his lurking presence, she was inclined to think Berg was right. And if anyone in Vertigon was dangerous, it was Zage Lorrid.

THE FIRE WARDEN

S IV had his head in the washbasin when the Fire Warden
entered the dueling hall. He shook the water out of his
hair and smiled at Zage Lorrid. He felt energized after his duel
with Dara. She was a tough opponent who made him work for
every point. It had been a long time since he'd sparred against
someone as good as her.

It didn't hurt that she wasn't bad to look at either. Even
better, it was fun to tease her. She was so serious and intense.

Speaking of intense people, Zage sat in the chair beside the
gear wardrobe and folded his hands.

"My prince."

"Warden. To what do I owe the pleasure?" Siv reached for a
towel and leaned against the washbasin.

"We have our lesson at this hour, my prince. I believed I
would find you here."

"Right. Of course. Good thinking." Siv blushed. He really
had meant to be better about attending his lessons after talking
with his father a few days ago. "Uh, let's go to the table in my
antechamber."

"Of course, my prince."

Siv led the way through the door beneath the balcony, which went directly to his rooms. He used to have much bigger chambers, but when he'd convinced his father to let him turn the quiet portico outside his room into the dueling hall, he'd had to give up most of his antechamber to make enough space. Now there was only room for a simple table, a low set of couches, an armchair, and a large Fire Gate, which drew a thin stream of Fire from the veins beneath the castle to circulate and warm his rooms before diverting to one of the workshops.

As usual, Zage went straight to the Gate and placed his hand on the ornate mantle above it. He leaned into it for a moment, fixing his eyes on the Fire flowing through it until it dimmed to a tiny molten thread. Zage hated being too warm, though it meant Siv would have to call for one of the Fireworkers on the castle's staff to turn the Fire up again later. It may be summer, but the stone castle was the highest, coldest point on the mountain.

Siv dragged his cushioned armchair over to the table with a screech and dropped into it. Zage sat across from him in one of the carved wooden chairs and pulled a sheaf of parchment from his robe.

"Shall we begin? I believe we should discuss how the unique magic properties of the Lands Below, Pendarkan Water-might in particular, influence the acceptance of some of our less specialized Works of..."

Siv did his best to listen politely. Zage was a quiet man with a penchant for sweeping about the castle in his dark robes and giving lectures in his raspy, papery voice. Despite his unfortunate lack of charisma, he had been the king's friend for decades. Siv had been afraid of him as a child, but as he grew older he had realized that Zage was actually quite shy. He was meticulous in his stewardship of the Fire of Vertigon, and he was earnest, almost fanatical, in his desire to give Siv a proper education in the nuances of Fireworking politics.

But today, Siv was distracted. Dara Ruminor had his attention. He went over their lengthy duel in his head step by step, looking for her weaknesses. She didn't have many. She was a precision instrument. They had stopped keeping score, but he was fairly certain he had lost the bout by a point or two—not that he'd ever admit that to her.

"My prince."

"Huh?"

Zage sighed, hissing like a furlingbird in deep winter.

"I said that when you are in Trure you must be sure to visit the palace of the Earl of Eastfell to ask his opinion on—"

"I'm not going to Trure anytime soon."

"Pardon me, my prince, but your royal father informed me you had discussed a visit to the home of your grandfather."

"He mentioned it in passing," Siv said, "but nothing has been decided."

Zage frowned. "I understood from my meeting with the king this morning that your journey is to commence before First Snow."

"First Snow! He wants me to spend the *whole winter* there?" Siv stood and paced in front of the Fire Gate. Or more accurately, he hobbled. He really was out of shape, and his muscles had seized up after sitting in the chair for hours. Well, maybe it had only been twenty minutes.

"If I may say so, I think it's a wise decision," Zage said soberly. "You would do well to better acquaint yourself with our closest neighbors and their noble families."

"I know everything about them, Zage. Trure is literally the only thing my mother talks about."

"The queen's reminiscences of the land of her birth are not without value," Zage said, "but you must learn of Trure's intricacies for yourself and begin building your own relationships. Its politics are more complex than those of Vertigon."

"Vertigon isn't simple, though," Siv said. He had nothing against Trure. His mother had taken lengthy visits there throughout his childhood, often leaving Siv and his sisters behind on the mountain. She was there now, in fact. Siv and his sisters had always known Trure was the only place their mother was truly happy. But when they accompanied her on visits, they hadn't seen her much more than during her long absences. Their time was always consumed by stuffy state dinners, preening cousins, and walks about the Truren Horesplains, which were every bit as plain as they sounded. Give him the heady heights and wild mists of Vertigon Mountain any day. Come to think of it, he *did* have a lot against Trure. He needed a better reason to avoid the trip, though—if he could refuse his father.

"The variety provided by such a journey would do you good," Zage said.

"I don't want to go for the whole winter," Siv said. "I'm making headway with a few noble families, including a certain lady who is our mutual acquaintance." Would he use that leverage? Oh, yes he would. It may be a little premature, but he was sure Lady Tull was starting to warm to him.

"True enough," Zage said. "But I believe now may be an opportune time for you to be out of the castle. There are dangerous games afoot. As you said, Vertigon isn't simple."

"Dangerous games?"

"Whispers fill the smoke of the mountain," Zage said. "We must all keep watch lest the whispers turn to shouts."

Siv sighed. "Oh, what shall we do?" He mimicked Zage's hoarse, papery voice. The Warden was getting paranoid. Constantly controlling massive amounts of molten Fire couldn't be good for the brain.

"Never fear," Zage said, either not noticing or not caring about Siv's mocking tone. "I will look out for your family while you go abroad."

"If I didn't know better, I'd think you're trying to get rid of me for the winter, Zage." Siv grinned.

The Fire Warden blinked slowly and shuffled the papers on the table. "Of course not, my prince. Shall we return to the lesson?"

Siv sighed and dropped back into his chair as the driest lecture in eternity resumed.

Dara was listening to a lecture of her own. She had been running down a sloping street toward Stork Bridge, which spanned the Fissure from King's Peak to Square, when she met her mother. Lima had been walking with Master Corren and his apprentice Farr. They were deep in conversation, but not so deep that Lima didn't notice her daughter trying to sneak past in the crowd.

"Dara Ruminor," her mother screeched. "What are you doing?"

Dara froze. "Uh, going for a run."

"Here?"

Dara glanced around the steep avenue bordered by upscale shops and taverns. Marble greathouses rose beyond them, and residents in well-tailored coats and finely embroidered dresses strolled past, servants in tow. They were far away from their home in the Village, but the Fire Guild was located in a greathouse here on King's Peak. Of course. Her mother had business there today. Dara hadn't even thought about that when she'd snuck out this morning.

"I run all over the place," Dara said. "King's is less busy than the Village, so there's more space." She pretended not to notice the crowds ebbing and flowing around them. It *was* busier on Village Peak, but King's wasn't exactly quiet at this time of day. Dara tried to hide her gear bag behind her. She didn't usually run with it, but maybe her mother wouldn't notice.

"What time did you leave the showroom?" Lima demanded.

Corren and Farr picked that moment to become politely engrossed in a display of Firejewels in a nearby shop window.

"I'm not sure," Dara said.

"Your clothes are soaked with sweat. You must have been running for a long time. So who is watching over the lanterns?"

Dara sighed. "Father is there."

"You know he can't hear anything from his workshop."

"I'm sorry," Dara said. "I thought you—"

"You thought I wouldn't catch you? Need I remind you, daughter, that the Ruminor name is not unknown in this city? You may spend most of your time thrashing about in that school on Square, but I am a recognizable figure." Lima adjusted her dark skirt over her broad hips. "Your father and I cannot have you darting about like this at all hours when everyone knows you should be watching over your family's interests."

"What family interests?" Dara said. "I can't Work the Fire. There won't be a family business when Father is gone."

Lima drew herself up. "You must think beyond mere lifetimes, Dara. We are building a legacy, one that will have repercussions for Firewielders for years to come. And you notice I say 'we,' even though my own fingers are every bit as cold as yours. I have never let that stop me, because I believe in your father's work."

"They're just lanterns," Dara mumbled.

At that moment a palanquin with a large troop of bearers processed past, forcing Dara and her mother to move closer to Corren and Farr. The noise must have covered Dara's words, because Lima didn't react. It was just as well. Dara didn't want to fight with her mother, and she knew she'd been wrong to skip out on her responsibilities.

She looked at the toes of her dueling boots. "I'm sorry, Mother."

"It's a burning shame that that young man over there is more interested in my work than my own daughter." Lima waved a hand to where Farr and Corren stood, still studying a bright Firejewel the size of a furlingbird's egg. Corren looked up and winked at Dara. Farr nodded to both of them, blushing to his hairline.

"Are you sure you can't take him on as a part-time replacement for me?" Dara said. "I was hoping to switch to training in the morning three days a week for a little while."

Lima swelled at her words. "You're not in a position to make requests right now. I've half a mind to stop paying for your lessons this very day."

"Berg says if I switch my schedule I can get some lessons for free," Dara said, barreling forward despite the unfortunate timing. She should have started this conversation when her mother was in a good mood. Such times were rare these days. "He wants me to help with the younger students' classes in the mornings. It'll save some gold, and it's just three days a week."

Lima pursed her lips tightly, but Dara didn't back down. She wasn't sure why she was fighting so hard to duel with the prince. Maybe she should drop it. Oat and Kel and the others at Berg's school were great training partners. She was curious about this prince, though. He had given her a hell of a bout today—possibly even tying with her, though she'd never tell him that. And she wanted to do something that was entirely her own, something that would get her further away from the pressures of her mother and the lantern business.

"Excuse me, Madame Ruminor?" Farr joined them, cracking his bony knuckles nervously.

"Yes?"

"I'd be honored if you'd allow me to spend a few mornings a week helping you. I enjoyed our conversation the other day, and I'd love to become more involved with the work of the Guild."

"Is that so?" Lima said.

"Yes, Madame." Farr looked over at Corren, who nodded encouragingly. He turned back to Lima, seemingly gathering strength. "Master Corren has told me of the new developments, and I wish to be involved. Someone needs to stop the Fire Warden from carrying out his damaging policies."

Lima studied Farr, sizing him up like an elite coach assessing a new pupil.

Corren joined them. "The boy is trustworthy," he said. "And perhaps you will like having him in your home on a regular basis." He winked at Dara.

Lima snorted. "Very well. If I can't trust my own daughter to be there when asked, perhaps you'll do. Walk with me." She took Farr's bony arm and steered him toward the Fire Guild without another word to her daughter. Dara was fairly certain that was a victory of sorts.

Farr glanced back at Dara and smiled nervously. He *did* have a nice face. She owed him after this. Corren apparently thought the same, because he strode after Lima and Farr as though he'd scored a victory of his own.

FOOTWORK

ABOUT ten minutes into their next practice, Dara was already seriously reconsidering her decision to train with Prince Siv. She ought to leave him to whatever Lorrid had planned for him. Or help the Fire Warden in his plot.

It started when Berg ordered them to do distance exercises to warm up. This involved facing each other, touching blades in the middle, and advancing and retreating up and down the dueling hall. They took turns leading the footwork and had to maintain the same amount of pressure on their blades. If the weapons lost contact, they lost.

Berg was still recovering from his cold. He dragged the chair over from beside the door and glowered at them while they did the exercise. Dara was already feeling annoyed. She wanted to do more useful drills in the lead-up to the Eventide competition. This was beginner stuff. But Prince Siv managed to make it more difficult than it should have been.

They had started slow. Dara's weapon rested in her palm, and she exerted gentle pressure on the grip with the tips of her fingers. She locked eyes with the prince through the mesh of his mask so she could tell which way he would move next. With each slight change of pressure or flick of the eyes, she advanced and retreated. At first it was okay. Advance. Advance. Retreat. Advance. Breathing steady. Feeling the pressure.

Then Siv stuck out his tongue at her. Dara was so surprised she eased up on her blade. Siv disengaged his own and whacked her on top of the mask.

"Focus, Dara," Berg growled. "Switch."

Dara clenched her jaw, ears ringing, but didn't reply. It was her turn to lead. She engaged Siv's blade, moving him up and down the strip, watching his eyes. She would not play games.

Siv followed her movements. Then he slowly began to shift his blade away from hers. He still followed her steps, but she had to constantly adjust her wrist to maintain blade contact.

"Take this seriously, will you?" she muttered.

"I am always serious," Siv said. Then he crossed his eyes and pulled a grotesque face.

Dara dropped her blade. "Look, I have a tournament coming up, and I can't afford to—"

"Dara!" Berg barked. "We are dueling, not talking."

"Yeah, Dara, we're dueling, not talking," Siv said. "My turn."

Dara gritted her teeth and raised her blade again. Siv took off immediately, retreating across the strip as though a mountain bear were chasing him. Dara nearly lost her balance as she darted after him, extending her arm as far as she could to maintain blade contact. As soon as Siv's back foot hit the end of the strip, he changed directions and started advancing just as fast as he had retreated. Dara leapt backwards, barely managing to stay on her feet. Siv ran them back and forth across the strip, end to end, until Berg called for them to switch.

Dara scowled at the prince. If that's how he wanted to play it...

She picked up the pace, taking no more than three steps in any direction before switching again. Advance, advance, retreat, retreat, advance, retreat, retreat, retreat, advance, retreat, advance, retreat, advance, advance. She knew she was in better shape than Siv. If he wanted to mess around, she'd make him work for it.

"Switch!"

This time Siv weaved back and forth, his blade wavering. Dara had to swing her arm wide to stay with him, but she kept her feet straight. She was so annoyed she could barely look the prince in the face. But it was harder to keep pace with him without the clues in his eyes.

"Enough!" Berg rose from the chair, his face a thunderhead. "You are worse than drunken bridgewalkers. Both of you."

"But Coach—"

"No talking!" Berg roared. He stood beside the strip and glared at them. "Dueling is a trust game. You must trust your instincts, trust the way your opponent moves. Even when you beat them, you must *feel* your opponent." Siv opened his mouth, no doubt to make a sarcastic comment, but Berg silenced him with a look. "Now. Engage the blades. Close the eyes."

"But—"

"Close the eyes. Feel the pressure. Trust the blade. Dara, you lead."

Dara shot an annoyed look at Siv before raising her weapon and closing her eyes. She didn't have time for this. She should be doing serious training, not trust exercises with imbeciles.

There was a faint click as their blades touched. Dara tried to slow her breathing and feel the pressure on her blade, but it slipped almost immediately.

"Keep eyes closed. Again."

Dara extended her blade, waiting for that click. When it didn't come, she opened one eye. Siv was waving his blade in front of him about two feet to the right of hers, eyes closed tight. Dara engaged his blade and shut her eyes again. Breathed. Then she advanced. Siv's response took a while, but he did respond, moving backward as she advanced. She changed directions. The pressure on her blade disappeared immediately with the first retreat.

"Pay attention, Prince," Berg said.

They tried again, moving up and down the strip at a tenth of the speed they'd used before. Dara realized she was going easy on the prince, even though he didn't deserve it. She sped up, and he lost contact right away.

"Be alert, Prince," Berg growled. "Is your head we must protect."

Dara felt somewhat vindicated that Berg felt free to lecture both of them. He called for them to switch again. She reached out her blade and engaged with Siv. It was his turn to lead. The pressure disappeared as Siv streaked backwards. She could hear the quick patter of his retreat, but it was too late for her to follow.

"Keep up, yeah?" Siv said.

Dara scowled and raised her weapon. Breathed. Listened to the creak of Siv's boots. Heard him exhale. Felt the pressure of his blade against hers. She held her sword lightly, ready to move at the first hint of pressure. She had to be quick, light on her feet, focused. This time when Siv moved, she stayed with him. They advanced and retreated, moving back and forth across the hall, staying in time.

"Switch!"

Dara took control of the footwork. She moved the prince up and down the strip, keeping her eyes shut and her hands light.

"Switch."

Siv picked up the pace, but Dara was ready for it. They moved like a dance. With her eyes shut, the rest of her senses were heightened. The sounds. The pressure. Every sensation was a clue to which direction Siv would move next.

"Switch."

The exercise seemed to go on for hours, but they found a rhythm. Tap. Pressure. Advance. Retreat. Advance. Breathe.

"Enough," Berg said. "Take a break. Then you will duel."

Dara opened her eyes to find the prince watching her. She held his gaze for a moment, neither smiling nor looking away. Breathing.

"Today, students," Berg grumbled.

Dara started then removed her mask and returned to the corner to retrieve her gear. She felt oddly warm, as though there were an extra burst of heat in each of her fingers and toes. She shook off the sensation, buttoned up her jacket, and rejoined the prince on the strip.

The bout that day didn't last quite as long as the previous one, but Dara found herself enjoying the challenge. The prince *was* good. At the end of the session, she didn't hesitate to confirm she'd be attending the next few practices.

Siv's youngest sister, Selivia, had watched the second half of their practice from the balcony. She bounced into the dueling hall as Dara was packing her gear bag. She still had those poorly dyed streaks in her hair, and her eyes were bright as she pestered Dara with questions.

"What did it feel like when you got hit in the leg? How about the head? Have you ever met Surri? Is she nice? What about Jur the Jurl? Do you have any pets? My favorite curdragon just had babies. You can come see the hatchlings! I think one of the kitchen cats might be pregnant too. Do you want a kitten?"

"Let her breathe, Sel. She must be tired after the workout I gave her." Siv grinned at Dara. He was leaning against the wardrobe, only half paying attention as Berg demonstrated a compound attack for him.

"I'm fine," Dara said curtly. She turned to the young princess. "Yes, I've met Surri, but Jur died before we were all born." Surri was the first famous female duelist. She still lived on Square Peak, and she ran a dueling school that rivaled Berg's in size.

"Good point," Selivia said. "Is Surri nice? She doesn't look that nice."

"Well, she is a little severe sometimes."

"Sounds like someone else we know," Siv called. Berg threw up his hands and stalked over to the washbasin, grumbling about fools and people who deserved to be assassinated.

"But Surri's still an excellent duelist even at her age," Dara said, narrowing her eyes at Siv. "She'd wipe the floor with you."

"Ah yes." Siv adopted a sober expression. "You must be jealous, as that's something you've yet to manage."

"You're on the floor after a bit of footwork," Dara said. "I don't need to waste the effort."

Siv chuckled. Then he turned around and pulled his shirt off over his head. The muscles in his back rippled as he used the shirt to wipe his face. Dara realized she was staring at the future ruler of Vertigon and looked down quickly.

"Sivarrion! There are ladies here!" Selivia squealed.

"Where?" Siv whirled around and pretended to look everywhere except at Selivia and Dara, offering a full view of his broad chest and muscular arms. There was a pattern of light bruises from Dara's hits forming on his body. She didn't quite look away in time before he caught her eye and grinned.

"Put your shirt on, Prince," Berg growled. "Only show off when you have something to show. Is cardinal rule of dueling."

Selivia giggled. Dara thought Siv might have made a face, but she was too busy trying desperately not to look at his shirtless form again. She packed up her gear and nearly ran for the door.

Dara began to fall into a new routine during her visits to the castle with Berg in the two weeks leading up to the Eventide competition. Selivia was often there when Dara made the trek up to the palace for more training sessions. She would cheer whenever they finished a bout, then hurry down to talk to Dara as soon as practice finished. Often, the princess escorted Dara all the way to the entrance hall afterward, dancing beside her on slippered feet. Despite their five-year age difference, she was eager to learn more about Dara and her life. Selivia had her studies and her motley collection of pets, but Dara gathered she was at loose ends much of the time.

As Dara spent more time at the castle, she found that the prince and princess were remarkably relaxed around her. They insisted on going by their first names, and they never once mentioned the fact that Dara did not belong to one of the noble families making up the royal court in Vertigon. It was a constant source of frustration for Dara's parents that Fireworkers weren't afforded aristocratic status despite their importance to Vertigon. Dara had been all too aware that Fireworkers were not part of the nobility throughout her childhood. But Siv and Selivia didn't seem to care. They spent far more time making fun of each other and their sister, the more reserved Soraline, than they did of Dara.

The prince was arrogant, though, and no matter how much Berg scolded him he still treated dueling like a game. He showed off with flying lunges across the dueling hall. He'd go for risky toe touches, even if he only made one in every five attempts. He insisted he could defeat half the professional duelists in Vertigon without even trying, and he teased Dara endlessly when she insisted on repeating her exercises until they were perfect. Dara didn't think she was helping him take the sport—or the potential danger—more seriously. Sometimes she finished their practice sessions wishing she could run a blade through his smirking eyeball. But at other times they were almost friendly. And she didn't mind admiring his tall, muscular form—at least when he wasn't looking.

In any case, Dara was training hard despite the change to her routine. Her mother and Farr were getting along well so far, and thanks to his help in the lantern shop she had more time to work out than ever before. She started doing two hundred perfect lunges before each lesson and spent extra time thinking about strategies to use against her primary contenders. As she ran the bridges of Vertigon, parries and footwork and compound attacks filled her thoughts. She felt in excellent shape as the Eventide competition neared. She was ready.

CUR-DRAGONS

S IV returned to his rooms after attending his father's council meeting, feeling unbearably restless. The only exciting part of the meeting was when they had approved the hiring of a dozen new Castle Guards to supplement the aging force. Many of the existing Guard had been recruited when his father was crowned, and it was past time their ranks were refreshed. But then the nobles had droned on and on about a policy that had been working perfectly for Siv's entire lifetime. If that's what being king was like, he wasn't sure he ever wanted the job.

Dara Ruminor hadn't come for practice that morning. She could only spare three days a week, and he found that he never seemed to train as hard when she wasn't there. Doing footwork by himself wasn't nearly as fun. He dropped into a few lunges in front of his Fire Gate, but his heart wasn't in it.

He still hadn't convinced his father to let him skip the trip to Trure. First Snow was still at least three months away, but winters were long in Vertigon. Traveling back up the mountain was always dangerous in the snows. Siv was afraid if he went to the Lands Below he'd be stuck there for months while his grandfather, the King of Trure, droned on about his youthful adventures with the Air Sensors of the distant plains and paraded eligible noblewomen before him. But Siv wouldn't repeat his father's mistake. He had vowed as a boy never to marry a lady who pined for another land.

He had plans to meet up with Bolden Rollendar at Lady Atria's parlor that evening. He always encountered qualified—and unattached—ladies in Bolden's company, but Lady Tull was the most promising of all. That was an alliance that would show Siv's father he was looking out for the good of the kingdom. Firelord take anyone who said he wasn't wise after he orchestrated that match!

Siv curled his fingers like he was holding a blade and lunged at the Fire Gate. He shifted back and forth on the rug, practicing a move he'd seen Dara do. Her actions were subtle, but he was starting to decipher a few of her tells. He had better luck scoring on her when she attacked than when she defended. She was patient as a morrinvole, though, and she knew to make him come to her.

Damn these long afternoons before the parlors opened! He paced around his rooms for half a minute more before deciding to see what his sisters were up to.

Pool followed him through the back of the castle and down to the winding tunnel leading into the cur-dragons' dungeon. Simple Firebulbs lit their way. He felt as if he were climbing into the depths of the mountain, but the tunnel was actually quite close to the outer cliff. The cur-dragons lived in a large cave open to the mountain air. A steep drop ensured that no one could access the castle through the opening—unless they could fly.

Siv reached the bottom of the steps and let himself through the gate to the stone platform where his sisters were playing with the cur-dragons. Firebulbs affixed to the walls gave the cave a warm glow. A crisp breeze blew into it from the opening, carrying hints of mist. The princesses' personal bodyguards lounged against the wall. They were brother and sister, burly, red-haired twins named Denn and Fenn Hurling. The Amintelle family had employed them for over a decade, just like Pool. Fenn idly stroked the scaly head of one of the cur-dragons as it purred smoke over her knees.

A dozen more cur-dragons napped on the warm stone floor or prowled back and forth in front of the cave opening. The creatures were the size of large dogs or smallish velgon bears. They had thick, scaly bodies and bony black wings, the joints edged with blunt spines. Their claws were filed down so they wouldn't accidentally hurt anyone, and they were trained to control their fire. The cur-dragons could carry packages and even small children in emergencies, but they were nothing like the dragons of legend. It had been generations since a true dragon was last spotted above the mountain.

Soraline and Selivia were sitting on the stone floor with a little pile of cur-dragon hatchlings crawling over their laps. Siv flopped down beside them.

"How was the council meeting?" Soraline asked.

"The usual."

"What did Lord Rollendar say about the changes to the Ringston Pact?"

"Uhh . . . favorable," Siv said.

Sora's eyes widened in her round face. "Really? Lord Rollendar? That's huge! If he's finally come around to Lord Nanning's way of thinking, that means—"

"Maybe he didn't say favorable," Siv said quickly. "I might not have been paying attention at that part."

Sora frowned and blew out a long breath. "Honestly, Siv, maleness is wasted on you."

"Um, thank you?"

Sora sniffed as Siv took one of her cur-dragon hatchlings

and held it up. The little creature looked at him with its beady eyes and sneezed a jet of smoke into his face.

"Careful," Selivia said, stroking its scaly head. "They're only a few weeks away from their first fire. Sometimes it comes early."

"Yes, you wouldn't want to singe that fine beard," Sora said disdainfully.

Siv poked her with his elbow. "It's better than yours."

Sora scowled, but one of the cur-dragons latched onto her finger, and she had to turn her attention to prying its toothless jaws loose.

"Did I miss Dara this morning?" Selivia asked. "I had my harp lesson."

"Nope. She's only here three days a week."

"So she'll be here on Turnday?"

"Afraid not," Siv said. "She has a competition." He felt an unexpected twinge of disappointment. He'd forgotten that was this coming Turnday. She wouldn't be back until next week.

"Oh, can we watch?!" Selivia squealed. "Where is it?"

"Square Peak, I think," Siv said. *Could* they watch? He usually went to the major competitions in the King's Peak Arena, but why shouldn't he drop by one of the smaller tourneys?

Sora scooted closer to them carefully so as not to disturb the mother cur-dragon sleeping near her. "We have our Eventide tea with Lady Farrow on Turnday, Selivia."

"Ugh. I hate all those stuffy old ladies. I want to watch Dara duel!"

"She is something," Siv said. There was elegance to the way Dara moved on the dueling strip. She had a powerful certainty that captivated him at times.

"You like her, don't you, Siv?" Selivia said.

"Sure, I like her." Siv shrugged and flipped the baby cur-dragon over to tickle its belly. More smoke wheezed out of its mouth.

"I mean *like* her," Selivia said. "She's pretty, isn't she?"

"Don't be ridiculous, Selivia," Sora snapped.

"I'm not!"

"Dara Ruminor is the daughter of a Fireworker," Sora said. "She's not even a member of the noble court. Siv simply cannot like her."

Selivia tucked a brassy strand of hair behind her ear. She was going to be in huge trouble for using that cheap Fire Potion when their mother returned.

"You're the one who was so excited to talk about her father the first time she was here, Sora," Selivia said. "He's very important, isn't he? More important than a lot of the nobles. You don't even know the names of all the nobles in the court!"

"Of course I do," Sora said.

"But I don't," Selivia said. "And I bet Siv doesn't either. Do you?"

"Uhh . . ." Siv became extra interested in the little spines of the cur-dragon's wings. They seemed longer and sharper than those of his brothers. The little guy preened under the attention.

"He should," Sora said. "The point is Fireworkers are crafts-men. They were denied nobility by our great-grandfather a hundred years ago precisely *because* they are as important as you say. Important. Powerful. The position of Fire Warden exists as a check on their power, and keeping their status beneath the landowning nobility is another. Siv should know that too."

"I do know that. Thanks for the history lesson, Sora." Siv shifted onto his belly and peered into the little cur-dragon's face, mostly to avoid meeting his sisters' eyes. He understood the importance of noble alliances in a royal marriage as well as

Sora did. Of course he would never consider courting Dara Ruminor. He would do what was best for Vertigon.

The thing that had him confused was why the thought twisted in him, like being stung by the spine of a zur-sparrow. He didn't *like* Dara, did he?

Selivia didn't seem ready to give up the notion. She began arguing with her older sister about marrying for love, citing the old stories of the Lands Below and the kingdoms across the Bell Sea that she had loved reading since childhood.

"We are royal princesses," Sora said. "Our duty is to marry the most powerful man we can find, whether he's a nobleman or a prince from another kingdom. Siv has to do the same, except he might have a bit more say."

"But—"

"You can dream about *Sallana and the Bridgeworker* or *The Legend of Teall and Darran* as much as you want, but that's reality."

"But you could love a nobleman, couldn't you?" Selivia's lip trembled. "It doesn't have to be this horrible duty. Mother and Father love each other."

"The point is that love or attraction isn't the priority," Sora said. "You'll only make yourself miserable or invite scandal down on the family because you're trying to live in a story—or get Siv to live in one." Sora flashed a look tinged with bitterness at her brother. "His alliance will be even more important than ours. *We're* just girls."

Siv was afraid Selivia would dissolve into tears if he didn't say something soon. Sora could be a bit insensitive. He really should say something soothing, but changing the subject was a lot easier.

"Hey, Sel, do you think this little guy is going to be bigger than the others?" he asked. The baby cur-dragon nipped at his ear then climbed up on top of his head. Its claws sank into his hair, the tiny, blunt nails like a massage.

Selivia giggled. "Maybe. He's feisty, isn't he?"

"Can I have him?" Siv hadn't had a cur-dragon of his own since he was a small boy.

"I don't see why not. You have to give him a good name, though."

"How about Rumy?" he said.

"You mean Rumy as in Ruminor?"

"No."

Selivia grinned. "You sure?"

"It has a nice ring to it. That's all." Siv pulled the creature off his head and held him up. Rumy snapped his little jaws, making a clicking sound that echoed around the cave.

"You never answered my question," Selivia said. She studied her brother with narrowed eyes. "Do you think Dara is pretty?"

Sora leaned forward a bit, as if she was eager to hear the answer in spite of herself.

"I just remembered I have somewhere very important to be," Siv said. He gave the little hatchling a squeeze and set him back beside his mother on the stone floor. "Have fun with Lady Farrow and her friends on Turnday." He grinned and strode away before his sisters could object.

He knew better than to entertain any thoughts about whether or not Dara Ruminor was pretty . . . or clever . . . or intimidating as hell. He was a prince. He had duties to Vertigon. That was as far as things went.

On the other hand, he *was* a prince. If he wanted to drop by a dueling competition over on Square Peak, who could stop him?

THE RIVAL

ON Turnday, Dara jogged through the morning mists to
Square Peak. Furlingbird Bridge thundered under her
boots, and her equipment bag thumped against her back. She
hurried along the wide avenues of Square Peak and around the
broad plateau at its crown. The dueling hall was located on the
far eastern side of Square Peak, one of the more sparsely popu-
lated parts of the mountain. She was early as usual, having
risen before the sun. She liked to give herself plenty of time to
focus before competitions. It was well worth the loss of a bit of
sleep.

She was among the first competitors to arrive at East Square
Hall, one of the oldest dueling venues in Vertigon. Built of
stone and fully enclosed, it could host competitions throughout
the winter. A few enthusiasts were already there when Dara
jogged through the narrow entryway beneath the stands. Firebulbs, coarser and more efficient than Fire Lanterns, lit the
cavernous space. Rough wooden benches for spectators rose on
one side, and dueling strips marked in chalk filled the wide
stone floor. The tournament officials gathered in a tight knot

near the athletes' entrance, their hands wrapped around steaming mugs of apple cider.

Dara headed for the trunk rooms at the far end of the hall. They were a bit dingy, and only a goat-hide screen separated the male and female competitors. Dara deposited her gear by her usual trunk and then began her warm-ups out on the main competition floor. Despite its age and austerity, this was Dara's favorite venue. The tap of boots and slap of blades echoed in a way that reminded her of the very first duels she'd watched as a child. The arched ceiling amplified the cheers of the spectators, giving the athletes an extra burst of energy when they needed it. Dara always dueled particularly well in East Square.

She settled into her pre-competition routine as other duelists began arriving. More spectators filed into the stands, including a few patrons who had come to see how their investments performed. Dara tried to ignore them and regulate her breathing. Focus. That's what she needed today.

The Eventide Open was the last major tourney before the Vertigon Cup. It came during the second half of the pro dueling season, which ran from spring to fall. Tournaments were typically held every two weeks during the season, usually on Turndays at the end of the week. Winter was a training time, when amateur tournaments and exhibition matches fulfilled the spectators' insatiable appetite for the duels.

The Vertigon Cup was an international competition, and it came with a particularly big purse. It was also late enough in the season that patrons usually made their final decisions about who to sign immediately afterwards. Patrons would then put up their chosen duelists for the winter with the understanding that they'd be the official representatives of their sponsor for the following season.

Dara needed a good result here if she wanted to generate interest from the patrons in time for the Vertigon Cup. They probably hadn't paid much attention to her when she was coming up in the youth division. She had won her fair share of tournaments, but many girls never made the jump to the adult league. Sponsors didn't want to invest in athletes who weren't planning to have long careers. Male matches tended to be more popular too, so it was harder for female athletes to prove they'd be a good investment. But today Dara would make sure they remembered her. They would have to take her seriously. She felt more nervous than usual, but she was confident. None of the twenty-four women who'd been on the roster last time she checked should be able to defeat her.

Other duelists soon joined Dara on the competition floor, each settling into their own pre-match rituals. Most jogged or did footwork back and forth across the stone floor, but a few had strange routines to help them get into a tournament mindset. One male duelist, Dell Dunn, was known for singing in a corner right up until the first match began. Another, Shon Quen, lay flat on his back, perfectly still, and stared at the arched ceiling until the moment before his first match. As soon as he started dueling, he'd shriek and shout after every single hit, an unnerving practice that had earned him the nickname Shon the Shrieker.

The chatter of the spectators pattered around the hall like rain. A handful of well-known retired duelists were in the stands, each with a small knot of fans surrounding them. A particularly broad old swordsman named Drimmez had a cackling laugh that carried over his crowd of admirers. Many of the fans had brought old dueling banners to get signatures from their idols. Some athletes would have helpers selling more of the banners outside the dueling hall. The spectators called out to their friends over the din and leaned on the barriers in hopes of getting a good look at their favorite athletes warming up. Dara did her best to ignore them all, willing the noise to fade into the background. The sponsors were all that mattered today.

"Hi Dara! I hear you're going to win today." Luci Belling fell in beside Dara as she did footwork up and down the hall. Dara had competed with Luci often in the youth category but hadn't seen her much since joining the adult division. Luci still had six months before she'd age out, but there was always a youth competition at the Eventide Open.

"Thanks, Luci," Dara said. She kept moving, but she glanced over at her friend as she advanced and retreated alongside her. Luci had cut her bronze hair short, as many duelists did. Dara had considered it a dozen times but could never bring herself to make the chop. "How's training?"

"Coach Surri is the same as always." Luci sighed, dropping into a lunge. "I never work hard enough for her."

"Ever think about training with Berg?" Dara asked.

"Doban? I'm terrified of him."

"He's nicer than he looks."

"Wish I could say the same for Surri," Luci said. "She looks *and* acts mean."

"We owe her for opening the sport up for women." Dara looked over at a tall, muscular woman with a pair of long scars across one side of her face. Surri was deep in conversation with a tournament official. She had been one of the first female duelists to compete in the Vertigon Cup, and her name was still legendary.

"You'd think she'd be happier about women having our own division now," Luci said, dropping into a lunge. "But I don't think she actually likes training girls."

"I'm sure Berg would love to have you at his school." Dara searched for her coach among the athletes and coaches milling around the competition floor, but he was nowhere to be seen. That wasn't like him. He often insisted on last-minute lessons before tournaments.

"I don't think I could afford Berg's fees anyway, unless I get a patron," Luci said.

Dara looked down at her feet and corrected her form. Luci's family wasn't as well off as Dara's. Luci's father, a bridge carpenter, often took extra shifts so Luci could keep training with Surri. Luci was a decent duelist, but Dara wasn't sure she'd ever be good enough to land a patron. Luci would end up working in a shop, or perhaps marrying a baker or a bridgeworker like her father. But at least her father came to watch her competitions. His booming voice was always recognizable at tournaments. Dara couldn't even remember the last time her own parents had watched her duel.

The stands were almost full now. Children crowded down into the first row and leaned over the barrier, waving at their favorite duelists and calling for tokens or signatures. Energy surged through the hall. It would be time to start soon.

Dara spotted Kel shaking hands with a ring of adolescent girls—and some older women—who had gathered to giggle and stare at him. He handed out tokens from a cloth bag at his side. Tokens were made of wood or stone, and each bore the markings of a duelist. Kel's, for example, were carved with a laughing mountain goat. Dueling enthusiasts collected the tokens from their favorite athletes. It was one of the many tools athletes used to increase their popularity and stay in the minds of their audiences when they weren't on the strip.

Dara had a bag of tokens too, but she had left it in the trunk room. Handing them out took time away from warming up. Also, her tokens bore an image of a Fire Lantern. She didn't like reminding people who her father was. They'd either wonder why she was trying to be a duelist instead of following in his footsteps or think she was using his influence to curry favor. She wanted people to know her for her skills and nothing else.

Luci veered off to put on her gear for the youth competition, which would begin before the adult divisions. Dara headed for one more lap around the competition floor. She was halfway around the hall when a commotion broke out near the eastern spectators' entrance. Trumpets blared, and drums pounded. Spectators pointed and chattered excitedly. A whirl of color, green and gold, swirled through the doorway.

It was Vine Silltine.

Great. Just what she needed. Dara didn't know Vine had entered this competition. She had been too busy over the past few days to swing by the sign-up posting.

A crowd grew around Vine as she floated through the stands. People squealed and reached for her tokens. Dara ran an extra lap, pretending not to notice Vine's grand entrance. *Why can't she come through the back like the rest of us?*

Vine reached the ground level and waltzed across the competition floor. Her lustrous black hair flowed loosely around her shoulders, and she wore a green dress made of a floating, shimmery silk. Veins of Firegold ran through the dress, gleaming in the light from the Firebulbs. She wore a dreamy, benevolent expression as she waved to the crowd. An entourage of companions followed, carrying her green velvet gear bag and blowing those ridiculous trumpets.

At the entrance to the trunk room on the far side of the hall, Vine whirled around, her dress and hair flying, and curtsied deeply to the crowd. Then she smiled beatifically and disappeared into the trunk room. The cheers continued even after she was gone.

"You look like someone broke your favorite blade."

"What? Oh, hey Kel." Dara had completed another circuit around the hall without realizing it. Her friend was waiting for her as she slowed to a walk. He had given away the last of his tokens, and there was a smudge of lip stain on his cheek.

"I see your archnemesis has arrived," Kel said.

Dara frowned. "She wasn't supposed to be here. I heard she was saving her energy for the Cup."

"You've never lost to her," Kel said. "I don't get what you have against her." He and Dara headed toward the entrance to the trunk room to retrieve their gear. He slung the empty token bag over his shoulder like a cape.

"She's just annoying," Dara said.

Vine Silltine was a relative newcomer to the duels. She was a minor nobleman's daughter from Lower King's Peak. House Silltine owned a scraggly peach orchard, a greathouse, and not much else. Dara wasn't sure what had possessed Vine to start competing in the opens, but she was rising quickly through the ranks. Worse, the fans seemed to love her.

Kel put a hand over his heart. "You mean you don't like talking about energy meditations, or whatever airy-fairy powers she claims help her focus? I always thought meditation would do you good."

"It doesn't matter." Dara grinned. "I'm going to win today."

"That's right. Now, I must depart to the other side of the screen." Kel gave a rather impressive imitation of Vine's curtsy before heading to his side of the trunk room.

The long, narrow space lined with trunks served as temporary lockers during competitions. There was a washbasin and latrine crammed at the end. A wrinkled serving woman supplied towels, drinking water, and dried fruits to the athletes. It was crowded in these final moments before the competition, the air crackling with nerves and adrenaline. They could hear the boasting and banter from the men's side of the trunk room. Someone crashed against the screen, causing it to teeter. Roars of laughter followed.

On the women's side, the other competitors gathered around Vine Silltine. She had removed her floating green gown and put on a tight pair of breeches embroidered with gold and green vines. She hadn't put on her blouse yet, showing off her impressive figure in a tight undergarment. The other women passed around Vine's glittering tokens and fawned over her.

Dara avoided them all and went straight to her trunk to put on her chest plate and white competition jacket. None of the other duelists even looked over at her. She was friendly with many of them from her youth competition days, though none had been as close as Luci. But they ignored her now. All of them except one.

"Is that Dara? Dara Ruminor?"

Mother of a cur-dragon. "Hello Vine."

Vine swept her arms wide, clearing a path through the other women, and danced over to Dara's trunk.

"When I heard you were entered in the Eventide, Dara, I just *had* to sign up," Vine said. She had a trilling voice and always seemed on the verge of singing.

"It's an open competition."

"I wanted to feel your aura before the Vertigon Cup. I've had a bout with each of the primary contenders in the past month, but you're the last one. I'm working on a new sensory technique that helps center my energy."

"Is that right?" Dara gave her a tight smile, working to disentangle the straps of her chest plate from her spare glove as quickly as possible.

"It involves the higher orders of Air Sense, and I think it's improving my accuracy immensely." Vine smiled serenely.

"Hmm."

"Do you mind if I sense your energy, Dara?"

"What?"

"May I place my hands on your temples and sense the—"

"No!" Dara ducked as Vine stretched out her jeweled hands and tried to place them on either side of her face. "Look, Vine, I'm glad you've got a new air strategy or whatever, but I need to focus on the competition."

"But this is all about focus, Dara. My energy coach says—"

"I'm sure that's great," Dara said quickly. "I'll see you out there, okay?"

Dara slung the rest of her gear over her arm and dashed out

of the trunk room. As she left, Vine was saying, "Hmm, I'm sensing a very stubborn aura, with . . ."

Dara stopped outside the trunk room to finish putting on her jacket. She wasn't sure why Vine annoyed her so much. Maybe it was because she hadn't been competing for long, and she was already doing *very* well. Dara felt wrong-footed. Focus. She needed focus. She had to win today. Nothing would get Vine Silltine out of her head like beating her in a match to ten.

The stands were packed now. The youth event was under-way, and cheers and screams filled the cavernous hall. There were a total of twelve dueling strips laid out for the competition, leaving enough space to run some of the divisions simultaneously. Blades rang, metal on metal, and coaches shouted instructions to their athletes. The smell of sweat and charcoal hung over everything.

Dara checked the list of matches posted on the wall and made her way over to the strip where she'd have her first bout. Two teenage boys were dueling there now, with much flailing and bluster. She scanned the crowd, especially the front row, assessing which patrons would have a good view of her bout.

Some key patrons were there in the audience, mostly noblemen and business owners. Dara knew them all by sight. There were also a few retired dueling champions who had used their winnings to establish themselves in Lower King's. Patrons sponsored athletes both as a matter of a pride and as a way of growing their own businesses. Of course, Dara's parents would never employ such a practice, but other business owners were more practical. Sponsored athletes would use their products in public places or appear at special events in their parlors, shops, and greathouses. Sponsors often arranged exhibition matches between popular duelists and took home a portion of the ticket sales from these private events.

Dara had her eye on one patron in particular who selected a female duelist every season. Wora Wenden made a name for himself as a duelist nearly thirty years ago, right at the beginning of King Sevren's reign. He'd used the prize money he accumulated throughout his career to start a highly successful garment business. Now his athletes wore his coats and dresses as a form of advertisement in return for his patronage. Master Corren was one of his primary textile suppliers. Corren was probably in the audience somewhere too, though he didn't sponsor any duelists.

Wora sat in the front row, near the strip where all the championship bouts would be fought. The strip for Dara's first bout wasn't too far away from his seat. She hoped he would notice her. But she couldn't think about that right now. She had to concentrate on the competition.

The last of the youth bouts ended, and the booming voice of the head dueling referee rang across the hall. It was time. The remaining adult competitors filed out of the trunk rooms, a parade of white jackets and flashing silver blades. The crowd cheered. This is what they had really come here to see. Soon, the clash of swords and thud of boots resumed, escalating the cacophony in the hall. Dara readied herself for her first bout, saluting her opponent and slamming her mask down on her head. She assumed her guard stance, awaiting the call of the referee. And she dueled.

Once the competition began, Dara felt more relaxed. She lost herself in the movement of her feet and the precise lines of her blade. She marked her opponents with charcoal, bound to the rhythm of the duel. This was what she was born to do. She couldn't Work Fire, but she could wield a blade with her own kind of spark.

Dara's standing in the rankings meant that her first few elimination bouts were relatively easy. She won them without difficulty, hardly needing any coaching. Berg had finally arrived, and he roved amongst the strips where his athletes competed. He had three youth duelists and seven adults in the tournament today, including Dara, Kel, and Oat. Competitions usually put him in a bad mood, but his growls of advice and admonishment were all part of the routine.

"Hold your weapon soft, but firmly, like baby's hand."

"Yes, quick reflexes! Keep awake."

"No! Is a sword, not a club!"

"If you want it more, you will be the winner. Want, students! Want!"

After winning her fourth bout, Dara took a break and looked over at Wora Wenden. Her stomach lurched when she spotted a familiar head of lustrous black hair in front of the old patron. Vine Silltine was leaning over the barrier, her hair cascading around her shoulders, and talking with Wora. Vine must have said something funny, because he threw back his head and laughed. Dara scowled, twisting her hands around the hilt of her favorite competition blade. If Wora chose Vine as his female duelist this year . . . *No. Don't think like that.*

Wora liked winners. It didn't matter how much Vine made him laugh. Dara would defeat her, and Wora would choose Dara for his patronage. She would be a true professional duelist, and she would be free of the lantern business forever.

Dara turned away from the pair, scanning the other patrons in the front row. Wora wasn't her only option. There was Lord Nanning. Gen Ribson. Bern and Tern Morn . . .

And there was Prince Sivarrion, sitting four seats away from Wora and looking right at her.

Dara's mask dropped to the floor. What was he doing here? The royal family never came to tourneys on Square Peak.

She bent down to retrieve her mask, schooling her expression to neutral, and looked again. Yes, that was definitely Siv. He wore a midnight-blue coat and a billowing white shirt, open at the neck. He grinned and waved at her. People in the crowd turned to see which duelist had attracted the heir-prince's attention. Dara's cheeks burned, and a flash of heat rose upward through her feet. More people were looking. The prince must have drawn quite a bit of attention when he arrived, but Dara had been too absorbed in her bouts to notice. How long had he been watching her?

Vine Silltine spun around then and winked at Dara. She didn't look surprised to see that Dara was the one Prince Siv was waving at. What did that mean? Flustered, Dara jammed her mask on her head and marched across the hall to where her semifinal bout would take place.

Wora. Siv. Vine. She had to focus. An uncomfortable heat wormed through Dara's belly and out toward her fingertips. The official was saying something to her. Her opponent was ready. It was a lanky redhead named Taly Selwun. She was okay, but she had a reckless, unpolished style that was easy to counter. Dara shook her head and assumed her guard position. Why was Siv watching the tourney? Was Wora watching her too?

The official raised his arms.

"Duel!"

Dara dueled, but her rhythm was off. She dropped the first point, and her opponent shrieked in victory. *It's just one touch. You can do this.*

"Taly, one. Dara, zero. Ready? Duel!"

Dara made the next few touches. Her hits weren't elegant, but she wasn't going to lose to some nobody.

Taly scored with a wild parry and a lunge to Dara's inner arm. She ripped off her mask and screeched out another victory call. *Amateur.*

Dara raised her blade.

"Duel!"

Back and forth they fought. The calls came fast. Taly's blade flashed in the light of the Firebulbs. Boots thudded. Shouts. Hits. Dara's muscles strained. The sting of metal connected with her body.

The score was now six to five, with Dara in the lead. *Four more. You just need four more.* Where was Berg? He was usually at her side during semifinals matches.

The crowd across the hall cheered. Something was drawing their attention. No one was even watching Dara's bout. Taly's next touch landed on her shoulder.

"Six to six!"

Dara retreated back to her starting line, chancing a glance across the hall. People were standing up, leaning over each other and the barriers to watch one of the central strips. Vine Silltine was dueling, her hair flying loose around her mask. She had improved since the last time Dara watched her. She was doing something unusual, a dancing floating lunge of some kind. She landed the touch, and the crowd went wild.

"Duel!"

Dara was barely ready. Taly hit her mask directly between the eyes and let out another victory yell. She had a right to shout. She shouldn't be ahead of Dara this late in the bout. Dara's ears rang from the impact.

"Duel!"

Taly scored a touch to the knee. It was a cheap shot, but Dara wasn't ready for it. The score was eight to six, and Dara was losing. Berg was nowhere to be seen. She had to calm down, to focus.

"Vine! Vine! Vine!" the crowds were chanting now. It was happening too fast. Dara couldn't think. Vine darted in and scored on her opponent's toe across the room. Wora Wenden was clapping.

"Point! Nine to six. Taly Selwun is in the lead."

No.

"Duel!"

Dara tried to shut out the chants. The cheers.

"Vine! Vine! Vine!"

"Point! That's the bout. Ten, six to Taly."

Dara looked down at her blade arm, at the neat round charcoal circle where Taly had just scored the winning hit. Dara had lost. She was out. She wouldn't even fight in the championship bout. She would be third or fourth place. She stared dumbly at the spot on her jacket.

"Duelist? Salute please," the official barked.

"Oh, sorry. Good bout, Taly. Thank you, sir." Dara saluted her opponent and the official. Her head seemed to be filling with smoke.

The crowds cheered across the stadium.

"Vine! Vine! Vine Silltine!" The other bout had ended. Vine was the victor. She danced and waved at her admirers. She would compete in the gold medal match on the center strip against Taly Selwun, the woman who had just *beaten* Dara.

Dara couldn't move as she watched Vine celebrate. She danced over to the barrier, and Wora leaned over it to kiss her on the cheek. She whispered something in his ear, and he grinned widely. Vine's entourage had somehow ended up seated in the third row. They handed out glittering golden tokens to the crowds. People climbed over each other in their haste to get their hands on one of Vine's tokens.

Dara forced herself to look at Siv, expecting to see him gazing at Vine along with everyone else. But he was staring at Dara. When she met his eyes, he shrugged and gave a half smile then mouthed something she couldn't make out. She felt heat rising in her cheeks. He had seen her lose after all her talk, after all of Berg's praise. She couldn't bring herself to go over and speak to him.

"Dara! What is happening?" Berg had finally appeared. He charged up to her, filling her vision like a big, square mountain.

"Where were you?" Dara said hollowly.

"Oatin was in a tie with Bilzar Ten on the far strip. I could not leave him. What is the result?"

"I lost."

Berg blinked. "You . . . you are doing what?"

"I lost to Taly Selwun."

"Taly Selwun?" Berg's face reddened rapidly, and he looked as if his head might explode. "*You* are not losing to Taly Selwun." He wheeled around and started toward the tourney official.

"No, Coach." Dara stopped him before he accosted the official. "It was a fair bout. I choked. I'm sorry."

Berg studied her for a moment and puffed out his cheeks. "We will talk later, young Dara."

"Yes, Coach."

Feeling numb, Dara gathered her spare blades and headed toward the trunk room. It was over. She was out. Vine would win the gold. Taly Selwun didn't stand a chance against her. She shouldn't have stood a chance against Dara either.

Shame boiled in Dara's stomach like rotten mountain root. She had lost. And she had lost to an inferior opponent with a dozen potential sponsors watching. With Prince Siv watching. There was no way she would get a sponsorship now. She had failed.

PLOTS AND PLANS

S IV felt a rather unpleasant sinking sensation in his
stomach as Dara trudged toward the trunk room without
looking at him. Her golden braid swung against her back like a
sad pendulum. She hadn't come over to say hello. She had
barely glanced his way during the entire competition. Was he a
fool for being here?

Siv lost interest in the tournament after Dara was knocked
out. He liked watching the duels, and today he had seen some
new competitors, real up-and-comers. But it was less exciting
now that his dueling companion was out and he had to deal
with all the people trying to curry favor with their young
prince. His arrival had created a stir. As they waited for the
championship bouts to begin, a steady stream of businessmen
and minor nobles paraded before his seat, offering him greetings and favors and making not-so-subtle requests for favors in
return. He'd end up having to explain this visit to his father,
and he still wasn't entirely sure why he had come.

Siv fiddled with a handful of athlete tokens that had been
shoved into his hands, tossing them in the air and catching as
many as possible at once. He didn't bother to chase after the

ones that got away from him. Maybe he could tell his father he had wanted to meet with common Vertigonians here on Square Peak. That could work, even though the actual commoners seemed more interested in fawning over the duelists than over their heir-prince.

"My prince," Pool said. "Will you be so benevolent as to bestow an answer upon this supplicant?"

"Huh?"

For Pool, that was the equivalent of a nudge in the ribs. Siv realized a young man stood in front of his seat, waiting for him to respond to something. He didn't recall the man's name, but he was dressed like a nobleman with a rich, Firegold-embroidered coat.

"Your Highness," the man said. "I wish to offer the compliments of House Zurren. We would be honored if you would allow us to hold an exhibition match in your honor. We represent the duelist Murv 'The Monster' Mibben." He gestured toward a large man with tattoos completely covering his bald head. "He is currently a top-four duelist in the rankings, and we are certain he would put on an entertaining bout for Your Highness. We have a number of candidates in mind for his opponent. Perhaps Lord Rollendar would allow Kelad Korran to participate, for example."

Siv rubbed a hand across his chin. He had taken the time to shave this morning, so the usual scratchiness was missing.

"Hmm, entertaining, you say?"

"Yes, Your Highness." The young nobleman twirled his hands. "Murv the Monster strikes fear in the hearts of his opponents and wonder in the eyes of his beholders. We believe Your Highness would not be bored. May I suggest a Turnday evening before First Snow for the exhibition?"

"You may be onto something," Siv said. A thought was starting to form in his mind. He was fairly certain it was a brilliant one.

"Your Highness?"

"Yes, Lord Zurren, I think an entertaining match might be just the ticket."

"Ticket? Of course, if you wish to have a larger match with ticket sales that could be arranged, but we had pictured a more intimate display for—Your Highness?"

Siv was busy studying the duelists drawing the most attention from the spectators as they milled around during the break. One man's hair was dyed a brilliant Fire Potion red, and he wore clothes that matched. Another had shrieked every single time he scored a hit and was now mumbling like a madman at the fans gathered eagerly around him (at a safe distance). Murv the Monster, with his tattoo-covered head and impressive stature, was glowering spectacularly at another macho-looking competitor across the hall. Lady Silltine's supporters were still handing out tokens and playing their ridiculous trumpets. And there was Kelad Korran chatting with his admirers in the first row, a few doe-eyed noblewomen among them, despite the fact that he too had been knocked out of the competition in the semifinals.

Ideas churned through Siv's mind like threads through a Firegold spindle. He was pretty sure he knew what Dara Ruminor needed.

Siv snatched up the blue coat he had dropped over his chair. "Let's go, Pool."

"Don't you wish to view the remaining duels, my prince?" Pool said.

"I have work to do."

The young nobleman was staring at Siv with an open mouth, but he didn't care.

"Enquire with Lord Bolden Rollendar about the match with Monster Murv, Lord Zurren. I'll show up. To the castle, Pool!"

"Yes, my prince."

Siv sauntered toward the entrance with a backward glance

at the trunk room entrance. Dara hadn't reemerged, but he had a feeling she wouldn't be coming back out to watch the final duel anyway. He had work to do before their next meeting.

A few hours later, Siv scribbled ideas at the table in his chambers. Technically, he was supposed to be visiting greathouses to extend Eventide greetings to the nobility, but this was far more interesting. Eventide involved endless rounds of small talk with jittery old ladies who still upheld the old-fashioned visiting tradition. Most young people would celebrate Eventide by getting roaring drunk later in the evening, but he ought to be able to accomplish a lot before then. Crumpled papers littered the floor around him. He was turning out to be a master strategist, if he did say so himself.

There was a knock at the door.

"Come in!"

"My prince, Sword Master Berg Doban requests an audience," Pool said as he cracked open the door. "Do you wish me to admit him to your royal presence?"

"Doban is here?" Siv wondered for a second if he had missed a lesson before remembering that his coach had been at the tournament at East Square earlier that day. "Let him in."

"Yes, my prince."

Berg strode into Siv's antechamber. He wore street clothes rather than his usual loose-fitting coaching attire, and he carried a crumpled felt hat in his hands. Siv had never seen him away from a dueling hall before. He towered beside the table, looking oversized in the cozy space.

"This is a surprise, Coach." Siv leaned back in his chair.

"My prince," Berg said gruffly. "I must speak to you about a danger you face."

"You mean Dara?"

Berg's jaw dropped. "Dara, my prince? You know—?"

"That she's going to kill me for watching her lose? Don't worry. I plan to head her off like a Truren stallion at Kurn Pass."

"A what?"

Siv grinned. "I want to help Dara get a patron, Doban, and I am a burning genius."

"My prince, this is not the danger I speak of. Not Dara."

Siv waved his eagle feather pen at him. "What's this about? I'm very busy."

"My prince, there is a plot," Berg growled. "Dangers on foot for you."

"You mean 'afoot?' You sound like Zage Lorrid."

"The Fire Warden? My prince, the Fire—"

"Yeah, he's always talking about dangers. He's got my back." Siv continued to scribble on his paper. He was on a roll. He couldn't let his ideas slip away while Berg talked to him about yet another nefarious and insubstantial threat he faced as the royal heir. He wondered whether he could get his hands on a Firetorch. Zage had never let him have one as a child, but now he might be able to make a case for it. He'd claim it was for educational purposes only.

"My prince, you must be careful," Berg said. "The city is not as safe for you and your family as it should be. It was a risk going to Square Peak alone. Someone there was . . . You cannot trust everyone you think you can trust."

"Doban." Siv looked up from his papers and met Berg's eyes steadily. "I understand you're trying to look out for me. Do you have any names? Any solid information to offer me about these plots? If so, I will listen."

Berg frowned, glancing around the antechamber as if he expected an assassin to leap out from behind the couch. Siv gave him what he felt was long enough and then bent back over his papers.

"It's okay, Coach. I know you're worried, but I have good

people around me. Pool takes care of me. The Hurling twins take care of my sisters. Captain Bandobar, the Guard, and the whole damn army take care of my father. We even hired a whole company of new Castle Guards recently."

"These new Guards were chosen by Bandobar?" Berg asked.

"Yeah." Siv didn't know that for a fact, but who else would have chosen them? He barreled on. "I'm not an idiot. If you know something, I'll listen, but if you want me to stop living my life for fear of some unknown danger, then save your breath."

"Bandobar is a good man," Berg said after a while. "If he trusts these new men . . . I have no certain knowledge."

"And Dara isn't going to run me through for watching her lose?"

"No, my prince. I do not believe Dara will hurt you."

"Good."

"In fact," Berg said slowly, "maybe you would be wise to keep her close."

Siv studied his paper carefully. "Keep her close?" Berg couldn't have seen something between them, could he? Not when Siv wasn't sure it was there himself.

"Dara is good, my prince."

"Damn right. She's way better than that Taly girl."

"I mean she is *good.*"

"Right. She'll make me a better duelist so I can defend myself against the dangers afoot." Siv was beginning to tire of this particular refrain. Next thing he knew Berg would be trying to send him off to Trure too. But the man was studying him, his expression thoughtful.

"Yes, my prince," he said. "Maybe she should train with you every day now."

"Yeah? What does she think about that?"

"I will tell her tomorrow," Berg said. "But she must not make excuses. Is okay for you?"

"If Dara comes here every day?" Siv did his best to fight

down the tiny flutter of hope in his chest, like the wings of a moth. He shrugged, keeping his voice casual. "Sure, why not?"

"I have business in the mornings, my prince. I cannot come every day, but Dara will train with you."

Siv raised an eyebrow. "You're skipping out on our lessons now, Coach? Just like that?"

"Only until I discover more," Berg grunted. "You will be okay with Dara, my prince."

"Sure I will."

"I take my leave." Berg jammed his felt hat down on his head. "Be careful, my prince. Do not go to Square alone as you did today. Vertigon is not so safe anymore."

"I wasn't alone." Siv frowned. There were limits. He was the heir-prince of Vertigon, and he didn't take orders from anyone but his father. And maybe Pool when he was extra insistent. He lowered his voice, knowing full well it still wouldn't sound as gravelly or intimidating as Berg's. "Is there anything else you feel you can order me to do or not do, Doban?"

Berg sighed. "No, my prince. You must be careful. As we say in my homeland: beware of the shadow as well as the fire."

Siv nodded, but he was already deeply engrossed in his plans by the time Berg left the chamber. He hoped the man would have a relaxing Eventide eve and calm himself down.

The light from the Fire Gate flickered across the pages spread across Siv's table. Yes, he was a genius. This would work. He would make Dara Ruminor a champion.

PARTNERS

DARA was sorely tempted to skip her training the day
after the competition. She hadn't lost that badly in
years. Ten, six to Taly Selwun? The numbers cycled around and
around in her mind. She couldn't sleep. She could barely eat.
She felt hot and feverish whenever she thought about what had
happened. She wanted to scream into the wind whipping
across Furlingbird Bridge as she jogged over to the dueling
school on Square.

She stretched with her friends, feeling stiff despite her
warm-up run. Oat and Kel knew better than to talk to her about
the bout with Taly, but they couldn't help regaling her with
their own stories of victory. Oat had won the men's division,
managing to defeat both Bilzar Ten and Rawl, Kel's biggest
rival. It was Oat's best finish ever. Kel had placed fourth, but his
patron had taken him out carousing in Lower King's afterwards,
and he'd scored a few victories of his own there.

Berg skipped the lecture she deserved when it was time for
their usual lesson. He simply said, "You are losing focus. You
know this."

It was worse than being yelled at.

After the lesson, Dara sparred with the other duelists for hours. Her muscles strained, burning and cramping, but she embraced the pain instead of thinking about her loss. She felt heat in her blood and channeled it into every hit. She could not fail again. She had to be perfect. She had to win.

She dueled until everyone at the school refused to give her another match.

"You've had enough for tonight, Dar," Oat said when she demanded he join her for just one more bout.

"I need to keep—"

"It's already dark," Oat said. "It's time to go."

Only then did Dara realize her limbs were shaking and her jacket was soaked through with sweat. She pulled it off and found a collection of new bruises patterning her arm. She trudged over to her trunk, avoiding the concern in Oat's eyes. Most of the other students had already left.

Berg approached as she knelt beside her trunk and slowly gathered up her gear to pack into her bag. She felt as though she were moving through molasses. Kel and Oat lingered at the door, waiting for her.

"Dara," Berg said.

"Yes, Coach?"

"This will not happen again, young Dara."

"No, sir."

Berg studied her from beneath lowered brows. "You must continue training with the prince."

"Please, no, Coach," Dara said, sitting back on her heels. "It's a distraction. If he hadn't been there in the crowd—"

"Stop!" Berg said. "You will not make these excuses."

Dara swallowed her retort. She had lost concentration during the tourney because of Vine drawing the adoration of the crowd and the prince disrupting her focus. She needed to get back to her normal routine if she had any hope for the Vertigon Cup now. With Farr proving so helpful to her mother, she had to make the most of the extra time to train.

But Berg wasn't finished. "I am busy, so you will practice with him alone from now."

"What? Coach—"

"Do not argue." Berg folded his arms over his broad chest and loomed over her. "You will go every day. Do not come back to the school in the afternoon unless you also train at the castle in the morning."

"I can't." He was punishing her after all. Sure, Berg said he was busy, but no business of his should take priority over training the heir-prince. He was trying to teach her a lesson.

"You will," Berg said. "This is not negotiation. You will go to the castle every morning. Start tomorrow."

Dara closed her trunk and hoisted her gear bag onto her shoulder, considering his words. His insistence that she train at the castle every day seemed to go beyond a desire to make Dara and Siv into better duelists. She had always trusted Berg's instructions, and she couldn't refuse him now. Training with the prince was still training. And dueling was still her only chance at the life she wanted away from the family business.

"Okay," she said. "I'll be there."

Berg gave a brief nod, as if he expected nothing less, and stalked away.

"What did he say?" Oat asked when Dara finally joined him and Kel at the door. He pushed it open, and the harsh mountain wind swirled around them, carrying promises of rain.

"He's punishing me for losing focus," Dara said as they descended the stone steps from the school.

"How?"

"He's making me . . . do extra workouts in the mornings."

"That's hardly a punishment for you," Kel said. "You love working out."

"It's different," Dara mumbled. She figured she still

shouldn't tell anyone she was dueling with the prince. Vine had seemed to know at the tournament, though. Could the nobles be talking amongst themselves about Siv's new training companion? How long would it take her parents to find out? Fortunately, because they didn't associate with Zage Lorrid and the Fireworkers in his employ at the castle, she didn't think word had gotten back to them yet.

"Are you coming to the tavern with us?" Oat asked as they headed down the winding stone path away from the school. Warm lights glowed across the three peaks of Vertigon. It was the second night of Eventide, so some people would still be engaging in the old tradition of visiting and bringing token gifts to their friends. They hurried through the wind, eager to get indoors before the rain began.

"I don't think I can."

"Come on," Oat said. "It's Eventide, and we're celebrating my win."

"Again," Kel put in. "Didn't quite get my fill of celebrations last night."

"Sorry. I've got an early start tomorrow." She didn't add that all she wanted to do was curl into a ball and forget how she had let herself down. She didn't want to ruin Oat's enjoyment of his moment by moping. She faked a smile for her friend's sake. "Have fun."

"Your loss," Kel said.

He sauntered ahead, but Oat was still looking at Dara hopefully. Suddenly he reached out and took her hand, entwining his fingers with hers, and pulled her closer.

"Come with us, Dara."

Dara looked down at their hands, surprised at the sudden intimacy. Oat's wide palm was damp, a look of hope on his face. Dara tugged her hand out of Oat's grasp, perhaps a little too roughly.

"Sorry, O, I'm beat."

He couldn't quite hide the hurt as he said, "No big deal. See you around, Dar." Oat turned and loped off after Kel, his practice weapons rattling in his bag.

Dara sighed. Oat had been sweet on her for a while, but she never thought he'd act on it. Why did he have to do it today of all days? She felt a little sick. Maybe she had overdone it at practice after all. She hadn't wanted to hurt his feelings, and she wasn't sure why she didn't return his affection. Like Farr, Oat would be a perfectly adequate match for her. He was kind and unassuming, and they'd been friends for years. But she wanted someone who made warmth and excitement spread through her, not someone who would be merely tolerable. She wanted Fire in her veins too. Real mountain Fire. And she wanted to win, to show her worth. She wanted so many things, but no matter how hard she worked, the lucky spark remained beyond her grasp.

Rain began to fall lightly over the mountain, making the Firelights shudder. Dara slogged home through the drizzle, passing huddled figures on the long bridge between Square Peak and the Village. She climbed the winding stairs toward her home, feeling tired and sad. The lanterns lit the front porch, bright and almost harsh. Her parents were in the showroom, their shadows distinct amongst half a dozen others. Corren's gravelly laugh rattled the window. Rafe and Lima must be entertaining their Fireworker associates. They were the types to keep to the old Eventide traditions. Dara skirted around the house, climbed through her bedroom window to avoid speaking to anyone, and went to bed.

Dara would rather throw herself off a bridge than face Prince Siv after he had watched her lose, but she hauled herself out of bed and up to the castle early the next morning. The rain still fell in a persistent drizzle. Her entire body ached, and the bruises from her last practice had darkened and expanded. She felt as if she'd rolled all the way down the mountainside in her sleep.

"Look what the povvercat dragged in," Siv said when she arrived at the dueling hall. He was on his feet for once, and he looked as if he had already been for a jog that morning.

"Prince Sivarrion," Dara said.

"All formal again, are we?"

"I had a rough practice last night," Dara said. "Can we postpone today's session?"

"You know how Coach Doban feels about rescheduling. He told me not to let you make any excuses when you came in today. I'm the prince of excuses, so I recognize them when I see them."

"You talked to Berg?"

Siv inclined his head, reaching into the wardrobe for his jacket. "He told me we'd be training exclusively from now on. Lucky me."

Dara didn't have the energy to argue.

"Let's just duel," she said.

"Not until we warm up. And not until you tell me what the Firelord happened at the tourney."

"I don't want to talk about it."

"Not so fast." Siv shrugged on his jacket. "Apparently you're now my official training partner, and I dragged my ass across the world's longest bridge to that grimy dueling hall to cheer you on. Now tell me why you lost to the shrieking sheyla."

"The what?"

"Shrieking sheyla, from Cindral Forest. I saw them at a fair in Trure once."

"Whatever." Dara pushed at the rug with the toe of her boot. "You could have warned me you were going to be there."

"Is that an excuse I hear? What, I distracted you with my dashing good looks?"

"That's not what I meant," Dara said quickly. She willed her cheeks not to turn red. "I wasn't expecting—"

"Were you expecting that knee shot?" Siv put his hands on his hips, his jacket hanging open. "How about when you launched yourself onto that last riposte. You're better than that."

"I lost focus."

"I don't think that's your problem. You're too focused. Seriously, you need to lighten up a little. You looked very tense, even in the bouts you won, tenser than a morrinvole in heat. Yeah, I've seen that too."

"I'll do better next time," Dara said. "I have to win the Cup now, or the patrons—"

"Oh, patrons this, patrons that." Siv took a step closer to her. "It's the crowd you need to worry about. You're not fun to watch."

"Excuse me?"

"Hate to break it to you, but you're so uptight and focused and serious when you duel that it's boring." Siv reached out and poked her arm. Dara stiffened. "This is a show," he said, and poked her again. "With spectators. If you get the crowds to like you, the patrons will follow. You have to entertain them, not just win a bunch of bouts."

"You've never competed," Dara snapped. She refused to step back, even though he was standing very close now. He had no right to lecture *her* about competitive dueling. She glared up at him. "You don't need a patron. Don't tell me about—"

"You don't need a patron either," Siv said. "You've got a wealthy father. What's the big deal?"

"I can't keep using my parents' money for dueling," Dara said. "They support it grudgingly as it is. I need to make it on my own." She met the prince's eyes fiercely. "You wouldn't know anything about that."

Siv blinked. "Is that what you think? That I don't want to make it on my own?"

"You're the uncontested heir to a prosperous kingdom."

The prince's face darkened, and he turned away from her. "Destined to be the Fourth Good King and all that." He finished fastening his jacket, nearly popping off the final button, and yanked on his glove. "You think I don't know? My father is a popular king in a long line of popular kings. I'm supposed to maintain the status quo and keep my mouth shut around the right people, nothing more." He whirled back to face her. "You think I don't sometimes wish I could make my own name? You don't know me, Dara."

Dara stared at the prince. She had touched a nerve. Despite the time they had spent together over the past few weeks, she was surprised he would talk to her about something like this, about his issues with his role and family. Maybe she and Siv were more similar than she realized.

"I'm sorry," she said quietly.

"Forget it." Siv noticed he had put his glove on inside out. He pulled it off again and rolled his shoulders as if shaking off the conversation. "Back to the dueling spectators. Did you see Lady Vine Silltine duel?"

"Ugh, I don't want to talk about Vine Silltine." Dara began putting on her own gear.

"She's a little over the top, but that stuff works. The crowds love her."

"Just because she flounces around in dresses before—"

"It's not just the dresses," Siv said. "It's the whole package: the grand entrance, the noise, the moves. She's sexy, and she uses that to stick in people's minds. Then she puts on a good show during the bouts. Your style is too utilitarian. You don't waste any movements. You save your energy. You're very precise. Vine moves more than she has to, but she does it because that's what people want to watch. She's like a thunderbird."

"So you think I should be more like what? A peacock?"

"You've got to be something, Dara, something more than a good duelist."

Dara sighed and pulled a blade from her bag. "I could wear a dress to the hall if it would help that much."

"No, no, don't try to be Vine."

"But you just said—"

"You need to develop your own style, something that will help you stick in people's minds, both on and off the competition floor. Don't do what she's doing." Siv finally righted his glove and headed for the dueling strip. "I have an idea or two up my sleeve for you."

"Look, right now I'm tired," Dara said. "I just want to bout so Coach won't kick me out of the school next time I go for my real practice."

"Real practice, eh?" Siv said with a wicked grin. "I'll show you real practice, but only if you promise to try out my idea. Otherwise, I'll make you waste every morning from here until the Cup with half-assed bouts. And because I'm the prince, you'll have to keep practicing with me anyway."

Dara gritted her teeth. "Fine."

"Good." Siv dropped his mask over his face. "We start your showmanship training tomorrow."

SHOWMANSHIP

W HEN Dara arrived in the dueling hall the following
morning, Princess Selivia was waiting.

"Siv told me the plan!" she squealed as Dara entered. "I
have so many ideas. We're going to make you the most memorable duelist ever! Not that you're not memorable now, of
course, but you'll be even better."

"What do you have in mind?" Dara couldn't help smiling at
Selivia's enthusiasm. Siv was sprawled on the floor with a book,
but he set it aside to listen to his sister.

"Well, Vine Silltine already has a very flashy, sexy image,
right?" Selivia bounced on her toes as she talked. "You're going
to be intense. Very intense."

"I'm listening."

"I was thinking about the Fire Lanterns your father makes,"
Selivia began.

"I don't want to do a Fire theme," Dara said.

"No, Vine already uses Firegold in her clothes and tokens.
You're going dark, the opposite of what people expect from the
Lantern Maker's daughter. You're very intense when you duel,
so let's use that. Black clothes, black tokens, black face paint."

"Wait, face paint?"

"Yes!" Selivia clasped Dara's hands and squeezed them tight. "And I want to dye black streaks in your hair. It'll look striking against the blond."

Dara eyed the amateurish streaks in Selivia's own hair. She wasn't sure she wanted to let the young princess have her way with any dye. Dara was secretly quite proud of her long golden locks.

"What does this have to do with the Fire Lanterns?" Dara disentangled herself from the princess's grip and glanced over at Siv, who still sat on the stretching rug. He grinned proudly at her, and she dropped her gaze.

"The ones in my chambers have super intricate iron-work panels, like lace made out of metal," Selivia explained. "When the Fire shines through them, it casts the most beautiful shadows on the walls. It's lovely, and it only works because there's something dark and solid in front of the Fire. You have this intense attitude about dueling, but we're only going to show people the shadows. You'll do the rest."

"I'm not sure I understand what you mean," Dara said.

"You'll be dark and mysterious and powerful. Use the shadows, not the Fire. You'll make Vine look crass." Selivia danced over to retrieve a basket from beside the door and began pulling out piles of black clothing: dresses, cloaks, even a pair of tall black boots with iron buckles. "Sora and I don't wear these anymore. We can have our dressmaker tailor some costumes for you."

"You'll be a badass," Siv said, standing up and joining his sister. "And you need a new name."

"What?"

"Not literally," Selivia said. "Siv, I was saving that part! I think you need a catchy nickname that will help people remember you."

"And you should trash talk," Siv said. "I can help with that. You just need to call Vine the daughter of a cull—"

"Siv!"

"Sorry, Sel."

"*I* don't think you should trash talk," Selivia said. "It's not unique enough. And some of the male duelists already do it well."

"Yeah, my friend Kel is one of them," Dara said.

"You're friends with Kelad Korran!" Selivia shrieked. "Can you introduce me? He's so funny and soooo handsome."

"Seriously, Sel?" Siv rolled his eyes. "And you think I get off topic?"

"We'll talk about that later," Selivia whispered to Dara with a wink. "Anyway, I don't think you should talk at all whenever you can help it. If we're going for dark and mysterious, you need to be silent. Like mist. Or smoke. Or nightfall."

"Nightfall. That's a decent name," Siv said.

"So let me get this straight." Dara held up a gown made of black velvet with a burn on the skirt. The material was heavy and much richer than anything she'd ever worn. "You want me to call myself Nightfall, wear all black, and never speak? And that will make the spectators like me?"

"You can speak," Selivia said, "but only when you have something super intense to say."

"Like what?"

Selivia shrugged. "You sleep with one eye open, or you eat Fireroot for breakfast. I don't know. You'll think of something."

"And you hate Vine Silltine's guts," Siv added. "You're planning to skewer her in front of everyone at the Vertigon Cup."

"I don't hate Vine." Dara put the black gown back on Selivia's pile.

Siv gave an exasperated sigh. "Yes, but don't go telling people that. Dueling spectators love a good rivalry. Think about

Shoven and Jur the Jurl. Or Wora Wenden and Drimmez. People still talk about their matches."

"But Vine—"

"She'll play along," Siv said. "It'll be good publicity for her too. I'm surprised she hasn't called you out already."

Dara frowned, but Selivia nodded eagerly, her curls dancing.

"That was Siv's idea, and I think it's brilliant. A rivalry is almost as good as a romance!" Selivia looked back and forth between Dara and Siv, her smile widening.

"The other thing you need is some new moves," Siv said quickly. "That's where I come in."

"I'm not doing a bunch of crazy leaps during bouts." Dara could already imagine the kind of moves Siv had in mind. He was not the subtlest swordsman she had ever met.

"That's fine, but you can add in some showier stuff," he said. "Your style will work with your new image, but you need to look more powerful and scarier while you're at it."

Dara studied the prince and princess. It made her feel strangely spoiled to have them putting so much effort into helping her find a patron. She had spent so much of her life trying to convince her parents that dueling was worthwhile. Their enthusiasm was an unexpected gift. She met Siv's eyes, and warmth sang in her fingertips.

"Look, you don't have to do all this stuff for me," she said. "I can just train harder."

"But it'll be fun!" Selivia said. "We're going to make you the most memorable female duelist since Surri herself won the first women's open."

Siv folded his arms and surveyed her like a master painter studying a canvas. "And I'm going to make sure you win."

Dara and Siv practiced while Selivia called in her dress-maker and began sorting through the piles of black fabric. Siv had come up with a new set of moves for Dara. She felt silly, but she gritted her teeth and did whatever he suggested. It was the least she could do when he had put so much effort into this new strategy. She resented the implication that he could "make her win" when she had been dueling for her entire life, but after her disastrous performance at the Eventide Open she was willing to try anything.

Selivia called Dara over every once in a while to hold garments up to her but wouldn't let her try anything on because she was too sweaty. Selivia seemed to be having fun, so Dara didn't object to the frequent interruptions. Unfortunately, Siv was having fun running her ragged too. When they were finished, she had a new collection of bruises on top of her old ones.

"Nice work, Dara." Siv pulled off his mask. The sharp slant of sunlight on the dueling floor indicated it was almost high noon. "We'll keep going on this tomorrow."

"I'm not doing that leaping thing again," Dara mumbled, loosening her jacket collar.

"Oh yes, you are," Siv said. "I better get going. I have a lesson with Zage, and he pouts when I don't bathe beforehand."

"Zage Lorrid?" Dara tucked her mask under her arm.

"The Fire Warden is teaching me the intricacies of Fire administration," Siv said. "Yes, it is as boring as it sounds. But I have to know how the kingdom works if I'm going to be the king."

Dara frowned as the prince disappeared through the door beneath the balcony, and Selivia dragged her over to try talking her into dyeing her hair again. So the prince had lessons with Zage Lorrid? That worried her, especially because he mentioned it without even a hint of caution.

Dara remembered how the king had kept Zage on as Fire Warden after the Surge that had killed Renna. Dara had been too young to follow the nuances at the time, but the king clearly thought the incident was an accident. And now he allowed the Warden to give lessons to his children? Dara couldn't help thinking that even if the Surge *had* been an accident, Zage was now in a prime position to abuse the king's trust. He was already mismanaging the Fire, as her parents said. What else was he capable of?

Selivia had gone back to sorting through clothes for Dara. One of her newborn kittens popped out of the basket and wound around her ankles, pushing its soft pink nose through the piles of black fabric. Selivia was thirteen years old, soon to be fourteen, her attention split between her pets and projects and her crush on a cute athlete. Renna hadn't even made it to thirteen.

Dara wondered what it would have been like to grow up with her sister, the warm, living person, not the shroud her memory had cast over their family. Dara was incapable of living up to her parents' expectations with her sister gone, and she constantly warred against the resentment threatening to rise in her heart. She often wondered how her parents would have treated her if Renna had survived. It wouldn't have mattered at all that she didn't have the Spark. And she missed her sister too. She had Zage Lorrid to thank for all of that.

Dara glanced at the door to Siv's room again, where he would shortly be meeting with the Fire Warden. Yes, Dara was worried for her new friends. Worried that her parents' old enemy could be preparing to move against them and destroy their lives—as he had Dara's.

Dara crossed Fell Bridge and climbed the winding steps up Village Peak to her home. Her mother was sitting on the porch, a platter of bread and goat cheese balanced on her knee. She wore a deep-purple dress with a tall collar framing her face.

"Where have you been, Dara?"

"Training."

"I didn't see you come in last night."

"I'm sorry." Dara set her gear down and sat on the steps at her mother's feet, feeling sore. The new moves used different muscles than she was used to. "I stayed late at the school. But I'll be here to help you all afternoon."

Lima handed her a piece of bread with cheese. "You must become more involved with the business, Dara. It's an important time."

"Mother, do we have to keep having this conversation? We made a deal that I could try to get a patron."

"Maybe it's time to accept this isn't going to work," Lima said. "I heard about the Eventide Open."

"You heard?"

"Corren was there. He said you lost to an easy opponent."

You could have asked me yourself. "You don't usually take such an interest in how I'm doing."

"Nevertheless, if you are not even winning the tournaments—"

"I'll win the next one," Dara said. "I'm training harder than ever." Why couldn't they ever talk without all this pressure? The hope that had begun to rise after the prince and princess offered to help her faded in the onslaught of her mother's disapproval.

"I need you to spend more time in the lantern shop and meeting members of the Fire Guild," Lima said. "Farr is making good progress, but my daughter must be involved."

"I already know how to balance the books," Dara said.

"I'm not talking about the books." Lima stood, pulling herself up to her full height. "This is a complicated business. You must nurture relationships, and not only with your clients. The Fireworkers are divided, and the mightiest among them are growing restless. They look to your father for leadership, and they must continue to do so. Zage Lorrid has grown too powerful."

"He can't split the Fires much further, can he?"

"Perhaps. He has the ear of the king."

Dara frowned, thinking of how the Fire Warden must even now be teaching the prince. What was he capable of?

"I thought you've always considered him incompetent after what happened with—"

Dara stopped at her mother's cutting glare. Lima hated it whenever Dara brought up her sister. She wished they could speak frankly about what had happened. They both missed Renna. They had both suffered from her loss. But it was no use.

"What do you think Lorrid will do?" Dara asked instead.

"Take your head out of your dueling mask and listen, daughter," Lima said. "There is much he could do." She swept into the house before Dara could respond.

She stared at the door long after it had closed. Her mother would be interested to know about her royal training partner's lessons with the Fire Warden. Lima might actually approve of Dara's presence in the castle if it meant she could get more information about what Zage was up to. If Dara could find out what the Warden discussed with the prince, the information could prove useful to her family—more useful than anything she had ever done in the lantern shop.

Dara popped the last piece of bread and cheese into her mouth and brushed the crumbs off her trousers. A light breeze blew over the mountain, carrying the sounds of Village Peak on the wind. It was a bustling, chaotic place, but the Ruminor house was far enough up the side of the mountain that there wasn't too much foot traffic going by, even at this hour. A boy led a pair of mountain goats past their front steps and up toward the crest of the peak. A workman trudged by with a basket full of Everlights strapped to his back. A peal of laughter rose from the tavern down the path on the way to Square Bridge.

Dara stood, her muscles seizing up, and looked across Orchard Gorge to King's Peak and the castle at its crown. Smoke hung over the ramparts, as if someone had been doing a particularly large Work that day. Similar pockets of smoke indicated access points to other Fireworker shops.

Would it be possible for Dara to listen in on one of Siv's lessons with Zage? She could actually contribute to the family business for once, and maybe find out whether he truly had designs on the king's power. But the idea of eavesdropping on Siv without his knowledge left an oily feeling on Dara's tongue. The prince considered her a friend, and with his help she was getting closer to breaking away from the lantern business for good. Maybe it was better that her parents didn't know whom she dueled in the mornings. For now.

LORDS AND LADIES

A FTER yet another lesson on Fire politics with Zage, Siv answered his father's summons to the royal library. It was a high-ceilinged room in the easternmost tower of the castle. Shelves clung to the walls, with ladders stretching into the shadows at the top. A pair of tall windows looking out over Vertigon broke up the shelves, and several couches and a large oak table covered in books completed the room. The king often received nobles here when delivering decisions that were likely to disappoint them. The informal atmosphere was better for hard conversations, and judgments made in the library were often received better than pronouncements from the royal throne. Naturally, Siv was rather suspicious of why his father had called him here.

The king sat at the oak table, and he pushed aside the large book he had been reading as his son entered.

"You wanted to see me?" Siv said.

"We need to discuss the details of your visit to Trure."

"Father—"

"This trip is overdue." The king removed his eyeglasses and cleaned them with a bit of cloth. "I think it's best if you stay the whole winter. Your mother has promised to winter on the mountain this year, but it would be good for you to be in Trure on your own."

Siv tried not to let his dismay show on his face. "I thought you were giving me a chance to work on a few prospects for alliances with important houses before we decide anything."

"Son, you keep talking about your big plans, but I haven't seen any evidence that they're moving forward. Eventide would have been the time to call on the eligible ladies of the kingdom —not to mention sample their staffs' cooking—and instead you disappeared to a dueling competition. You continue to avoid your duties. Trure isn't so bad, you know."

Siv paced back and forth in front of his father's table. This was so sudden! He had no warning! Well, he supposed he had some warning, but things were just getting started with Dara's dueling project. He hadn't been as excited about anything in a long while. He didn't want to leave before he'd had a chance to admire his handiwork.

"If I can arrange something before First Snow, will you let me stay on the mountain for the winter?"

"You need to tell me more, Sivarrion," the king said. "Who is this brilliant match you keep hinting at?"

Siv grimaced. That was a project he should have been working on more. It had been far more interesting to plan for Dara's transformation into Nightfall than to arrange his inevitable marriage of state. It was time to show his cards, though.

"The Widow Denmore," he said at last.

"Lady Tull?" The king looked surprised but not displeased. "I'm intrigued."

"Her mourning period is coming to an end this month. With her husband's untimely demise, she's an even more promising prospect than when she was still the Lady Tull Ferrington." Lady Tull's husband had been the sole heir to the

Denmore Estate, as she was to the Ferrington Estate, and now it all belonged to her.

"You may be right about that," the king said thoughtfully. He pulled a map of the mountain toward him showing the holdings of all the major landowners. "She controls the Denmore Estate now, and her link to the Ferringtons is as important as ever." The king traced the lines indicating the Ferrington lands. Lady Tull's family holdings included Second Slope, where an important road led down into the Fissure. "She'd be a good match for any man in the kingdom."

"That's what I thought," Siv said. "And I happen to be the most eligible bachelor in Vertigon." He'd no doubt be letting down a host of adoring maidens, but a Denmore alliance would be the best scenario for the Amintelles.

The king put his eyeglasses back on and studied his son.

"And how do you like the lady herself?" he asked. "I hope you would find some joy with her."

"She's sad, but lovely." Siv had given it a lot of thought. Lady Tull Ferrington Denmore was a good match no matter how he looked at it. He had let his efforts to endear himself to her fall by the wayside in recent weeks, but he couldn't allow his dueling with Dara to get in the way of the good of the kingdom any longer. It was time to renew his efforts to woo the young widow.

"Sivarrion, I'm impressed by your forethought," the king said after a moment. "But I don't wish to rush you or the young lady. You needn't marry right away. Perhaps you should spend the winter in Trure, and we can revisit the idea of a match with the Widow Denmore when you return."

"Don't worry about that," Siv said. If he was being honest with himself, he didn't want to drag this out. He had to marry anyway. He might as well maintain some control over the process. He stopped pacing and met his father's eyes. "I might be ready to announce our engagement by First Snow. If I do, will you allow me to remain on the mountain?"

"Very well," the king said. "If you entreat Lady Tull to accept your proposal before summer's end, you may forgo the trip to Trure."

"Thank you, sir." Siv would need to work on Lady Tull, but at least he wouldn't be leaving right away. He'd have to get out to the parlors more. He hadn't been as often since he started getting his ass kicked in the dueling hall. Speaking of the parlors, that was another area where Dara was lacking. He could remedy that. And there was still the matter of launching Dara's rivalry with Vine Silltine.

A knock sounded on the great wooden doors of the library, and Bandobar, Captain of the Castle Guard, stepped inside. He was a stone-faced soldier, a few years older than Siv's father. One of the new Castle Guard recruits hovered behind him, his wide eyes darting around the king's library.

"Lord Rollendar is here to see you, Your Majesty," Bandobar said. "And his son, Lord Bolden, is asking after the prince."

"Ah, good. Send them in."

Bandobar saluted, and then glowered at the young guardsman until he did the same. The rookie blushed to his hairline. He hurriedly stepped back as Bandobar admitted the two noblemen.

The king turned over the map he had been perusing as Lord Von Rollendar entered the library. He was a powerful man with thick sandy hair going white at the temples. As always, he wore a formal red coat embroidered with ebony thread and the Rollendar House sigil. He took in the library and its occupants with sharp eyes, including Siv's slouch and unbuttoned coat, before bowing to the king.

"Welcome, Lord Rollendar."

"Your Majesty. May I present my son, Bolden?"

"Of course. A pleasure to see you again."

"Majesty." Bolden bowed to the king and nodded at Siv. Like his father, Bolden had thick sandy hair. He also had a long, sharp nose and blond mustache that made Siv think of a furlingbird poking its beak out of a nest. "I understand you have important matters to discuss with my father, Sire," he said. "May I entreat the prince to join me for a walk about the castle while you talk?"

"Yes, yes, of course," the king waved his hand, still holding the cloth he had used to clean his eyeglasses. "I'm sure you young men have schemes aplenty. You're free to go, Sivarrion."

"Thank you, Father." Siv offered a polite bow to his father and nodded at Lord Rollendar, though with less warmth. When Siv and Bolden had gotten into trouble as boys, it was always better to be caught by the king or one of the guards than by Bolden's father. Von Rollendar had darkness boiling beneath his skin, and he let it show when he was angry at even the most innocent of pranks.

This was convenient timing, though, as far as Siv was concerned. Bolden always knew where the important players would be on any given night. He would definitely know when and where Lady Tull was likely to be socializing. He was also a dueling patron himself. He could help with the Dara project.

Siv and Bolden left the library, the heavy wooden door closing behind them. Bandobar stayed in the library to watch over the king and Lord Rollendar, but two more new Castle Guards stood at attention beside Pool in the corridor. One was young. The other looked like a seasoned soldier. Perhaps he'd been recruited from the army. Siv and Bolden waited to speak until they had moved away from the Castle Guards. Pool followed at a polite distance.

"Do you know why the king called my father in today?" Bolden asked.

"No idea," Siv said. "Hey, do you know when—"

"My father thinks the king is angry with him."

"He didn't seem angry to me," Siv said. And if his father were angry, Siv certainly wouldn't tell Bolden.

"Maybe you can find out for me," Bolden said. "My father has reservations about the Ringston Pact, but I'd like to know for sure what the king thinks."

Siv smiled, but it was forced. He didn't appreciate Bolden trying to use him for information. He wasn't stupid.

"I wouldn't worry about it," Siv said. "Are you going to the parlors this coming Turnday?"

"Obviously."

Siv resisted the urge to chide Bolden about his tone. He needed the man right now. In truth, keeping company with Bolden wasn't quite as easy as it had been when they were boys. Bolden was far too ambitious, and their friendship had become lined with barbs.

"I need a good night out," Siv said. "Is Atria's still the place?"

"That it is," Bolden said.

"Will Lady Tull be there, by any chance?"

Bolden looked up sharply. The smile he gave Siv wasn't entirely friendly.

"I suspect she will," Bolden said after a moment. "She has come out with me often of late."

"Good," Siv said. Lady Tull may technically still be in mourning, but she was also quite young. He wasn't surprised to find she was joining the parlor gatherings already. "Let's raid the kitchens and see if we can't finish off a bottle of wine before our fathers are done." He'd need it to keep the mood light. Bolden also had designs on the Widow Denmore, but Siv was the prince. He'd have first pick. Bolden knew that and undoubtedly resented him for it.

They walked down the spiraling tower steps on their way to the kitchens. Lanterns and Firelights glowed across the mountain, visible through the narrow windows. Vertigon was beautiful, with its three peaks and the endless shadows and slopes.

The bridges connected everything, and people moved along them like insects far below the castle. Siv rounded the corner to another window. On the far peaks of the Village, he spotted a string of lanterns leading the way along a stairway. That was common outside Fireshops. He wondered if Dara's home was near there and what she was doing.

A cur-dragon swept through the sky, reminding Siv that he hadn't been down to visit little Rumy yet that week. He would do that just as soon as he got Bolden to tell him where every dueling patron on the mountain liked to socialize. With any luck, a few of them would be at the same parlors as Lady Tull, and he could kill two zur-sparrows with one stone.

Siv decided to share his latest idea with Dara when she came to the castle for their regular practice session a few days later. He stopped the bout with a raised hand and pulled off his mask. Dara lowered her blade.

"I've been thinking about the next tourney," he began.

"It won't be like the Eventide match," Dara said quickly. Strands of golden hair fell around her face as she removed her mask. Her eyes were bright and fierce, like Firejewels.

"It's not that," Siv said, reminding himself to focus. *Damn, she's pretty.* "Your image isn't your only problem for getting a patron after the Cup."

"I've been working on the new moves," Dara said. "And as long as I win—"

"Patrons turn down winners all the time. The guy who won the Eventide is still a free agent, isn't he?"

"For now," Dara said. "I think Oatin Wont has a decent chance at the Cup. He trains at my school."

"Oh. Right." Siv sometimes forgot that Dara had other dueling partners besides him. He was sure he was her favorite, though. So what if that other guy had won a stupid tournament?

"Anyway," Siv continued, "I bet Vine would have ended up just as cozy with Wora Wenden even if she'd lost the final. She networks with influential people. It's probably as important as playing to the crowd, if not more so. She goes to parlors and drinks with the patrons and makes them like her."

"It's just like politics," Selivia said, coming over with an armful of gear. She had been poking around in the wardrobe, looking for a black glove. Eager to help with the Nightfall project, she was often there when Dara came to practice. But Siv sometimes wished he could have Dara to himself.

His little sister came closer. "Sora goes to dinner parties all the time so she can talk to the right people. She loves that kind of thing."

"The right people? You sound like my mother," Dara said.

"It's very important," Selivia said, handing Dara a black glove with ornate silver stitching to try on. "Kings aren't the only ones with power. You have to know people with money and influence too."

"And know what they want," Siv said. "People are always trying to get something from each other. It's part of the game."

"Where would I even find these influential people?" Dara asked. "I'm not part of the royal court."

"You don't have to be," Siv said. "It's no fun anyway."

"Yes, they'd prefer to meet you in a casual setting, I'm sure," Selivia said.

"A casual setting?" Dara asked. She looked suspicious. Good. She was in for a surprise.

"No one wants to feel like they're at a courtly hearing all the time," Selivia said. "Those are dreadfully dull."

"I've decided exactly what you need." Siv grinned, thoroughly enjoying the worried look Dara gave him. "Dara Nightfall, tomorrow night we're going drinking."

LADY ATRIA'S PARLOR

I T was evening, and Firelights already lit the way across Fell Bridge when Dara left the Village and approached King's Peak. The mists were thick tonight, giving the world an unearthly glow. Crossing the bridge felt like walking over a river of cloud.

On the King's Peak side, stone steps led down from the foot of the bridge to the broad expanse of Thunderbird Square. The bridge guard's house loomed beside the stone steps. Dara didn't recognize Siv standing in its shadow until she had almost passed him. He wore simple black breeches and an open-necked shirt, but his elegant green coat embroidered in Fire-gold made him look more regal than he usually did in the castle. An ornate sword was buckled at his waist.

A lanky middle-aged man stood beside him, a pair of long knives in his belt. He had dark hair with a sweep of gray at each temple and a somber face.

"This is Pool," Siv said, nodding at the bodyguard. "He'll back us up if we get into a tavern brawl."

"That is inaccurate, my prince," Pool said. "I shall endeavor to keep you safe should we encounter any unsavory elements during the evening's excursions, but I can't condone any untoward brawling."

"Isn't he fun?" Siv grinned. "Now, let me look at you. You went with the black theme. That's good."

Dara adjusted her long black skirt over her hips as Siv studied her. She had rushed home after practice to bathe and hadn't put much thought into her clothes. She wore a simple blouse with Worked steel buttons. Still warm from hurrying across the bridge, she carried the fine black cloak Selivia had given her over her arm.

"Can you do something to make your hair not so tight?" Siv gestured to the golden braid slung over her shoulder. Her hair was still damp, and she had pulled it taut against her scalp. "When you've been dueling it falls around your face in wisps and looks nice."

Pool's eyes flickered toward the prince, then he went back to scanning the square around them.

Dara hesitated. She still wasn't sure whether she bought into this whole scheme. She was nervous that she wouldn't be able to accomplish whatever the prince thought she would tonight. Siv tapped his foot impatiently. With a sigh, she dug her fingers into her braid to loosen it, pulling a few strands away from her face.

"Yes, that's it!" Siv looked her over once more. "Onward to the pub!"

Dara followed him across the broad square and up the street into Lower King's Peak.

"In here," Siv said before they'd gone far, indicating an unassuming establishment called the Bridge Troll Tavern.

"I thought we were going to a parlor," she said.

"It's still early. We can't be the first ones there. Let's have an ale and talk about our plan of attack."

Siv swept open the door and led the way inside. Bridge Troll Tavern was quieter than similar establishments on Square Peak around the dueling school—and much cleaner. A trio of well-dressed men leaned close to an open window, puffing on long pipes inlaid with Firegold. The smoke curled out into the evening. A man and a woman with heavy cloaks and tired faces gazed into plates of roasted mountain goat. A few soldiers sitting at the bar glanced twice at the prince as he strode across the polished wooden floor and slid into a back booth, but he didn't draw as much attention as Dara would have expected. The soldiers merely straightened their uniforms a bit and resumed their conversation.

Pool collected three mugs of ale from the tavern keeper and sat beside Siv on the outer edge of the booth. He looked like just another drinking companion, but he positioned himself so he could watch the door. Eyes alert and shoulders tense, he didn't touch his ale after setting it down.

Dara studied her own drink dubiously. She took a sip, and the taste made her tongue curl. She set the mug back on the table.

"So, when we get to the parlor," Siv said after taking a long draught from his own mug, "you can't be too eager."

"But the patrons—"

"Don't refer to them as patrons," Siv said. "No one wants to feel like you're trying to get something out of them. These are just people, and by the end of the night you're going to be their friend."

Dara frowned, scratching at the rough grain of the table. "I thought everyone is trying to get something out of each other."

"Yes, but no one *says* it." Siv took another sip of his ale. "There's a subtlety to it. Like your dueling style, actually. You make tiny adjustments to your hand position, and your opponent basically impales themself on your blade. If you can do it during the bout, you can do it in a parlor."

"It's not the same."

"Just relax, and try to make friends. People help their

135

friends." Siv tapped Dara's hand with a long finger, and she stopped scratching at the wood. For a second she thought he was going to take her hand. Instead he rested his hand beside hers on the table and leaned toward her. "Don't worry about the patron part right now. This parlor will be an easier crowd because you'll probably already know a few people who spend time there. It's Zage's crew. Fireworkers."

"So my parents' colleagues? Great." Dara was pretty sure the Fireworkers who kept company with Zage Lorrid would *not* be the ones she knew through her parents. Hadn't her mother said they were divided? Dara pushed the ale farther away from her. Siv raised an eyebrow but didn't comment on it.

"Some of the Fireworkers support duelists," he said. "The sword smiths, obviously, and a few of the distributors. Zage has powerful contacts."

"Isn't Zage Lorrid sort of . . . sinister?" Dara said.

Siv chuckled. "He's a little strange, but the man is a genius. He's been teaching me ever since I learned to read. I'm sure you'd like him if you got to know him."

"If you say so." Dara remembered the shadowy figure who had emerged in her path the day she decided to run through the castle. She couldn't reconcile the image of a beloved teacher with the Fire Warden her parents had despised for as long as she could remember. She wondered if Siv knew about the Surge.

She glanced at Pool, who was still surveying the tavern. He obviously took his bodyguard duties seriously, and the castle had plenty of guards. She shouldn't worry about Siv. But if the greatest threat came from one of the prince's teachers, a confidante with the run of the palace, there wasn't much Pool—or all the dueling training in the world—could do about it.

Dara considered telling Siv what had happened to Renna, but she feared he would have the same response the king had:

pardoning Zage on the grounds that it must have been an accident.

Instead, they talked about dueling strategies as darkness wrapped around the mountain. Siv gave her a few pointers on what she should and shouldn't say to the patrons, but he seemed to think she would know what to do when she got there. Nerves worse than any pre-competition jitters warmed her skin.

She also couldn't help noticing the way Siv leaned in to talk to her, and the way he kept moving his hand closer to hers on the table. Did she want him to take it? She shifted her hand a little closer to his, just to see what would happen. She scanned the tavern briefly, hoping none of her parents' friends would see her.

"We can probably go out now," Siv said abruptly. "You going to finish that?"

Dara snatched back her hand and pushed her ale, still more than half full, across the table. Siv downed it in one long gulp.

The streets of Lower King's glowed with the Firelight pouring from the windows. The dinner hour was long past, and the residents of King's Peak were either making their way home or heading into the taverns and parlors along the steep street. Servants carried loaves of bread and bundles of cured meats home for their employers. Members of the noble court sauntered along with attendants in tow. Vertigon was all steep streets and staircases, so nearly everyone was on foot. The only horses, small, tough mountain ponies, were nothing like the elegant steeds ridden by noblemen in the Lands Below.

Siv made no effort to hide his face. A few passersby noticed him and bowed or dropped brief curtsies. Dara stayed half a step back, closer to Pool, who blended into the crowd despite his stiff mannerisms. Siv sauntered with his head high, sword swinging at his low-slung belt, and Dara remembered that he literally owned these streets.

The higher they climbed, the more the crowds of tavern-goers thinned. The streets, wider and quieter here, wound between fine greathouses, many built directly into the mountainside.

The dwellings closer to the castle were made of polished marble, which had to be quarried near the foot of the mountain and hauled all the way up the Fissure. The houses shone faintly. Fire-infused tiles topped the richest ones. As the moon rose, its light caught the Fire veins and reflected across Lower King's Peak. Dara slowed and looked back. Deep shadows stretched across the mountain. The mists had thickened, but she could still see the Village on the opposite peak, a jumbled warren of terraces and rooftops. Her family's house stood out even at this distance because of the lanterns leading the way.

Siv stopped when they reached a walled greathouse with an elaborate Fire-formed gate. He turned to Dara, shadows cutting across his high cheekbones.

"Zage told me the story of these doors when I was a little boy," he said. "Forged by my great-grandfather."

"The First Good King?"

"One and the same," he said. "The last Amintelle to have even a hint of the Firespark. When he realized his son didn't have the Spark, he appointed the first Fire Warden to control the mountain source and keep the peace amongst the Firewielders of old."

"You mean this is the Fire Warden's greathouse?" Dara examined the intricate swirls on the gate. There was no discernible picture, but the abstract designs suggested Fireworks far grander than the ones performed these days. This house sat atop the Well deep in the heart of the mountain, the mysterious source of the Fire itself. This house was where the Fire Warden parsed out the flows of Fire, disbursing it to all the Fireshops across the three peaks. She could almost feel the heat of old Vertigon in her blood as she thought about the raw power the Fire Warden controlled from here, the kind of power she had never been able to touch.

"I'd expect the daughter of Rafe Ruminor to have been here before," Siv said, turning to walk alongside the Fire Warden's high-walled home. Dara fell in beside him.

"My parents don't get along very well with Zage Lorrid," she said quietly, wondering again if she should tell him about Renna.

"And you don't get along with them."

"I never said that."

"Call it a hunch." Siv nudged her arm with his elbow then didn't pull away, keeping contact as they walked. Pool blinked.

"They're pressuring me to get more involved with their business," Dara said. "They think dueling is a waste of time. But it's all I've ever wanted to do. When I was a little girl and discovered I couldn't—" Dara stopped. Some hurts didn't need to be aired. She remembered the hours she had spent trying to draw on the Fire all too well, sometimes sneaking to her father's workshop in the middle of the night. She had cried on her knees in front of the access point, unable to understand why the Fire wouldn't come to her. She hated letting on how much it bothered her that she couldn't Work the Fire, and she didn't want to get into all that with Siv. "Never mind."

The prince didn't press her further. He led the way past an elaborate pillar at the corner of the Fire Warden's wall to a smaller greathouse beside it. It was bigger than her parents' dwelling and shop combined. Marble columns rose beside the door, and light and laughter tumbled through the window.

Parlors had a long and venerated history in Vertigon. Those who deemed themselves too important to be seen in simple taverns congregated in the front rooms of the greathouses on King's Peak. They'd engage in the same drinking, gambling, and socializing activities as in any other tavern, but around a more affluent set. The hosts would be repaid many times over through the business contacts and goodwill they cultivated in their parlors.

"Here we are!" Siv rapped on the door. It flew open immediately, and a voluptuous woman in a pink silk gown stood before them.

"Prince Sivarrion!" she crowed, her rich voice seeming to issue from the depths of her body.

"My Lady Atria." Siv kissed her hand gallantly. "Always a pleasure. May I introduce Dara Ruminor, my dueling partner, and you know Pool."

"My lady." Pool bowed stiffly, his ears going red.

"Come in, come in!" Atria cried. She squeezed Dara's hand. "A dueling partner, eh? Glorious. And Pool, you must call me Atria."

"Of course, my lady," Pool said.

A servant whisked away Dara's cloak, and they followed Lady Atria through a brightly lit entryway. Dara glimpsed people in the front room, laughing and drinking in tight groups of three and four. Servants bearing trays with goblets of wine, delicate cakes, and fruit tarts wound among them. A grand suit of armor decorated one corner of the room, and finely dressed ladies draped themselves over puffy couches—and over finely dressed gentlemen. It was a warm, colorful scene, enriched with the smell of perfume and spices.

But they didn't go into the main parlor. Atria led them toward the back of the house, chatting to Siv and rattling off the names of those who had already arrived. Dara walked beside Pool, who ducked his head into rooms as they passed, always keeping an eye on Siv and Atria.

"Are you looking for someone?" Dara asked.

"It's wise to assess the landscape for potential threats," Pool said. "It is a Castle Guard's primary imperative."

"Do you think someone *here* would harm the prince?"

"What I think is irrelevant," Pool said. "We must be alert for every eventuality. You would do well to remain ever vigilant."

This man is as paranoid as Berg, Dara thought. She didn't think they'd find any threats in Lady Atria's parlor, but she kept her eyes open just in case. She didn't want to lose her "dueling partner," as Siv had described her.

At the back of the greathouse, Lady Atria led them down a short flight of stone steps to a door set into the rock of the mountain. Inside was a low-ceilinged, musky space lined with couches and clusters of tables. People lounged about, engaged in more staid conversations than the revelers in the rooms above.

"This is where the true influencers gather," Siv said. "Lady Atria collects them."

"Nonsense." The big woman smiled beatifically. "They are simply my good friends. Enjoy yourselves, dear hearts." Atria swept off to talk to a diminutive man in a bright-red coat sitting alone in a corner. Pool chose a spot to stand guard beside the door and didn't join them as he had at the tavern.

Siv offered Dara his arm. She took it after a second's hesitation. She had never spent time with the prince outside the dueling hall, and she wasn't sure how they were supposed to act toward each other in mixed company. She was still a craftsman's daughter, and he was still the heir-prince. But when she rested her fingers on the green sleeve of his coat, he smiled down at her, and a surge of warmth went right through her.

Siv led her to a low table against the far wall where two men and a woman lounged on low couches covered in bright cushions. Smoke from a pipe drifted above them.

"Evening," Siv said. "Have you started the game without me?"

"Wouldn't dream of it, my prince," answered a young man with smooth dark skin. He was dressed in sturdy traveling clothes, and a cloak was draped on the couch beside him. "Who is your lady friend?"

Siv straightened, and Dara could have sworn his chest swelled. "May I present Dara Ruminor, one of the finest young duelists on our fair mountain."

"Ruminor? As in the lanterns?"

"Yes."

"Pleased to make your acquaintance." The man stood, his movements crisp, and offered her his hand. "Chala Choven. I'm with the Below Lands Trade Alliance. I come from Soole."

Dara released her grip on Siv's arm to take Chala's hand and felt instantly colder. Chala bowed low.

"Never mind your schmoozing," said the other young man, who had remained seated. "I've seen you duel, Dara. You're quite good."

"This is Lord Bolden Rollendar," Siv said.

"You're Kel's patron!" Dara burst out, remembering too late that she wasn't supposed to mention the word patron.

"That I am." Bolden had sandy hair and a neat mustache beneath a long, sharp nose. "Kelad talks about you all the time. I've won a bet or two on that fellow. Good duelist."

"You've probably lost a bet *to* him too," Dara said.

Bolden laughed. "That I have. Are you joining us for tiles, Siv?"

"Of course. Oh, and this is Lady Tull, the Widow Denmore." Siv bowed to the final member of the trio, a woman who couldn't be more than four years older than Dara. Lady Tull was beautiful. Stunning, actually. The traditional mourning veil she'd worn since her young husband, Lord Denmore, was killed in a tragic fall from Orchard Bridge didn't hide that fact. The accident had been the talk of Village Peak for much of last year, and it had left Tull the head of one of the most powerful noble families in Vertigon.

"A pleasure to meet you," Tull said. She held out a tiny, soft hand. Dara took it, feeling ungainly in her presence. She wished she could hide the way her muscles, ordinarily a source of pride, rippled in her hand and arm when she greeted the delicate lady.

Siv flopped down onto the cushions beside Lady Tull and indicated that Dara should sit between him and Chala Choven. An elegantly dressed serving man appeared and poured goblets of wine for each of them. Dara took a single sip of hers then set it on the low table. She twisted her hands in her skirt, unsure what to say in the presence of so many young nobles.

Chala began distributing the tiles for a game of mijen while Bolden filled Siv in on the latest gossip. Apparently earlier in the evening someone had tried to sneak into the back room uninvited.

"He'll be on Atria's blacklist for eternity," Bolden said. He laughed, a loud, braying sound.

"She's not especially forgiving," Siv said.

"She forgave you for that incident with the Fireroot," Bolden remarked, "but then you are the prince."

"You do love to bring that up, don't you?" Siv grinned at Bolden, who grinned back, all teeth. Neither one looked happy somehow.

"You can go first, Dara," Chala said, handing her the starting mijen tile. "You're our guest."

"Which rules do you play by?" she asked.

"Bern's, of course," Bolden said.

"I prefer Riiv's myself," Siv said.

Mijen could be played with two different methods. Riiv's method was favored in the Village. Dara suspected Siv was trying to make her more comfortable by suggesting the more common version of the rules.

"We needn't always do what you prefer," Bolden said, "my prince."

Siv laughed, but it sounded forced, not at all like his usual jovial tone. He wasn't happy to have Bolden speaking to him like that. Dara wondered, briefly, when she had learned to tell Siv's laughs apart.

"Bern's method it is, then," Siv said.

Dara laid her first tile. Siv met her eyes and gave her a reassuring nod. But there was a tightness in his eyes that wasn't usually there.

The five players laid tiles as the servants poured more wine. Chala relit his pipe and puffed smoke over their heads. Members of other groups came over to speak to the prince, mostly just to wish him well. A few had actual requests: for audiences with the king, for special dispensations, even for opportunities to buy the prince a drink at a later date. He handled the interruptions graciously. Although these were apparently his friends, he was also performing his royal role as the heir-prince. Dara had never seen him do that before. He looked older and more regal somehow, and far more serious than when it was just the two of them in the dueling hall.

Dara listened to the conversation around the mijen table, but she didn't have a lot to add. She was more comfortable with her dueling friends and their straightforward exchanges than in this smoky back parlor, where she wasn't sure exactly where everyone stood. Chala laughed a little too loud at the noblemen's jokes, acting solicitous and accommodating. Bolden kept trying to provoke a reaction from Siv. Dara wondered what they were each getting out of this supposed friendship. Lady Tull didn't speak much either, but whenever she did the three men leaned close to hang on her every word, even Siv.

At least Dara was winning the game. She may prefer Riiv's method, but even using Bern's rules she was an excellent mijen player. Lady Tull was the worst of the bunch, and Dara didn't feel bad at all about taking control of nearly a third of her tiles with one move.

Chala raised an approving eyebrow at that and leaned in to

study the game more intently, his pipe forgotten. While he contemplated his next move, Dara studied the other people in the parlor. They were an eclectic mix, some dressed in their best finery and others looking as if they'd just climbed the Fissure. The nobles were easy to spot because they each had a hovering ring of attendants waiting to serve them. A handful of Fireworkers gathered at a center table, clinking glasses of spiced wine and warming their contents with pocket Firesticks. Showing off their wares, no doubt. At least one of those men, Jara the Gilder, was a close associate of Dara's father. What was he doing here?

As she scanned the dark edges of the room, she spotted a glint of silver in the far corner. There was something familiar about it, but it disappeared into the shadows before she could get a good look.

"So, Dara, what does your father think about the Fire Warden's latest regulatory actions?" Chala asked, drawing her attention back to the group. He had made a move that was clearly intended to take away her lead. He must think he could distract her from the game. He was in for a surprise.

"Yes, I'm curious about that as well," Lady Tull said. "My advisors tell me Lantern Maker Ruminor opposes regulation."

"Oh, we don't discuss business at home," Dara said. That wasn't strictly true, but she doubted her father's opinion would be welcome amongst Zage Lorrid's friends.

"Don't be coy, Dara," Bolden said. "We all know Rafe Ruminor wants fewer restrictions."

"It's not about that," Dara said. "He doesn't want the Fire to be diluted by people who haven't studied the art enough." She moved a tile casually, hoping Chala wouldn't catch on to what she was doing.

"If you ask me, he's right," Chala said. "There are many who want policy changes . . . and not necessarily in the direction they're going. The more rare the Fireworks are, the better it is for our profit margins. It's hard to transport and trade high quantities of less valuable Works. The Below Lands Trade Alliance is willing to support those who see things our way."

"Come now, we're not discussing politics, are we?" said a dry, papery voice behind them. "This is a quiet gathering among friends."

A hand landed heavily on Dara's shoulder. It was cold as ice. She shuddered involuntarily, looking up to find that the hand and the voice belonged to none other than Zage Lorrid.

"Just making conversation, Fire Warden," Chala drew back, adjusting his tall collar. He hadn't reacted to Dara's move yet.

"I don't think we need to bore our young friend here. And some things needn't be discussed in mixed company." Zage's whispery voice made it sound as if he were speaking through smoke. He wore all black, like the last time Dara had seen him, and the silver leaf pin glinted at his throat.

"Of course not," Chala said slowly. He adjusted his collar again, his hands moving nervously.

"Join us for a drink, Warden?" Siv asked. He scooted closer to Lady Tull to make room on the couch.

"I have business to attend to with my associates," Zage said. "My prince, where is your bodyguard?"

Siv shrugged, reaching for his wine goblet. "Pool's around here somewhere. Probably making eyes at Lady Atria."

"I see," Zage said softly. "You would do well to be careful."

"I always am!"

Zage studied the prince for a moment before saying good-bye to the others. His dark eyes flitted to Dara before he joined the Fireworkers at the center table. She shivered. The Fire Warden seemed awfully interested in whether or not Siv had a guard. She wished the prince hadn't told him about Pool's preoccupation with Lady Atria.

"He's a good man, Zage," the prince said when the Fire Warden was out of earshot. He moved a mijen tile, opening himself up for Dara to take a few of his tiles. "But he has a hard time relaxing."

"Another round?" Chala said. He frowned at the table and gave Dara an appraising look. There was no way he could catch up to her score now. "I spend enough time worrying about the Fireworkers. Not another word of business." He waved his arm for another bottle of wine, and soon everyone had a full goblet. Dara didn't even need hers topped up. She didn't like wine much more than ale. At least she had won the game.

Bolden called for a toast, and Dara held her goblet up with everyone else.

"To wine, friends, and the two ladies who have graced us with their presence," Bolden said. He nodded at Dara and Lady Tull, keeping his eyes on the latter as he sipped from his goblet.

"And to me!" said another voice behind them. "Can't start the toasts without me."

"Kelad!" Bolden said.

Dara spun to see that her friend had arrived. He wore finer clothes than usual. If she was not mistaken, the red and black embroidered into his silk coat were the colors of House Rollendar. Bolden stood and clapped Kel on the back.

"It's the man of the hour," Bolden said. "Kelad won me a pile of firestones in the Eventide Open. Finished in the top four. It almost made up for his dismal performance in the Square Tourney."

Kel shrugged. "I'll never live that one down."

Bolden kept his hand on Kel's shoulder in a proprietary manner and turned to the others.

"I don't think you've met Prince Sivarrion before. Kelad Korran, may I present the heir-prince and future Fourth King, Sivarrion Amintelle. And you know us, his faithful lackeys." There was something mocking in Bolden's tone. Dara hadn't imagined it.

Kel bowed to Siv and the others. Then his eyes fell on Dara.

"That is not Dara Ruminor in a dress, with a drink in her hand. I must have died and waltzed into the realm of the Firelord."

"Hey Kel," Dara mumbled, blushing. "Not a word of this to the guys."

"Have you seen this girl duel?" Kel said. He raised his voice a bit, and people at the other tables looked over. "This is the second coming of Surri herself. Did you know she runs all the way across Furlingbird Bridge from Village to Square every single day? Sometimes twice! She trains harder than any other duelist on the mountain."

"Including you?" someone shouted from another table.

"Half the mountain trains harder than me!" Kel called. "No, Dara Ruminor is the duelist you'll be telling your kids about in twenty years. She's the real thing. A round on me in honor of Dara Ruminor!"

"Hear, hear!" Siv called immediately, and the others followed his lead. Siv winked at Dara and whispered, "He knows how it's done."

During Kel's speech she had been sinking deeper and deeper into the couch. If the patrons in the parlor hadn't paid attention to her before, they would now. She wished she could act as nonchalant about the attention as Kel did. She'd still rather have a sword than a goblet of wine in her hand.

Kel plopped down on the couch between Dara and the prince.

"Want to spot me the gold for the round, Dara?"

"I—"

"Just kidding," Kel said. "I won at cards earlier. I'm good for it."

"Was that necessary?" she asked.

Kel picked up Dara's goblet and took a long sip. "It's high time you got noticed by the right people, Dar. That's what it takes if you really want a patron."

"That's what I've been telling her!" Siv said. "That's why I brought her here tonight. You did my job a lot more efficiently, though."

If Kel was surprised to have the prince of Vertigon congratulating him, he covered it well.

"She needs to be a more dynamic duelist too," Kel said. "Patrons love that."

"Exactly." Siv leaned around Kel, eyes bright. "See, Dara. This'll work. We've been going over some new moves."

"New moves, eh?" Kel raised an eyebrow at Dara.

Lady Tull touched Siv's arm, pulling his attention away from the two duelists. Kel waited until Siv was fully engaged in conversation with the comely widow before turning back to Dara and hissing in her ear.

"What in the name of the deepest gorge are you doing here with Prince Sivarrion of all people? And what does he mean you've been working on moves?"

"I've been dueling with him," Dara said.

"Dueling," Kel said flatly. "With Sivarrion. The future Fourth King. And now you're drinking wine and schmoozing with lords and ladies? What's gotten into you?"

"Berg asked me to," Dara said, fiddling with the folds of her skirt. "The prince needed a training partner."

"You're partners now? When were you going to tell me?"

"It was supposed to be sort of a secret," Dara whispered. "Coach Berg offered me free lessons in exchange. He thinks the prince needs to take dueling more seriously for his own safety."

"Berg's a head case, but that's not the point." Kel looked over at the prince, who was still deep in conversation with Lady Tull. "The cur-dragon is obviously out of the bag. You could have told me in the spirit of our long friendship. I almost had a heart attack when I saw you here."

"I'm kind of embarrassed," Dara said. "Parlors aren't usually for me, but he thinks I should try to become friends with potential sponsors."

"He's right about that," Kel said. "Though I'll warn you that a friend who pays for your living is never quite the same." He finished off Dara's wine and waved for another goblet. "I can't believe this. Oat and I thought you might have a secret lover because you're late to practice so often now." Kel's eyes widened. "Wait. He's not your secret—"

"No! Of course not."

"You sure? He's going to a lot of effort to—"

"I'm sure."

Dara looked past Kel to make sure Siv hadn't heard them. The prince was still engrossed in whatever Lady Tull was saying. Tull laughed and laid a hand on Siv's arm. Dara felt a painful twinge in her stomach, but she ignored it.

"Well, this has made my night," Kel said as a servant appeared with a goblet for him and refilled Dara's wine as well.

"Please don't tell Oat," Dara said. "He's looking for a patron too, and I don't want him to think I'm holding out on him."

"Don't worry about it," Kel said. "I tried to get him in with Bolden, but he's not a fun enough drinking buddy for the tastes of our young lord."

Bolden was talking to Chala on the opposite side of the table, the game of tiles forgotten. He kept looking at Siv and Tull out of the corner of his eye. Chala was making some sort of business pitch, but Bolden barely listened. He interrupted Chala to call for something stronger than wine, his attention still focused on the widow and the prince. Lady Tull was playing with the fabric of Siv's coat now. The sight made Dara feel slightly sick. She took another sip of her newly refilled wine, but the taste wasn't getting any better.

"Hopefully I'll do well enough in the Cup to get a patron even if all this stuff doesn't work out," Dara said.

"You'll be fine, Dar." Kel drained his goblet in one gulp.

Dara raised an eyebrow, but he just shrugged and said, "I've got some catching up to do with my liege."

Dara wondered whether Kel really enjoyed Lord Bolden's company. On the one hand, Kel got to visit exclusive back-room parlors, but he had little choice in the matter. He was essentially singing for his supper. Every patron expected something different for their support. It was Kel's responsibility to be good entertainment and good company for the young lord.

"Speaking of patrons," Kel said, keeping his voice low, "if you and the prince are so chummy, have you considered asking him to sponsor you?"

"The royal family never sponsors duelists."

"There's a first time for everything. He's got the gold."

"No." Dara didn't hesitate. The idea had crossed her mind once, but once was enough. "I'm not asking him for money. We're training partners. At least inside the dueling hall, we're on an equal footing. I'll help him become a better duelist, and he'll help me do whatever it is we're doing here, but that's it." Dara did not want to start down the path of accepting money from Siv. Somehow, she knew it would change things between them.

Kel glanced at Bolden. "Understood."

THE BRIDGE

A S the hour grew late, the revelers trickled out of the parlor, many of them swaying and stumbling. Kel and Bolden left with their arms around each other's shoulders, singing loud drinking songs. Dara made Kel swear not to tell anyone about her and the prince, but she wasn't sure he'd remember in the morning. Chala curled up on a couch beneath his traveling cloak, determined to stay the night with his arm wrapped around a bottle of wine. When Lady Tull rose to go, Siv kissed her hand and offered her an elegant bow. He sauntered over to speak to the Fire Warden, who hovered in the corner like a dark bird, while Dara searched for her cloak.

She found Pool sitting on a bench in the entryway with his arms wrapped around Lady Atria. Atria sat partway on top of Dara's cloak, but she didn't seem to notice Dara waiting politely beside them. Pool and Atria kissed in the half-light from the lanterns, making wet smacking sounds. Feeling embarrassed, Dara cleared her throat a few times to get their attention, but they didn't budge. Finally, she grasped the edge of her cloak and tugged on it until Atria shifted onto Pool's lap and the cloak popped loose.

She returned to the underground parlor, where Siv was taking leave of Zage.

"I'm just going to walk my dueling partner to the bridge," Siv was saying.

"Take care, my prince," Zage said. "The night is dark, even on the Fire Mountain."

"Never fear," Siv said, throwing his arms wide. "I'll be bright-eyed as a burrlinbat at our next lesson."

"Farewell, then."

Siv lurched slightly as he joined Dara at the door. Zage's eyes glittered in the semi-darkness behind him. Once she was sure the prince was following, she hurried up the steps, wanting to get away from Zage as soon as possible.

"You don't have to walk me home," Dara said.

"Nonsense," Siv said. "I could use a bit of fresh mountain air. Where's Pool?"

"He and Lady Atria are . . . busy."

"You don't say? He's been pining after her for ages."

They walked toward the front of the greathouse together. Siv grinned widely when they reached Pool and Atria.

"Pool!" he shouted.

Immediately, Pool leapt up, his face smeared with Atria's red lip stain.

"My prince! I am at your service, ready to defend your life at every moment, Sire!"

"Sit back down, Pool," Siv said. "We're just walking to Fell Bridge. Take your time, and catch up to us."

"My prince, I couldn't possibly—"

"I've got one of the best duelists in Vertigon with me," Siv said, forcing Pool back down on the bench with both hands. "Say a proper good-bye, and I'll see you in a few minutes."

"Yes, my prince. I will take my leave of my most benevolent and sublime lady and join you shortly."

"As you were." Siv chuckled as he and Dara headed out the door.

It was the hour past midnight. The street outside the parlor was empty. Siv and Dara's footsteps tapped a quiet music in the stillness as they passed the elaborate gates of the Fire Warden's house. They walked side by side, closer together than they had before. Something about the dark and the night made it seem like the right thing to do.

"Thank you for the invitation tonight, my prince," Dara said.

"You're starting to sound like Pool," Siv said. He began to hum tunelessly, his steps weaving a bit.

"No, really, I had a lovely time."

"Sorry you didn't like the wine."

"I don't like any wine," Dara said. "It makes morning training sessions easier, at least."

"Well, I'll be at practice tomorrow no matter what," Siv said.

"I know. You've been working hard over the past few weeks."

"Have to stay ahead of Berg's mythical assassins, don't I?" Siv smiled, his prominent cheekbones carving strong shadows on his face. His eyes shone bright in the moonlight, and his meandering steps brought him a hair closer to her. Dara looked down to avoid his gaze, but she didn't pull away from him.

The streets of Lower King's were deserted, and as they strode through the darkness together it felt as if they were the only two people on the mountain. Mist and quiet drifted around them as they crossed Thunderbird Square and approached Fell Bridge. There was no sign of the bridge guard, except for a single light burning in the window of his house. The stillness was eerie. Pool should have caught up to them by now.

"Lady Tull was nice," Dara said to fill the silence.

Siv looked at her sharply.

"What makes you say that?"

"She seemed to enjoy your company, that's all."

Siv was quiet for a moment. Then he sighed. "Lady Tull is the head of a powerful house," he said. "A rich house."

"And her mourning period will be over soon," Dara said.

"That's correct." Siv didn't need to say any more. Dara knew what wealthy young widows looked for after their mourning periods—and what heir-princes looked for when they reached adulthood. Denmore was a powerful house, even by Amintelle standards.

The mist thickened around them. The lights of Village Peak on the other side of the Gorge were barely visible as they crossed the final stretch of the square toward the bridge steps. There was a chill in the air. Summer was almost at an end, and it would only get colder in the mountain heights. Dara shivered despite her cloak. Without hesitation, Siv put his arm around her shoulders. She was almost as tall as him, but his arm fit comfortably around her body.

"This all right?" he said, his voice husky.

Dara didn't answer. A strange, warm feeling was spreading through her. It was more than just Siv's arm around her shoulders. She felt stable somehow, as if she were connected to the very roots of the mountain. She realized she had stopped walking. Siv turned toward her and brought his other hand up to rest on her waist, inside her cloak. They were so close Dara could feel the heat coming off him in waves. She was breathing heavily, as if she'd been running, and her breath mixed with his.

Dara put a tentative hand on Siv's chest. He curled his arm closer around her, so his hand rested on the small of her back. She leaned into him. She couldn't help it. A voice in her head told her this shouldn't be happening, but still she didn't draw away. Heat hummed in her body. She could feel Siv's heart racing through her fingertips.

Slowly, he lowered his face to hers, his eyes a mix of

shadows and light. Pulse quickening, she glanced around to make sure no one could see what they were about to do.

That's when she saw the man darting toward them, a large knife raised.

Dara shouted as the man lunged toward the prince's back.

She shoved Siv sideways, grabbing the ornate sword from the sheath at his belt as he fell. The attacker was almost upon them. Dara swept the prince's blade up in a crude parry, knocking the assailant's knife aside. The man rammed into her, cursing as he stumbled.

"Run!" Dara shouted at Siv.

The attacker recovered his footing. He wore the simple clothing of a tradesman: brown trousers, brown coat, well-made boots. Dara raised the tip of the prince's blade, adopting her dueling stance. But the attacker didn't pay her any attention. He whirled around, between her and Siv, who was just getting to his feet. He was tipsy, his movements sluggish.

"Dara!" Siv said, eyes widening at the man with steel in his hand.

"Get behind me," she said. Then she attacked.

The assailant spun and met her blade with a swipe that barely kept the point from his chest. The attacker bared his teeth in a silent snarl.

Dara shouted for help, but no one came to their aid. The emptiness of the square was suddenly ominous. Even the bridge guard's house remained still. They were alone.

Dara and the knifeman circled each other as Siv groped for something to use as a weapon, but he couldn't pry up any of the cobblestones. The attacker lunged for him again. He scrambled backward, still struggling to stay balanced.

"Run to the bridge," Dara shouted.

Still unarmed, Siv obeyed, clambering up the stone steps. Dara jumped in front of him, sword at the ready. The attacker stalked nearer. There was a glint of Firegold on the hilt of his long knife, at odds with his plain appearance. Dara stabbed at his eyes to keep him from getting any closer. All of her dueling experience screamed that this was wrong. She couldn't jab out an opponent's eyes! Where was Pool?

Fear clutched at her, but she couldn't let that blade anywhere near the prince. Dara's sword wasn't blunted, but she doubted its tip was very sharp. She had to be precise. The knifeman jabbed at her again, and Dara struck, cutting a thin line down the length of the man's weapon arm. He cursed and switched the knife to the other hand. Blood dripped on the cobblestones.

Dara and Siv retreated up the steps to the bridge as the attacker edged closer. He moved quickly, jabbing and slicing. He obviously knew what he was doing, and he wasn't afraid of a girl with a sword. No help came, despite their shouts. The attacker advanced.

"Dara, let me—"

"Shh, don't distract me," she snapped. Siv didn't argue. His boots thudded on the boards of the bridge as they retreated further.

The attacker seemed to be waiting for something. If there were more of them, Dara wasn't sure how long she'd last. She had never been in a real fight before. This sort of thing didn't happen in Vertigon. And in Lower King's no less!

They edged out onto the bridge, and the mist closed in around them.

"What do you want from me?" Siv said. "Allow me to speak with my father about your complaint. Perhaps we can come up with a solution."

"We're done dealing with Amintelles," the man hissed. "Your time in Vertigon is finished."

"Let's just calm down and talk about it," Siv said. "I'm sure we can—"

"My prince!" a voice shouted through the mists. "Halt, you!"

Pool was running down the steep street toward the square, his long legs pumping. Half a dozen men in uniform followed.

The attacker glanced over his shoulder and cursed.

"Die, Amintelle," he hissed. Then he hurled the knife straight at the prince's heart.

Dara reacted, unthinking, her training kicking in. She parried, lightning fast. The knife sparked against her sword and flew away, tumbling down into the depths of the Gorge. The attacker cursed again then rushed toward the edge of the bridge and jumped after his knife. He fell without a word into the mists below.

The world was silent for a heartbeat.

"Nice move, Dara Nightfall," Siv breathed.

"My prince! Are you injured?" Pool stormed onto the bridge and skidded to a halt in front of them. Dara stared numbly after the man who had just leapt to his death. What *was* that?

"I'm all right," Siv said. "Thanks to Dara. Do you know who that was?"

"No, sir, but we will investigate immediately."

Siv said something in response as they accompanied Pool back toward the square, but it faded to a buzz in Dara's ears. She sat shakily on the steps leading down from the bridge. A Fire Lantern glowed above her. A powerful heat sang in her fingers, still clutching the prince's blade. She ground the point into the stone step beneath her feet and tried to breathe.

Pool took charge, ordering the men he had brought with him to scan the area for evidence of more attackers. Others arrived, both guards and people who lived nearby. Someone shouted from the bridge guard's house. Something about a body.

Dara felt far removed from the commotion. Tension hummed through her veins. Slowly, the heat leeched out of her fingers, as if it was draining through the blade in her hand. She felt a bit nauseous.

After a few minutes, the cold of the night slipped around her again, clearing her head. As she came to her senses, she realized she was still clutching the prince's sword. She held it out to him shakily. Siv met her eyes and grasped her hand as he took the weapon. They stayed like that for a moment, her hand on the hilt, his hand on her hand, as Pool and the guards bustled around them.

"I owe you my life, Dara Ruminor," Siv said. She had never seen him more serious. A bit of that strange heat flashed in her veins, but it was gone in an instant.

"My prince, we must relocate to a safer position immediately," Pool said. "I must express my humblest and most sincere apologies for failing in my duty. It will never happen again, my prince, for I shall insist upon my resignation the moment we get you to safety."

"Don't be ridiculous, Pool," Siv said, turning away from Dara at last and returning the sword to its sheath. "I ordered you to stay. It's my own damn fault for being a fool. Let's find out who that man was. Have someone escort Miss Ruminor to her home. Under the circumstances, I probably shouldn't cross the bridge."

"I can get home on my own," Dara said.

"I won't have it, my lady," Siv said. "Two of these men will make sure you get safely to your door." His usual grin had vanished, but he remained calm despite the circumstances. Dara didn't argue. She didn't want to walk home alone in the dark after this. She could still hardly believe what had happened. Who would attack the prince? Who even knew he would be here without a guard tonight?

Zage Lorrid. The answer was glaringly obvious. Zage and his cronies knew exactly when the prince left Lady Atria's greathouse. And they knew he would be walking toward Fell Bridge instead of going straight up to the castle. Dara thanked the Firelord that the attacker had made his move while she was

with the prince. If she had already started to cross the bridge . .
.

Dara shuddered as Pool dispatched two Castle Guards to escort her home. Berg was right. The danger to Prince Siv Amintelle was very real indeed.

THE CASTLE

S IV was stone-cold sober by the time he returned to the castle. Nothing like nearly being stabbed in the back to clear your head. He was still kicking himself for not being the one to fend off the attacker. Dara had saved him with his own blade because he had been too inebriated to react. He vowed never to let that happen again.

He still felt tenser than a Soolen elephant crossing a rope bridge. No one had ever tried to kill him before, as far as he knew. It didn't feel real, even though the glint of that knife flying toward him in the moonlight would likely be imprinted on his brain forever.

He distracted himself by trying to talk Pool out of falling on his own sword on the way up to the castle. He'd do his best to keep the man from being dismissed from his post, but he didn't think there was any way he could hide what had happened from his father. Too many people had seen the commotion at Fell Bridge. He could already imagine the gossip that would descend upon the mountain like a hailstorm. An assassination attempt! In Vertigon! He couldn't quite believe it, and he had been there himself.

Word traveled even faster than Siv expected. His father met them in person in the entryway of the castle, flanked by the solemn men of the Castle Guard. He wore a robe, a pair of chamber slippers, and a sword buckled at his waist. Several of the Castle Guards carried small Everlights, and they formed a neat box around the king. Shadows cloaked the upper reaches of the entry hall.

"Siv, are you hurt?" the king said as Siv entered the pool of light surrounding him. The king's face was pale and his hair disheveled.

"No, sir."

"Pool," the king snapped. "Report."

"My men are scouring the area, Your Majesty, but the assailant appears to have acted alone."

"Inform me as soon as they return with more information."

"Yes, Your Majesty. And may I express my deepest and most excruciating penitence for—"

"We will discuss it later, Pool." The king spoke to his own guards in a low voice. Bandobar saluted sharply and strode out of the castle, taking several of his more seasoned Guardsmen with him.

The king turned to Siv. "Accompany me to my chambers."

"Yes, sir."

They spoke formally, but as Siv fell in beside his father, the king gripped his shoulder with a heavy hand.

"Are you sure you're all right, son?" he said. "I received word that you were attacked only moments ago."

"I'm fine. My dueling partner was there. She protected me."

"She?" The king raised an eyebrow. "You'll have to tell me more about that another time. Did you get a good look at your assailant?"

"It was dark. He was dressed like a common tradesman, but he could have been anyone."

"Vertigonian?" the king asked, lowering his voice.

"I think so."

"I see."

They reached the stairwell to the king's chambers and began to climb. As they rounded the familiar corners, the tension began to drain from Siv's body. He had been flexing every muscle since the moment someone started trying to stick a piece of steel into his body. Damn. That had been scary.

But Dara had protected him. Protected him when he could barely walk straight.

"Father?" Siv said.

"Yes?" the king wheezed, concentrating on the steep steps of the tower.

"I . . . wasn't as alert as I could have been tonight." He didn't mention the drinking but figured it was implied. "I should have listened to your advice."

His father didn't answer at first. They rounded the spiral staircase, footsteps whispering on the stone.

After a moment he said, "Thank you, son. Your willingness to admit that does you credit. If anything had happened to you tonight . . ." The king didn't complete the thought, and they finished the climb to his chambers in silence. They waited on the landing while his men scoured the room for intruders.

"These next hours and days will be crucial in gathering information," the king said. "We'll get to the bottom of this. Why don't you stay here tonight? You'll be the first to hear any news and . . . well . . . I'd like to keep you close." The king cleared his throat gruffly.

"Yes, sir," Siv said. "Thank you." He hadn't really wanted to go back to his own chambers in the western tower of the castle tonight. In truth, he was shaken by what had happened. He'd never admit it out loud, of course. The king patted him on the shoulder with a warm hand.

When the guards were satisfied that the room was safe, the king called down to the kitchens for a midnight snack, and they settled in the antechamber to discuss what had happened. They spent the next few hours going over the incident in exhaustive detail, including the names and possible complaints of every single person Siv had encountered that night. When the guards finally left it was nearly dawn. Siv stretched out on the couch in his father's antechamber, knowing he'd sleep like a cur-dragon hatchling. He was safe in the hall of the king.

Climbers searched the Gorge for days for the body of the attacker, hoping it might yield some hint as to why the man had attacked the prince. In the meantime, Captain Bandobar made good use of the new company of Castle Guards, dispatching them to patrol the castle more frequently than ever before. Siv couldn't turn a corner without bumping into one of the men, their uniforms still freshly creased, their expressions keen at the chance to protect the royal family from real danger.

The king made Siv attend every meeting with the men investigating the attack, and he found excuses to keep Siv and his sisters close. He even insisted that Siv attend all the royal council meetings, which used to be optional. Well, Siv used to think of them as optional. He was starting to think his father was overreacting to the threat to his life. It had been a single assailant, probably some crazy man who blamed the royal family for his lot in life. Yes, it had been scary at the time, but in the light of day, surrounded by the Castle Guard, it was hard to believe he was still in any danger.

Worse, the council meetings took place in the mornings when Dara was supposed to come to the castle, and he had to cancel a few of their dueling practices. He wanted to see her again, but he was being swept up in his royal duties, which apparently became more extensive after someone tried to kill you. He hoped everything would calm down in a few days so he and Dara could get back to work. Of course, that meant Siv's courtship of Lady Tull would have to resume as well, but he tried not to dwell on that.

Siv scribbled a letter for Dara on a spare bit of parchment to leave with the guards at the front gate. He felt bad about disrupting her training routine. And they were going to get behind on the Nightfall project unless she continued to work on it herself. He needed to nudge her a bit to make sure she proceeded according to plan. If only he weren't so busy reassuring his father that he wasn't going to be assassinated! At least, he hoped he wasn't.

Siv doodled ideas for the project on parchment during the interminable meetings, his thoughts drawn back to Dara like an arrow in Cindral Forest. He couldn't forget the intensity in her eyes that night, the way her body had warmed in his arms as he held her close. She had looked surprised, but she hadn't pulled away from him. Or at least, she hadn't pulled away until she'd shoved him to the cobblestones and saved his life. That meant something, right?

He knew he should never have held her like that at all, should never have even begun to imagine what her lips might feel like. He definitely shouldn't be wondering whether she'd close those intense eyes if he kissed her.

Vertigon was his duty. He reminded himself of that fact every time his thoughts strayed back to Dara. He would take whatever steps were necessary to guide it well one day, even if that meant steps side by side with the most strategically advantageous noblewoman he could find. Tull was the right match for the kingdom, no matter how he felt about it. But he still wanted to find some way to repay Dara for what she had done for him. And he wanted to see her again.

HOUSE SILLTINE

DARA could hardly wait for her next practice with Siv. She didn't go over to King's Peak the next day, assuming the prince would have more than enough to do in the aftermath of the attack, but she was dying to know what had happened after the two Castle Guards escorted her home.

She still felt shaken by the incident, but she fended off the lingering fear by analyzing what had happened as if it were a tournament match. Who had the attacker been? Or more importantly, who had hired him? There would be an investigation; surely they would realize that Zage Lorrid had been the last person to see Siv before they headed out into the night. He must have sent the assailant down to Thunderbird Square as soon as they left the parlor.

Dara was certain the king's men would get to the bottom of the plot. In the meantime, she and Siv needed to train harder than ever. Berg was right: he couldn't be caught unawares again. She was already thinking about which defensive parries they should work on next time.

Of course, Siv might have been more alert if he hadn't been looking at *her* quite so intently before the attack. If he hadn't put his arm around her and . . . Dara still didn't know what to think about that. They were training partners and—she thought—friends, but that was as far as it could ever go. He was the heir-prince of Vertigon, after all.

Still, she couldn't stop replaying the moment when Siv put his hand on her waist and leaned in, couldn't steel herself against the feelings that arose each time she remembered how his body had felt against hers. It had left her almost as breathless as the attack.

And then there was the way heat had flashed through her fingers when she held the prince's blade. The way it had seemed to leak from the sword into the stones at her feet afterwards. She barely dared to think about that. It was probably the fear. The adrenaline. It didn't mean anything. It couldn't have been . . .

She shook off the thought before it formed, resolving to focus on dueling and on finding out whatever she could about the prince's enemies. She was a duelist. Nothing more.

But when Dara arrived at the castle for training on the second day after the attack, the guard at the sally port refused to admit her.

"Extra security."

"But I come for practice every day," Dara said.

"You're not on the approved list," the guard said. He was a barrel-chested man with an iron-gray beard. Dara was quite certain she had met him before. Yeltin was his name. There had been new Castle Guards around of late, but this one should know who she was.

"I duel with the—"

"I am aware of that, my lady, but the prince is busy. The king requires his attention to important matters of state today. The prince left a letter for you."

"A letter?"

Yeltin held out a piece of parchment sealed with wax. Dara

took it, feeling the rich texture of the paper beneath her fingers, and read:

Dara Nightfall,

I am trapped in a meeting with stuffy nobles and not nearly enough sharp, pointy objects. They don't even have good refreshments. Any chance you can rescue me?

In all seriousness, thank you for what you did. I'm glad you were with me. I owe you one.

Fortunately, because I have the cunning of a thunderbird, I know how to repay you! We are going to make Nightfall the most feared and admired name on the mountain. I don't know when I'll be free, so you have to keep working on our scheme. Time is running out before the Vertigon Cup. The next step is Vine. Can I entreat you to go see her about your rivalry?

We also need to come up with a way to introduce the New You to the masses. It has to be big. Any ideas? I'd do it myself, but I fear I will be stuck in this meeting until my hair turns gray. Think you'll still want to duel me then? I hope so.

See you next time, swordswoman. And be nice to Vine, at least until you declare your everlasting hatred of her in front of the citadel.

Yours in training,

Siv

Dara smiled at the paper. The prince's handwriting was surprisingly elegant, much nicer than her own cramped style. But his requests were more challenging than he realized. He was supposed to be the one with the Nightfall ideas. And she did *not* want to go ask Vine for help with anything.

She looked up at Yeltin the guard. "Could I speak to Sel—Princess Selivia, by any chance?"

"I can only allow pre-arranged appointments. Perhaps you can return in a few days."

Dara sighed. "Okay."

"My lady," Yeltin said as she started to turn away.

"Yes?"

"On behalf of the Castle Guard, I want to thank you for what you did two nights past. You have the respect of our ranks, my lady."

Dara blinked. "Thank you. But I'm not a lady."

"You are a friend to the Amintelles. That means something among the Castle Guard, my lady."

Dara inclined her head, not sure what else to say. She had acted on instinct. She couldn't imagine doing anything else. The old guard went back to scanning the mountain for possible threats, the Amintelle sigil prominent on the breast of his uniform. She was glad to see that men like him were protecting her friends.

As Dara descended the steps leading away from the castle, it occurred to her that if all the Castle Guards knew she had been with the prince that night, word would spread through King's Peak and eventually reach the Village—and her parents. They would find out she was training with the prince. Now that she thought about it, Farr had given her an odd look when he passed her on the way to the lantern shop that morning. Maybe the news had spread faster than she thought. He would almost certainly mention the rumors to her mother while they worked together. Dara grimaced, wondering if she could sleep at the dueling school tonight.

She retraced her steps to Thunderbird Square, not needing to hurry for once. She hadn't anticipated being turned away at the gates. Her mother wouldn't expect her back at the lantern shop for hours, and she was keen to delay the inevitable conversation for as long as possible.

Fell Bridge looked different in the daylight, not as chilled and spooky as it had the night of the attack. If it hadn't been so dark, there would have been a good view of the bridge from many of the balconies and terraces bordering Thunderbird Square. Help would have come much sooner. She might not have had to stab that man in the arm. But she had a feeling nothing would have stopped him from throwing himself into the mist and silence beyond the bridge when he failed to carry out the assassination.

Dara tried to shake off the memory. It was a bright, safe morning, and she and Siv were both fine. She took out the prince's letter and read it through again, tracing the elegant script with her fingers. He wanted her to come up with a way to introduce Nightfall to the masses. Something big.

Dara studied the porticos and balconies overlooking the broad expanse of Thunderbird Square in front of the bridge. Yes, there really was a good view of it from most of those houses. And many prominent families lived in this part of Lower King's. It gave her an idea. It would require her to swallow a bit of pride, but she had a feeling Siv was going to be impressed. He wanted something big, and she knew just the thing.

The Silltine greathouse was located off a quiet thoroughfare near Pen Bridge, which connected the eastern outskirts of Lower King's to Square Peak. Dara had asked in a few shops and taverns to find it. Despite being a nobleman's dwelling, it wasn't large. Dara had the sense that it was quite old, perhaps built during the reign of the First or Second Good King, but the family hadn't expanded it. They hadn't even added marble trim when it became popular several years ago, leaving it a house of gray stone. A wide terrace on the second level stretched most of its length, and rows of large windows looked out on the Fissure.

There was a pleasant breeze blowing over King's Peak. It swept from the distant ranges of the Burnt Mountains beyond Vertigon, carrying hints of the colder weather to come. They weren't far from the drop-off that descended behind the castle, making it a quieter area than most of King's. It would be a nice place to have a home.

When Dara knocked on the door and asked to see Lady Vine, a slim butler led her up an old-fashioned staircase to the second floor and out onto the terrace. The open-air space was set up like a dueling hall, with a standard tournament strip marked across its length. A practice dummy guarded one end of the terrace, and there was a gear trunk and a set of weights beside the door.

Vine Silltine herself sat cross-legged on a luxurious carpet facing out toward the Fissure. Her long hands rested palm-upward on her knees, and she was humming softly.

"My lady?" the butler said. "Dara Ruminor is here to see you."

"Dara, Dara! I sensed something different in the air today." Vine rose gracefully to her feet. She wore flowing trousers and a tight top that left her shoulders and midriff bare. Her long, dark hair was twisted up in a practical bun.

"Hello Vine. Sorry to disturb your . . . whatever you were doing."

"Meditations. It is part of my training," Vine said. "I must learn to calm my mind and sense the Air. It helps my performance in the duels."

"Uh, right," Dara said. "Well, it seems to be working."

"You are referring to the Eventide Open?" Vine laughed gaily. "Yes, I believe my mind is becoming ever more in tune with my body and with my opponents. It allows me to claim the points better than ever. But what can I do for you?"

Dara gritted her teeth, resisting the urge to turn and walk away. "Oh, well, I was just thinking . . . I had this idea that maybe we could have a match before the Vertigon Cup."

Vine's gaze dropped to the gear bag slung over Dara's shoulder.

"I'm afraid I can't duel any true opponents in my training space." She swept her arms wide to indicate the terrace. "It is sacred, and I don't wish for any insecurities to invade the aura—"

"Not right now," Dara said. "I mean a public bout. It could drum up some attention for both of us before the Cup. And, well, I think the crowds would like it."

"Interesting." Vine studied her, head tilted like a bird's. "I can't say I expected this from you, Dara. What did you have in mind for this public duel?"

"I thought it could be a surprise. One of us could, you know, call the other out when there's a crowd around." Dara hoped she wouldn't have to say more. Siv had seemed to think Vine would be in favor of the idea. If he was wrong, and she had come here for nothing . . .

But Vine clapped her hands. "A rivalry! I see what you're saying. Yes, we must build anticipation among the people before the main event. It will be like Shoven and Jur the Jurl!"

"I was thinking we could have a bout on Fell Bridge," Dara said. "That way lots of people could see us. A duel on a bridge would be pretty dramatic."

"Brilliant!" Vine said. "Oh, you have made me so happy this morning. Let's coordinate the details, but leave the outcome up to skill and fate."

"Right. I don't want a *fake* duel." The last thing Dara wanted was to purposely lose a bout to Vine in front of everyone. Or know that Vine was purposely losing to her.

Vine smiled and touched her nose. "Of course. Oh, Dara, I've always wanted a rival. This is a great gift to me. From now on we must ever be at odds. This is a wonderful strategy."

"I hope so." Dara sighed. There was no stopping it now. "Shall we get started?"

Vine insisted on calling for tea and cakes. Her butler, whose name was Toff, set up a table in the far corner of the terrace looking out over Square Peak and the Fissure. Dara and Vine drank their tea and discussed Dara's ideas for the public duel. Vine's suggestions for spicing it up would have made Siv proud. Dara was finally coming around to the idea that this might be kind of fun.

After the main details had been decided, Vine leaned in, clasping her hands around her delicate celadon teacup.

"Now that's out of the way, you must tell me everything about your encounter with Prince Siv the other night."

"My what?" Dara looked up sharply. The memory of the warmth of Siv's arms, the brightness in his eyes as he leaned toward her crashed down, leaving her breathless.

"You saved his life!" Vine said. Dara covered her relief by taking a long sip of her tea. Of course Vine meant the fight, not the almost-kiss.

"It's the talk of Lower King's," Vine said, "but I want the real story. I *always* get the real story."

If people were talking about it already, Dara's parents were sure to find out. *Great.*

Vine waited eagerly, so Dara outlined the basics of the encounter, right up to when the attacker threw his knife at Siv. She saw the flash of steel in the moonlight, felt the surge of speed in her arm as she reacted without thought. The spark of steel on steel. She had been ready to finish him off.

"I was scared, to be honest," she said, looking up at Vine. "I've never tried to hurt anyone before, but I would have killed that man before I let him stab the prince."

"Magnificent!" Vine didn't seem to understand that it was her absolute willingness to kill the attacker that had scared Dara so much. "Oh, I love this story. I must admit I thought you would be a great public friend after this and had planned to seek you out. I'm even happier to have you as a public enemy." Vine sipped her tea, and Dara wondered if she might be a bit mad. "So how did it all end?"

"The guards arrived, and the knifeman jumped off the bridge before he could be caught."

Vine nodded, as if she already knew this part. "There's a search underway to retrieve the body and the knife. I hope they will identify him soon. We can't have any threats to our *dear* prince, now can we, Dara?" Vine winked. "But did anything else happen *afterwards*?"

"No . . . I just went home."

"That's it?"

"Yes. Two members of the Castle Guard escorted me."

"Hmmm . . ." Vine dipped her finger in her tea and drew circles on the table as if waiting for Dara to reveal something more.

Dara frowned. Did Vine know more about that night than she was letting on? Either about her and the prince—not that there was anything to know—or about the attack itself? She said she always got the real story.

"Vine, what do you think about the Fire W—the Fireworkers?" Dara asked. Vine may know what was going on in the city, but Dara didn't want the Fire Warden to find out she was asking questions. Who knew what Zage Lorrid was capable of?

"They're a restless bunch," Vine said. "I understand there's a growing faction that's dissatisfied with Amintelle control over the Fire, given that the Amintelles haven't had a Fireworker among them in over fifty years. I don't know that they would try to kill the prince, if that's what you're getting at."

So much for subtlety. "I was just thinking about who knew

when Siv was leaving the parlor. There were a lot of Fireworkers there." *And Zage. We can't forget Zage.*

"You're in the right family to talk to Fireworkers, Dara."

Dara sighed. "I suppose so." Her parents were definitely not in Zage's faction. She doubted they would be much help. The Ruminors might not have a great love for the royal family, but she was sure they'd rather see Zage Lorrid brought down than the king himself, maybe even for treason.

A breeze blew across the mountain, carrying the scent of peach blossoms from the orchard beneath the greathouse, mixed with the ever-present smoke of the mountain Fires. Vine sighed and gazed out at Square Peak.

"It is so nice to talk like this," she said. "I fear some of the other duelists don't like me because of my noble status. They talk to me at tournaments, but I couldn't call us true friends."

"You're a threat," Dara said. "That's the truth of it. They know you're competition, both for the medals and the patrons."

Vine beamed. "What a nice thing to say. Here. You must have the last piece of cake."

Dara accepted the cake and took a bite, the tart blackberry filling bursting on her tongue.

"Vine, why *are* you trying to get a sponsor?" she asked. "You are a noble, after all." Something about seeing Vine all alone on her pretty little practice terrace made Dara feel comfortable enough to ask.

Vine's smile faded. "My father is not well, nor is he wealthy. He's had to sell most of our land to House Rollendar. I fear House Silltine will be no more soon. The income a patron would provide may actually exceed that of our remaining holdings. I wish to support my father in his twilight years without selling the last of his legacy."

Dara was surprised. She had assumed Vine was doing it for the glory and the pageantry, not the gold.

"You have suitors, don't you?"

"Yes, though not as many as you might expect. They know the size of my dowry." Vine stood, brushing crumbs off her flowing trousers. The morning sunlight shone golden on her shoulders. "But if I have the option of earning patronage through my own means and on my own feet, why would I buy it with my hand?"

Dara didn't answer, finishing her tea in silence. She still wanted to defeat Vine, but she understood her a little better. When it was time to say good-bye, Vine hugged her and then swore never to speak another kind word about her. Dara crossed the bridge to Village Peak feeling rather good about her new enemy.

FIRE

D ARA jogged home, thinking about how to explain what had happened to her parents. She had managed to avoid them this morning, but her mother would undoubtedly be waiting for her when she returned. Her parents would not be happy that she had kept her new training partner a secret. They'd be upset with her for staying out so late too, partly for her safety, of course, but also because of the potential damage to their reputation. She was not looking forward to the conversation at all.

But the lantern shop and the house were empty when Dara returned to the Village. Her mother had left a note on the desk beside a pile of paperwork for her to complete.

Emergency meeting at the Fire Guild. Your father and Farr are with me. Finish these delivery slips and watch the shop.

Dara breathed a sigh of relief and sat down at the desk, preparing to go through the paperwork. She fiddled with the edges of her mother's note, rereading it for some hint of what they might be doing at the Fire Guild. It was unusual for them to be called to the Guild in the middle of the day without warning. She wondered if the emergency meeting had anything to do with the attack on the prince. Could the Fireworkers finally be deciding to stand up to Zage? Dara hoped she wasn't the only one who suspected him. Jara the Gilder had been at the parlor. Perhaps he had been trying to gather information about what the Fire Warden was up to.

Maybe Dara could actually help her parents with this. They could use what she had seen that night to make their case against Zage. She almost wished she had been going to the Fire Guild meetings lately to hear about their plans. She liked the idea of working with her parents for the good of Vertigon and the royal family. They could be part of something together in a way they hadn't been since Renna died.

Speaking of being part of something . . . Dara looked up at the lanterns hanging around the walls, a question that had been at the back of her mind for two days becoming ever more concrete. Was it possible?

Stillness reigned in the lantern shop. The shadows painted the walls in static shapes, the Fire burning steadily behind the intricate metal lacework.

Dara went to the window. The Village was quiet. There was no sign of her parents and Farr returning from the Fire Guild. They would likely be gone for hours.

She raised her fingers, turning her hands this way and that. They looked the same as always. Her right hand was rough with distinct calluses from her swords. She curled it into a ball. It felt the same as it always had. No warmth. No power. No Fire.

A breeze whispered against the windows. The emptiness of the house was like a living thing.

Dara remembered the burst of fear, of adrenaline, of heat she'd felt as she wielded the prince's sword against the attacker. The *heat*. Again she wondered, *Was it possible?*

She barely dared articulate her suspicions, but she had to know. She locked the door to the lantern shop. Then, with a deep breath, nerves thrumming in her chest, she walked down the tunnel toward her father's workshop.

By the time she reached the end of the tunnel, Dara's heart was racing. Heat surrounded her as she pushed open the door. The light of the Fire was a solid thing, so unlike sunlight or the even the light of a normal, wood-burning fire. She stepped inside and closed the door behind her.

The workshop was neatly organized. Rafe Ruminor did his best work in a precise space. One side of the room had stacks of raw metal ore that could be melded with the Fire to create the lanterns. Partially finished lanterns were neatly arranged on stone tables on the other side of the room, some of them already glowing.

And in the center was the access point to the Fire itself. It was basically a crack in the stone, a deep hole that tapped into the veins of molten power running through the mountain. A shallow stone trench led away from it. When Rafe worked, he would stand before the crack and draw the liquid Fire into his body from the channel in the stone. He would then transfer some of it to the trench so he wouldn't have to hold all of the power within him while he sculpted the lanterns and infused them with everlasting flame. Powerful Fireworkers could draw Fire from the spidery veins in the mountain no matter where they stood, but they required an access point like this to create works on any meaningful scale. In the olden days, Wielders would have been able to summon extraordinary amounts of Fire at will from the stones of the mountain, but now the flows were too tightly controlled.

Dara remembered watching her sister, Renna, learn to Work. It required concentration and will to control the Fire. It was possible to Work without touching the Fire directly, but it was easier to shape it if the Worker drew it into their veins first.

They had to manage a delicate balance, like filling up a cup of water. When Renna had died, the Surge had filled her cup far beyond its capacity, and she lacked the control to let it drain out of her body.

Dara considered this idea, which she only knew about in an academic way. The Fire filled up the Worker like water or blood, coursing along the veins and into whatever substance was being formed: a Fire Lantern, a thread of Firegold, a blade. Fire and metal were natural companions, and most Workers learned to form bits of metal into tiny beads when they first started training with the Fire. Renna had made Dara an entire necklace out of tiny spheres of Fire-forged steel. She hadn't worn it since Renna died, but she still remembered watching the pride in her sister's face as she completed the final lopsided bead.

One thing Dara remembered clearly from listening in on Renna's lessons was that Fireworkers anchored themselves to the stones of an access point to help them connect with the flow of Fire. She had spent hours trying to do just that before she accepted that she didn't have the Spark.

Again, Dara thought of the feeling of heat flashing through her body during the attack, the way it had seemed to drain into the stones of the bridge afterwards.

Had she pulled a bit of Fire from the mountain when she fought to defend the prince? Or had she imagined that sensation of heat filling her and coursing through the sword in her hands? She had to know before the possibility ate away at her. Her fingers were supposed to be cold. She had no Spark. She was long past this.

And yet.

Dara approached the access point, feeling the heat intensifying. Though it was hot, it didn't scald her face. She drew closer to the crack in the rock. Nervous energy filled her, making her limbs shake. She stretched out a hand, the light seeping from the stone illuminating her fingertips.

Her hand hovered above the crack, but her skin didn't burn. She couldn't stop herself. She had to know.

Dara closed her eyes, placed her hand on the stone, and willed the Fire to come to her.

Nothing happened. Her whole body shaking, Dara tried to summon the power that sang deep beneath the mountain, the molten river that flowed beneath the crack in the stone.

Nothing.

She opened her eyes. The workshop looked the same as always. Neat. Empty. This was silly. She couldn't Work. She had never been able to touch the Fire. Why would it be different now?

Dara turned to go and was almost at the door when she spotted a slim piece of steel about the length of a dueling rapier lying on top of the orderly pile of metal. She pictured that night, when she'd clutched the prince's sword and felt that strange heat in her blood.

She picked up the steel, hefting it like a blade, and returned to the crack. She laid the tip of the metal against the stone and closed her eyes again.

She concentrated, stretching out with her will, with her heart, with all the desperation and fear that had filled her that night. She used the concentration she had honed during count-less hours of dueling. Dara had always known she was fighting a losing battle for her parents' respect. She had always known she could never replace her sister. But when she dueled, she felt powerful. She felt in control. Now, Dara used that feeling, that focus, that power. She breathed.

And a hot bolt of Fire shot straight through her.

Dara gasped and dropped the metal. She took three steps backward and fell to the ground, fingers sizzling.

She stared at the piece of steel. It glowed, faint but distinct. Already the heat was starting to fade. She had pulled Fire from the mountain. Pulled it through the steel and into her body for an instant.

It couldn't be true.

She could Wield.

~

Dara closed the door to the workshop, darted back up the tunnel, and snatched her gear bag from the kitchen. Then she ran.

She didn't care that she was supposed to be watching the shop. She had to keep moving. She ran through the Village and down toward Furlingbird Bridge, nearly knocking people over as she passed. Voices rose in her wake, calling out for her to watch where she was going. She ran faster, as if the churning of her legs could clear the cacophony in her head.

Soon, her boots pounded on the bridge. It was less crowded here, quieter, and she settled into a steady jog as she crossed toward Square Peak.

She had accessed the Fire. How was she suddenly able to do that? What did this mean? She had spent so long wishing for the Spark and trying to touch the Fire throughout her childhood. Why now? She had only been able to draw Fire through the steel bar, but that wasn't necessarily unusual. Some Fireworkers used aids to help them focus and control the molten flow.

Fireworker. She had never been able to claim the word. She had been denied the ability long ago, denied the place in her family, in her legacy. Instead, she had found something to fill the burning hole in her life without the Fire. She had given herself to dueling without reserve.

What would happen now? Could she simply abandon dueling and learn to Work?

Dara reached the other side of the bridge and jogged up Square, her strides becoming labored. She was too old to become a true Fireworker, the only kind her father took seriously. Some who discovered their abilities later in life tried to teach themselves the basics instead of learning the formal discipline. Her father had always dismissed them. Rafe Ruminor had trained from childhood in the noble Art, and he rejected anyone with a lesser education on the principle that true Fireworking must be studied from the first moment the Spark appeared.

Dara's breath caught in her throat. What if he wouldn't accept her into the discipline? With such a late start to her training, would he cast her away? Would he consider her unworthy after all?

She ran faster, dodging a herd of mountain goats being ushered along the road on Square Peak. The breeze cooled her skin. She turned a corner, and Berg's dueling school loomed before her. Lights glowed in the windows, and the sounds of shuffling boots and clanging blades rang across the mountain. Dara loved that sound. She loved how this big stone building had been her refuge. She had cried and sweat and bled and laughed in that school. In many ways, it was more a home to her than the Ruminor dwelling had been for years.

Dara slowed to a walk. Did she even want to train to be a Fireworker now? What if her parents forbade her from dueling when they found out she had the Spark? Could she give it up when she was this close to achieving her goals?

Everything was shifting around her, the pieces of her life falling like an avalanche.

Dara couldn't tell her parents the truth. At least, not yet. The news was too momentous. She needed time to consider the implications and decide how she felt about it all. She couldn't afford a distraction of this scale, not with everything already going on with the prince and Vine and Nightfall. And the Vertigon Cup was only a few weeks away. She needed to focus on her dueling right now. She would wait until after the competition to tell her parents what she discovered.

Until then, she would stay far away from the Fire.

RETURN OF THE QUEEN

THE mountain crawled with rumors about who could have been responsible for the attack on the prince. It was the most exciting thing that had happened since Lord Samanar's wife announced she was leaving him for the butler in front of the entire court at a royal feast. Speculation was rife in the taverns and parlors about who disliked the prince enough to make such a drastic move. A bitter former servant? A foreign assassin? An uncommonly ambitious (not to mention unscrupulous) nobleman?

Siv's best guess was that the attacker had acted alone. "Die, Amintelle" sounded like the sort of thing a nutty disgruntled subject would shout. He didn't think it implied a larger plot. It was probably a personal complaint, something a prince or king might never hear of until it was too late. Perhaps some injustice or perceived slight had caused resentment to worm its way into the attacker's mind until he thought the only solution was to assassinate the prince. They might never know why it had happened.

When the attacker's body was finally found on the slopes of Orchard Gorge, no one stepped forward to claim it. His battered face made it hard to draw an accurate likeness to post around the kingdom. The knife with the Firegold hilt had disappeared entirely. Strange, that.

Siv's days were still uncommonly busy, though. Captain Bandobar's men investigated tips about possible threats to the Amintelles, and they delivered frequent, lengthy reports on their progress. Bandobar recruited even more Castle Guards, and Siv no longer recognized half the men who marched about the castle, eager to protect him and his family.

Pool in particular took the threat extra seriously. He felt personally affronted that someone would dare attack his prince. And of course, he was mortified that he hadn't been there. Siv had convinced his father not to fire Pool given that Siv had ordered the man to let him and Dara walk ahead alone that night. Besides, the new hires needed a veteran Castle Guard to guide them. Not that Pool was a particularly good example at the moment. He had taken to tramping back and forth in front of Siv's door around the clock, looking as morose as a pullturtle. This led to exhaustion, and eventually Bandobar had to order him to let someone else guard the prince for a while.

In the midst of all the excitement, Queen Tirra returned from Trure. It was strange, perhaps, but Siv was often surprised to see his mother. She spent so much time away from Vertigon that it was as if she didn't live in the castle at all. When present, she floated through the halls, wraithlike, unless the king was around to anchor her to the ground.

But she sought out her son the very day she arrived on the mountain. Siv had escaped a council meeting to visit Rumy the cur-dragon. Selivia had informed him breathlessly that the hatchlings had begun sneezing out their first bursts of flame, and he didn't want to miss it.

He was sitting on the floor of the cur-dragon's cave waving a fern leaf in front of little Rumy's snout and coaxing him to set it on fire when his mother arrived.

She moved silently as mist and had placed her hand on Siv's shoulder before he even realized she was in the cave.

"Burning Firelord!" he leapt to his feet.

"Hello, Sivarrion."

"Mother! When did you arrive?" He hugged her, feeling the bones of her shoulders in his embrace. Queen Tirra was a wisp of a woman, tall and thin and pale.

"A short while ago. I learned of the attack from a courier when I was still traveling the Fissure. Are you well?"

"I'm fine. It's old news. How was your journey?"

Siv's mother looked tired, her mousy-brown hair falling out of the long scarf around her head. She bore little resemblance to her three dark-haired children. Sora had inherited their mother's lighter Truren eyes, but otherwise, the siblings were Amintelles through and through.

"It was lovely," Queen Tirra said. "Your grandfather sends his regards. He'd love for you to visit him again soon. He wishes to arrange a marriage match for you."

"Did Father talk to you about that?" Siv said suspiciously.

"He's in a council meeting. I will go to him soon."

"Well, don't worry about the match. I've got a Vertigonian noblewoman in mind." Siv hadn't thought of Lady Tull in days. There'd be no chance to get out to a parlor again until the excitement over his death-defying adventure subsided. He hoped she would be amenable to the match even if he didn't have quite as much time to woo her. He supposed he could invite her up to the castle, but then he was a very busy prince.

Dara's intense eyes rose before him, but he brushed away the vision.

"I'm not sure that's wise." The queen was frowning. "There's restlessness in Trure, rumblings from Soole and Pendark. Our alliance with my father's kingdom may be more important than ever."

"There'll be plenty of time to talk about it," Siv said. "But you should rest. You've had a long trip."

"I will rest soon enough. Who is this handsome creature?" Queen Tirra slid gracefully to the floor and folded her long legs beneath her. She still wore a traveling cloak, and little Rumy immediately stuck his nose in its soft folds.

"This is Rumy." Siv flopped down onto the floor and tugged the cur-dragon out of his mother's cloak by his spiny hide. Rumy bared his empty gums and snapped at Siv's fingers.

"How old is he?"

"Nearly six weeks."

"He's going to be big. Look at those feet." The queen reached out to the little dragon, and he flipped onto his back so she could stroke his belly.

"I know. I'm going to train him up to be a guard dragon as soon as he's grown."

"Like you trained that velgon bear when you were thirteen?"

"Uhh . . . This'll be different. I'll delegate some of the responsibility." Siv remembered the pet in question. He hadn't disciplined the beast strictly and consistently enough. It grew too wild to approach by the time it was full-size. They had released it on the slopes beyond Square to live as a free bear.

But Rumy would be different. Siv could already tell he was going to be a smart, strapping creature.

"Where are the girls?" his mother asked.

"Sora is having her lesson with Zage, and Selivia went up to the library. She's still trying to think up names for the rest of the cur-dragon litter. She's looking for ideas."

"I'll go say hello, then." The queen stood and brushed off her skirts. Her personal guard, a grim warrior from Trure, snapped to attention at the cave entrance.

"Let me walk you," Siv said. He lifted Rumy up to return him to the dragon keeper. As he held the creature around the middle, Rumy burped, and a tiny flame puffed out of his mouth.

"There it is! Well done, Rumy! I knew you had it in you!"

Rumy snapped his gums triumphantly and swished his tail back and forth like a cat.

When Siv and his mother returned to the castle, a servant awaited them at the entrance to the cur-dragon tunnel.

"Prince Sivarrion, a letter was delivered for you a few moments ago."

"Thank you."

Siv plucked the parchment from the servant's hand and examined the plain wax seal. He only knew of one person who would write to him without impressing a noble house crest into the seal. He cracked it open and checked the signature. Dara. Oh, he was good. He was damn good. He couldn't keep a grin from creeping onto his face as he read.

Prince Siv,

Thank you for your letter. I hope the meetings aren't too bad and that you'll be able to return to practice soon. If you get too out of shape I'm afraid I'll have to decline our next duel for fear of hurting you. I wouldn't want anything to happen to you.

I visited Vine as you requested. She has agreed to the rivalry. We made arrangements to stage a public duel to drum up attention. It will begin in Thunderbird Square and range onto Fell Bridge. Hopefully there will be a lot of people around to see it.

The duel will take place in the afternoon this coming Turnday. If you are free to train again the following week, I'll tell you how it goes. Unless it goes poorly, in which case we will never speak of it again.

Dara

PS. Please tell Princess Selivia I will be wearing the face paint.

Siv continued to grin at the paper after he finished reading. The writing was dark and cramped, as if Dara had leaned into her pen and focused on the words with as much intensity as she employed in the duels. And the plan! It was such a good one that Siv started to think he had come up with it himself. He couldn't wait to see how it played out.

"A letter from your Vertigonian lady?" Queen Tirra said. Siv jumped. He had forgotten his mother was there.

"No. It's just my dueling partner." He rolled up the letter and tucked it into his pocket before his mother could take it from him.

But she was studying his face. Siv hooked his thumbs in his sword belt, trying to keep his stance casual, but he found himself wanting to touch the letter in his pocket. What had his mother read in his expression while he read Dara's letter?

"I've heard about this dueling partner," she said after a moment. "Am I to understand she saved your life?"

Siv nodded. "She's a fine swordswoman."

"You think of her as more. I can see it in your eyes, son."

"She's a Fireworker's daughter," Siv said shortly. "She's not the match I had in mind."

"But you care for her." A swift stroke of sadness crossed the queen's face. It made Siv's throat constrict.

"I know my duties, Mother," he said. "You don't need to remind me."

"I don't want to deny you happiness, son."

"Dara is my friend, nothing more." Siv turned and started walking toward the library. The queen glided along beside him.

"I wish you joy in your marriage," she said. "Even if a match is not meant to be, perhaps you can find other ways to include this Fireworker's daughter in your life."

Siv stumbled over an uneven floor tile. His mother couldn't be suggesting that he take a mistress. His *mother*?

"I've compromised in my own ways throughout my marriage," the queen said.

No, no, no. They were not having this conversation. He did not want to know.

"You may find solace in ways that are separate from your wi—"

"Mother!" Siv finally got out a strangled cry. "You're not saying that you . . . that you . . ."

"Goodness, Sivarrion," the queen said. "Don't look so scandalized. You know very well that I have compromised by spending much of my time in my beloved Trure with my family even though I live with your father. Perhaps your friend can have a role in your life beyond that of a dueling partner. As a guard, perhaps. What did you think I was suggesting?"

"I thought . . . I didn't think you were . . . I'm sure Selivia is still in the library, but I have to take care of . . . something. I shall see you at dinner, Mother." Siv bowed to hide the redness in his cheeks. Of course his mother wasn't advising him to take Dara as his lover! He pretended to be very interested in a sconce in the wall so he wouldn't have to meet her eyes.

The queen smiled gently and continued on to the library. She did look tired. Siv always had the sense that mountain air was heavier for her than for others. He watched her until she disappeared from view.

No, Siv couldn't give his future wife the halfway marriage his mother had given his father. She called it a compromise, but Siv didn't think it had been fair to his father or to him and his sisters that her allegiance was to Trure and not to their family. When the time came, Siv would be as devoted to his partner as he was to Vertigon itself. Even if that partner had to be Lady Tull.

But the idea of making Dara a more permanent presence in the castle lingered. He wasn't ready to give her up just yet.

Of course, she would be far too busy being a champion duelist to have time for guard duty. After her showdown with Vine, she would be more popular than the king himself. The duel was going to set Vertigon on fire for Dara Nightfall Ruminor. Siv only wished he could be there to see it.

DUEL ON THE BRIDGE

I T was uncommonly sunny on the Turnday Dara and Vine had selected for their duel. Summer was drawing to a close, and they wagered people would want to take advantage of one of the last truly warm days. They'd be strolling through Lower King's and the Village in large numbers, and people on both slopes would have a great view of Fell Bridge.

Dara waited on the porch outside her parents' home for the moment to arrive. Her father was hard at work, even though it was a rest day. Her mother was meeting a foreign distributor over on Square, so there was a good chance Dara could get through the day without her parents stopping her from making a spectacle of herself. They'd find out after the fact, but by then it would be too late.

Dara was dressed in one of the all-black outfits Princess Selivia had put together for her. The trousers were too tight, but Dara could still move. That was the important thing. The swirls of black face paint were absolutely ridiculous, but the overall effect wasn't too bad. The hood of her cloak would hide the paint until the big reveal anyway. She'd even braided a few black ribbons in her hair.

She had enlisted Kel and Oat to help with her scheme. They should be getting into position now. She tapped her feet on the porch steps, watching the slant of the shadows over the peaks, waiting for the right moment to head to the bridge. She would show the world she could be more than a good duelist. The mountain would have to pay attention to her. The people would know her by her own name, not her parents'.

If the reports of her dueling friends were any indication, people were already talking. Word had gotten out that Dara was with the prince the night of the attack. Some of the gossips even declared that she had saved his life. This could only help her cause with the people. Well, all of the people except her parents.

Dara's mother had been strangely cold toward her lately. Dara had expected a fiery lecture at the very least. Instead, Lima had been formal and polite. The only evidence of anger had been when she vigorously cleaned and polished Renna's chair, jostling Dara roughly while she ate breakfast.

Yesterday Dara had finally cornered Farr the apprentice to ask for hints about what her mother might be thinking.

"She asked me not to talk to you," Farr had said, cracking his bony knuckles.

"At all?"

"Well, about business stuff."

"She said that?"

"I think she's worried you might report back since . . . well . . . . I guess you're friends with the prince now."

Dara frowned. "The prince doesn't have much to do with the Fireworking business. He knows the Fire Warden, but I doubt he tells him everything."

"Maybe." Farr had clammed up after that and told her not to worry. He had said her parents knew what they were doing.

Dara had barely seen her father, and she avoided going down to the workshop at all costs. She figured it was only fair that they cut her off from talking about their work after she had hidden the truth from them. They must think she was fraternizing with their enemy, even though the Fire Warden was the one they truly hated, and she certainly wasn't talking to him. Even so, she was sad to see her hopes of a partnership between her and her parents evaporating. It was ironic that they had finally stopped demanding she get more involved with the business the very week she discovered she could Work after all.

She'd agonized about telling her parents the truth, but she knew they'd make her give up dueling to study the Work. She would have to abandon the rush of competition for the hot confines of the workshop and plant her feet beside her father's for hours on end. She would have to say good-bye to the fast action of the duel, to her friends and her coach. To Siv. Once, the ability to Work the Fire had been all she ever wanted. Now, she was no longer sure.

She had to see her plans through, at least until the big competition. She would be able to make the right decision after she found out whether or not she was going to be offered a patronage. With any luck, the duel today would launch her into the public eye so definitively that the sponsors couldn't possibly ignore her. She'd patch things up with her parents after the Vertigon Cup.

Dara glanced up at the Ruminor Lantern hanging above the porch. Her father's Work. Solid. Magic. It hovered there, singing with power and heat.

No one was around. The Fire burning in the core of the lantern called to her. The shadows around it were faint, almost nonexistent in the sunlight, but the Fire pulsed, matching the beat of Dara's heart.

The temptation was unbearable. Dara looked around once more. The pathway beside the house was empty. Farr didn't come to the lantern shop on Turndays. Her mother was still on

Square. Her father was deep inside the mountain, consumed with his own work. No one would see.

Dara reached up and touched the metal lattice of the lantern, concentrating on the Fire core within it. Almost immediately, warmth sprang into her fingers. Heat spread up her arm and down through her stomach, her legs, her feet, finding root in the mountain. The lantern dimmed as Dara drew the Fire out of its core and through her fingers. It was easier this time, a slower burn. And it was magnificent. Dara's body became a conduit for the Fire between the lantern and the mountain itself. As the Fire passed through it, the metal lacework of the lantern melted and twisted. Dara pulled out more Fire and kneaded the metal with the tips of her fingers. It curled and formed beneath her hands.

Stop.

Dara released the Fire. Her head whirled with dizziness, gone in the space of a few breaths. The metal lace of the lantern stilled. She checked to make sure the walkway beneath the porch was still empty. She couldn't let anyone see her touch the Fire, not when she was so close to making a name for herself. She turned the lantern so the panel she had touched and altered couldn't be seen from the porch.

Dara glanced at the sky. It was time. She hoisted her gear on her back, pulled the hood of her cloak over her head, and started down to Fell Bridge. She slipped into doorways whenever anyone passed her. She was about to reveal herself to the mountain, but it would be embarrassing if someone spotted her in costume beforehand. Besides, she was supposed to be stealthy and mysterious.

Dara crossed Fell Bridge at a jog. They had agreed to start the duel in Lower King's Peak to draw the attention of the "right people," but the contest would range across the bridge if all went well. With luck, people from Village Peak would gather to watch the fight from the other bridges too.

Thunderbird Square was as crowded as she and Vine had hoped it would be. Palanquins and mountain ponies eased their way through crowds. Servants scurried by with packages, and tradesmen sold their wares to the throng. Children darted underfoot, racing each other across the cobblestones. Ladies strolled, brightly colored skirts swirling, and guardsmen drank with casual abandon in the shade of a tavern. Dara wound through the mob, keeping her head down. She approached the elegant greathouses looking out over the square. Nerves played in her stomach. This was a performance, not a competition. She wasn't used to this.

The fine weather had brought the nobility out onto the terraces and rooftops of their greathouses. The clink of glasses and peals of laughter drifted out over the mountainside. Dara scanned the greathouses until she located a head of lustrous dark hair. Vine Silltine stood on the balcony of a particularly fine house. She wore an elaborate green dress woven with Fire-gold. Her thick black hair hung loose around her shoulders, lifting and swirling in the breeze. She did not look ready for a duel.

Dara took up a position in the shadows near the greathouse so she could hear what was being said above her. Dozens of people crowded the balcony with Vine. It sounded as if they were having quite a big party. Dara fervently hoped Vine wasn't planning to humiliate her.

She spotted Kel leaning on the terrace beside her rival. Good. He had insisted he would have no problem getting an invite to the terrace party. The greathouse belonged to a Lord Zurren, who was a big dueling fan. As soon as Kel spotted Dara waiting in the shadows, he touched Vine's arm. She glanced down and winked at Dara.

"So," Kel said in a loud voice. "I hear you're going to win the Vertigon Cup, Vine Silltine."

"That is my goal." Vine's voice carried well. A few people in the street looked up.

"Is that Vine Silltine and Kelad Korran, the champion duelists?" said the loudest stage whisper Dara had ever heard. She spotted Oat in the crowded street. He waved.

"Are you worried about any of your competitors?" Kel called.

"No one can touch me," Vine said. She hoisted herself onto the balcony railing and stood. Firegold flashed from her dress. She swirled it about her ankles and pranced along the balustrade. "No other female duelist has made me bat an eyelash all year."

"There's another swordswoman making a name for herself," Kel said.

More people were looking up at the pair on the balcony. A portly lord waved for his companion to be quiet so he could hear them better. A pair of young girls pointed at Vine, whispering her name like a prayer.

"I heard she saved Prince Sivarrion with her blade skills," Kel continued. "She's really something."

"Rumors!" Vine tossed her hair dramatically. "Where is this duelist? If she's that good, why don't I know her name?"

"Wasn't it the Ruminor girl?" someone near Dara called out.

"That's what I heard."

"Ruminor!" Oat shouted from the street.

"What's that you say?" Vine wrinkled her nose prettily. "Blooming Door?"

A few people laughed, including the portly nobleman. Vine tossed her hair again.

"I'm not afraid of a duelist who won't even let her name be known. I am Lady Vine Silltine, after all."

One of Vine's mysterious assistants appeared beside her. He tossed glittering tokens into the air. People in the street cheered and scrambled for the tokens on the cobblestones. Three teenage boys had joined the two girls, and they were hurriedly telling them everything they knew about Vine Silltine's famous moves. The crowd beneath the balcony was growing.

"Where is this supposed prince savior?" Vine called. "I don't believe she exists. If she does, will she be brave enough to answer my challenge? Vine Silltine won't tremble before some Blooming Door."

Chuckles rippled through the spectators. The audience waited eagerly to see what else the famous Lady Vine Silltine would do.

"Nightfall," Kel said. He was quiet, but not too quiet. "I hear she's called Nightfall."

"I heard that too!" a man in the street shouted. He wasn't even one of their friends. More people were strolling up to the group beneath the balcony to see what the commotion was about. The cluster of teenage dueling fans had multiplied, with both boys and girls eagerly telling their friends about their favorite competitors. A lady ordered her palanquin bearers to halt so she could get out and see what was going on. The nobles at the party above all had their gazes fixed on Vine.

"Nightfall?" Vine scoffed. "Is she asleep? I want her to show her face."

Wait for it. Wait for it. Dara had to get the timing just right. She pulled her mask and weapon out of her gear bag and pushed it beneath the front porch of Zurren's greathouse.

"I hear she doesn't sleep at all!" came another voice nearby. There was something familiar about it. "She's too busy saving lives. What have you done lately, Vine? Pranced around like a Truren peacock?"

That voice. It couldn't be. Suddenly there was a hand on the small of Dara's back. She whirled around and looked up into the eyes of none other than Prince Siv. He wore a hooded cloak, but there was no mistaking those high cheekbones, those bright eyes. She felt a jolt of fire in her toes.

"It's time," he whispered, just for her.

Vine strutted back and forth on the balcony. Somewhere, her musicians had started blowing trumpets.

The prince squeezed Dara's waist for the briefest instant. "Knock her down," he said. Then he spun her back around and gave her a push.

Dara swept off her hood, revealing her face paint in all its glory, and swirled her cloak.

"Vine Silltine!" she shouted.

The people around her noticed her theatrical appearance and took a few steps back, eagerly clearing a space for the show. Siv melted back into the crowd, whispering "Nightfall. It's Nightfall," in people's ears as he went.

"Vine, you called for me?"

"That was quick," Vine said. The crowd laughed. "Is that you, Blooming? I've heard all about you."

"Enough talk, Vine. I challenge you to a duel. Now." Dara remembered what Selivia had said about remaining mysterious and didn't say anything more. That was easier than hamming for the crowd anyway.

"Can't you see I'm enjoying myself at a party?" Vine stuck out her lower lip and sat on the edge of the balcony, swinging her feet out over the crowd.

"I challenge you," Dara said again. She hadn't expected Vine to make her talk her into the duel.

"Maybe later." Vine leaned back on the balcony's edge, draping her skirts expertly as she did. It made a pretty picture, Vine lying in the sun above the crowd, seemingly not bothered by the drop, Firegold skirts fanning out beneath her.

"Now," Dara said.

"What was your name again?" Vine asked.

The spectators chuckled. More and more people joined the assembly, some running all the way across the square to investigate the commotion.

Dara gathered herself and growled. "I am Dara . . . Nightfall . . . Ruminor. I challenge you to a duel."

"Well, if you insist." Vine rolled off the balcony. A woman screamed, but before anyone could move Vine turned gracefully in the air and landed on her feet. Then she ripped off her skirt, revealing tight breeches underneath. Applause erupted through the crowd.

An assistant appeared at Vine's elbow and handed her a mask and a sword, the hilt edged in Firegold.

Dara slammed her own mask onto her head, threw off her cloak, and raised her blade. People stepped back to clear a bigger space. Wide eyes and eager faces surrounded them.

"Duel!" Kel shouted down from the balcony.

Dara attacked, wasting no time. Vine had her moment on the balcony. Now it was Dara's turn to make an impression. She would show people what it was like to watch a real duelist. For all Vine's talk, Dara was the one that wanted it more. This duel was hers and hers alone.

Dara drove forward, stabbing and lunging, fast and accurate. Steel rang against steel. Boots scraped and tapped on the cobblestones. Vine met her parry for parry. Dara hadn't had a bout with her in nearly a year, and Vine was much better than she had been then. But Dara was better too. Vine tried her usual dancing, showy steps, but each time Dara cut her off. She forced her back relentlessly. This might be a show, but it wasn't a game.

Dara and Vine fought back and forth across Thunderbird Square. The crowd pulsed and surged around them. They had agreed not to go easy on each other. They leapt from barrels and wove in and out of porticos, making the match as dynamic as possible. Their swords flashed in the sun. The sting from Vine's blunt-pointed weapon bit into Dara's arms, but she refused to react to the pain. She would be cold like steel in the face of Vine's flashy Firegold assault.

The crowds loved it. Most shouted for Vine, but there were calls for Ruminor and Nightfall in the crowd. Siv and Oat weren't the only ones cheering for Dara now.

Dara landed a solid hit on Vine's stomach, feeling the sensible padding underneath the flashy outfit. Vine grunted and thrust the blade away. Dara retreated toward Fell Bridge, narrowly avoiding the riposte.

The duelists picked up speed, each hit harder and faster than the last. More spectators ran down the slopes of Lower King's to watch. Vine twirled around and launched into one of her elaborate dancing lunges. She caught Dara on the hand with a shot that made half her wrist go numb. Dara retreated farther, almost to the foot of the bridge. Vine followed.

Thunderbird Square was packed now. The crowds roared with each clang and thud. But Dara kept her attention on Vine, watching for her weaknesses, learning her timing.

Vine lunged for her mask, and Dara leapt up the stone steps at the head of the bridge.

"It's where she fought the prince's attacker!" someone shouted. Dara was pretty sure it was the prince himself. "Nightfall! Nightfall!"

Dara took the cue and lingered on the steps, keeping the higher ground. Vine paced in front of her for a moment then hurtled forward up the steps. The image of the man with the knife flared in Dara's mind. This felt a little too real. But she would not allow the memory of fear to get in her way. She raised her blade, stopping the assault, and launched a rapid counterattack. She went for the head. Hand. Heart. Vine slipped off the steps, landing in an ungainly sprawl.

Dara paced on the bridge platform while Vine recovered. Kel would have used this moment to taunt his opponent, but Dara stuck to her plan. She was shadow and steel. She planted her feet in front of the bridge and waited for Vine to rise.

She didn't have to wait long. Vine lunged straight for her

feet, and Dara jumped backward onto the bridge to avoid the hit. She had lost count of the score, but she was pretty sure she was winning. It didn't matter, though. Today was all about the show. Then she would obliterate Vine in the Cup.

Dara retreated. People from Village Peak had gathered on the bridge at the commotion, but they ran back across it to leave room for the duel. Dara glanced across the Gorge at the nearby Orchard Bridge and Cherrywood Bridge beyond it. People filled them from end to end. They would have a full view of the final act.

Dara reached the middle of the bridge and waited for Vine to catch up. They faced each other, blades raised, keeping distance as the crowds shouted their support. Wind whipped across the Gorge, streaming through Vine's hair, ruffling Dara's loose blouse. The sun was beginning to set, and shadows stretched out from Dara's feet like smoke.

Dara and Vine dueled back and forth. The bridge swayed under their feet. The clang of their swords echoed across the Gorge. Dara tried the moves Siv had given her, driving like an arrow for the toe and head with an exaggerated intensity. The spectators on the other bridges called her name.

"You will never defeat me!" Vine shrieked. She whirled her golden blade in the dying light, and for a second it looked as though she were wielding Fire like the sorcerers of old.

"I am Nightfall, and this is my bridge," Dara shouted. She lunged, catching Vine's whirling blade and driving her own point toward her chest. It landed on Vine's breastplate with an audible thunk.

The crowd cheered.

"Nightfall! Nightfall! Nightfall!"

"Halt!" someone shouted. There was a flicker of movement beyond Vine, a voice raised in anger. "How dare you engage in such a ruthless display on a public bridge!"

A slim man in a bridge guard uniform ran toward them

from the King's Peak side, shouting admonishments as he neared. Dara thought she recognized Vine's butler, Toff.

"Cease this violence immediately!" he bellowed.

The people on the other bridges booed and hollered, "Let them finish!"

"I will call the army. You cannot duel here!" the man's face reddened with the effort of shouting loud enough for all the spectators to hear.

"We will finish this, Nightfall!" Vine called as the butler dressed as a bridge guard made an elaborate show of restraining her. "No one challenges me and walks away!"

"We'll settle it at the Vertigon Cup," Dara said. She placed her blade across her shoulders like a yoke and watched calmly as the guard drew Vine back along the bridge. When Vine was halfway to the end, Dara swept her sword into the air and saluted the crowds on the bridges and on the two slopes.

"I am Dara Nightfall Ruminor!" she announced. "I shall return at the Vertigon Cup!"

Then she turned and jogged back to Village Peak. Cheers followed her all the way home.

THE LANTERN MAKER

T HE duel was the talk of the mountain for days afterward.
The event replaced the attempted assassination as the
favored topic of debate and speculation in Stone Market. Fist-
fights broke out in taverns over who had the upper hand. Young
women wore black or gold hair ribbons to indicate which
duelist they supported. Dara's public persona had been born.
She was a force to be reckoned with, a duelist who rescued
people from assassins and fought on bridges.

Dara was surprised at how quickly her fame spread.
Strangers stopped her on runs to ask about her strategy for the
showdown with Vine at the Cup. The younger students at the
dueling school watched her complete her hundred lunges as
though she were some magical creature. Famous duelists
nodded to her when they passed each other on the bridges.
Betting on the results of the Cup grew fierce. Tickets were
selling fast. It was going to be one of the biggest tournaments
Vertigon had ever seen.

Unfortunately, with all the added attention it was only a
matter of time before Dara's parents addressed the subject. She
had assumed her mother would be the one to confront her

about the spectacle, but instead it was Rafe Ruminor who called her into his workshop early in the morning a few days after the duel.

Dara took the winding tunnel into the mountain from the back of their house. She hadn't seen much of her father lately. She had been going for morning runs in place of her still-suspended practices with Siv to avoid seeing him at breakfast, and she often stayed late at the dueling school at night. She was afraid she'd let something slip about her secret. Her father had been almost as busy as her anyway. With his access to the Fire becoming increasingly limited, it took him longer to complete the same amount of Work.

There was still plenty of power deep in that tunnel, though. As Dara neared the workshop, she felt the Fire sense deep in her body. It hummed in her blood, a slight vibration like a pinched nerve after a precise hit from a blade. Her newfound ability was either growing stronger or she was becoming more aware of it. It made her uncomfortable to be this close to the access point and all that raw magic. What if her father noticed something different about her?

Dara took a deep breath, as if facing an unknown opponent in a championship bout, and pushed open the door to the workshop. Her father stood over a half-finished lantern on a stone table. He didn't look up when she entered. He was in the most delicate phase of the Work: imbuing the metal center with a Fire core that would keep its warmth and light for a hundred years. This was where the magical art went beyond mere metalworking. It required a combination of carefully honed skill and natural ability to capture the Fire in a core without melting the metal that held it. Her father had both skill and exceptional strength. His lanterns never succumbed to cold and dark, and they never lost their shape, as cheaper Firebulbs were known to do. Ruminor Fire Lanterns had been discovered after being lost in the high mountain snows for years, still burning a patch of warmth around them.

Dara waited beside her father, watching the lantern glowing beneath his hands. Rafe didn't even have to touch the metal. He drew the liquid Fire from the mountain and channeled it into the core with sheer will. The heart of the lantern glowed, and Dara's blood pulsed in time with it. The metal lattices usually tempered the intensity of the Fire, but before they were installed the naked power of the Fire shone bright.

Dara edged a few steps farther away, resisting the urge to reach out and touch the Fire.

After a while, her father's broad shoulders relaxed. The core burned, steady and bright, and the Fire within looked as solid as a bar of gold. Now that he had completed the core, Rafe used more of the molten power to shape the rest of the lantern. He attached plain steel plates around the glowing core and then kneaded them like clay. He began to weave the molten metal into the intricate lacework for which he was so famous.

Shadows from the top of the lantern, not yet fully formed, made Rafe's face look ghoulish. Dara shifted her boots on the stone floor of the workshop, long since worn smooth, and cleared her throat.

"I know you are there, my young spark," Rafe said. He was quiet for a moment longer. The pattern on the lantern beneath his fingers began to take the shape of a dragon—not the mangy cur-dragons that lived in the caves of the mountain, but a true dragon the likes of which hadn't been seen in a generation. "I understand the whole of Vertigon knows of your display on Fell Bridge this past Turnday."

"It was just an act," Dara said quickly. "Vine Silltine and I thought a showy rivalry would help draw a good crowd at the Vertigon Cup. We want to make sure the patrons are watching our final bout." She left out the part about the rivalry being Prince Sivarrion's idea.

"It was crass," Rafe said. "You are a Ruminor. You should not abase yourself in the streets."

"It's part of the sport," Dara said.

"It is time to put away childish games, Dara. There are more important things happening on this mountain."

"What important things?" Dara leaned against another worktable then stood quickly when she felt the heat coursing through the stone.

Rafe looked up from the lantern. "If you paid closer attention to our family affairs, perhaps you would know. As it is, you have proved yourself too young for confidences."

"I'm eighteen."

"You do not act it," Rafe said. "You brawl in the streets. And you sneak around behind our backs when you should be attending to our business. I understand you have been dueling with Prince Sivarrion."

Dara grimaced. She knew that would come up soon enough. Farr had said her mother no longer wanted him to discuss the business with Dara, but the silent treatment couldn't be expected to last forever.

"Coach Berg asked me to practice with the prince," she explained. "He's been giving me free lessons in exchange. That's why I switched to working in the shop in the afternoons instead of the mornings."

The dragon on her father's lantern burst out a tongue of flame. "Berg Doban," Rafe said. "You have spent more than enough time with that man. I don't want you to take any more lessons with him."

"What's wrong with Berg?"

"He does not have our family's best interests at heart."

Dara frowned, surprised at this statement. Berg had been her coach for her entire career. He cared about her. She thought back to his insistence that the prince was in danger, which had been proven correct.

But what could Berg be involved in that had allowed him to know about it before anyone else? What if he was on the wrong side? What exactly *was* the right side?

"You must trust me, daughter. Cease your lessons with this man."

"But I have to train," Dara said.

"Then you will do so without our support," Rafe said. He used his thumb to curl a bit of steel into a winding tail for the dragon then allowed it to cool from orange to black. "Your mother and I have decided it is time for you to quit dueling."

"The Cup is only a week away!"

"Then it will be your last duel."

"Please." Dara took a step closer to her father, ignoring the heat flaring in her chest. "I've worked so hard."

"Our decision is final."

Dara bit her lip, nearly drawing blood, as indecision warred through her. Should she tell her father about her newfound Spark? The temptation was fierce. She almost promised to turn to Fireworking if he would let her keep dueling too. The news about her ability would change everything. But she didn't know if it would serve as a bargaining chip or a shackle. She wasn't ready to tell him yet.

"I'm sorry I kept my practices with the prince a secret," she said instead. "I didn't think it would do any harm."

"You truly believed that?" Rafe lowered his voice to a whisper. "After what happened to your sister in this very room?"

"What does that have to do with the prince?" Dara asked. "It was the Fire Warden's fault."

"And it was the prince's father who allowed him to get away with it."

"What?"

"The king denied us justice," Rafe said. "The king allowed the Warden to diminish the power of Vertigon with his dilution of the Fire. And you think it does no harm to play with this king's son like a child?"

Dara shivered at the dangerous quiet in her father's tone, despite the intense heat of the workshop.

"None of that is Siv's fault," she said. "He could change things one day."

Her father scoffed. "He is young. Young, and under the thrall of Zage Lorrid. Do you really think Sivarrion will change his father's Fire regulation policy when he becomes king? The Fireworkers have enough difficulty challenging Zage's actions. We can hardly count on a foolish young prince to do it."

"What does all this have to do with me and my dueling?" Dara asked, wondering what it would mean for her Working too. Until a week ago, what the Fireworkers said about the regulation policies hadn't mattered to her. Until a week ago, none of it had truly affected her.

"The winds are changing," Rafe said. "Do not be surprised if you find your priorities change as well. It is time for you to grow up, my little spark."

Dara studied her father's strong profile, bathed in light and shadow. What was going to change? What did her father think was going to happen? Could Zage's efforts to gain more power over Vertigon take a more drastic turn?

And what of what Rafe had said about the king? Dara had assumed he would warn the king if he knew anything about Zage's plans. But it sounded as if his dislike of the Amintelles ran deeper than she realized. But he wouldn't want any of them to die. Would he?

"What do you think is going to happen?" she asked.

"I cannot say." Rafe waved a hand, dismissing her. "Trust no one but your own flesh and blood and Fire." It was an old saying, one her father only used in his gravest moments. Dara took that as her cue to go.

She hesitated when she reached the door, and turned back

toward her father. He was a darkened shape against the light of the Fire Lantern on the table. The Work was important to him, but she had worked hard too. She couldn't give up now.

"I have to keep training until the Cup," she said, her resolve strengthening with each word. "I have to see it through."

"So be it. But do not expect to remain under this roof if you continue to duel after that."

"You'd . . . you'd kick me out?" Dara's breath caught, coming short and sharp.

"It would be your choice." Rafe studied his lantern, speaking without emotion. "Duel or remain under my roof. I will no longer have an irresponsible young woman sullying our family name."

Pain flashed in Dara's heart at his words. A tiny spark of Fire moved through her body for an instant, but her father didn't appear to sense it. She shut the door to the workshop and trudged up the tunnel, feeling hollow and cold. A line had been drawn. If she wanted to keep dueling after the Cup, she needed a patron. Otherwise, she would have nowhere to live. Her footsteps dragged, echoing dully in the corridor.

She went through the lantern shop on her way out. Her mother wasn't there, but Farr was bent over the ledgers, scribbling eagerly.

"Hello, Dara," he said as she passed. He sat back and stretched his arms, his limbs unfolding like tree branches.

"Farr."

"Are you off to join your mother at the meeting? The Guild is talking about the king and the Fire Warden."

Dara slowed. "What about them?"

"The plan, of course."

"What plan? The Fire Warden's plan?"

"The . . . It's . . . I thought that's what your father wanted to talk about . . ." Farr glanced toward the workshop. He cracked his scarred knuckles nervously.

"No, that was something else. What is the Guild discussing? Is he finally going to make a move?" She sincerely hoped the Guild had enough power to act against Zage before he hurt anyone, even if her father apparently had little interest in helping the king himself.

"I'd better not say," Farr said. His face split with that nice grin of his. "Your parents have been really good to me. They're giving me opportunities I never dreamed of, Dara."

She thought of what her father had just said, about how he would turn her out of his house. He had effectively threatened to disown her unless she bent to his will. She blinked back tears, thinking of her mother's coldness since she saved the prince. Maybe it would have been better if Farr were their flesh and blood, not Dara.

"I'm going to practice," she said. "See you later, Farr."

"Bye, Dara. Oh, and good luck with the dueling show." Farr returned to his work as she closed the door behind her.

THE SAVVEN BLADE

W HEN Dara arrived at the castle gates, the guard—one of the new ones—didn't turn her away. The prince had sent her a message letting her know he was finally free to resume training. She crossed the uneven courtyard to the castle, its walls glowing with thin Firegold veins. It was strange to think that crossing this courtyard had become routine over the past two months. A cur-dragon swept overhead, its call sharp through the wind. The first hints of autumn tinted the leaves of a gnarled old tree beside the castle wall.

Princesses Selivia and Soraline accosted her inside the ornately wrought doors.

"Siv told us everything!" Selivia gushed. "I wish I could have been there to see you duel!"

"It was fun, actually," Dara said. "Thank you for your help with the outfit."

"You must have looked dazzling! In a very intense way."

"I've heard several members of the nobility discussing you over the past few days," Princess Sora said, her round face glowing. "I think you have a solid chance of earning a patronage."

"Thank you. That's kind of you."

"They'll be fighting over you!" Selivia said. "Just wait."

"I hope so." Dara was grateful for their unabashed confidence in her. If only Dara's own family could be as supportive. She tried to put thoughts of her conversation with her father out of her mind.

"Are you coming to practice today?" she asked the two princesses.

"We're on our way up to the library for a lesson," Sora said, "but we wanted to make sure you're coming to the Feast. It's two days before the Cup."

"The King's Feast? Ordinary duelists aren't usually invited." The annual feast before the Vertigon Cup was primarily for visiting dignitaries and nobles. The athletes would go out to the taverns for their own celebration after the competition was over.

"We're inviting you now, of course," Selivia said. "And you have to get here early so I can dress you."

"You don't have to—"

"I insist," Selivia said. "Vine will be there too. We can play the two of you off each other. It will be brilliant!"

Dara brushed her fingers against her sensible gray trousers and avoided looking at her scuffed boots. She was pretty sure Vine would make a better impression than her in a ball gown. It might not help Dara's cause to attend the feast. But maybe Selivia could work a bit of magic.

"Okay. I'll be there," Dara said. "Thank you."

"Yay!" Selivia hugged her tight and then darted off down a corridor on the opposite side of the entrance hall. "Hurry, Sora. We're going to be late!"

"I'm looking forward to speaking with you later, Dara," Sora said. She smiled and followed Selivia while Dara headed for the dueling hall.

The prospect of attending the King's Feast cheered her up a bit, but Dara couldn't shake the memory of her father's words. He had drawn the final line. He had told her to abandon everything she had worked toward. She had been on the brink of telling him about her Fire sense, perhaps promising to study the art with him if he would only allow her to duel too. But could she simply give in to him now?

She wanted him to be impressed by her dueling, the thing she loved most. She wanted him to see that her work was paying off. She wanted to feel valuable to him as his daughter completely apart from the Fire. She wanted him to embrace her, acknowledge who she was and what mattered to her. If she told him about the Spark now, she would never have that. She couldn't concede when she was this close to victory.

Pool stood guard in front of the dueling hall. Dark shadows underlined his eyes, and the straight wrinkles around his mouth had deepened.

"Welcome back, my most eminent and agile lady," he said, offering a stiff bow.

"Hello, Pool. Nice to see you again."

Pool opened the door for her. "He is waiting for you."

Siv leapt out of his chair and strode over to meet her as she slung her gear bag to the floor in her usual corner. For a second Dara thought he was going to hug her, but he stopped short when he reached her.

"That was spectacular, Dara! Sheer utter magic."

A thrill of pride and warmth filled her at his words. It was amazing how much light Siv could add to her day. She had missed him. It felt right to be back here in the dueling hall, more right than being anywhere else on the mountain—or with anyone else.

"I can't believe you came," she said, meeting his eyes.

"You didn't tell anyone I was there, did you?"

"I wasn't even sure myself."

"I snuck out," Siv said proudly. "I haven't done that in ages, but I was as stealthy as a gorlion in a lightning storm. My mother and father will kill me if they find out, never mind what Pool will do! You didn't tell him?"

"No," Dara said quickly. "But Selivia and Sora—"

"They know all about it. Selivia would literally murder me if I didn't describe every single instant of the duel. It was all I could do to keep her from coming along."

"You shouldn't have risked it," Dara said. "What if you had been attacked again?"

"You'd have saved me," Siv said lightly.

Dara took a deep breath. It was time to voice the worry that had been tugging at her from the first time she met Zage Lorrid. She couldn't lose Siv, not now.

"I think someone is plotting against you and your father."

"That attack was a one-off," Siv said. "Don't worry so much."

"I've been hearing things lately from the Fireworkers, and a bit from Vine too. I think something is going to happen."

"Look, I appreciate that you're spending your free time worrying about me," Siv said, "but the people love my father. He's a good king, just like my grandfather and his father."

"I think . . . I think Zage Lorrid wants to usurp him."

"Zage?" Siv chuckled and began putting on his dueling gear. "My father has given more power to Zage Lorrid than anyone else in the kingdom. It's not in his best interests to try anything."

"But—"

"Zage has served my family for years. He's a good man."

"Siv." Dara swallowed. She hated bringing this up, but she had to impress upon her friend the seriousness of what could happen, what this man he trusted had done in the past. "Do you remember the Surge from about ten years ago?"

"The Surge? Is that a duelist?"

"The Fire Surge. When the Warden lost control of the Well, and the Fire he'd been restraining burst out through the access points in the Fireshops?"

"That sounds vaguely familiar. Must have been quite a light show."

"Did you know that a Fireworker's apprentice died when it happened?"

Siv stopped putting on his gear and turned toward her, suddenly serious. He waited patiently, as if he could tell she wasn't finished. Dara took a slow breath and met his eyes.

"It was my older sister. Her name was Renna, and she was only eleven years old. Zage should have been removed as Fire Warden after it happened. But he manipulated your father into keeping him on. Now he has been reducing each individual Fireworker's access to the Fire. He could be planning to take control once and for all."

Instead of answering, Siv walked over to her. He took her hand between both of his, holding it gently. She took a shuddering breath, feeling annoyed as her vision blurred with tears.

"I'm sorry about your sister, Dara. I didn't know."

"It was a long time ago." She sniffed, fighting to regain her composure. "But Zage ..."

"I understand why you must hate him," Siv said softly, "but I don't believe Zage would hurt any of us."

"How do you know?"

"If he wanted to hurt us, he's had plenty of opportunities over the years. And like I said, he already holds the highest Fireworker position in Vertigon. I've known him for a long time, and I don't think he'd want to be king."

"But what if he's the one who hired the assassin?"

"Dara, it'll be okay. Bandobar and the Castle Guard will get to the bottom of that." He squeezed her hand, and she wished he wouldn't ever let go. At the same time, she felt that he was dismissing her concerns because she was upset. He was trying to cheer her up, and he wasn't taking this seriously enough.

"Zage has been causing friction for a while now," she said. "I think you should look into it in case he has something bigger in the works."

"Plots and intrigues are for the Lands Below," Siv said. "Vertigon is better than that."

"Then at least be more careful," Dara said, her grip tightening on Siv's hand. "I don't want anything to happen to you."

"I'll be fine," Siv said. Suddenly he looked down at their hands, still clasped, as if he realized what they were doing. Instead of releasing her, he stood very still. His breath was warm on her face, his grip firm. Dara's heart sped up, and heat spread across her skin. Then his eyes dropped to her mouth.

"Prince . . ." Dara whispered.

He dropped her hand as if it burned. "Let's focus on your training for the Cup," he said, clearing his throat. "I've had some ideas for new moves since the duel with Vine."

There was a heavy knock on the door, and Berg Doban strode in without waiting for a response.

"Coach! It's been a long time." Siv turned away from Dara and went over to shake Berg's hand. The coach's face was solemn, but he gave no indication that he'd noticed how close together they'd been standing a moment ago.

"You are training well without me, I hear."

"Dara's great!" Siv said. "She's making me a more boring duelist, but she's keeping me alive."

"Hmm," Berg grunted. "Today I will teach you a lesson. Dara, you will watch. You are next."

"Yes, Coach." Dara took a seat on the rug to stretch while she waited. It had been a while since Berg had been here for a practice session, and she was surprised to see him. He seemed to be in a foul mood as he shrugged on a jacket and glove.

Siv was unfazed, though. He rotated through each set of exercises, his arms moving in clean lines, his thigh muscles flexing. Dara couldn't help sneaking glances at him while she stretched. He was definitely getting better.

But Berg was harsher than ever. Whenever Siv missed a parry, Berg riposted, letting every hit land with a thud. Siv would be bruised after this practice. Berg wasn't as fast as he used to be, but he was still brutally strong.

Soon, the prince was sweating and swearing. They worked longer than a typical twenty-minute lesson, but Berg didn't let up. He continued to land almost as many hits as Siv did. He was supposed to be conducting a lesson, not a thrashing. Something wasn't right here. Dara stood.

Siv must have realized something was amiss at the same moment.

"What's gotten into you, Doban?" he said, straightening and pulling off his mask. "Mother of a cullmoran! Are you trying to kill me?"

"I am trying nothing," Berg growled. "You must be ready." He tossed his blunted practice blade onto the floor and stalked over to the rack of weapons by the door. He pulled out one of the ornate swords. The tip was sharp, winking cruelly in the late morning light.

"Coach . . ." Dara said. "Maybe you shouldn't."

"You must understand," Berg said. He returned to the dueling strip and faced the prince. Siv stood his ground, face grim, sweat dripping from his hair.

Dara took a step forward. "Coach, you—"

"Silence," Berg barked. "Dara, you too."

"What?"

"On your guard. Both together."

"Coach, no tourney—"

"No more arguing. We will fight now."

Dara hurried to the strip, shrugging on her own jacket and mask, and exchanged worried glances with Siv. She assumed her on guard stance, her blood humming with tension. Berg faced them, a big, square mountain with sharpened steel in his hand. Dara fought down the fear curdling in her stomach. This didn't feel like a game. What was he doing?

Berg advanced, the sharpened blade at the ready. Without a word, Dara and Siv separated so their swords wouldn't tangle. Dara tapped at Berg's blade tentatively with her own, testing his defenses. Like lightning, Berg lunged and nicked Dara's arm. Blood fell on the stone floor.

"What the hell, Berg!" Siv attacked, arm wheeling wildly. Berg parried each stroke then thrust his blade through the prince's dueling jacket. He pulled the blade out again, leaving a neat cut in the fabric. An inch to the left and he would have stuck him in the ribs.

"Do not lose focus!" Berg roared.

Siv retreated, and Dara engaged Berg, more carefully this time. Her defensive game changed completely in the face of a real weapon. She traded a handful of parries and ripostes with Berg and then retreated. Siv joined her and did the same. Both of them breathed heavily. Fear and confusion gripped Dara. Berg wouldn't really hurt them, would he? The warm trickle of blood dripping inside her sleeve suggested otherwise.

Berg attacked the prince, and Dara acted on instinct, stepping in front of him and sweeping her coach's blade aside. Berg's counterattack barely missed her mask. One wrong move with a weapon like that, and she could lose an eye straight through the wire mesh of her mask.

Siv followed Dara's move with an attack to Berg's shoulder, steering clear of his mask-less face. The hit landed with a thud.

Dara and Siv fended off Berg's rapid counterattacks. Any thoughts of showmanship evaporated. They kept their movements small, controlled. Defense was all that mattered. Berg's eyes bored into them like awls. Dara studied every inch of him, every tense and shift of muscle, watching for clues to where he would move next. Some sort of burn marked his left hand, the one not protected by a glove. When had that happened?

The bout continued unabated. Dara's limbs shook, but she didn't dare suggest a break. She had a feeling Berg wouldn't stop if she asked. Siv swore steadily under his breath beside her, but he didn't make any more reckless attacks.

Back and forth they fought. Every moment felt as if it lasted an hour. Dara was reaching the point of exhaustion, unsure whether she could keep her blade up much longer. She felt as though she were being ripped back and forth in a snowstorm today, between her father's ultimatum, Siv's hands on hers, and now this.

Again, Berg attacked. Dara clenched her teeth in frustration, but she met his attack blow for blow. She landed a hit on his arm and immediately recovered, ready to duel again. Siv stood ready beside her.

Suddenly Berg lowered his guard. Dara and Siv kept their blades up. There was no telling what he would do.

But Berg only studied them for moment. Then he turned and replaced the sword in the weapons rack. He moved stiffly, as if the intensity of the duel had finally caught up with his aging bones. The shiny patch of the burn glinted on his left hand.

"This is what a real attack feels like, students. You must be ready." Then he stalked out of the dueling hall and slammed the door behind him.

Silence reigned. Dara's weapon arm shook as she lowered her guard. Then Siv let out a string of curses and tossed his blade aside. He went straight to the water basin and stuck his head into it. Dara slid down to sit on the floor. What was that about? She'd always thought Berg was a little crazy, but to face them with a sharpened blade? He was taking this training far too seriously.

Siv returned with a wet cloth and knelt beside Dara. He helped her remove her jacket and cleaned the blood from her elbow, long fingers curled gently around her arm to keep it steady. Neither of them spoke. She could smell the sweat on his body, mixed with the coppery tinge of her blood. The cut wasn't deep, but it stung. Siv wrapped a strip of bandage around it and tied it tightly. Then he sat back on his heels and wiped a sleeve across his face.

"What the hell was that?" he said.

"Another lesson?" Dara thought of the burn on Berg's hand, and the way he always insisted an attack was imminent. He hadn't been wrong. "I told you something's going on. Why else would he suddenly be so concerned about your safety?"

"I thought he just liked me," Siv mumbled. "I know you suspect the Fire Warden, but if I didn't know better, I'd wonder if Berg was trying to orchestrate a training accident." He touched the bandage on her arm, his thumb brushing her skin. "He had no right to do that."

Dara frowned, remembering her father's reaction when she mentioned Berg earlier. But it was *Berg*. He couldn't have meant to hurt them.

"I don't believe he wants you harmed," she said, not feeling quite as confident as she sounded. "You need to be careful, though. Please."

Siv met her eyes. "I will. I promise."

"Good." Dara returned his gaze, heat rising into her through the stones on the floor. She wanted to reach out to him. She wanted him to touch her again. But they had bigger things to worry about. And he was still the prince.

Siv seemed to be having a similar struggle, for he stood abruptly. "So, do you want to keep practicing, or can we call it a day?"

"I've had enough dueling for once," Dara said.

"Likewise. Listen, I've got something for you before you go. I'd hoped to give it to you under more jovial circumstances."

Siv led her to the weapons rack by the door. He pulled one of the blades out with a flourish. It was a fine rapier with a Fire-forged steel blade. The hilt and guard were black iron, wrought with an intricate pattern. The point was deadly sharp.

"Here," Siv said, thrusting it into Dara's hands. It was heavier than a sport dueling weapon, and the grip was cold to the touch. Dara's breath caught in her throat. The sword was little short of spectacular.

"It's beautiful, but I can't use this." She hefted the blade, feeling the perfect balance, admiring the glittering steel edge. "It's not blunted."

"It's for show," Siv said. "Dara Nightfall, the mysterious dark duelist, needs to carry a weapon to match her name. Wear it whenever you're not competing. You can use your regular gear for tourneys, but show this off whenever you can."

Dara ran her fingers over the black guard with its elegant, twining pattern. "Where did it come from?"

"It was made by Drade Savven."

Dara nearly dropped the weapon. "I can't accept this." This was the work of a true master sword smith. A priceless weapon. There were only a handful of Savvens left in the world.

"I insist," Siv said. "Otherwise it'll just sit there. Savvens deserve to be shown off."

Dara looked closer at the intricate iron of the hilt. A tiny S was etched in the pommel. It was the most beautiful sword she had ever seen.

"Thank you," she whispered.

"Wear it to the feast," he said. "It'll look good on you."

His gaze fixed on hers, perhaps a little too intently. Dara cleared her throat and took a small step backwards.

"That was quite a training session," she said. "You're dueling really well."

"Of course I am!" Siv grinned. "Now get out of here."

"See you at the feast?"

"Indeed." Siv bowed, flourishing an imaginary cape. "Until tomorrow, Nightfall."

Dara left the castle at a jog, feeling lighter on her feet despite the solid heft of the Savven blade at her hip.

THE ROYAL FAMILY

S IV was ambushed that very afternoon. Sora sent him a
note asking him to meet her in the Great Hall after the
noon meal. She neglected to mention that their parents would
be there too, with alliances on the brain.

As soon as Siv entered the hall, Sora grabbed his arm and
dragged him up the long carpet leading to the dais.

"Sorry, but you've been avoiding them for too long," she
said brusquely.

"Traitor."

Sora wrinkled her nose. "You smell of sweat, Sivarrion.
Can't you bathe after you duel?"

"I had more important things on my mind."

"The kingdom is important."

"I know. Believe it or not, I'm more dedicated to Vertigon
than a velgon bear is to finding soldarberries."

Sora sniffed but didn't respond. They passed their mother,
Queen Tirra, who was directing the preparations for the feast
the following night. The hall sparkled with ornamentation.
Glass baubles hung from the arched ceiling, and it looked as if
every Fire Lantern in the castle had been brought in for the

occasion. Workmen were dragging the long wooden tables away from their usual places along the walls. The scrape and screech of activity filled the space. Tomorrow would be a big night.

"I'm afraid your time is up, son," the king said when Siv and Sora reached him. "Thank you, Soraline, you may go."

Soraline began to protest. "But—"

"I promise to fill you in later," the king said, eyes twinkling.

"Fine." Sora jutted out her lip and sulked all the way to the door.

Siv turned to face his father alone.

"Yes, sir?"

Sevren Amintelle stood before his throne, looking every inch the king. Well, except for the pastry dusted with sugar in his hand.

"Your mother and I have been talking," he said, his tone serious. "Your grandfather has heard rumors of dissent all the way down in Trure. It is time to take decisive action to protect our hold on Vertigon."

Siv straightened. "What kind of dissent?"

"The Fireworkers. We knew a day would come when the power enclosed within this mountain would cause us difficulty. Our efforts to contain it have not been enough. Drastic actions are even now being planned in concert with a handful of noble houses that see the Fireworkers as their ticket to a better position."

"Which noble houses?"

"I believe Lord Von Rollendar is the likeliest candidate at this stage." The king put the last of the pastry in his mouth. "What say you to that?"

"It wouldn't shock me," Siv said. Dara might suspect Zage, but Lord Rollendar fit the bill better. And Bolden had known Siv would be out late the night he and Dara were attacked. Despite their long friendship, Siv had no doubt Bolden would choose his house's interests over him. "And he has Fireworker allies?"

"He does." The king glanced at the workers preparing the Great Hall and lowered his voice. "He has been seen in their company often of late. My informants are establishing a case against him."

"Are you going to have him arrested?"

"Not yet. House Rollendar is powerful. His brothers would not take such an action lightly."

Siv pictured Bolden's three uncles, proud and cruel. There was a time when no Amintelle king would have worried about a handful of Rollendars. The Peace of Vertigon may have been good for the people, but it didn't lend itself to kingly demonstrations of power. It was rather inconvenient, really.

Siv looked up at his father. "You don't think we're strong enough to stand against them?"

"The majority still supports us, but we must protect our alliances now more than ever. I . . . I'm afraid I've grown complacent over the years." The king grimaced. "These maneuverings have taken me by surprise."

"So, I'm out of time." Siv had already figured out where this was going.

"You must confirm your marriage alliance with Lady Denmore within the week. The Denmores and Ferringtons, together with the Amintelles, are more than a match for the Rollendars. Otherwise, we will need to seek an immediate link with a powerful Truren lady to strengthen our position. We cannot delay."

Siv mirrored his father's tall, straight posture, allowing the mantle of duty to settle over him like frost.

"I understand."

The queen drifted over to join them. She put a hand on Siv's shoulder.

"Sivarrion," she said. "I'm sorry you—"

"It's all right, Mother. It's time." Siv met his father's eyes. The king nodded, gravely. He was dignified even as he admitted weakness. Still, Siv wished he didn't have to see it.

"I'll do it at the Feast," Siv said, scrabbling for a positive angle as his parents' expectations and the needs of his mountain tightened around him. "Vertigon deserves a queen truly its own. And the people will love that Lady Tull's tragic story ends with a royal marriage. It will help our cause in more ways than one." Dara wasn't the only one who needed to build up their public persona. His family had to be strong—and they had to make sure the people continued to love them.

The thought of Dara sent a painful jolt through Siv's chest, but he endured it. Duty. He would bear his duty with as much dignity as he could muster. Apparently she had been right about the threat, even though he still didn't think Zage was at the heart of it.

"What are we going to do about those rogue Fireworkers?" he asked.

"I have arranged a meeting with Lantern Maker Ruminor in a few days to discuss the current tension," the king said. "Perhaps he can shed some light on the other Fireworkers' morale."

"That was my idea," the queen said.

"Dara's father?"

"That alliance has great potential," the queen said. "As I think you've discovered." She squeezed his shoulder.

"Hmm, I might actually want to attend that meeting," Siv said. Now that was a first. Sivarrion Amintelle, asking to attend a meeting. Miracles did happen.

"It's the morning of the Cup." The king smiled. "I'm sure you'll want to watch your dueling partner in the preliminary matches."

"Fair point." Siv wouldn't miss Dara's Cup bouts for the whole burning mountain.

"We'll be there for the championship, though," the king

said. "Perhaps Dara's father and I can watch the match together from the royal box. Doubtless we'll have resolved everything by then."

Siv hoped that would actually happen. From what Dara had revealed about her relationship with her parents, it would mean a lot to her if her father showed up for the championship bout. The championship she had better win, for Firelord's sake!

"In the meantime, make your suit to Lady Denmore. The younger Lord Rollendar has designs on her as well. You must act before he does."

Siv bowed his assent, not quite holding in a massive sigh. Bolden would hate him even more for stealing his rich lady, but it had to happen. An alliance between the Amintelles and Denmores would keep Vertigon strong. A Denmore-Rollendar pairing would fracture it further. And the Rollendars weren't just too powerful. They were cruel. He could not surrender a single stone of Vertigon into their hands.

That was the crux of it. His feelings for Vertigon, his iron-clad duty toward Vertigon, had to outweigh any other feelings he might have for a certain enchanting woman with strength in her hands and fire in her gaze.

Captain Bandobar approached Siv's father and whispered in his ear. The king replied, his answer making Bandobar grin despite his usually serious demeanor. He and the king had been friends for many years. Bandobar had entered his service before Sevren Amintelle had even become the Third Good King. When Bandobar finished his report, the king clapped him on the back before sending him away. Siv watched the man stride across the hall, his gait crisp and athletic despite his advancing age. A true Fire Blade was strapped to his hip. Bandobar would defend the king to his dying breath. More than anything else, he was the reason Siv did not worry about his father.

Bandobar reminded Siv suddenly and forcibly of Dara. The

friendship shared between the king and his guard was genuine, their loyalty absolute. Siv may need to marry Lady Tull, but that didn't mean he had to lose Dara's friendship. He trusted her without question. No matter what threatened his family, he was sure he could handle it with Dara at his side.

Siv bid his parents farewell and left the Great Hall. He would have more than one proposal to offer at the feast.

THE CUP FEAST

T HE day of the feast, Dara spent a few hours helping her
mother in the morning when she usually went to the
castle. She could have been using that time to get in an extra
workout, but she wanted to see if there was some hope of
reconciliation with her parents. Maybe her father hadn't truly
meant what he said the other day.

But Lima was distracted, and she barely seemed to notice
Dara was there. She puttered around the lantern shop, not
accomplishing much as far as Dara could tell. Lima didn't
broach the subject of Dara's recent activities or the ultimatum
her father had given her. Her continuing silence on the matter
was unnerving. Dara couldn't help feeling as though her
mother had washed her hands of her daughter.

The lanterns hummed with an extra intensity, the Fire cores
singing in Dara's increasingly heightened senses. She was only
too glad to finish her work and dart out of the shop. She bathed
quickly, twisted her damp hair in a braid on her back, and
strapped the Savven blade to her waist. Then she began the
now-familiar trek across the Gorge and up the slopes of King's

Peak. The Savven drew glances in Lower King's. It wasn't common to see a pitch-black hilt.

At the castle, the door guard—Yeltin again—raised an eyebrow at the weapon, but he recognized Dara and let her pass. The entrance hall bustled with servants and stewards preparing for the feast. Workmen carried barrels of ale and wine down the widest central corridor. Gold-embroidered fabrics hung from the vaulted ceilings, and huge clusters of early-autumn foliage were being arranged in glass vases around the entrance hall.

Dara had arrived early as Selivia requested, but she wasn't sure what to do from here. She wondered if she should wait in the dueling hall. She had never been anywhere else in the castle. As she shifted her feet on the tile, the workers bustling around her, a young woman tapped her on the shoulder.

"Excuse me? You are Dara Ruminor?" She wore the Amintelle crest stitched on her simple brown dress.

"Yes, I'm Dara."

"Princess Selivia asked me to bring you to her chambers." The woman had a faint accent, and she had eyes as light as a summer sky. She must be from the Lands Below.

Dara followed her through the bustling halls. Fire Lanterns in elaborate sconces lined the walls. Some of them were Ruminors, but other lantern makers were represented as well. Many of the lanterns were very old, the ancient Fire burning strong as ever. Shadows flickered on the walls. Open doorways revealed glimpses of elegant rooms that must serve all manner of royal functions, reminding Dara that she had actually seen very little of the castle so far.

"What's your name?" Dara asked her guide as they turned at the end of the corridor and climbed a winding stone staircase. Dara was pretty sure they were entering the westernmost of the castle's three towers.

"I am Zala Tolan."

"You're from the Lands Below?"

"I am Truren. From the Far Plains folk."

"How did you end up in Vertigon?"

"I arrived with Queen Tirra after her last visit to my home."

"Really? Why did she bring you back?" Dara had rarely seen the Queen of Vertigon. Tirra Amintelle had come from the Lands Below to marry King Sevren but spent many months each year visiting her home country. Rumor had it the queen was perpetually homesick.

"I am to work for her daughter, the Princess Selivia, to teach her more of the Plains tongue."

"Not Princess Sora as well?"

"She already speaks our tongue very well."

They reached the next landing, and Zala rapped on a large wooden door carved with an intricate pattern of vines and flowers.

"Come in!"

The wide, bright room was indeed decorated with Ruminor Lanterns. Three tall windows, little more than arrow slits, cut into one wall. Low couches covered in brightly dyed pillows filled the room. Books were stacked high around the floor, and a stand with a pitcher of soldarberry juice and plates of delicacies waited beside a pair of ornate double doors. These doors were flung open, revealing a canopied bed covered in richly embroidered cushions.

Princess Selivia rushed to take Dara's hand when she followed Zala inside. "I'm so excited you're here, Dara!" she squealed. "The dressmaker and I were up past midnight getting your gown ready. We almost forgot to fix the tear I put in mine last time I tried it on."

"Well, you look very pretty," Dara said, glancing at Selivia's bright-yellow dress. The princess's dyed streaks were gone, leaving her hair sleek and black again. Dara wondered if the queen had ordered it for the feast.

"Oh, this isn't my feast dress. I'll put that on later. We're starting with you today."

The princess grinned and pulled Dara through the double doors to the inner chamber. In the corner was a massive wardrobe. A long black dress hung over the wardrobe door. At least, Dara thought it was a dress. It looked like no more than a swath of black fabric. Dara had secretly hoped the dress would be a bit fancier. She would die before she told anyone, but she had been looking forward to wearing a beautiful dress to the royal feast. She'd imagined embroidery and silk at the very least, maybe a jewel or two. Instead, the dress appeared to be a long, straight column with a black cloak falling from the high shoulders. There was a bit of embroidery on the sleeves, but this too was black on black.

"Wait until you see it on!" Selivia said. "You're going to look so elegant!"

Dara changed into the gown, struggling a bit to pull her muscular arms through the sleeves. Once the dress was on, though, she could see that the sleeves were nearly transparent. The embroidery showed on her arms like shadows. The effect was quite pretty. Zala and Selivia buttoned up the back of the dress and put the cloak on Dara's shoulders.

"Don't look at the mirror yet," Selivia commanded.

She directed Dara to sit on a low stool while she went to work on her hair. Dara had vetoed the black dye, so Selivia wove shiny ribbons of black silk into her hair instead. She did the work herself while Zala put rouge and kohl on Dara's face. Selivia critiqued her progress, chattering rapidly.

"More above the eyes! She has to look shadowy and mysterious, not tired. Draw it out at the corners more. Yes, like that!"

When Selivia was satisfied, she made Dara stand and approach the mirror. None of her shoes had fit, so Dara wore her own tall boots hidden beneath the dress. She strode to the mirror beside the wardrobe, pleased to find that the skirt didn't restrict her movements too much. The fabric was airy and silky, but the thick cloak was velvet. It would keep her warm in the mountain air.

Dara blinked in surprise. An imposing woman stared back out of the mirror, a woman who looked remarkably like Dara's mother. Rather than being alluring, the kohl made Dara's face bolder, her features sharper. It was a handsome look rather than a beautiful one. The black strands woven into her golden hair were reminiscent of the patterns on a Ruminor Lantern. Her hair piled into a crown-like coil on top of her head. Combined with the slim, simple lines of the black gown, it made Dara look even taller than she actually was.

As a final touch, Selivia retrieved the Savven blade from the outer room and moved the sheath from Dara's plain leather belt to one made of black metal, linked like a chain. Dara buckled it on. The belt sat low on her hips, and the elaborate hilt peeked out from the cloak when she moved.

"Oooh, you look like a witch queen from a story," Selivia gushed.

"Um, I'll take that as a compliment."

"You should. You're striking, Dara. You'll look magnificent and strong next to Vine's flashy colors."

"Thank you for all your help, Selivia. This is . . . this is wonderful." Dara couldn't describe how she felt at the sight of this transformation. Emotions welled up, gratitude and nerves and pride and sadness. Why did she have to look so much like her proud, cold mother? She cleared her throat. "Don't you need to get ready too?"

"Oh yeah!" Selivia waved her arms frantically at Zala. "I almost forgot! We're going to be late. Wait in the sitting room if you like. We'll be quick."

Dara returned to the antechamber with the heavily cush-ioned couches. She didn't want to sit, afraid she'd knock some-thing loose from the pile of hair on her head. She strode around the room, practicing how to walk without tangling the cloak and sword. She'd never be able to duel in something like this, of course, but she would look impressive as long as she didn't stumble.

It was almost time for the feast. The three windows revealed a red-gold sunset over the mountain. Dara stalked back and forth through the burning patches of light, turning and twirling and enjoying the feel of the dress swirling around her legs and the blade hanging from her hips.

"Having fun?"

Dara whirled around. Siv was leaning in the doorway, grinning. He must have seen her flouncing back and forth.

"When did you get here?" she demanded, cheeks burning.

"I live here, Miss Ruminor."

Dara cleared her throat and swept the cloak back, trying to show she didn't care. Despite her practice, the cloak tangled in her blade, and she had to fight to pull the velvet free from the intricate hilt. She cursed under her breath until it yanked loose.

"That's no way to talk to a Savven blade, Dara. Or should I call you Nightfall?"

Dara glared at Siv as he crossed the room toward her. He too wore all black, and a high, stiff collar drew attention to his high cheekbones. His boots shone brighter than the steel of her blade.

"I still think the name is silly," she grumbled.

"We'll see if you feel that way when the crowds are chanting it at the Cup."

Siv reached Dara and straightened her cloak, which had been pulled to the side during her tangle with the blade. After adjusting the cloak, Siv let his hands rest on Dara's shoulders, his thumbs near the dip in her throat. Dara met his eyes, her breath quickening. His hands tightened on her shoulders.

"You look stunning," he said.

"It's all Selivia's doing."

"No, Dara. You are . . . And even if we can't . . . You're . . ." Something like sadness flickered across Siv's face, but it was gone in an instant. He uttered a foul curse about the blood of some sort of zur-creature or other. Then he cupped her face in his hands and drew her closer. Dara's heart flickered like a candle.

"When did you get here, Siv?" Selivia's bright voice sang out.

Siv dropped his hands with a look of raw frustration and spun to greet his sister. Dara stepped away from the prince quickly, her blade tangling in her cloak again, her steps off balance.

Selivia sailed into the room in a grand dress that was the blue of a mountain lake. Her hair was piled up like Dara's, with a few dark ringlets bouncing free. She looked fresh-faced and sweet, every inch the princess.

"I have come to escort my darling sister to the feast," Siv announced, bowing with the dignity of an aged lord.

"Why, sir, I'm flattered." Selivia dropped a playful curtsy and then strutted around the room to make her dress swirl. Zala hurried after her with a pair of dancing slippers in her hands. The young princess hiked up her skirt and stood still just long enough to allow the maid to finish dressing her. "Is Sora coming too?"

"She's already downstairs," Siv said.

"Of course. She always likes to be there early so she can corner her favorite diplomats," Selivia explained to Dara. "She's been raving about the envoy from Soole for a week."

"Shall we descend, ladies?" Siv offered one arm to his sister then turned and offered the other to Dara. His smile was warm and confident. After a split-second's hesitation, she took his arm. He was being polite. Nothing more. She must have imagined the warmth of his hands on her face, his breath mixing with hers.

They walked down to the Great Hall together. Fire Lanterns blazed along their path. Colorfully dressed people milled in the entrance hall before the wide-open doors to the Great Hall. Strains of music and laughter drifted out around them. The crowds parted, and the three of them swept through the double doors together.

The Great Hall was massive, almost as big as Berg's dueling school, and it sparkled like a fairy kingdom. Glass baubles hung from the ceiling like droplets of rain. Banquet tables stretched the length of the room, and a head table sat on a raised dais at the far end. The space in the middle was clear of tables, and lords and ladies greeted each other with elegant bows and trilling laughter. Colors, lights, and voices swirled around them.

Selivia explained they would eat the feast first, followed by dancing until late.

"I don't usually get to stay up for the dancing," she said, "but this year Mother says I'm old enough."

"The queen will be here?" Dara asked.

"Oh, yes. She rarely misses the Cup Feast." Selivia exchanged a brief look with her brother. "There are always visitors from Trure."

"She spends a lot of time there?"

"She visits twice a year and stays for a month or two, sometimes three," Selivia said. "Oh, look at the Widow Denmore's dress! Her mourning period must be over."

The crowds shifted to reveal the beautiful, sad woman Dara had met at Atria's parlor. Lady Tull's dress was wine red and cut quite low. A group of admirers orbited her like moons. When she noticed the prince and princess, she dropped a deep curtsy. Her neckline dipped lower still.

"You'd better get her to save a dance, Siv," Selivia said.

The muscles in Siv's arms tensed for a moment. Then he relaxed, a quiet sigh escaping in Dara's ear.

"You're right. Wait for me?" he said to her. Then he released her arm and strode away without waiting for an answer.

Lady Tull brushed aside her other admirers with a stately wave as the prince approached.

"She's sooo pretty," Selivia said. "It was so sad when her husband died. My dressmaker told me it was a suicide, not an accident. I hope that isn't true."

Dara didn't answer. She felt a twist of jealousy as Siv took Lady Tull's hand and leaned in to speak to her. It was a ridiculous thing to feel. He had a right to dance with whomever he wanted. And she was certain he wasn't looking at Tull the way he had looked at her a few minutes ago.

A group of noblewomen rushed up to Selivia to compliment her on her dress. Dara stepped aside and waited patiently. The princess may like to dress her up, but she wasn't obligated to introduce her. They couldn't truly be friends. Not here with the royal court surrounding them.

Dara scanned the hall for anyone she recognized. She felt out of place in her somber black, no matter how dramatic it made her look. Most of the women wore colorful dresses with elaborate Firegold embroidery and fantastic jewels. Some were clearly visiting from the Lands Below, their gowns exotic and strange. Dara rested her hand on the hilt of the Savven blade, gripping it for comfort. She had nothing to fear from these people. She didn't need a noble house or her father's famous name. She had worked hard, and she was about to prove herself in her own right.

She became aware of a young girl around Selivia's age staring at her intently.

"Dara Ruminor?" she whispered.

"Yes?"

"You're really her?"

"Yes, I am."

The girl continued to stare. Not looking away from Dara's face, she tugged on the sleeve of the man standing next to her.

"Papa, look who it is!"

The man turned to see where his daughter was pointing. He strode over and offered Dara his hand.

"Tellen of House Roven," he said. "I saw your bout on the bridge the other day. Brilliant work!"

"Thank you," Dara said.

"Maraina, look, it's Nightfall!" the girl squealed to a passing friend.

The friend gasped. "Nightfall? Dara Ruminor!"

"I can't believe we get to meet you in person!" said the first girl. She twisted her hands shyly in the folds of her pink gown. "My name is Jully. I'm . . . I'm a huge fan." The girl's face turned as pink as her gown.

Jully's friend Maraina waved a few other young noble-women over, and whispers spread through the crowd.

"It's Nightfall. Nightfall came to the feast!"

More people hurried over to Dara. Some greeted her, others stared openly, awe and excitement on their faces. A space cleared around Dara. She did her best to act unconcerned, but she looked about for any sign of her companions, feeling self-conscious.

"Oh, Jully, you found Dara!" Selivia had returned. Dara breathed a sigh of relief as the princess began introducing her to the growing crowd of young noblewomen.

"I'm a fan of Vine myself," one said to Dara, "but the way you're both making female dueling more exciting is so inspiring."

"What do you think the score will be at the Cup?" Lord Roven asked over the heads of the gaggle of young women. "I want to place a bet!" He laughed richly.

"Are you going to make Vine cry?"

"Ooh, have you seen her yet today? She looks so pretty!"

"May I see your sword, Nightfall?"

"Did you really save Prince Siv?"

"What was it like to fight on the bridge?"

The crowd spun around Dara. Princess Selivia had disappeared again into the milling onlookers. Dara didn't have time to answer every question being tossed at her before three more took its place. Wait, was she supposed to be quiet and mysterious here too? Or was she supposed to make friends? She fought down panic.

Suddenly Siv was at her elbow.

"It's absolutely true that Dara Ruminor saved me on the bridge," he said. This sent the young noblewomen into a tizzy of giggles. Lady Jully's mouth dropped open, and she tugged on her father's coat again.

"May I escort you to your seat?" Siv said, his lips brushing Dara's ear.

"Thank you." She took his arm and kept her head high as they wove through the crowd. "I didn't expect that."

"You're famous." Siv grinned, puffing out his chest as they walked. "This is working."

He led the way toward the long table to the right of the main entrance. Fine stone plates and goblets covered the surface, along with an ornate Firegold-trimmed tablecloth that Dara recognized as Master Corren's work.

"You're sitting next to Jully Roven," Siv said, "but I wanted a minute with you before I send you back into her fawning clutches."

"Oh. Okay." For some reason, Dara had pictured herself sitting with Siv and his sisters at the feast. But this was an official royal function. Of course she wouldn't be seated on the dais. However casual they were in the dueling hall, there was still a division between her and the future Fourth King. There always would be.

"Listen," Siv said. "I've been thinking about something since our duel with Berg. We're a good team, and I wanted to talk to you about—"

"Sivarrion!" A voice boomed, seeming to fill the Great Hall with warmth like a Fire Gate. Dara turned and found herself face to face with King Sevren himself.

"Father." Siv bowed formally, but he was clearly pleased to see his father. "May I introduce Dara Ruminor?"

"You must be this Nightfall I've heard so much about!" King Sevren had a pleasant face, deep voice, and a smile that put Dara immediately at ease. She curtsied.

"Thank you for having me at the feast, Your Majesty."

"Oh, a pleasure, my dear," the king said. "I understand I owe you my thanks for keeping my son from being skewered."

"I was in the right place at the right time, Your Majesty."

"Nevertheless, I don't know what I'd do without my boy." King Sevren clapped his son on the back. Siv went a bit pink, but he was grinning. "Now if you'll excuse us, I need my son for an important matter of state involving a toast with some exceptionally good wine."

"I'll talk to you about that thing later, Dara."

"Make sure you try the orchard pies," King Sevren said. "I've sampled them, and we're in for a treat."

Dara curtsied again, the king and prince already moving off through the crowd of nobles. She wondered what Siv had been about to say. They *were* a good team. Was it possible he wanted to be something more? For an instant, she felt the warmth of his hands on her face again. Had he been about to kiss her? Did he want to suggest that they'd make a good team in ways that had nothing to do with dueling? The idea was silly, but Dara couldn't help indulging it. Despite the fact that he was a prince, she felt on an equal footing with Siv. They complemented each other, at least in the duels. And he made her feel like running and flying and wielding Fire all at the same time. Was it possible he felt the same way?

FIRST DANCE

DARA took her seat halfway along the hall from the high table. Each place was marked with a polished stone with the name of the guest written in infused Firegold. Dara's simply read "Nightfall." She touched the smooth stone. A tiny drop of Fire leapt from the Firegold word into the tip of her finger. She pulled back, wrapping her fingers around the hilt of the Savven. She'd have to be more careful about that. Her connection to the Fire was advancing at a more rapid pace than it was supposed to based on what she'd seen of Fireworker apprentices. She might not be able to hide her newfound ability for much longer.

When young Lady Jully joined her, she chattered non-stop about Dara and Vine's duel. It was certainly having the effect they had hoped it would. People who hadn't even seen it could describe the whole thing move for move.

When Vine Silltine flounced to a seat directly across the hall from them, Jully gasped loud enough to make people five seats away turn to look at her. Vine was dressed in her signature green and Firegold, and the neckline of her dress plunged almost to her belly. Unlike the other women with their elaborate up-dos, her dark hair was loose about her shoulders and woven with flashing threads of gold. She raised an appreciative eyebrow when she saw Dara then immediately scowled. The people around her noticed, and soon everyone was darting eager glances back and forth between the two rival duelists.

Dara chose not to react. She simply stared across the hall at Vine. She thought about their upcoming duel, about how she would cut through Vine's defenses and put her prancing to an end. She allowed as much of that focus and determination to show on her face as she could manage. Berg said the first person to break eye contact always lost the duel. Dara's eyes never wavered until the serving men and women brought out the food.

The feast was magnificent: juicy roasted hunks of mountain bear, blue pigeon eggs stewed in Fireroot, orchard pies and bird's nest soup and sweetened spice cakes. Wine flowed freely. Dara took a few sips from her goblet, but she still didn't like the taste. The clink of silver on stone filled the hall.

Siv and his sisters sat at the high table with their parents and a handful of honored guests. Dara got her first good look at the queen in a long while. She was dressed in a pale-green dress that was almost white, like her light Truren eyes. She looked unhappy, despite the warmth and frivolity around her. She only smiled when she looked at King Sevren, and even then it was a shadow of an expression.

The others sitting at the high table with the royal family were mostly the heads of important noble houses. The beautiful Lady Tull Denmore sat between Soraline and Siv. He spoke animatedly to her, making her smile. But Dara was sure the prince's gaze drifted across the hall to her a few times throughout the meal.

Zage Lorrid sat at the end of the table nearest to the dais. He was deep in conversation with Bolden Rollendar's father, whom she recognized by his sandy hair and sharp nose. Zage glanced up and met Dara's eyes once, a frown twisting his thin lips. She looked back at her plate quickly, wondering if Siv had shared her suspicions with him. Siv wouldn't do that, would he?

No. She trusted him. She could hardly wait to find out what he had been about to say to her before the king whisked him away.

As they finished the orchard pies and started in on the sweetened spice cakes, Lady Jully explained the importance of the First Dance.

"Each nobleman will ask one lady to join him for the opening dance." Jully took the last cake and broke it in half, offering a portion to Dara. "It's a mark of honor, and who they choose at each feast is important. Most are married, but they'll offer First Dances to the wives of men they're trying to make trade alliances with or whose daughters they're hoping to marry off to their sons. It's not usually romantic, but it's delightfully juicy. My father is going for Lady Nanning this year. He and Lord Nanning are thinking of sponsoring a new dueling school next year."

"Really?"

"Yes. Oh, it would be magnificent if you decided to train there!"

"I'm pretty happy with my own coach." Dara looked up at the high table as the servants dressed in crisp white uniforms emerged to clear away the dishes. "Will the royal family choose partners?"

"King Sevren chooses Queen Tirra whenever she's here for a royal feast. He's the only one who always picks his own wife for the First Dance. But we've all been talking about who Prince Sivarrion will choose. He selects a different lady at every feast. He's quite diplomatic actually. *I'm* too young for him." Jully sighed deeply. "I'll probably end up dancing with my cousin again."

"Has he ever asked Lady Tull?" Siv was deep in conversation with the comely widow. He only stopped chatting with her to take long sips from his wine goblet.

"Yes, while she was married to poor Lord Denmore," Jully said. "He looks like he might ask her again, doesn't he? Oh, they'd have the most adorable babies."

Dara coughed and reached for a stone water pitcher to refill her goblet. The prince *was* leaning quite close to Lady Tull. It made sense. The king was hale and hearty, so Siv couldn't be under immediate pressure to choose a wife, but he'd need one eventually. And House Denmore was prominent. It would be the right move for Siv to ask her to dance. To dance, and maybe more. Dara gulped down her water, fighting desperately against the urge to keep watching him.

King Sevren rose, and the Great Hall fell into an expectant silence. He lifted his goblet and thanked everyone for attending the feast.

"I believe we will have one of our most exciting Vertigon Cups yet," he said after acknowledging each of the visiting dignitaries by name. "May the athletes show their quality and make their lands proud. Now, if my lovely wife will join me, let us dance!"

Applause thundered through the assembly, making the glass baubles shudder, as King Sevren guided his ethereal queen to the center of the dance floor. As the first notes rose from the musicians in the corner, men began to stand and offer their hands to the other ladies around the hall.

Dara couldn't help it. Her eyes snapped back to Siv. He was downing the last of his wine, a look of grim determination on his face. He had set down his goblet and put his hands on the arms of his chair to rise when another man strode up to the high table so fast he was almost running. Lord Bolden Rollendar extended a hand to Lady Tull. Dara couldn't be sure, but she thought he was smirking at the prince as he invited the wealthy young widow to dance. Lady Tull accepted. Siv stopped halfway out of his chair and watched them walk to the dance floor with a slight frown on his lips.

"Ooh," Jully squealed beside Dara. "Can you believe that? Lord Samanar is dancing with Vine Silltine!"

She hadn't noticed the exchange between Siv and Bolden. Siv poured himself another goblet of wine, swallowed it in a single gulp, and slammed it back onto the table. Most of the other noblemen had claimed their dance partners by now. Vine twirled across the center of the floor with a distinguished older man, hair and skirts swirling. Princess Soraline danced with a light-eyed Truren. The king and queen cut a regal figure, their elegant shapes standing out in the crowd.

Siv strode around the now-vacant head table. He made a sharp, deliberate turn at the corner and headed directly toward Dara and Jully. The latter finally noticed him with a gasp. Siv stopped in front of them and offered his hand.

"May I have this dance, Dara Ruminor?"

Ignoring the borderline apoplectic look on Jully's face, Dara accepted. Siv led her around to the other side of the table, steering her faster and more firmly than before. His face was flush with wine and abandon. Dara felt suddenly shy.

"I don't dance very often," she said.

"It's easy. Keep distance with me, like we're dueling." Siv put his arm around her waist and took her other hand in his.

They turned slowly around the dance floor. Dara's black cloak swept behind them like a dream. The Savven blade creaked at her waist. Dara kept her eyes on Siv's chin as she concentrated on not stumbling or getting tangled in her skirt.

"You're very focused," Siv said.

"Don't want to fall."

"You'll be fine." He squeezed her hand, warmth growing between their palms. "No one will notice."

But heads were turning to look at them all across the Great

Hall. It was one thing for them to be seen together at a parlor, but the First Dance was something else. If anyone hadn't been talking about Dara before, they would be now.

As the churn of the dance floor brought Vine closer for a moment, she met Dara's eyes with her lips pursed. Then she mouthed something that might have been "nice move."

Lord Bolden and Lady Tull swayed into view. Bolden was whispering in her ear. Although Siv wasn't looking around for his dinner partner, Dara couldn't help wondering if he was disappointed about the outcome of the dance. But he would have plenty more dances with Lady Tull. He was kinder and funnier and more handsome than Bolden. Even if he hadn't been a prince, Lady Tull was sure to choose Siv. The more she thought about it, the more Dara was convinced such a match would serve her friend well.

"Loosen up, Dara. You're going to break my hand," Siv said.

"Sorry." Dara relaxed her grip, surprised, and finally looked up into Siv's eyes.

"It's just a dance." Siv grinned and whirled her a bit faster. A hundred eyes followed them as they swept across the floor.

Dara wanted to say something, but Siv was pulling her closer, holding her. His breath was on her face, sweet with wine and sugar. Heat filled her body like the heat in a Fire Lantern. Their steps quickened. Across the hall, Vine executed some sort of dramatic twist to draw attention back to her, but Siv and Dara were in their own little swirl of movement and energy and heat.

Unbidden, hope bloomed in her chest like lightning. He *did* look at her differently. He *was* holding her closer, arms around her as though he could block out the world. Castles and Fireworkers and kingdoms and royal matches couldn't touch them. It was just her and Siv and the magic of the dance.

The music faded away like morning mist, and they twirled to a stop. Siv was breathing harder than he should have been, his eyes bright. He didn't release her. Time seemed to stop, captured in glass.

The music started up again, livelier this time. Vine spun a new dance partner out onto the floor, a young man who was almost as sprightly as Vine herself. People gathered to watch them. They had stopped paying attention to the duelist and the prince.

"Walk with me," Siv whispered against Dara's ear.

She followed. Maybe she had been wrong about Lady Tull. Maybe there was something more to her friendship with Siv than dueling. There was no mistaking the spark between them now. She could barely think straight as the implications of what he might be feeling, what she was feeling, rose within her like molten gold.

Siv marched her toward an alcove set with low stone seats at the edge of the Great Hall. The curve of the wall lessened the noise of the music. At the back of the alcove, a window looked out over the lights of Vertigon.

"Right." Siv took a deep breath. "I have something to ask, as I mentioned. Now I'm not so sure . . . We've been at this training thing for a while. You have goals, and I have . . ." Siv grimaced. "Actually, it doesn't matter what my father wants me to do. It's my choice. I'd like to make our partnership more permanent. That is to say, I know you've been looking for a patron, but—"

"Wait. Please don't." Dara felt reality thudding down on her. He was going to offer her a patronage. She was so stupid. Of course the prince didn't *want* her. What had she expected? That's what this was about, not . . . anything else. She tore her hand out of his grasp, feeling embarrassed and foolish. "I don't want gold from you."

"Can I finish?"

"You can't be my patron." She choked down a lump in her throat. "That'll ruin everything."

"I didn't mean—"

"Look at how Kel and Bolden are. They act like friends, but Kel can't say no to anything because Bolden pays for his living. I don't want to be in debt like that. Not to you."

"Dara—"

"I'd better go. I need a decent night's sleep before the tourney."

Siv raised his hand to touch her face, but Dara dodged it as though she were avoiding a hit from a dueling sword. "Dara—"

"Thank you for the dance. I'll see you at practice."

She fled before Siv could say another word, feeling like she'd been stabbed. Her pride hurt the most. She thought they had something special, something more than a hired duelist and a potential patron. She never wanted it to be like that. Not with him.

Dara hurried along the wall, staying in the shadows. Couples were tucked into other alcoves, their giggles piercing her like arrows. Dara didn't speak to anyone. Her early departure could add to the mystery of Dara Nightfall. Selivia broke through the crowd and tried to wave her over, a question on her lips, but Dara didn't slow. She slipped out of the hall and disappeared into the night.

NIGHTFALL

S IV watched Dara walk away from him. He couldn't stop
looking, but he didn't follow her either. In fact, he had felt
nearly incapable of rational decision-making and coherent
thought from the moment he first laid eyes on her tonight.

He had spent all damn day getting himself ready to propose
to Tull Denmore. It was the right thing to do. It was what his
father wanted and his mountain needed. He had been planning
to do it, he really had. Sure, he'd needed a few drinks to help
warm up to it. Maybe he could have asked the necessary question during the hour they'd spent sitting beside each other at
the feast, but he hadn't been quite ready. He figured there'd be
plenty of time that evening.

But then there was Dara. Stunning, intense Dara. She spun
his brain like a tornado on the blasted plains of Soole. By
rights, they should have nothing more between them than a
friendly camaraderie. She had helped him out. He had master-
minded a brilliant public relations strategy for her. That should
have been the end.

But Firelord knew there was more to it.

When Bolden had swept in like a vulture to whisk away

Lady Tull, something had cracked in Siv. He didn't want to dance with Tull anyway. He'd already let his father down by not asking her for the First Dance. What did it matter if he threw the whole damn plan out the window?

. And so he had chosen Dara. He had taken her in his arms and danced as though they had no titles, no families, no limits. He was barely conscious of what he said to her, but he remembered every flash in her eyes and every brush of her skin against his.

He'd pulled her into the alcove to declare . . . something. His love, his undying loyalty, his wish that he could throw himself onto a blade for her if she'd only look at him the way he looked at her. He wanted to lay the whole kingdom of Vertigon at her feet for a smile. He desperately wanted to kiss her proud, intense mouth.

And then he'd gone and blown it. He was supposed to be educated and damn eloquent. He was supposed to be charming. He should have taken her into that alcove and offered her his soul in the palm of his burning hand.

Instead he'd babbled until she was offended, and then he'd let her walk away. Of course she didn't want him, didn't need him the way he needed her. She was becoming something wonderful and strong. She had worked her whole life to get exactly where she was. He had no right to ask her to be anything but Dara Ruminor, champion duelist.

He had no right, but he was going to burning try anyway.

Siv ran for the exit.

He made it almost to the double doors before Pool leapt into his path. Siv pulled up at the sight of his bodyguard.

"You are retiring already, my prince?"

"I have to talk to Dara."

"My prince, I cannot allow you to depart this fair fortress. You must not wander about in the hours of darkness." Pool dipped his head apologetically then wrapped his hands around Siv's arm in an iron grip.

"Let me go, Pool." Siv tried to pull his arm away, but Pool dug in his heels and didn't budge. "That's an order."

"My deepest apologies, my prince, but your regal father has given me strict instructions never to allow you to stray into peril again."

"So come with me," Siv said through gritted teeth. People were looking up at the rather unprincely tug-of-war they were having with Siv's arm.

"Oh. Perhaps the king would approve of such an arrangement."

"Let's go, then." Siv shrugged Pool off and continued toward the door.

They made it three strides into the entrance hall before Zage Lorrid intercepted them. Siv slowed at the sight of his teacher, wondering if there was a way to get past him extra quickly without being rude.

"You are following the Ruminor girl," Zage said. He wore the same dark cloak as always, his hands folded within it. "You must not, my prince."

"Out of my way, Zage." So much for not being rude. Dara was getting farther and farther away by the second.

"My prince, you cannot be alone on the mountain with the Ruminor girl."

"Pool will protect me. I need to talk to her."

"I urge you to reconsider, my prince. Have you spoken with Lady Tull yet?"

"No."

"Your father led me to believe that tonight you would finalize your arrangement with—"

"Well, I didn't. Damn it, it's my decision."

"Please, my prince," Zage said. "Choose another lady.

Choose an old crone or a scullery maid. But do not choose a Ruminor."

Siv stopped trying to make a break for the door and whirled to face him.

"Why the hell not?"

"My prince, nothing is certain."

"You have to do better than that if you mean to stop me."

"Very well." Zage closed his eyes and stretched out his hands. Molten threads of Fire burst out from each of Zage's fingers, like liquid tentacles. Siv could barely shout before they twisted into glowing rings around his wrists and ankles. Siv had seen him Work Fire plenty of times. He had even gone to the Well deep within the mountain to watch him maintain the elaborate magical containment system that ensured the Fire was doled out in measured amounts. But he had never expected Zage to raise a hand of Fire against him.

Zage's eyes narrowed in concentration as the Fire flowed from his fingers, strengthening Siv's bonds. He must have drawn an awful lot of Fire from the mountain and carried it with him to the feast. Dara's warning about Zage suddenly seemed a lot more plausible. The threads of Fire didn't touch him, but Siv had to stand absolutely still to avoid being burned. He knew without asking that if he tried to push through the Fire it would hold him as surely as iron shackles.

A glance to the left confirmed that Pool had been restrained in the same manner. He had a hand on each of his long knives, but bracelets of molten Fire held his wrists still.

Siv thought of the very worst curse he knew and hurled it across the entry hall.

Zage sighed deeply at the epithet. "I understand why you feel that way, my prince, but I am afraid I cannot allow you to go out into the night with Dara Ruminor again. The last time that happened you were almost lost."

"Are you insane?" Siv growled. He was already sweating

from the heat of the Fire hovering around his limbs. "Dara saved my life."

"Perhaps. But she also separated you from your guard. You were vulnerable with her. I cannot allow you to expose yourself again this night."

"Let me go, Zage, or so help me—"

"Your father told you there is a Fireworker plot, my prince. Need I remind you that Dara is the daughter of a Fireworker?"

"What? You think the Fireworkers are using her to get me alone or something?"

"I cannot be sure, but I am unwilling to take risks with your life," Zage said. "I am sorry. I'm sure whatever you have to tell the Ruminor girl can be said at the Cup in the presence of an appropriate contingent of guards and witnesses."

Siv engaged Zage in what he thought was a rather impressive staring match, but the Fire Warden didn't budge. Of course Dara wouldn't hurt him. He hesitated at the thought of her Fireworker connections. But that was ridiculous. Dara had nothing to do with it. Her father was even coming to the castle for a meeting the day after next. He and the king would clear things up, and Zage would give up his absurd mistrust of Dara.

"Fine, fine. I'll stay in the castle," Siv said. He'd humor Zage for now. He knew the man was capable of standing there all night long if he had to.

"Very well." Zage finally released him, the bonds melting away and dripping into the stones of the castle.

Siv straightened his clothes and marched away from Zage with as much stately dignity as he could muster. But he wasn't returning to the burning feast. And he definitely wasn't speaking to Lady Tull. Instead he nicked a bottle of wine and headed down to the cur-dragon cave, Pool following him like an overanxious shadow.

Siv picked up little Rumy from the slumbering pile of hatchlings and settled down at the entrance to the cave, swinging his feet over the sheer drop. He spent the rest of the night—and the rest of the bottle—watching the stars travel through the sky, the cur-dragon's warm head resting on his knee. By morning, he knew exactly what he would say to Dara next time he saw her.

THE VERTIGON CUP

D ARA woke early the morning of the Cup. She gathered
her gear and ate a quick breakfast at the family table.
When she was nearly finished with her bread and goat jerky,
her father entered the kitchen. The familiar smell of Fire and
metal swirled in with him. He wore his nicest coat, a well-
tailored garment he usually saved for formal Fire Guild
assemblies.

"Daughter," he said.

She didn't answer, unsure what to say. They hadn't talked
since he'd told her she could no longer live under his roof if she
continued dueling after the Cup. After that, she didn't know
what else they could possibly say.

Her father took a seat across the large stone table. He rested
his elbows on it and studied her. Dara avoided his gaze, looking
instead at his coat pocket, where a faint glow indicated that he
was carrying a Work containing a small measure of Fire,
perhaps a Firestick.

The silence stretched between them, a Fissure with no
bridge. Finally, her father sighed, his barrel chest swelling.

"Good luck today, my young spark. I hope you duel well."

Despite herself, Dara looked up. There was something grave and sad in her father's eyes.

"Thank you," she said.

"I may even come watch you in the afternoon."

"The tickets have been sold out for days," Dara said. She regretted the sharpness in her tone immediately. Her father was offering her an olive branch. She should take it, but she couldn't resist the urge to riposte. It was too little, too late.

"That's unfortunate. I have a meeting on King's Peak this morning. I hope it won't take long. Perhaps I can take you for a nice meal afterwards."

Dara stood and put away the rest of the jerky. She brushed breadcrumbs from the table. A few landed on Renna's chair, and she cleaned them off before pausing beside her father.

"Who are you meeting with?"

"No one of significance." Rafe reached out and took hold of her wrist lightly. Dara froze. Would he be able to sense the Spark within her? She focused on cold thoughts and avoided looking at his pocket containing that infusion of Fire lest she draw on it accidentally. She didn't want him to find out like that. Not when she knew how it would change the way he treated her. Not when today was the day she would finally prove herself a worthy duelist.

If her father could sense anything different in her, he didn't mention it. He tightened his grip.

"Dara, things will be different after today," he said. "No matter what happens, I want you to remember that you will always be a Ruminor."

"I know that," Dara said.

"Sometimes I may have made you feel that because you can't Wield the Fire you are somehow less my daughter. I have never believed that in my core. You are my flesh and blood and Fire. Remember that in the days to come."

"Of course I will, even if I win." Dara tried to smile and pulled her hand gently out of her father's grasp.

When Dara gathered the rest of her gear and left the house, her father was still sitting at the stone table, staring at Renna's chair. She sighed. He was right. Things would be different after today.

Dara jogged to the King's Arena, the huge dueling hall on the western side of Lower King's, not far from the steep drop-off cutting into the peak beneath the castle. It was the grandest venue on the mountain, used for all the most important tournaments, especially the ones that drew foreign competitors. The Fireworkers of old had constructed the arena in the days when they still carried out large-scale stoneworks. The sheer walls appeared to be growing out of the stone, and they concealed the vastness of the structure within.

The crowds were thick already as hopeful would-be spectators waited outside the gates in case extra tickets became available. Hawkers wove among them, offering jerky and spiced ale, banners with the names of the duelists blazoned across them, and rare and popular duelist tokens. Little knots of people formed around the duelists making their way into the stadium. Some competitors hired assistants for the day to make sure their tokens got into as many hands as possible. Dara wasn't the only one hoping to make a big impression today.

Wora Wenden paraded by with the duelists he had sponsored this year, all decked out in his most elaborate finery. Murv "The Monster" Mibben stalked through the crowd, bigger men giving him a wide berth. Training partners Rawl and Yuri swaggered toward the arena, stopping to speak to the onlookers as they went. Bilzar Ten, who was even better looking than Kel, posed amidst a tittering mob of female fans. Shon the Shrieker lurched by, muttering under his breath as a group of spectators followed him eagerly.

A palanquin bearing the Zurren House sigil pushed

through the crowd of commoners, its bearers shouting curses at anyone who got in their way. Other lords and ladies, some familiar to Dara from the feast, mingled with the rest of the spectators as they waited to be let inside. Some had traveled from the Lands Below, and they wore their country colors proudly. Dueling was more popular in Vertigon than in any other land, so this was likely the biggest competition they had ever seen. They stared at the surrounding throng with wide eyes.

Dara carried the black Savven blade and wore the same outfit she had in the duel on the bridge. She had stopped when she was halfway to the arena to apply some of the paint to her face. Instead of the elaborate swirls, this time she smudged dark streaks under her eyes like war paint. Dara was going to battle.

Heads turned as she jogged up to the arena. She slowed to a strut, staring down the gawkers in true Nightfall fashion. When she reached the center of the crowd milling outside the entrance gates, she stopped. People fell silent when she paused in their midst. She looked at the faces surrounding her: men and women of all ages, orchard tenders and bridge carpenters, tradesmen, nobles, ore miners, brightly dressed foreigners, children carrying wooden swords. They waited for her to say something. But she didn't speak. She only stared at them, feet planted, hand on her Savven blade, until ripples of silence spread through the crowd.

This was it. All the work she had done up to this point, both on the training floor and with the theatrics of the past weeks, had led to this moment. She had wanted all of Vertigon to pay attention to her, and it was. Not with shouts and swirls and dramatics. She simply stood there. Confident. Ready. The people remained silent, watching her, waiting, and she didn't have to say a word.

Finally, she nodded once, short and sharp, and took out her

bag of brand-new tokens—a last-minute gift from Kel and Oat. They were simple black stones etched with her initials in an elegant script. She began handing them to the people closest to her. One by one, they took the tokens with awe. No one moved as she walked through the crowd. The calls of people too far away to see what was going on filtered through, but Dara held this particular crowd under her spell.

When the bag was empty, she raised the Savven blade in salute.

Then she turned and strode into the dueling hall through the athletes' entrance. Murmurs followed until the doors clanged shut behind her.

The duelists in the changing rooms were quieter than usual. This tournament was important for all of them. Luci Belling gave her a tentative wave, but she looked as though she might be sick. The foreign athletes who had traveled from the Lands Below sat in their own bubbles of space as the Vertigonian duelists watched them warily. Dara put all her things in a spare trunk, except for the Savven blade. It would be her lucky talisman. She left it buckled to her hip as she headed out to the arena to warm up.

King's Arena was vast, with broad windows to let in as much daylight as possible. The gates had been opened while she was changing. Spectators streamed into the stands, filling them up with a hundred colors. The women's event always took place before the men's, and the stands often didn't fill completely until the men started dueling. But this time, no one wanted to miss the first event. The ticketholders hurried to claim their seats. People pointed and shouted for Dara. The rhythm of her name filled the arena. She waved but tried not to pay too much attention to them. She had her routine. She was a professional. And she would not lose focus this time.

But as Dara jogged around the dueling floor she couldn't help looking at one particular spot in the stands: the royal box directly in front of the championship strip. It was empty. The king and queen were sure to come down later in the day to watch the finals, but there was a long time to go before then. None of their children had arrived yet either.

Dara focused on her breathing, on her feet. She had thought Siv would be here by now. She shouldn't have run off after the feast. He had hurt her by offering to be her patron, but he couldn't have known how that would make her feel.

Still, she had thought he was going to suggest something else. That was the real reason she had darted from the hall. The real reason she felt hurt. Hurt, and embarrassed for being foolish. *Stop, Dara. You need to concentrate.*

She scanned the floor for Berg, trusting him to smack sense into her if she lost her focus this time. There. He was talking to Oat and Kel and a few other students near the men's trunk room. He looked up, as if he sensed her watching him, and raised a hand in greeting. After a moment's hesitation, she returned the gesture. They hadn't discussed that strange training session in the prince's dueling hall. The nick on her arm hadn't finished healing yet. The incident—combined with her father's words—still made her feel nervous around Berg.

She jogged around the arena, willing the nerves and the fear to sweat out of her. She was here to do the one and only thing she had ever truly cared about. This, at least, was simple.

Fanfare and trumpets blared, announcing Vine Silltine's grand entrance. Dara had planned for this moment. She slowed, waiting until Vine reached the center of the arena. She wore a new dress today, bloodred and billowing, and she looked magnificent. She blew kisses at the crowd and twirled her scarlet skirts dramatically. She'd added dancers to her entourage, and they flailed around her in a manic parade as she crossed the dueling hall.

Dara picked up her pace, veering just a bit, and bumped roughly into Vine as she jogged past.

"Oh, sorry!" she said, loud enough for her voice to carry. "Didn't see you there."

Vine's smile slipped. The crowd waited with bated breath.

"Just keep your eyes clear for the bout," Vine said. "You don't want to go tumbling into the officials. Or the stands."

Dara bowed mockingly. "I'll leave the theatrics to you. I'm here to duel."

A low "oooohhh" rumbled through the crowd. Someone started chanting, and others quickly joined in. The shouts for Nightfall and the chants of "Vine Silltine" competed for dominance. Hands drummed on knees, the energy in the stadium palpable. Their build-up had worked. They were ready for a showdown. Dara waved once more and went to gather the rest of her gear before the first bout.

Vine met her in the trunk room. She glanced around to make sure no one was listening then whispered, "This is great fun, Dara. We should have started a rivalry years ago!"

"May the best duelist win," Dara said.

"You're so good at this animosity thing." Vine giggled. "Now, you have to tell me about you and the good prince. Princess Selivia told me how he's sweet on you, though anyone with half an eye could see it at the Cup Feast. But the big rumor is your father has it in for King Sevren."

"What?" Dara felt the ground shifting in strange directions.

"I have to know. Are you involved in a forbidden romance, or are you part of your father's plot? Or both!"

"Vine, there's no—"

Horns rang out, calling the duelists for the first round of competition.

"Tell me after!" Vine said and darted back out to the arena.

Head reeling, Dara followed. The prince was sweet on her? Enough to tell his sister? Her father was involved in a plot? There was no way. Her father would never work with Zage Lorrid.

In a daze, she reentered the arena. The crowd roared her name, the sound drumming through her like thunder.

She shook her head to clear it. Her father couldn't be plotting against the king. He wouldn't work with the Fire Warden, and he definitely wouldn't have sent an assassin after her and Siv. Vine was trying to mess with her by bringing up the prince's affection and rumors about her father now. Vine could giggle about their rivalry in the trunk room, but she wanted the Cup too. This was part of the game. Dara had to keep her head in the competition. There would be time enough for answers later.

Siv and his sisters were sitting in the royal box now. They waved and cheered along with the crowd as she crossed the competition floor to her first bout. Siv looked happy to see her, despite their recent unpleasant parting. Was it possible he had been trying to say something that wasn't about a patronage after all? Could he really have feelings for her? In the same way she had feelings for him?

The prince stood up, revealing that he was wearing all black once again. He reached for something at his feet, and Selivia helped him unfurl a strip of black satin. It was a banner nearly the length of the royal box with the word Nightfall painted in gold across it. The crowd noticed whom the royal family was supporting, and their shouts reached a fevered pitch.

Dara raised a hand to acknowledge the gesture, overwhelming emotion threatening to rise through her. Siv grinned across the hall. Even though she knew it would conflict with her Nightfall image, Dara smiled back.

But then she looked down at the toes of her sensible dueling boots.

Breathe. She had to block everything else out. *Just breathe.*

Her first opponent was Taly Selwun. Dara's vision narrowed to a tunnel. She took the strip, bending her blade into shape across her knee, and snapped her mask down onto her head.

The official waited until both duelists had saluted. Then he raised his hands.

"Ready. Duel!"

It was over quickly. Dara never should have lost to Taly Selwun. She commanded the bout start to finish. She didn't throw in any fancy moves, but now was not the time to show off. She obliterated Taly ten to two.

Cheers filled the arena. Taly sobbed through her salute. Dara refused to look at the royal box. Refused to ask how Vine had done in the first round. *Concentrate. Next bout.*

Her second opponent was from the Lands Below. The referee made the calls in two languages. Dara focused. She imagined the opponent was Berg. Any hits she allowed would rip her skin or gouge her eyes. She wouldn't let this woman get through her.

"Bout! Ten, four to Ruminor!"

On and on the bouts progressed. Dara forgot everything but the competition. She didn't bother with fancy moves or pageantry. She got the job done using her own precise style, enhanced by all the training she had done with Siv. Fast. Accurate. Deadly.

And the crowd loved it. They chanted her name as she barreled through one opponent after another. No one could touch her.

Berg stalked amongst the dueling strips, offering his usual tips whenever he passed Dara's strip.

Against a sprightly Truren: "Invite, invite, invite, then crush!"

Against one of Surri's best students: "Good endurance. Lightning reflexes. Intense focus. This is it. You know the way."

Against a Pendarkan champion with muscles like iron: "Must be like tiger! You are not afraid!"

Dara let his words spur her forward. She would not lose. Not today.

In what felt like no time at all, she whipped off her mask and saluted her penultimate opponent. The woman limped forward to shake her hand, leg no doubt going numb from the last hit. Dara had won the semifinals. She would compete in the championship bout. She would fight for the Cup.

"Good, Dara," Berg growled from the sidelines. "Keep doing this."

"Yes, Coach."

Berg gave a short nod and stalked over to check on his male students, who were preparing for their first round.

With the rest of the competition eliminated, Dara slowed to watch Vine's final bout, the other semifinal. It was closer than any of Dara's bouts had been. Vine and her opponent were tied at eight. Dara crossed her arms and loomed as close to the strip as she could get. People in the stands pointed gleefully at her as she glowered at her rival, enjoying the display of animosity. Secretly, Dara was afraid Vine would lose. They had to have this final contest. It had to be Vine.

And it was. Vine executed two identical shots to the wrist to claim the victory. They were beautiful hits. Clean and precise. Dara hid a smile as the crowd went wild.

The spectators couldn't be happier. They were about to get the bout they'd been anticipating: Dara Nightfall vs. Vine Silltine, the first true female dueling rivals. The duelists who fought in public squares and jumped from balconies and danced with princes. It was a dream match-up.

There was a short break between the semifinal and final bouts. Vine sat cross-legged in the middle of the dueling hall to meditate while Dara ran laps. She tried not to look at the audience, at the patrons, at the prince. People would be buying snacks and replenishing their drinks. The betting on the final results would be growing to new, possibly record-breaking heights. Anticipation built around the stadium.

Dara blocked it all out as she jogged. She was tired, but her extra training sessions over the last months had paid off. She had energy left for the championship duel.

On her second lap around the arena, she couldn't help looking up at the royal box. Siv waved at her to come over. Dara hesitated. She shouldn't be distracted, but she couldn't resist. She had to know if Vine was right. She jogged up to the box. Siv leaned down over the balcony.

"You're doing great!" he shouted. "Sel has been clawing marks in my arm she's so excited."

Selivia noticed that Dara had joined them and bounced over from where she had been sharing salt cakes with Sora. She leaned so far over the balcony that Siv had to grab her shoulder to keep her from pitching over it. She had painted black swirls on her face.

"You're amazing, Dara! You're going to win this! This is the best day ever!"

"Thank you." Dara smiled at the princess's enthusiasm. "Just trying to stay focused."

Selivia clapped both hands over her mouth.

"Of course!" she said through her fingers. "I won't distract you. Siv, come on, we have to let her focus!" The young princess tugged on her brother's arm, trying to get him to move away from Dara.

"Just a sec, Sel." Siv shook her off and leaned back down, the height of the box keeping them separated by a few feet.

"Listen," Dara said before he could say anything. "I'm sorry I stormed off the other night. That was immature."

"Yeah, it was," Siv said, but there was no sting in his words. "Look, I wasn't going to offer to be your patron. I knew you wouldn't like that."

"Really?" Dara's heart beat faster. "What were you going to say?"

Siv glanced around. People in the stands had noticed them talking, and they were pointing and chattering behind their hands. The two princesses watched them with bright eyes.

"I don't want to distract you or make you mad," Siv said. "I'll talk to you after you win the championship, okay?"

"Okay. I'll hold you to that."

"You should." Siv grinned and executed a perfect salute with an imaginary blade. "Cut her down, Dara Nightfall. This bout is yours."

The horns rang out again. Cheers and shouts erupted around the stadium. It was time.

Dara took her place at one end of the championship strip, which sat on a raised platform directly in front of the royal box. She felt flush with triumph and anticipation, but not enough to distract her from the bout. She placed the Savven blade beside the strip. Her good luck charm.

Dara strode to the center of the platform and shook Vine's hand firmly. Sweat glistened on Vine's forehead, and her dark eyes were fierce and determined. Theatrics aside, she would give Dara a good bout. She strutted back to the starting line, still prancing for the crowds.

A profound calm descended on Dara as she saluted Vine, the officials, and the spectators. She gave an extra salute to the royal box. Selivia dug her fingers into her cheeks, the swirls of paint smudged beyond recognition, and bounced up and down on her seat. Soraline had a death grip on the crumpled black banner in her lap. Siv winked at her and smiled.

"Let's see what you've got, Dara Nightfall!" Vine called.

"You will."

The official stepped forward. The spectators held their breath as one.

"On guard."

Dara was ready. She had worked too hard for this. She was going to win.

Vine tossed her hair.

The official raised his arms.

"Ready?"

Dara lifted the tip of her blade, settling into the guard position she knew so well. No matter what Siv was going to say to her afterwards, this bout was hers.

The official took a deep breath. "Du—"

Someone screamed, shattering the silence in the stands. Shouts filtered through the back of the audience, confused and distressed. The official hesitated, hands still raised. Dara didn't move, trying not to listen to whatever the crowds were shouting.

But then guardsmen began to run into the dueling hall, their boots thundering on the stands. People were standing, looking around, trying to figure out what was going on.

Then one voice shouted above the others.

"The king is dead! Someone killed King Sevren!"

THE DUEL

CHAOS tumbled through the arena. Shouts. Pandemonium. Cries of anguish. Dara only felt confusion. It didn't make sense. It had to be a trick. A bad joke. The mountain was peaceful. Assassinations were for the Lands Below. This couldn't happen in Vertigon.

Castle Guards surrounded the three young Amintelles up in the royal box. Siv and his sisters sat stunned, disbelieving. Dara could see their stricken faces through the guards sweeping around them. Then they were being ushered out of their seats, pushed toward the exit.

There was something strange about those men. They wore the Castle Guard uniform, but Dara didn't recognize any of them. Were they *all* new? Where was Pool?

"I'm afraid we will have to postpone the duel," the official was saying. But Dara didn't wait for him to finish. She started toward the royal box.

"Wait!" Vine called. Dara ignored her. There would be no more dueling today.

"Siv!" she shouted.

The prince didn't hear her. He looked rattled, fractured, but

270

he put one arm around each sister and pulled them close as the guardsmen guided the three of them out of the royal box. One of the guards pushed back onlookers with bony limbs, stretched out like tree branches.

Dara dropped her competition weapon to the floor with a clang and dashed back to the strip to snatch up the Savven blade. She had recognized that bony guard leading the young royals away after all.

It was Farr, dressed as a Castle Guard. Something was very wrong.

Farr and three other guards formed a tight cluster around the royal family and rushed them out of the dueling hall. Dara hurtled after them. Spectators and other duelists lurched in front of her, asking what was going on as if she were some sort of authority. She forced through the crowd, snapping at anyone who got in her way, but she soon lost sight of her quarry. Panic spiked in her heart.

She finally broke through to the outer doors, where more crowds gathered, their faces worried and mournful. Dara scanned the streets and staircase leading away from the arena. She caught a glimpse of Siv and his sisters again. The guards were hurrying them down the street, too far ahead. People stood aside to let them pass, calling out questions in their wake.

"Is it true?"

"Where is the king?"

"It cannot be!"

At the far end of the road a steep staircase climbed upward toward the castle. But instead of taking the royal family up, the four guards gathered in closer and shepherded them downward. Dara hurried toward them. They were too far ahead, and they were going the wrong way.

"Hey!" Siv's voice rose on the wind. "Take us to the castle. We have to see our father."

The lead guard shook his head.

"You must come with us."

Dara broke into a run, drawing the Savven blade. The sheath clattered to the cobblestones.

"I said go to the castle," Siv commanded.

Instead of obeying, the guards wrenched the princesses away from their brother. Sora screamed. Selivia sobbed and struggled against Farr, who held her by both arms. Two guards moved in closer to Siv. One drew something from his belt. Metal glinted.

"What's the meaning of this?" Siv shouted.

"The king is dead," the man growled. "You are next." He raised his arm, a large knife clutched in his fist, and lunged toward the prince before he could react.

Dara hurled herself down the steps. At the last instant, she sliced her blade between Siv and his attacker. The man let out a bloodcurdling scream, and his knife dropped to the ground. His hand dropped with it.

Sora shrieked. The man whose hand Dara had cut off teetered backwards, stumbling farther down the steep stairs.

Siv wasted no time. He punched Sora's captor and pulled her away as he fell to the ground. Siv pushed his sister up the stairs.

"Run, Sora!"

Then he tackled her captor before he could draw a weapon.

Farr was dragging Selivia farther down the winding stone steps. The hem of her skirt bloomed red with the blood of the man cradling the stump of his arm.

The final guard stalked closer to Dara, blocking her way. He had golden-brown hair, longer than the standard Castle Guard cut, and he had the lean, powerful look of a seasoned duelist. He drew a rapier from his belt. It was deadly sharp and edged with a thin, burning strip of gold. A Fire Blade.

Dara raised the Savven.

Siv swore as he slammed into the wall of a nearby

greathouse, exchanging shoves and punches with Sora's erstwhile captor, but Dara kept her focus on the man with the rapier. He moved smoothly, comfortable with the deadly weapon in his hand.

Though tired from the competition, Dara's senses sharpened like a razor. She studied her opponent's stance, his exploratory taps at her blade. He moved well, but his weapon was thicker than the Savven blade, heavier. She would use that.

Dara attacked. The clang of steel against Fire-infused steel rang over the mountain as the swordsman parried. His riposte missed her by a hair. Dara retreated then counter-attacked as the swordsman lunged for her again. Fast as lightning, he blocked her hit. His lip curled in contempt.

Dara had the higher ground, but it was hard to move on the steps. She held the swordsman off, jabbing at his face when he got too close. She could still see Farr beyond her opponent, holding Selivia by the arm and trying to drag her down the steps. The princess went limp, forcing him to bend down to lift her dead weight.

Dara bounced on the balls of her feet, looking for an opening in the swordsman's defenses.

Behind her, Siv managed to subdue his man with a heavy-handed punch to the jaw. As the guardsman crumpled to the ground, Siv scrambled back down the steps and plucked the knife from the grip of the severed hand on the ground. Then, still breathing heavily from the scuffle, he took a position beside Dara. They faced the swordsman side by side.

They didn't speak, didn't need to. Siv edged one way, Dara the other, then they both attacked.

The Fire Blade blurred with unnatural speed. The swordsman met their combined assault, somehow managing to block both Dara's sword and Siv's knife. He retreated downward another step, awaiting their next move.

The man was outnumbered, but all he had to do was hold

them off. Selivia and her captor were getting farther away despite her efforts to slow him down. They would be beyond reach soon. This had to end now.

"I'll handle this guy," Siv grunted. "Get Sel."

"Take the Savven," Dara said. The prince wouldn't stand a chance if he tried to fight a true swordsman with a knife.

She retreated a few steps and moved the hilt of her blade toward the prince so he could take it from her. As soon as she opened her guard, their opponent lunged for her exposed wrist. She knew he would fall for the feint. She countered with a sudden shot to his upper arm, a pure sport dueling move. The Savven bit into him. The man cursed.

Siv took the opportunity to hurl the knife directly at his heart.

The swordsman's eyes widened as the blade pierced his body. He dropped the sword from his injured arm and clutched at the hilt sticking out of his chest, disbelief painting his face white.

"Now get Sel," the prince said, jumping forward to grab the fallen sword. "And keep the Savven! I'll make sure Sora's safe."

Without hesitation, Dara ran headlong down the steps after the fleeing pair. She caught a glimpse of the princess's skirt swishing around a corner as they left the stone staircase and rushed along a wooden walkway bordering a quiet row of houses. The pounding of their steps echoed across the Gorge.

They were going in the direction of the Fire Guild. *It can't be!*

Farr was taking Selivia to the Fireworkers. Farr, a known ally of Dara's parents. Farr, the young man who had become such a big supporter of the Ruminors at the Guild of late.

The princess screamed for help. Dara ran faster, despite the shock hammering through her.

The Fire Guild was immense. They would disappear into it.

Dara would never be able to save the princess unless she reached them before they got through the doors. But they were too far ahead. She had to do something.

She clutched blindly at the Spark growing inside her, the connection to the power of the mountain that she barely knew how to use. She drew on her fear, her adrenaline, every ounce of focus she had saved up for the Cup championship.

At first nothing happened. She was running on wood, with no time to gather residual power from the stones of the mountain. But the wall beside the boardwalk was lined with Fire Lanterns. Ruminor Fire Lanterns. Dara knew what she had to do. She needed a conduit. The Savven. It would have to work.

Dara stabbed the blade upward, piercing one of the Fire Lanterns as though it were the head of a practice dummy. She yanked the power contained in the core along the blade and into her body. She gasped at the prick of heat as it was injected into her blood. Then Dara curled the Fire into a tiny molten ball inside her and hurled it forward, out of her body and up the sword. It gathered a coating of molten metal as it blazed along the blade. Then she whipped it forward, like flicking a zur-wasp off the tip of her sword.

The little bead of Fire and steel struck Farr on the back of the head and stuck to his scalp, burning a ring in his hair. He cursed and stumbled in surprise. Selivia fell to the ground. Farr spun around, bewildered. He would know someone had just attacked him with Fire.

"Let her go," Dara yelled.

"Dara?" Farr said, facing her across the walkway. "Don't you know this is part of the plan? I have my orders from your fa—"

"No!"

Dara pulled. She wasn't sure how she did it without direct contact with a steel conduit, but she yanked the bead of Fire and hardening steel back toward her. It passed straight through

Farr's skull on its way to her. His eyes widened for an instant, then the life went out of them like a candle being extinguished. He fell.

Dara caught the bead of Fire in her palm and dropped to her knees. She crawled across the rickety boards to the wall and forced the bead of Fire into the stones with trembling hands, leaving the steel residue behind like a thumbprint. Horror filled her. It couldn't be true. Her father couldn't be the one behind all this. Not Rafe Ruminor, the city's most respected practitioner of the Fire Arts. He couldn't have ordered the prince and princess to be kidnapped, perhaps killed. He couldn't have been involved in the murder of the king.

Selivia was sobbing incoherently. She didn't seem to have followed the exchange between Dara and Farr, who now lay dead beside her. *Dead.* At Dara's hands.

Dara approached them on trembling legs. She took Selivia's arm and helped her up.

"We have to get back to the castle," she said urgently. "There may be more of them."

"You stabbed him?" Selivia gasped.

"You're safe now," Dara said, choosing not to correct her. "That's all that matters. Quickly."

"Are Sora and Siv okay?"

"They're fine. We need to move, Princess."

"It's not true about my father, is it?" Selivia said. "He can't be dead."

"I don't know," Dara said. Her heart constricted in her chest at the sorrow and pain on the young princess's face. This had been Dara's father's doing. He had been the one all along. She made herself look down at Farr's blank face before she walked away.

They hurried back along the boardwalk. They had to get far away from the dead Fireworker before someone spotted them.

If her father found out she had been the one to thwart his plans
... Dara was afraid to follow that line of thought.

They climbed back up the stone staircase. Siv was waiting
for them, his eye turning purple from the fistfight. He held the
man whose hand had been cut off in a headlock. A trail of
blood splattered on the steps indicated he had tried to crawl
away. He fell unconscious from Siv's headlock as Dara and
Selivia approached.

The man Siv had punched was still out cold. The
swordsman with the golden-brown hair lay dead on the stairs,
his comrade's knife still sticking out of his chest. Sora sat a few
steps up, knees pulled up to her chest. Siv had given her the
Fire Blade, and she was pointing it at the dead man as if she
was afraid he'd rise again.

Selivia cried harder when she saw her brother and sister.
She dove into Sora's arms and sobbed into her shoulder. Siv
met Dara's eyes, full of grief and gratitude. Without speaking,
she lowered the Savven and sat on the stones beside him,
helping him keep watch over the unconscious men.

Pool and a host of Castle Guards found them moments
later. None of the more recent hires were among them. They
took charge of the two living prisoners and spread out to search
for additional threats.

Pool's face was thunderous, and he had a bandage hastily
wrapped around an ugly wound in his side.

"We have been betrayed!" Pool said. "The Guard is compromised. Heads will roll in the very literal sense of the word. Is
that Dara Ruminor?"

"She saved me," Selivia said.

"You are most fortunate to have such a competent protector.
As for this blackguard," Pool kicked the unconscious man, "he
is one of the offending treacherous men in our cohort. When I
find the remaining traitors responsible for this grievous—"

Siv stood, and Pool stopped speaking abruptly.

"Is it true?" Siv said. His face was grave, and he looked ten years older in that moment.

Pool inclined his head.

"I am sorry, my prince," he said. "Your father is dead."

THE KING

SIV walked through mist toward the castle. Twilight descended over Vertigon. Cold wind swept around the little group as they climbed and climbed. The air crackled with electricity, promising one hell of a storm.

Shouts rang over the mountain. Siv's people were still unsure what had happened this day. The guards murmured amongst themselves, tense and wary. One of their prisoners moaned but didn't manage to regain consciousness. It didn't matter. There'd be time to question him later.

Siv's sisters had stopped crying. Both were breathing in shuddering, shocked gasps. They clung to his sleeves, which were dampened with mist and the blood of his attacker. They clung as if Siv could protect them from the truth they were about to face.

He kept his eyes turned toward the castle. Lights blazed in the tall windows as night fell slowly around them.

Dara walked behind them. He could sense her, even though he didn't turn his gaze from the castle. She was a solid, warm presence at his back. A burning torch in the darkness.

They had been betrayed. Pool explained it as they trudged

onward. The new company of Castle Guards Bandobar had hired were false. The traitorous guardsmen had subdued Pool and the Hurling twins and taken over their posts at the Cup, along with additional conspirators dressed in Amintelle colors. As soon as the news of the king's death reached the arena, they had whisked Siv and his sisters away. The news had struck Siv dumb, blinding him to the fact that some of the men escorting them were strangers. Dara hadn't fallen for it, though.

And his father. His father had dropped dead over his noon tea. Poisoned. Siv had always known that was the greatest danger to his family. Not swordsmen. Not duelists he could best if he trained hard enough. A sneaking, treacherous drop of death.

When they reached the gates of the castle, the mists had settled in, thick like smoke. Bandobar, his father's friend and guard, stood before them.

He dropped to his knees on the stones and held out the hilt of his sword. Siv knew what Bandobar expected him to do. Bandobar had failed. His king, his friend, had fallen. He had hired untrustworthy men. He hadn't protected the lives in his charge.

Bandobar's face showed no fear as Siv took the sword from his grasp.

Siv studied the blade as the mist swirled around them. It was a Fire Blade, like the one borne by the swordsman he and Dara had fought, the one he had killed. It could be wielded faster and more accurately than a cold steel weapon. Bandobar had carried it with honor for decades. But it hadn't been enough.

"Please," Bandobar said. He stretched out his arms, leaving his chest and throat exposed.

Selivia started crying again. A chill wind whipped across Siv's face. He remembered what his father had said about wisdom, about the mantle of responsibility for which he should have been prepared.

"Please, Sivarrion," Bandobar said, using his name the same way his father always had. "Do it."

Siv stared at Bandobar for a long time. Then he lowered the blade to the stones.

"Go," he said. "I will spare your life. Leave Vertigon before first light."

Siv walked past the man on his knees without waiting for his reaction and entered his castle. The entrance hall loomed eerily, unfamiliar now that everything had changed. Decorations from the feast still adorned the walls, and foliage wilted in vases by the windows. The lighted space was at odds with the mist surrounding the castle, but it held no comfort. An unearthly keening came from somewhere deeper in the castle. The queen.

Shuffling footsteps sounded, and Zage Lorrid hurried into the entryway from the Great Hall. Pool raised his sword as if he wasn't sure whether or not Zage was a threat. Dara tensed too, clutching her Savven blade.

Siv didn't move. He recognized the stricken expression on Zage's normally impassive face: grief. The man looked as distraught as Siv felt.

"My prince," Zage said. "I am so sorry."

"Where is my mother?" Siv said, fighting to keep his voice calm.

"A few of my trusted associates are escorting the queen to her royal chambers. I've asked them to administer a sleeping draught. Is that acceptable?"

"Yes," Siv said. "Sora, Sel. Will you go to her?"

"What about you?" Sora asked.

"I have work to do," he said. "Stay in Mother's rooms tonight. I'll join you when I'm done."

He hugged each of his sisters quickly, hardly able to look at their heartrending faces. They went with a pair of guards, who were personally dispatched by Pool. His side was still bleeding, and he looked ready to drop. There would be time enough for that later.

Siv turned back to Zage, who waited like a looming bat.

"Tell me."

"Your father's body has been moved to the dais in the Great Hall," Zage said. The man's dry, whispering voice was a comfort as the damp of the mist chilled Siv's bones. "A spark of Fire was visible in each iris for a few moments after his death." Zage took a shuddering breath, like a death rattle. "Cause of death was a concentrated dosage of Firetears."

Dara shifted her feet on the tile floor.

"Firetears take effect within anywhere from one to four hours, depending upon the strength of the dosage," Zage said. "Your father had several meetings this morning with assorted dignitaries, nobles, and Fireworkers. Any one of them could have been responsible for the poisoning, if it wasn't one of the servants. Everyone who handled your father's meals today has already been taken into custody."

"Understood. We will make sure Vertigon is secure before beginning the investigation. Send me General Pavorran. Bandobar is gone. Pool now leads the Castle Guard."

"Very well. And there's the other matter—"

"I know." Siv felt an iron band tightening around his chest. Vertigon's kings were always crowned immediately in the presence of their deceased predecessor's body. They could not leave the mountain without a ruler even for a day. As the next king, he would pledge himself to the service of Vertigon that very night. "We'll uphold the tradition. Call for the required number of noble witnesses. No Rollendars, no Zurrens, and no one who met with my father today."

"Sir." Zage drew his cloak closer around him like a blanket, suffering still evident on his face. He had served the king for years. He loved him. Any suspicions Siv briefly held of Zage faded as the grief-stricken man swept away into the shadows.

Siv turned to Dara. "Wait for me?"

She inclined her head, eyes burning with sorrow. Siv wanted to hug her, to seek out her warmth, but he could not allow his own sorrow to reign. It was time to take up his crown.

Siv straightened his back and strode into the Great Hall.

CASTLE GUARD

D ARA waited in the castle entryway as midnight neared. Beyond the double doors, the tables of the Great Hall were draped in black. On the dais where King Sevren had so recently offered his hand to his wife for a dance, his body lay, cold and lifeless.

Dara knew her father was responsible. She knew it as surely as her own name. Farr's words on the boardwalk had been unmistakable. Farr, Lima, and Rafe had been working on something big at the Fire Guild for weeks. Dara had been too wrapped up in her own schemes to pay attention to what they were doing. And they had stopped asking her to be involved when word got out that she had protected the prince. They hinted more than once that something was going on, but she had assumed they were working against the Fire Warden, not that they themselves were the ones planning to take down the king.

That morning her father had said things would be different after today. He wasn't talking about the Cup at all. It was Rafe Ruminor, not Zage Lorrid, who plotted treason. He was the one with the most to gain from the demise of the Amintelles and their long-held policy of restricting the Fire. He still resented the king for pardoning Zage Lorrid, for not bringing him to justice for Renna's death. He must have decided that rather than kill Zage and have another Amintelle-appointed Warden take his place, he would change the whole balance of power in the kingdom. He had started with King Sevren and his children.

Dara thought back to that morning in the kitchen. Her father had carried an object in his pocket that glowed with concentrated Fire. She'd thought it was something innocuous, like a Firestick, and she'd worried about letting on that she could draw the Fire from it. But what if it wasn't so harmless after all? Dara had seen a bottle of Firetears once. It had been as bright as the core of a Fire Lantern.

Whether her father had been the one to deliver the poison or not, there was no denying he was involved after what Farr had said. It made sense that he and Lima would be at the core of the plot. But part of his plan had gone awry. Dara had arrived in time to prevent the capture and murder of the king's children. The Fireworkers' efforts to remove the entire royal family in one day had failed. If the royal children had fallen, he might have made his next move. He might have shaken the very stones of the mountain with Fire and thunder.

Instead, Sivarrion Amintelle was being crowned king that very night.

Siv had asked Dara to wait for him. She couldn't go home and face her father after what she had discovered. Everything would be different after this night. And so she waited. She sat cross-legged outside the Great Hall as servants, guards, and nobles darted back and forth, their voices echoing around the cavernous entry hall. Fear and frenzy reigned. Nothing like this had happened in a hundred years. Siv directed the chaos from the dais where his father's body lay, taking charge of the castle and the crown. And Dara waited.

When the preparations were complete, a handful of nobles gathered to witness the coronation of their new ruler. The rite only required the presence of ten members of noble houses, and they arrived without ceremony. Lords Roven and Nanning. Lady Denmore. A few others. Vine Silltine was one of them, resplendent in black. Her aged father hobbled beside her. She acknowledged Dara waiting in the corridor with a nod, but she didn't speak to her.

Dara stayed in the entrance hall until the ceremony was over. Vertigon tradition required that the new king be crowned immediately beside the body of the old. It was not their way to waste too much time with pomp and circumstance. The king was dead. Long live the king. Dara couldn't help but think it a cruel tradition. She wondered what Siv was feeling as he stood before the body of the father he loved and accepted his crown.

When it was all over and the nobles had left, Pool came for her. His face was pale, and blood had crusted over the bandaged wound in his side. Dara had learned that several old Guardsmen were killed when the new recruits turned against them. Pool was luckier than some.

"He is ready for you, Miss Ruminor."

"How is he?"

Pool shook his head sadly. "He is our king."

Dara gripped the hilt of her Savven blade for strength and followed Pool into the Great Hall.

Siv sat on the steps of the dais with his back to his father's body. He twirled the Amintelle crown between his long fingers, a ring of burnished silver set with Firejewels. The hall was still. Moonlight peeked through the tall windows. It was a clear night above the low veil of mist, unusual for this time of year.

"Your Majesty." Dara bowed before the new king, turning her feet at right angles so it was more like a dueling salute than a curtsy. "I . . . I'm sorry for your loss."

"I have something to ask you," Siv said. His eyes were dry,

his face the most serious Dara had ever seen it. It was heart-breaking.

"Anything, Your Majesty."

"You saved me again today. Me and my sisters."

"Your Majesty—"

"Please don't call me that," he said softly, sounding sad and restrained. "Siv is still fine, even though everything else has to be different."

King Sevren's body seemed to glow in the moonlight. It loomed behind the prince—the new king. Dara remembered how King Sevren had clapped an affectionate hand on his son's shoulder at the Cup Feast, how Siv always spoke so warmly of his father. And now he was gone.

"What can I do?" she whispered.

"The Castle Guard is compromised. I don't know how deep the treachery goes. I want you to be one of my guards, to help me protect my family and my . . . my kingdom." Siv looked up and met her eyes steadily. Somehow, she knew this wasn't what he had been planning to ask her in those bright, happy moments before the final bout at the competition. It was hard to believe it was still the same day. "I need you, Dara. I'm sorry I can't offer you anything else now."

A terrible guilt cut into Dara at the sight of the naked grief in Siv's eyes. Whatever she had hoped they would have together had been stolen from them along with his father. She wanted to tell him how she felt about him, how she would do anything to bring him the same joy he had given her over the past few months. But the guilt held her back. Her father had caused this. Her father had taken away the man Siv loved and admired more than anyone in the world. Sevren, The Good King. The good man.

But why? That was the real question. Was it pure vengeance for Renna's death, or did he want to rule the mountain like the Firewielders of old? An image of her father striding through the castle, his eyes brimming with Fire and blood, flashed before her, filling her with dread. What would he do next?

"The job wouldn't leave much time for sport dueling," Siv said when she didn't answer him. "I know how important that is to you, but I need someone I can trust at my side."

Dara's heartbeat caused her physical pain. Her father had taken the joy and humor from Siv's eyes. She would do anything to keep anyone, even her father, from taking his life. She had been selfish for too long, wrapped up in her own desires and goals. She should have seen it coming, should have paid more attention. She would give up the world to atone for it now.

"I'll do it." Dara knelt on the cold floor and presented the hilt of the Savven blade. "I pledge my life to protect you and your family."

Siv stared at her for a moment.

"Are you sure, Dara? You can say no. Dueling is your dream."

"I'm sure. I will serve on your Guard." She swallowed but kept her voice steady. "I swear to defend you against all threats. I will give my life to guard yours. You won't do this alone."

"Thank you." Siv put one hand on top of the Savven hilt and the other over Dara's hand, holding it firm around the grip. His fingers tightened on hers, and gratitude and sadness and determination fought their way across his face. "I accept your service and appoint you, Dara Ruminor, Castle Guardian."

Siv released Dara's hand. She stood and saluted with the Savven blade. Moonlight flashed on the night-black steel. She would protect this man, the Fourth Good King. And she would find out the truth about King Sevren's death.

No matter what it took, she would pay for what her father had done.

EPILOGUE

BERG Doban waited in the shadows outside the castle. He listened to the rumbling in the streets as news and rumors, grief and anger made their way through the people of Vertigon. Berg clenched his fists as if he could beat back the descending darkness. He had lived on the mountain for nearly twenty years. It was his refuge, his place of peace after the fractured, war-torn life he had led before fleeing his homeland. But the man who had made it so was dead.

A dark figure stumbled down the steps from the castle, weaponless and reeling. As Berg watched, the man tore off his coat, marked with the Amintelle sigil, and threw it to the ground. His shape was familiar, even slumped in grief.

Berg stepped out of the shadows and into his path.

"Bandobar," he growled.

The man looked up, anguish and despair on his face.

"Doban?"

"Tell me true."

"Sevren is gone," Bandobar said. Berg nodded, accepting the weight of the mountain as it settled on his big, square shoulders.

"And the children?"

"All three survived. Your student was with them. You were right about her."

"Yes," Berg said shortly. Dara wouldn't let him down. Despite her parents, despite her faults, Dara was good. Putting her in the company of the prince was the only way he knew to save him. And to save her.

"But what of the king?"

"Fireteaars," Bandobar said bitterly. "I didn't catch them in time. The children were taken by some of my guardsmen, aided by imposters. I did not inspect the men thoroughly enough. I failed."

"I saw one of the dead attackers," Berg said. "He was one of those we saw training in the caverns. It is as we feared."

"A true swordsman?"

"Yes," Berg said. "I saw the wounds. My students bested him."

Bandobar nodded. Mist and darkness swirled across his craggy face. He had grown old in the past few hours.

"But will they be strong enough for what is coming?"

"This I do not know," Berg growled. "They must be."

"I pray it will be so," Bandobar said. "But I failed my king. Sivarrion would spare me, but you must know that is not the way. Will you give me justice?"

Berg nodded. This was why he had waited in the shadows. Bandobar was a man of honor, not one to accept exile when he had failed. He wouldn't be able to live with himself anyway.

It pained him, but Berg would do it. He owed it to Bandobar after their many years working together to protect the king and his family. He would do whatever he had to for the son of Sevren Amintelle, no matter the cost. He had a debt to pay.

"The sword or the bridge?" he asked.

"The sword." Bandobar didn't hesitate.

Berg drew the sharpened blade from the sheath at his waist. Bandobar stood before him, arms held wide.

"You must protect them, Doban," he said. "And continue to teach them as you have been. The fate of Vertigon depends on it."

"Yes, my friend," Berg said. Then he drove the point of the sword through Bandobar's heart.

ACKNOWLEDGMENTS

Thank you for reading *Duel of Fire*! In the five years since this book was first released, I've had a wonderful time getting to know you all. Thank you for your reviews, fan art, and notes of encouragement. Your support for this series means more to me than I can express in writing. I truly couldn't do this without you.

I'd like to thank the people who gave me feedback and advice when I first started this series and who have continued to be there for me in the years since. They include Sarah Merrill Mowat, Brooke Richter, Rachel Andrews, Willow Hewitt, Laura Cook, Jennifer Deayton, Amanda Tong, Betsy Cheung, Rachel Malham, James Young, and Ayden and Julie Young. Special thanks to my first editor, Marcus Trower, who taught me so much and is gone too soon.

Thank you to the fencers in my life for the good times, inspiration, and *Princess Bride* movie nights. Thank you, Kimberly Young, for checking the details and giving me some great lines for Coach Berg.

On the publishing side, I'd like to thank Susie and Lynn at Red Adept Editing, Rick Gualtieri, and my wonderful audiobook narrator, Caitlin Kelly, who brings these characters to life. The team at Deranged Doctor Design are responsible for the original covers and the show-stopping new designs for the special edition hardbacks. Thank you for making my books so beautiful!

As always, I'm grateful to the most important people in my life: my husband, my family, and the staff at my local Starbucks. I love you all.

And again, thank *you* for reading. I'm so glad you decided to spend a little time with these characters. I hope you enjoy the sequel!

If you want to receive a free 50-page story featuring Berg Doban and King Sevren, kindly sign up for my mailing list at JordanRivet.com. You will also get discounts when new books launch.

Now, I hope you'll keep reading for a bonus story that only appears in this special edition!

Jordan Rivet
Hong Kong, 2021

DARA'S FIRST DUEL

The door was locked when Dara arrived at the dueling hall. She squinted at the rising sun, which had barely crested the flat top of Square Peak. The tournament wasn't supposed to start for hours, but Dara hadn't wanted miss any part of her first real competition.

She pulled on the heavy wooden door in case it was stuck, bracing her feet against the stone foundation.

"You are late."

Dara spun on her heel at the sound of her coach's voice. "What? I thought the first round wasn't until midday! I'm sorry I didn't mean to—"

"Is okay, young Dara. I am only joking."

"Oh. Right." Dara bounced on her toes as Berg Doban strode up the steep path to meet her. She'd been taking group classes with Coach Berg for two years, and she was still a little afraid of him. He was a big, square man from the Lands Below, with a quick temper, gravelly voice, and high standards. His jokes were rare—and always unexpected.

He peered at her in the dawn light. "Why are you coming here so early?"

"I didn't want to miss anything."

"Hmm." He rubbed the gray stubble on his chin and glanced at the path meandering past the dueling school toward a row of shops. "I am still needing my breakfast."

"Go ahead," Dara said quickly. "I can wait here."

"Do not let your muscles get too cold."

"Yes, Coach!"

He stomped off toward a nearby pie shop, leaving Dara jogging in place by the dueling school. It wasn't much to look at, just a big gray box made of local stone, its broad windows covered in unpainted shutters. Dara had hoped Berg would let her inside to do some drills with a practice dummy, but he hadn't looked quite awake yet.

Might as well do footwork while I wait. She picked a spot where the slope wasn't too steep and dropped into the guard position Coach Berg had taught her—bent knees, feet at right angles, right arm partly extended. She took a deep breath, imagining an opponent before her, and began.

Advance. Retreat. Advance. Lunge.

She settled into a rhythm, her boots scraping the dirt. Her long golden braid swung against her back as she shuffled forward and backward. Footwork was satisfying in its own way, but she couldn't wait to compete for real. She wanted to show Coach Berg what she could do. So far, she hadn't distinguished herself in the large group classes, and she hadn't gotten up the nerve to ask her parents to pay for private lessons.

She'd told them she was competing today, and she hoped they'd make the trek across the bridge to see her. Her father was the one who'd suggested she take dueling classes, but he tended to get lost in his work in the Fireshop beneath their house. Her mother thought dueling was frivolous. Maybe she'd feel differently if she saw Dara win a tournament.

She picked up her pace, twisting her empty hand this way and that to try out the parries she'd been learning. She didn't own a dueling sword yet. She'd use one of the school's weapons as soon as Coach Berg returned and let her inside.

"Oi! New girl!"

Dara turned as a pair of boys from her dueling class sauntered up the path toward her. One was even taller and gawkier than her, and the other was as small and wiry as a mountain goat. The smaller boy, Kel, was the one who'd called out to her.

"I'm not new," Dara said. "I've been in your class for a year."

Kel chuckled. "That counts."

"Are you here to help out?" asked the taller boy, whose name was Oat.

"With what?"

"Coach has us sweep the school and get the fire going before competitions to earn extra lessons."

"Really? Can anyone do that?" If Dara could pay for her own lessons, maybe her parents would agree to buy her real dueling gear.

"Not so fast." Kel gave her a mischievous grin. "First you have to answer a riddle."

"What kind of riddle?"

"A dueling riddle, obviously."

Dara frowned. "And if I get it right, Coach will let me work in exchange for private lessons?"

Kel's grin widened. "Exactly."

Oat gave him a shove. "Don't tease her, Kel."

"I'm not!"

"There's no riddle," Oat said. "Anyone can help with the setup."

Dara looked at Kel, confused. "So you made that up? To mess with me?"

"You don't need to take it so seriously. Sheesh. Haven't you ever heard of banter?" Kel moved forward to unlock the door to the school, and Oat gave Dara a sympathetic look.

She avoided his gaze, cheeks burning. She couldn't always

tell when people were teasing her. Even if they didn't mean to be cruel, she hated feeling like everyone was in on the joke except for her. She wasn't going to let these boys get away with it.

I'll beat them in today's tournament. They'd *have* to take her seriously then.

∼

The dueling school was cavernous inside and smelled of sweat and boot leather. Trunks were arranged along one wall, where the students could stash their gear, and dueling strips were marked on the floor. A rack of rapiers sat across from the main entrance, the battered bell guards catching the morning light.

Kel started building a fire while Oat grabbed a pair of brooms from the corner and handed one to Dara. They set to work on the vast stone floor, sweeping up the dust and ash that could hamper their footwork during the competition. It was as good a warm-up as any.

"I've seen you in class," Oat said shyly as they worked their way down the competition strips. "You've got good form."

"Thanks." Dara glanced at the gangly boy, who had dark hair and a good-natured smile. "You have great point control."

Oat rolled his shoulders. "Coach keeps telling me I can't rely on my height the whole time. He says the other boys will catch up to me soon."

Dara wasn't so sure about that. Most of the men in Vertigon probably weren't as tall as Oat, and he couldn't be older than thirteen. "How many competitions have you done?"

"This'll be my third. You?"

"It's my first."

Oat's face brightened. "No way. Hey, Kel! It's Dara's first tournament."

"Why didn't you say so?" Kel jogged over to join them,

brushing ash from his hands onto the freshly swept floor. "You know, the entry fee for a tournament is three sweetened salt cakes and a soldarberry tart from—" He ducked as Oat swung a broom at him. "Okay, okay. No teasing."

Dara didn't want them to think she was gullible, but it would be worse if they thought she needed people to stand up for her. She summoned her courage. "I'll bet you each a salt cake I can beat you in the rankings today."

The two boys looked at her in surprise. Dara sensed she'd said something wrong—or at least foolish.

"Uh, Dara," Oat said gently. "It's your first tournament. Most people don't win any bouts their first time. You're only getting experience."

"Let the girl bet." Kel studied Dara through narrowed eyes. "I've seen her in class. I reckon she has a chance."

Dara tightened her grip on her broom and met his gaze defiantly. "Or you're just desperate for a salt cake."

Kel laughed. "Or that. Tell you what. If you finish ahead of either of us, all the salt cakes are on me."

Dara stuck out a hand. "You're on."

They finished cleaning the dueling hall and freshened up the lines on the floor marking the competition strips. Coach Berg returned, licking pie grease off his fingers and looking only slightly more awake than the last time Dara had seen him. She didn't have time to ask about the free private lessons before a chattering group of older students arrived to help officiate the youth tournament. Some were real professional duelists Dara had watched from the stands at major tournaments.

"That's Bilzar Ten." Kel pointed out a particularly handsome young man. "I hear he's already had two different coaches."

"He worked with Surri," Dara said. "The first woman ever to win the Vertigon Cup."

"Wouldn't it be grand to compete in the Cup?" Oat asked.

Dara imagined the roar of the crowds at the biggest dueling hall on King's Peak, the lightning-fast moves, the athletes who were as popular as King Sevren himself. "I hope I get good enough for that someday."

Soon, the other competitors began pouring through the doors. Some were Dara's classmates, like Oat and Kel, and the rest were students from youth classes at the other dueling schools around Vertigon. There would be no adult or advanced divisions at this competition and no hefty prize purses. This tournament was strictly for amateurs.

Dara picked out her favorite weapon and white competition jacket from the school's stash, then she did more footwork as a cacophony of stomping feet and anxious chatter filled the hall. She was too nervous to register the other competitors as more than white-clad blurs carrying clattering bundles of swords, masks tucked under their arms. She focused on the heat in her muscles and the scrape of her boots on the floor, trying to remember everything she'd learned in her classes so far.

When it was time to begin, the officials gathered everyone together and explained the rules. This competition was designed to maximize the number of bouts the young duelists would have. They'd compete in three rounds of six-person pools, where they'd fight all the people in their pool in bouts to five points. After each round, the competitors would be divided into new pools based on their performance, and they'd again fight all the people in their pool in five-point bouts. By the end of the third round, every duelist in the competition would have fought fifteen five-point bouts. The top four competitors would then fight ten-point bouts to determine the overall winners. It was a different format from the elimination rounds they'd find in more advanced competitions.

"The purpose is to give you all as much tournament experience as possible," explained Bilzar Ten. "You also won't have any duelists from your own school in the first round. After that, it'll depend on your results."

While Bilzar fielded questions, Dara scanned the group of adults gathered at one side of the hall. Berg's school wasn't set up to host spectators, but some of the duelists' parents had come to watch their children. Dara's mother and father weren't among them.

Shoving down her disappointment, Dara wished Oat and Kel luck and went to join her first pool.

Most of her competitors were already at their dueling strip near one of the large windows. The other young duelists tested the bends of their weapons and tightened the laces on their boots, chattering animatedly. Dara set down her mask and blade in the corner, too nervous to introduce herself to anyone.

An official with sword calluses on his hands arrived to announce the first bout.

"Dara Ruminor. You're up against Luci Belling."

Dara quickly dabbed charcoal on the blunted end of her sword and jogged to the center of the strip. She shook hands with a slim girl with bronze hair, who gave her a friendly smile. A bronze-haired man who must be Luci's father watched proudly from the sidelines.

"Good luck," Luci said.

"You too." Dara's voice came out as a croak.

They saluted and put on wire mesh masks to protect their faces. Dara's breathing quickened, and her blade felt unusually heavy. This was it. Her first bout in her first real competition.

The official took his place beside the strip and raised his hands. "On guard."

Dara's heart pounded.

"Ready?"

Her hands shook.

"Duel!"

Dara launched forward and threw herself into a deep lunge. The blunted tip of her blade hit Luci's shoulder with a loud *thwack*.

"Point! One, zero to Ruminor."

The vibration went right up Dara's arm, resonating like a hit during practice never had before. A neat charcoal dot had appeared on Luci's white jacket.

Dara smiled and retreated to the starting line. Already, her nerves were abating. She had a feeling she was going to like this.

The official raised his hands again. "On guard. Ready? Duel!"

Dara won two out of her five bouts, including the first against Luci. Even though she'd lost more matches than she won, Dara felt elated, as if she were walking along a bridge railing high over Orchard Gorge. Dueling was *fun*. The action was fast and fiery, and competition made it ten times better. She could hardly wait for the next round.

Her results put her firmly in the middle of the pack when the pools were reshuffled for the second round. Oat had won three of his bouts, and he ended up in Dara's second pool.

"How's your first tournament so far?" he asked as they waited for the round to begin.

"It's great!" Dara said. "I scored points in all the bouts I lost. And I think I could have won the last one if I figured out that boy's timing sooner." She waved to a stocky young fellow adjusting the bend of his sword nearby. "I want to watch him duel again to analyze his style. He does this interesting parry I haven't learned yet."

"Easy there," Oat said with a laugh. "Focus on this pool first."

"Right." Dara turned to size up their competitors, who were assembling their gear and refreshing the charcoal on their sword points. "How did Kel do, by the way?"

"Won four out of five."

"Nice."

"It's his best result so far." Oat grinned. "You wouldn't know it from the way he talks, but he lost all but two bouts in our last competition."

"Oatin Wont." The handsome Bilzar Ten had arrived to officiate their pool. "You're up first against Shon Quen."

"Wish me luck." Oat took up a position on the dueling strip, preparing to face his first opponent.

Dara watched their duel closely, trying to work out what she'd do when she faced these two. The rest of the hall seemed to fade as she concentrated on the rhythm of their feet, the timing of their feints and lunges, the angles of their blades. Shon shrieked in triumph every time he scored a point, but Oat held his own.

As Dara looked for weaknesses, she found she could identify openings in the duelists' defenses, but she wasn't sure how to take advantage of them yet. She still had so much to learn.

"How is Oat fighting, young Dara?"

She jumped, surprised to find Coach Berg standing beside her. He'd been moving through the dueling hall all morning, shouting hints to his young students and grumbling at the older ones helping to run the tournament. So far, he hadn't shown much interest in Dara's bouts.

"He's doing well," Dara said. "He keeps dropping his arm, though."

"Yes. Oat has this problem." Berg glanced down at her. "What do you do when you see an arm drop like this?"

"Stab it?"

Berg chortled. "More specific, please."

Dara watched Oat and Shon's next exchange closely. Shon scored and let out a shriek that shook dust from the rafters.

"I guess you have to time it right," Dara said. "Oat usually drops his arm when he retreats, and he's too far away for his opponent to reach anyway. But sometimes he doesn't lift his hand again before he moves forward. That's when I'd hit him."

"Indeed."

Dara looked up uncertainly. "Is it okay for you to tell me how to beat one of my own classmates, Coach?"

"You are both here for learning. If you hit him in that hand, he will not be dropping it so often." Berg wiggled his eyebrows at her. "And you are telling me. I did not tell you anything."

Dara grinned, pride surging through her. She *had* figured it out, hadn't she? Before she could ask Coach Berg for more hints, he moved off to check on another group of students. She wished he'd stayed to watch her put her idea into practice. She wanted to show him what she could do. She wanted him to take as much interest in *her* performance as in her analysis of someone else's.

Oat won his bout against Shon, and then Dara was up against a boy from Surri's school. She was still thinking about how to beat Oat, so it took her by surprise when her next opponent didn't show any of the same weaknesses. He fought fast and wild, and it was all she could do to parry his hits. She lost the bout five to one and earned a handful of bruises in the process.

Good thing Coach Berg wasn't watching after all.

Dara felt flustered after the loss, and her next opponent, another girl, defeated her five to three. The joy she'd felt in the first round started to slip through her fingers. Two losses already. Maybe she'd lose every match in this round. Maybe she wasn't any good at this and she'd just had some beginner's luck. Worse, she'd have to buy salt cakes for the boys after all.

She reapplied charcoal to her blade, trying to gather herself. Her blood was racing and her head buzzed, making it hard to concentrate.

"Dara Ruminor and Oatin Wont," Bilzar called. "You're up."

Already? Dara hurried back to the starting position, and her boot caught on the stone floor, making her stumble. Her mask crashed to the floor and bounced out of her competition strip and into the next one ten feet away. Bilzar raised an eyebrow.

"Sorry. One second." Face burning, Dara rushed over to the strip and apologized to the official and the two duelists there. One of them was Kel. She didn't dare look him in the eye as she retrieved her mask and jogged back to her own strip.

"Are you ready now?" Bilzar asked dryly.

"Yes, sir." She saluted Oat and crammed her mask onto her head, covering up her blazing cheeks.

"On guard."

She bent her knees and assumed the dueling position, feeling unbearably awkward.

"Ready?"

She raised her blade, gripping it so tightly the tip shook. Her hand felt hot and sweaty in her glove. Across from her, Oat dropped into his guard position, all long skinny limbs and unlimited reach.

Bilzar cleared his throat. "Duel!"

The bout started slowly. Dara and Oat pulsed back and forth, advancing and retreating as if doing a footwork exercise during class. Tentatively, Dara jabbed at his arm with the point of her weapon.

With a great sweeping motion, Oat parried her blade and landed a hit in the dead center of her chest. The wooden plate she wore beneath her jacket gave a loud *thunk*.

"One, zero," Bilzar said, sounding bored. "On guard."

Dara retreated to the starting line. Her sword arm trembled.

She felt as though everyone in the dueling hall was watching her fail.

"Ready? Duel!"

Dara advanced, three, four, five steps in rapid succession. Oat blocked her first attack. Her second. She retreated. Advanced. Lunged.

Oat's blade hit her mask hard enough to make her ears ring. She'd misjudged his reach and lunged right onto his sword.

"Point! Two, zero to Oatin Wont."

Back to the starting line. Dara felt the bout careening out of her control. People shouted all over the dueling hall. Steel rang against steel. Footsteps. Heartbeats.

Focus. You need to—

Oat's blade hit Dara's wrist just behind the guard.

"Point! Three, zero."

Dara shuffled back into position. Sweat stung her eyes. Maybe tears too.

Movement to her left caught her attention. Kel's bout had finished, and he was standing beside their strip, watching them. Coach Berg loomed beside him. He was watching Oat and Dara too.

This is your chance, Dara thought desperately. She was good at footwork and exercises, and her form was solid, but none of that mattered if she couldn't keep her head in a competition. *Show him you're worth paying attention to, too.*

"On guard. Ready? Duel!"

Dara advanced slowly, making sure every step was clean, every angle correct. *Keep it simple. Stay focused.*

Oat lunged, and she parried the attack. Her riposte missed the mark, and Oat retreated out of reach. His hand drifted downward, leaving him exposed. He was too far out of her range. But she watched that hand. Waited for her moment.

Oat started forward, his hand still hovering down near his hip. Before he could raise it, Dara struck.

The tip of her blade landed neatly in the crook of Oat's elbow as he brought his arm forward.

"Point to Ruminor. The score is one to three."

Yes! Dara retreated to the starting line.

"On guard. Ready? Duel!"

Dara advanced carefully. She bounced on the balls of her feet, staying loose, focusing on Oat's hand, on her charcoal mark on his elbow. He feinted once, twice, trying to elicit a reaction. She stayed calm.

Oat retreated a step, then two, his hand lowering as he studied her for an opening.

Wait for it. Don't act too soon.

Oat advanced much faster this time, going for another wrist shot. Dara got there first. She struck the top of his hand a split second before he hit her.

"Another point to Ruminor."

"Woohoo! Go new girl!"

Dara looked up in surprise. On the sidelines, Kel pumped his fists in the air. He was cheering for her? Coach Berg was still watching, though she couldn't interpret the expression on his blunt features.

"On guard."

Back to the starting line. Feet at right angles. Knees bent. Arm raised. Blade at just the right tilt.

"Duel!"

Dara and Oat met in the middle of the strip and traded attacks and parries. The clang of steel echoed around them. Dara's blood roared in her ears. She couldn't lose focus. Couldn't hold back. She knocked Oat's blade aside with all her strength and stabbed him straight in the chest. Her sword bent at the impact, and once again she felt the reverberations right down to her toes.

"Point to Ruminor! The score is three to three."

"Go Dara! Go Oat!" Kel crowed, dancing along the edge of

the strip. "You can do it! Fight for those salt cakes."

"You know only one of us can win, right?" Dara called out.

Kel grinned. "Is *that* how this game works?"

"Duelists," Bilzar said, a warning in his tone. "On your guard, please."

"Sorry." Dara returned to her starting position. *Tied.* That wasn't good enough. Dara wanted to win this.

At the word from Bilzar, Dara and Oat began their next exchange. They covered more ground, moving up and down the strip, using the rhythms they'd learned in training. Dara tried out the moves she'd practiced over and over again with her classmates and the practice dummies. The moves she'd replayed in her head the night before the competition. The moves that would one day become as natural to her as breathing.

Oat scored again. Then Dara. They were tied at four. Only one point to go.

Dara glanced to the side. Coach Berg was still observing them, still unreadable. Kel chewed on all his fingernails at once. Behind him, his own official was calling him for his next bout, but he didn't notice.

"On guard. Ready?"

Dara bent her knees. Raised her blade. She wanted this badly. Not just to beat Oat and show Coach Berg and Kel what she could do. She wanted dueling. She wanted to feel this rush every day, to know that if she worked hard and focused and kept her head in the competition, this could be her whole life.

"Duel!"

Dara advanced. She tried one attack, then another, but Oat's hands were too fast. He parried and blocked, never letting her through his guard. She needed him to make a mistake.

Dara retreated, pulling out of Oat's range. He jabbed at her a few times, and she moved farther back. She was almost to the end of the strip. If he pushed her past the back line, he'd get the point and win the bout anyway.

Noise filled the hall. The smell of sweat. Someone on another strip hollered in triumph.

Stay calm. Focus.

Dara continued to block Oat's attacks, not following them up with her own counter attacks. She retreated farther still.

Oat's stance grew wobbly, as if her actions unsettled him. He looked worried that she might have a plan. Why else would she let him push her all the way to the back of the strip?

He retreated a few steps to regroup. His weapon hand lowered as he studied her from well out of her reach. Even with her best lunge, Dara couldn't hit him from here.

But she didn't need to. Oat advanced, preparing for his next attack, his hand not yet fully into position. As he lunged, his great gawky limbs flying toward her, Dara struck where she knew his wrist was about to be.

Oat's hand came up, and the tip of Dara's blade was there to meet it. The blunted point caught on his jacket, bending the blade.

"Halt!" Bilzar shouted. "Point to Ruminor. Ruminor wins five to four."

"Yes!" Dara ripped off her mask and pumped her fists in the air as if it were the championship bout. She didn't care who teased her for it. She had won!

"Nice bout." Oat removed his mask and offered his hand. "Looks like I owe you a salt cake."

"Only if I finish ahead of you in the rankings." Dara shook his hand firmly, flushed with triumph. "That was the deal."

Oat shrugged. "I reckon you earned it either way."

They left the strip to make room for the next competitors, and Coach Berg stomped over to them. Dara looked up hopefully, but Berg addressed Oat instead.

"I am telling you to watch that hand. You must not be dropping it like that."

"I see what you mean now." Oat wiped sweat from his forehead. "I'll work on it."

Berg harrumphed doubtfully, and Oat winced.

"We can work on it together, if that would help," Dara said. "I think I know what you need to do differently."

"That'd be nice," Oat said. "Thanks."

"Don't forget about me!" Kel jogged over to join them, earning an annoyed glare from Bilzar when he took a shortcut across the competition strip. "I can help too."

Dara raised an eyebrow. "Aren't you supposed to be dueling right now?"

"I just got demolished in about twenty seconds," Kel said. "I'll get him next time."

"You are needing to focus," Coach Berg said. "Like young Dara here. She is focused like an arrow. You must be doing this too. She knows the way."

Kel sighed. "Yes, Coach."

Berg grunted then stomped off to yell at another group of students.

Dara watched him go in disbelief. "Did he just compliment me?"

"Don't get used to it," Kel said.

Dara shoved him lightly, a smile welling up from her gut to fill her whole face. Coach Berg had seen her. He'd used her as an example for her classmates even! She almost didn't care where she finished in the rankings after this. She was going to get those extra lessons and be twice as good by the next tournament.

"Let's get back to work," she said to her new friends. "We have more duels to go before any of us gets cake."

～

When the third round ended, none of the three ranked high enough to compete in the championship bouts. They sat on the equipment trunks near the competition strip to watch the more advanced fighters, sharing a whole box of sweetened salt cakes between them. Coach Berg had bought some for all the students, growling that they'd better not drop any crumbs on the floor.

Dara sat between Kel and Oat—which was where she'd finished in the rankings, incidentally—and she didn't even mind when they teased her a bit. She was too busy watching the top duelists charge back and forth across the strip, blades flashing almost too fast to see. The clash of steel rang loud around the dueling hall and reverberated through Dara's core. Now that she'd gotten a taste of competition, she wanted more.

She vowed silently to be in one of those top spots next year. She'd work harder than every duelist in Vertigon to get there. She'd show everyone—her competitors, her coach, her parents—that she was born for this. Most of all, she'd prove it to herself. Dara Ruminor was a duelist.

ABOUT THE AUTHOR

Jordan Rivet is an American author of swashbuckling fantasy and post-apocalyptic science fiction. Originally from Arizona, she lives in Hong Kong with her husband. She fenced for many years, and she hasn't decided whether the pen is mightier than the sword.

www.jordanrivet.com

Lightning Source UK Ltd.
Milton Keynes UK
UKHW011949080721
386870UK00010B/566/J

9 781087 964638